By David Wagoner

Poems
Dry Sun, Dry Wind (1953)
A Place to Stand (1958)
The Nesting Ground (1963)
Staying Alive (1966)
New Selected Poems (1969)
Riverbed (1972)
Sleeping in the Woods (1974)
Travelling Light (1976)
Collected Poems 1956-1976 (1976)

Novels
The Man in the Middle (1954)
Money Money Money (1955)
Rock (1958)
The Escape Artist (1965)
Baby, Come On Inside (1968)
Where Is My Wandering Boy Tonight? (1970)
The Road to Many a Wonder (1974)
Tracker (1975)
Whole Hog (1976)

Edited
Straw for the Fire: From the Notebooks of
Theodore Roethke, 1943-1963 (1972)

Whole Hog

Whole Hog

by David Wagoner

An Atlantic Monthly Press Book

Little, Brown and Company   Boston · Toronto

First Edition
T 11/76

Library of Congress Cataloging in Publication Data

Wagoner, David.
  Whole hog.

  "An Atlantic Monthly Press book."
  I. Title.
PZ4.W1354Wi   [PS3545.A345]   813'.5'4   76-16526
ISBN 0-316-91702-8

Atlantic-Little, Brown Books
are published by
Little, Brown and Company
in association with
The Atlantic Monthly Press

Designed by D. Christine Benders
Published simultaneously in Canada
by Little, Brown & Company (Canada) Limited

Printed in the United States of America

For Patt
who made it
with love

Chapter One

I HADN'T MUCH WANTED to go to California—the land of Milk and Molasses—because I was just barely getting used to Clay County, Missouri—the Land of Muck and Chitlings—but if I'd known how far that Unpromised Land was and what was laying and running and crouching inbetween, I wouldn't of let Ma and Pa start me and the hogs walking that direction at all but would of dug in my heels like a hauled mule or maybe run off. Yet once they'd sold our mostly washed-out farm and commenced emigrating, it was too late for me to do anything but tromp along with my none-too-blissful ignorance and treat that journey like some more education.

I had known hogs all my twenty years (bar the first few which I don't recollect too good, though I must of been smelling them even then), but we hadn't been on that long, crowded California Trail with fifty-one of them more than about a fifth of the way—seven weeks—before I'd honed an edge on what I thought I knew previous, which had now become as follows:

1) A hog don't much care to go no place.

2) Once he gets started, a hog don't care where he's going as long as he don't *have* to go there.

3) Once he figures out he *has* to, he turns sulky and more pigheaded (that last not necessarily being too bad a way to look at the world if you're not running it), and what he wants to do then mostly is lay down.

4) He don't want to go in a straight line because he lives by his nose, same as a dog, and smells come crossways more often than longways.

5) He don't want to mind nobody's manners but hisn.

6) He don't want to listen to orders or mind any jab in the hocks or keep his nose out of other people's business or keep it clean neither.

And I spose I'd turned half hog myself, trying to keep the drove bunched up behind our wagon where Ma or Pa could take a head-count and didn't have to strain their voice whiles hollering at me. I wanted to lay down on the job too, but as long as Pa was leading the way into our Glorious Future Way Out West, I couldn't do nothing but grunt about it.

But my job was giving fair signs of laying down on *me*. By the time we was a hundred and fifty miles past Fort Kearny in Nebraska Territory, we didn't have but twenty-seven hogs left, most traded for grain to feed the ones left or fodder for our mules, Speck and Long Tom, but some just straying off in the night to mix in with the buffaloes or maybe get theirself roasted by the Pawnees or wolfed down raw by wolves or maybe just plain rendered by the sun.

I felt bad about it, but it didn't seem like my fault. These was woods hogs, not sty hogs, and they couldn't help it if they felt born to roam as they pleased. A woods hog is narrower

and faster and smarter than a sty hog and can jump through a
hoop three foot off of the ground if it *wants* to (only customarily it don't want to), and they look like where they mostly
spend their time, same as a bird might that wants to hide in
speckled brush or up amongst yellow and green leaves: spotty
brown, which is what our woods amount to generally back
home.

But out on the dang prairie and now here on this mostly
flat, bare, sandy valley of the South Fork of the Platte River,
they didn't look like nothing but strangers, too lumpy for
bushes and too lively for rocks and too small for buffaloes, yet
too bunched up to miss. Short as they stood, even laying down,
they was higher than what might be growing. I think it worried
them, and it done the same to me. Back home, you could see
where you wanted to get to next, even if it was only a rise or a
hollow on the way to town, but here you could look as far as
you could see and walk all day to get there, and once you was
there, it was the same as where you'd been at before and none
the wiser.

And if you don't have nothing to back them up against at
night like a clift or a blind gully after you've made them walk
all day, you're likely to lose a few, specially when you don't
have enough swill or fodder to keep them thinking they've got
a home away from home. The river was helping some to keep
them hedged in: at least there was *one* direction they wouldn't
stray. A hog don't mind drinking water if he don't have nothing better to do such as sleeping or eating, but he don't go
slogging into running water unless he's got a blamed good
reason, which ours didn't—least not till the night I'm going to
start telling you about, namely June 5, 1852, when everything
changed for better or for worse, for richer or for poorer. My
name's Ezekiel (Zeke for short) Hunt, and by the time that
night was over, it was about all I had left besides Colonel
Woppert.

Colonel Woppert was a spotty-brown scissor-bill hoggaster
(which is a three-year-old boar in case you don't know nothing

about hogs, and most don't, even them that say they do like
me) of a breed Pa become partial to back in Missouri, probably
because they ain't worth as much as sty hogs, being smaller
and stringier. But I can't say as I blame him. There's some that
says your Mexican racer is a better rooter for tough times and
less likely to catch swine pox when you don't happen to need
more trouble, but I'll stick with scissor-bills myself. Colonel
Woppert had been about the size of a squashed pickle barrel
when we started out, but he'd leaned in even more, same as
the others, not being used to all this walking.

A hog has got a small stomach and big ideas, though to look
at, you'd think it'd be the other way around. A hog likes to
eat *often*, and the less time wasted between meals, the more
sense he makes out of life. And he likes his food with a good
heft to it, not just cow fodder, though he'll hog off a field of
it if there's nothing else.

But out here on the Trail with all our belongings heaped in
one wagon, and money short, and no place to buy nothing if
we'd had it, and fearful of trading more hogs, and no farms
and few stores, and all the thousands of folks ahead of us and
behind fighting for anything that man or beast could chaw up
and get down, there wasn't no such a thing as a head of cab-
bage or a bucketful of corncobs and no heap of swill at the
end of a day. A hog is willing to cooperate on the subjeck of
slop. He'll do the best he can, even if it's got rags and paper
and what-all mixed in with it for a *while*. A hog has got forty-
four teeth in that mouth of his, and forty of them is good hard
grinders, but the other four can be worse than a bear trap if he
turns mean, so it's best to keep him eating if you can.

But Colonel Woppert and Shaver and Granddaddy Rockwell
and Miz Atlas and the other twenty-four that hadn't been
traded off or strayed or been stole was beginning to look kind
of cow-hocked from behind, which was the view I'd become
most customed to. And they wasn't much sunnier in their
thoughts than me. If you've ever walked behind a drove of
swine for seven weeks, you get a pretty clear idea what they

been eating if anything, and they hadn't been giving me much trouble stepping over their droppings since back at the trail junction before Fort Kearny when the bottom fell out of an Army feed wagon and our hogs got their first good long munchers of grain in a month or more.

Bringing up the rear gives you time to think, same as being last in a foot-race, spite of Ma and Pa taking turns to look back and give advice free of charge about which of our dwindling bunch to poke with my staff next or saying, "Mind that Lucy June there" or "What's Miz Atlas got stuck to her left-front trotter?" or, if we was in amongst a grove of cottonwood stumps (stumps being all that was left of trees most everyplace), "See if you can't make them root here" and on and on, never letting no slack form in the halfway peace and quiet, saying, "About five more mile today, Zeke" or "Don't scuff them shoes so, Zeke, they got to last" as if I didn't know which end of my foot to put on the ground, or "Fetch me a pail of that crick water," which meant me doing a little hopscotch back and forth and all the time making sure some grout-headed sow hadn't taken a notion to see what was happening on the other side of the sand slopes or some overgrowed shoat hadn't caught hold of a dry teat on the run.

Or like right then, when it happened to be Pa leaning over the tailboard in the shade of our raggedy canvas duck, his straw hat shoved back to air his skinny red forehead, and he says, "What you scowling at, boy?"

"Nothing," I says. "Just thinking."

"Well, if it's that hard to do, leave off," he says. "We're going to be at the ford pretty soon, and you'll need all the muscles you got, even them in your head." And he spit like he always done when he thought he'd got off a good one.

I didn't argue, but truth to tell, I always scowl when I'm thinking because it makes me mad not being able to do it better. And what I was thinking was *I'm no better than one of these hogs because I don't know why I'm doing all this walking, yet I don't seem to have no choice but do it.* It don't seem

like much of a thought when it's wrote down, but that was
why I was scowling. Now, a hog don't like to travel no further
than he has got to trot to the trough, and what good's the
wide open spaces to him?—not being able to see past fifty
yards except for blurs and no good swill to snuff at. He don't
have nothing to gain but exercise.

And I was in just about the same fix. I'd looked at the
prairies and the sand hills and the Platte River Valley and the
hind end of the wagon and the hind ends of hogs, and now and
then taken a look at folks camped near us and give a few
howdies and seen a few Injuns far off, but for all I'd learnt,
I'd might as well of been as squint-sighted as Colonel Woppert.

Pa'd had the idea to bring along live hogs instead of hams
and sides of bacon like many another done, and he had it all
figured out and could scratch the numbers in the dirt for you
anytime you'd care to listen to it all over again: with Miz Atlas
doing her normal farrowing and us eating some of the shoats
(though the idea had commenced making me sick) and trading
off others and with gilts like Lucy June and Pattycake coming
up to the time when they could do some farrowing theirself,
Pa could prove we'd make it all the way to California and still
have enough of a herd to start the hog farm and orchard he'd
been talking about for a year or more. The only trouble was
the hogs wasn't on paper but right there in front of me, getting
less and less as the weeks went by.

And there was only two kind of people amongst the thousands and thousands moving along that Trail same as us that
summer: them that wanted a hog for theirself, to swap for or
swipe and slaughter, or the kind that couldn't abide the sight
and smell of them and tried to drive us off every campsite we
lit on. Pa'd be standoffish and wary with the first kind and
either red-face mad or scairt white with the second kind, depending on how good they was at yelling and how they
handled their guns. So we hadn't made no friends along the
way yet and didn't look likely to, and when you've been
rained on and windblown and near hamstrung from walking

and hollered at for a slow fetcher and fed just enough beans and bacon to hold your pants up and told to hush, you are likely to have a scowl on your face whether you're thinking or just eating dust.

And Pa had his mind absolutely dead sunk on going on.

Chapter Two

THE PLATTE RIVER is famous for being a mile wide and an inch deep, and it's both sometimes. But there's other times—like this stretch along the South Fork—when it narrowed up and deepened down and hurried along looking even siltier and soupier than usual, too thick to drink and too runny to eat. We'd already passed up the lower ford and the middle ford past the place where the river forked: Pa didn't like the look of them nor the busted wagons (one of them upside down on a sandbar midway downstream), so we'd headed on for the upper ford, hoping last was best.

But the bank hadn't improved none: it was about five foot high, sheer and crumbly both, and the river was a good five hundred yards wide and too swift-looking for comfort, and

the first two fords hadn't looked no shallower than what was
inbetween, so me and the hogs plodded and plopped along,
thinking about suppertime and not getting our hopes up any
too high.

When he seen where the wagons was trying to cross *this* time,
Pa reined in and just set there watching. Three rigs was at it
(one almost all the way across but wrenched around and aimed
upstream whiles the two oxen had went jackknifing downstream), and three more wagons (two with cows tied to the
back) was waiting on the bank to see if the first ones was going
to touch bottom often enough to keep from sailing back East.

"Not much sunlight left," Ma says, which meant if we got
stuck halfway or commenced enjoying some of the other
splendid events that could happen when you had a river running through your wagonbed, she might not be able to see
good enough to cook our bacon.

"It's deeper than I thought," Pa says, which was such an
unusual confession from him I felt dumbstruck.

To hear him talk ordinarily, there wasn't nothing he hadn't
foresaw and took into account. All the weeks traveling and
all the weeks before that when he begun to brood on getting
us out of scratch-and-scrape country and into the Land of
Strawberries and Goat Cream, I'd listened to the squaring-out
and toting-up and hear Pa being *reasonable* (which meant *shut
up and learn something*) all the livelong day and night, naming
our supplies and figuring which hook or crook we could use to
get us fifty pound of sea biscuit and a couple extra hickory
shirts.

But never once had I heard him say he might just possibly
been mistook, not even when our hogs begun disappearing.

"I believe they're having a little trouble," Ma says, which
meant she seen the nearest wagon tipping over half-sideways
in the current and the mule sposed to be pulling it doing his
level best to climb backwards over the footboard and get in
the wagon with the rest of the family.

The hogs was getting restless and wandering a little, snuffing

this way and that in case there might be something worth
thinking about in the breeze, and I had to touch them up
here and there to keep them herded in.

"We'd best camp and get a fire going," Pa says, which meant
I was sposed to start rounding up some firewood in a territory where probably fifty other people that same day had
been scraping for anything that'd burn, and fifty the day before, and the same or more before that, every dawn and dusk
back to the spring thaw. It looked like there was going to be
plenty of scrap wood out in the river before long, mainly busted
wagons and barrel staves and such, but it might be a long while
before it would strand itself good and proper downstream and
most likely it'd be somebody else's suppertime godsend.

"Zeke," Ma says, which meant it was all settled and I had
best start passing a miracle if I didn't mind.

I must of been scowling again because Pa says, "Zeke," with
a kind of little warning in it. Meanwhile, the furthest-off
wagon had got itself aimed for the other shore again, but the
yoke of oxen had busted loose from the middle wagon and
was floundering this way and that, trying to decide whether
they was coming or going (a problem most folks around that
ford, including us, wouldn't of been able to give them much
help with), and the wagon itself looked to be stuck in the
sand. The young man setting in it still had the empty reins in
his hands like he was running a trot-line for catfish, and the
woman beside him appeared to be doing a good deal of talking, her mouth right up next to his ear so's he wouldn't miss
nothing important. The people waiting their turn on the bank
did some pointing and waving and hustling back and forth
without getting their feet wet.

"How'm I sposed to get them hogs across a stretch of river
like that?" I says. It was the first time I'd asked it out loud,
though it had been running through my mind for days.

"I don't expeck you to do nothing," Pa says. "That way I
keep off a steady diet of disappointment."

I was tempted to sass him on the sore subject of steady diets,

but Ma says, "Firewood, Zeke," which meant hush up and
stay practical and mind your pa.

And I done so, just to keep peace. But that river was real and
so was the hogs, and it wouldn't do to pretend one or the
other didn't exist.

I gawped around, and Pa says, "Try the crick over yonder."

I done what he told me, herding the hogs along (since they
and me didn't have nothing better to do and lots worse), using
the ring in Colonel Woppert's nose now and then, which he
didn't appreciate none (Pa'd put it there in the first place to
keep him from rooting up our carrots), and the rest moseyed
along in a loose clump. They wouldn't *always* do what he
done, but half the time they figured he might know best, long
as nothing extra bothersome was going on like too much noise
or stray dogs.

Before I was out of earshot, I heard Pa say, "There was
sposed to be a ferry," in a kind of wondering voice with a
slump on the end of it, which must of meant that's how he'd
counted on getting our hogs across this jumble of a South
Fork so's they could commence climbing California Hill and
cut over to the North Fork at Ash Hollow and along towards
Fort Laramie if they didn't wither up on short rations first.

I hung back a few seconds to hear how maybe he was going
to invent a ferry where there wasn't none.

"How much did it cost?" Ma says.

"I don't know," Pa says. "But it was sposed to be here."

"Well, least we can save whatever it was," Ma says.

Which shows you the general class of thinking goes on in our
family, though I don't claim to be much better myself, having
no good examples to go by except maybe Colonel Woppert in
a cornfield who can shake a stalk with his nose and tell how
many ripe ears is on it. (Your ordinary hog has to knock a
stalk over to make sure if it's full or empty.)

I drove the hogs into a bend of the crick (it was deep enough
to discourage them) so's I could keep them still without having
to run a circle around them like a sheep dog, and then I used

my staff to poke around in three or four ash heaps other
parties had left behind, hoping somebody'd flung sand on their
fire to put it out and buried something I could burn. I dug up
a half a dozen usable sticks finally and, what with an armload
of buffalo chips I beat the hogs to, I had the makings of a
cook fire by the time Pa brung the wagon over.

There's no use telling you what all them hogs had been eating. There's no use spoiling your dinner, even if you don't
have none. But I *will* say they had learnt to put buffalo chips
and mule apples where they'd do the most good. We'd only
seen buffalo from far off (Pa not being much for hunting on a
mule that wouldn't do nothing but walk, if that), but their
chips was most everywhere, and if folks on the trail chipped
off a campsite bare, it wouldn't be long before there was a
fresh crop. I don't know what the buffalo left in them chips,
but if they'd burn in a fire, they must of done something
wholesome inside a hog too. And there's no use telling a hog
to leave some kind of mess alone if you haven't got a better
mess to call him off with.

"There was sposed to be a ferry," Pa says to himself, like he
wanted to get it memorized proper in case the governor of the
Territory come by and asked if there was was any way he
could improve the Trail for us.

"Well, maybe it's a blessing in disguise," Ma says, which
meant it might be best to leave off thinking about a vexation
in case you'd be tempted to blaspheme the Almighty, who was
getting so good at disguising His blessings lately, you'd might
suspeck He got a powerful lot of fun doing it.

She clumb down and began making the fire herself. It was
one chore she *had* to do because we had so little to burn, if
she wanted to get any cooking done at all or any water boiling, she had to have the pan on before anybody struck a
match.

So I had a little time, while Pa unhitched the mules and hob-
bled them and give them each a handful of the bale of hay
we'd grudged off of a sutler back in Dog Town near Fort

Kearny and a handful of corn each, which was mighty poor pay for what they'd done since the last handfuls at noon—I had time to look over this here Upper Ford which we had to make if we was interested in getting to California at all instead of commencing to curve south and climb Pikes Peak.

We was on a little bit higher ground now, so I had a better view of the folks baptizing theirself by the last of the good daylight. The first wagon I'd watched had finally made it across with all four wheels still on and no broken ox legs, and the second one was still two hundred and fifty yards from dry land in both directions whiles their oxen had went a quarter mile downstream to think things over, and the third had got its mule convinced it should aim forward instead of trying to stick the whiffletree up through the canvas top and was at least moving, though mostly sideways with the current, and one of the boys on the near side had got up his nerve enough to slide his rig down the bank with the cow still tied on back and not looking too anxious for a swimming lesson, but he appeared like he was going to set there a spell with his back wheels still on the shore whiles his team of horses got a little better acquainted with this yellowy muck churning under their nose.

If it'd been the River Jordan and us and them the Lost Tribes, it might of made some sense.

"Well, if there ain't no ferry, I expeck we'll just have to do without," Pa says.

"I don't spose it'd hold many hogs anyway," Ma says.

And she was right there, far as she went. You go shoving a hog into anything, you'd better be sure you got the other end plugged or shored up, and I wouldn't of much cared to find out how they built the butt ends of ferries way out here. The hogs'd behaved theirself on the ferry across the Missouri at St. Joe, but it was most as big as a barnyard and not something knocked together out of scraps.

I had convinced them hogs to ford many a crick, including some that had ambitions to be rivers, and sows and boars and shoats and gilts alike had wet their belly on many a cold morn-

ing just because I was there to poke them into it and holler
them out the other side. But except for that one ferry and
some plank bridges, they'd never had their trotters off of solid
mud or at least muck for more than two seconds all the lum-
bersome hundreds of miles between here and Clay County. I
had begun my half-awake life as a droving fool (the main
trouble with hogs is they don't never seem to be at where
they're most wanted, so there's got to be a drover like me—
what they call a "pig pelter" because you get in the habit of
chunking clods at a hog to get its attention—to move that
drove to market or maybe to new territory like now), and you
don't need much in the way of brains for it, just a good hickory
staff as tall as you and a set of lungs for calling, and I had
penned hogs and styed them and marshed them and rounded
them out of hickory hollows and jack-hauled them out of
sloughs and even thumped a few out of rotten logs that thought
they'd try being raccoons for fifteen minutes, and I had kept
bigger droves than this together for long spells of uphill and
downhill commotion.

But I had never before tried to get a drove to drowned itself
in anything like this South Fork of the Platte. They say a hog
will cut its throat with its back trotters sooner than swim, and
it seemed like Pa might be going to find out if it was true or
just another back-country lie.

"Why don't we hogtie them and ship them over a few at a
time in other people's wagons?" I says.

"I don't believe folks would be that obliging," Pa says,
sounding quiet and disgusted with such a fool notion.

"We could pay them," I says.

Ma flattened her mouth at me and shook her head in the
smoke that was starting to puff out of the little fire.

"If you don't want to pay money, you could give each
wagon two hogs and let them keep one on the other side," I
says. "Least we'd have *some*thing left."

"Hush up that kind of talk," Ma says.

Pa had rounded on me and was staring at me hard like somebody else had swiped my voice when I wasn't looking. "Zeke," he says, which meant I was heading into razor-strop territory, though he hadn't lifted a hand against me for three years now, ever since I come up to six foot tall.

"Because I'll tell you them hogs won't make that crossing on their own, and I don't aim to make them try," I says.

"You'll do what you're told," Pa says, using his quietest, softest, most dangerous voice.

"We'd do better to set here and sell them off one by one, then take the *money* across," I says, not being able to shut my mouth, even if it meant a licking, which I didn't plan to take as long as I had two good feet to run on. "Or let's just turn around and go back home."

"I decide what gets done in this family," Pa says.

"Zeke," Ma says, fanning the smoke with her cooking fork. "You listen."

"I'm listening," I says. "But I don't hear no sense being made. Why don't we at least go back to Fort Kearny where we can buy or beg or scrounge or swap for feed to keep these pigs alive and build up the drove again? Why do you want to drowned them?"

Pa had turned redder than the sunlight. "I don't notice nothing or nobody drownding around here," he says. "Now you just keep your place and leave the thinking to me."

"I want to hear some thinking," I says, and maybe somebody *had* stole my voice and started using it unbeknownst. I had never talked to him like this, even in my head. "I'm the drover. *That's* my place. And I say they can't ford that river."

Pa wasn't used to arguing with nobody and me neither, so we just stood there a while, feeling kind of embarrassed, him pretending to give Speck and Long Tom's hooves a look-over and me giving a yearling gilt named Seldom (because that's how often I could catch her in the woods back home) a poke in the rump to keep her from wandering off up the edge of the crick. But what we was really doing was calculating where this here discussion was going to wind us up. Pa knew full and well he couldn't even *try* to get the drove across without me, and I knew full and well he wouldn't do no turning around once he'd got his big busted-looking nose aimed at that California he'd been talking about for what seemed like forever and a week.

Ma says, "Do what Pa tells you," warming up a chunk of bacon on one side whiles the buffalo chips lasted.

"He hasn't told me nothing yet but to keep my place," I says. "All right, I'm keeping it. And I'm waiting for some of this *thinking* to start."

"I *am* thinking," Pa says, scanning over the wet scenery between us and the north shore. "Just hush up that big mouth. Save some of it for calling hogs."

I give him about five seconds, then I says, "Well, sir, why don't we build our own ferry?"

"All right," he says. "Why don't you just walk on down to the lumber mill and buy us enough timber?"

"Looks to me like there's going to be at least one wagon left for trash in that river," I says. "Maybe there'll be another tomorrow. You could build some kind of ferry out of two wagons, I expeck."

"How you going to haul anything out of there, sposing the owners'd even let us try without a gunfight?" he says.

"We've got two good mules, don't we?" I says. "And them people won't just set around admiring their wreckage forever."

"And what did you figure on using for nails and tools?" he says, turning sourer and raspier because he wasn't having no luck backing me into a pen and slamming a gate on me.

"Don't need nails," I says. "There's such a thing as pegging and wedging and mortising."

"There's such a thing as knowing how to do it too," he says.

"We got a saw and a hammer," I says. "I expeck I could learn. That way, we'd only be risking a few hogs at a time."

"I've had enough of this backtalk," he says. "Give me a yip when supper's fixed. And see if you can let a little daylight into the thick skull of that son of yours before I do it with an ax handle." And he went stalking off, stiff in the butt from setting all day, toward the other wagons on the near shore. There was seven of them now, four more having trundled along in the meanwhile, trying to make up their mind to cross or camp with the sun going. "I'll see if I can find out anything," he says.

Which might of been a pretty fair idea back about seventy mile at the lower ford instead of waiting till now, but I didn't say so.

"I never in my life heard anybody cross him like that before, not even Uncle Fred," Ma says. "Whatever's got into you?"

"He's led us all into a big mistake, and he won't admit it nor try doing something sensible about it," I says.

"Why should he have to admit anything?" she says. "Why can't you just let him go ahead and make his mistake—if that's what it is—and keep still about it? They're his hogs."

"Seems like they're part mine too," I says. "I kept still whiles we've been losing this drove little by little, but I can't stand to see the rest go all at once." It was hard to say, but I tried. "I—I love them hogs, and he don't. Maybe that's what's wrong."

She stared at me like I'd just confessed some kind of sin she'd never heard of. "You can't go loving hogs," she says.

"Well, I do," I says.

I don't think I'd ever said I'd loved nothing out loud before except maybe something to eat, and it felt strange as a dream. It scairt me a little, and I didn't know how I could love hogs neither. They have set ideas, what there is of them, just like' me and Pa, and they're stubborn, but they *think*. People don't like the notion, but take a look in a hog's eye and you'll see something you might hope to see whilst shaving or primping but won't. They're doing something better than you and me can do, and I'd caved in and let my admiration for them break out of hiding and follow them into the kind of thickets they liked, where I could root and nuzzle and hunt wild windfall apples and nuts too. I'd opened out a little and didn't care no more if it seemed dumb.

And these hogs felt unhappy, and it wasn't just being hungry.

A hog can't sweat, even if he feels like it. Sweat just can't get through that thick skin of his which feels more tender and soft to him than pigskin gloves to a lady setting in a brougham with her beaux all lined up along the shady way, specially if he gets sun scald or the scroffs. And a hog can't scratch hisself as good as a dog (though he'll try, but can't bend and double around to reach everyplace), so he has to find hisself a post or a stump or the side of a shed or anything rough to hunch up against and keep his spirit from going to sleep on him, and these hogs had come hundreds of miles now without seeing nothing worth scratching up against but our wagon which Pa wouldn't allow for fear they'd wear it out or heave it over or shear off a wheel-spoke being too enthusiastic. So I felt sorry for them.

In a quiet, long-faced, wispy-haired, bent-headed pose over the frying pan, with her bonnet shoved back and her freckles looking dark after the days of wind and sunshine, Ma says, "You're eating bacon for supper as usual."

"I know it," I says, hanging my head too. "And I'm beginning to disenjoy it more and more. But I can't root like them, and I got to stay alive."

"And you help to slaughter and dress and cook pudding and render," she says.

"You started me on that so early, I can't remember *not* doing it," I says. "I only began to think *lately*. It took time." I watched Pa giving his howdies to the other men down at the riverside and even shaking a hand or two and starting to talk and point and get it all figured out. "But I'm not going to do it no more. Somebody else can do the slitting and trussing up and butchering. Not me."

"Well, I don't like it neither," she says. "But if I only did what I liked, I wouldn't have nothing to do."

"I'll tell you how it is, Ma," I says, getting down on one knee. "Either that river dries up by tomorrow or Pa figures how to part the waters or a ferry shows up or we parcel this drove out in separate wagons like I said or we stay on dry land

and head for someplace else—one of them—or there's going to
be Hell to pay. And we're all three going to pay it, and there's
going to be twenty-seven hogs paying it too."

"You watch your language," she says.

"I mean Hell with a capital aitch," I says. "The kind in the
Bible."

"You'd best starting reading the Ten Commandments," she
says.

"I'm honoring my father and my mother with my best
thoughts on all subjecks great or small from here on in," I
says. "And right now the subjeck is drownding hogs."

Just then I seen a man taking a swing at Pa down by the
crick's mouth where the wagons was in a loose cluster and Pa
backing up and seeming to try to talk sense. But the other man
wasn't about to smoke no peacepipe just yet, flinging his hat
off sideways and offering both fists up to Pa like he was
sposed to pick the one he'd sooner be knocked down with,
and I was running along that loose, sandy, gentle slope before
I knew I'd picked up my feet.

But I wasn't even halfway there when Pa commenced running back towards our wagon, leaving the other man standing
there yelling and some of the others heehawing and whooping
after him, and I felt shamed to see him working that hard to
get out of a fist fight. Truth to tell, he wasn't any too good at
it (I'd only seen him trade punchers twice before, and he got
the worst of it both times from bigger men), but he'd never
backed up whiles he was getting his nose busted and a tooth
chipped off crooked.

I had my staff with me, which is a pretty good persuader
even if you're ganged up on, but there wasn't nothing I could
do with him making tracks at me, his face gone white, either
scairt or icy-mad.

Before I could open my mouth, he says, "Get back to the
hogs!" He was winded already, running through sand not being
one of the chores he ordinarily did, but he made like he was
going to tackle me when I didn't switch around right away and

start back but just stood there trying to make sense out of him. "Go on, git!"

And he made a lunge at me, so I turned and trotted along-side of him, looking back and seeing nobody was following, just a clump of lunkheads down there, shouting and waving, including the one who done the swinging.

"There's a man says he's going to kill all our damn hogs," Pa says, panting inbetween times.

I'd never heard him swear before, and it was like hearing Colonel Woppert recite Psalm number 49.

Chapter Three

SOME OF THE HOGS had strayed off a ways, so I had to call them in. The way you call hogs (sposing you should want to) is you start out high as you can go up in the roof of your nose kind of wailing louder and louder and coming down the scale a ways where you can get up to full volume, and then you hang on there long as you need to without losing your last bellyful to hit down hard on the end like a grunt. There's all kind of words you can use doing that, but I found best for me was Seeuuboy, which I used to hear our neighbor Lum Partridge calling out three mile off when I was buckle-high, only you stretch it out till it's like SeeeeeuuuuuBOY! Or even longer. I don't know why hogs like it just so, but they do. And I don't know why some's better at it than others, but they are. I'm

21

just fair. Ed Hostetter back home, he can make hogs come
from so far off, he has to call long before dark or they'd be
butting at his back door in the moonlight after he went to
sleep.

But all I needed now was a medium-size call, and I got them
clumped up again in that barren crickbend where there wasn't
nothing for them to root at but a few weeds. Ma's mouth fell
open when she seen Pa running and then rummaging up in the
tailbox and hauling out our Allen revolver wrapped up in a
bandanna.

"Where's them bullets?" he says, since he didn't believe in
keeping loaded guns around and hadn't fired it at nothing during the whole trip nor for a year before when he missed a
skunk in our henyard and couldn't hit nothing with it apurpose anyway because it kicked as hard as Speck and Long Tom
together. "I seen them just last week." And he tossed out
some ripped calico Ma'd been saving for rags and one of my
three books, namely *Aesop's Fables*. It landed safe.

"What happened down there?" Ma says, looking set to pack
up and haul off.

"I asked a perfeckly simple question," Pa says. "I acted like
a gent, and I got swang at for my pains. *Where'd* them bullets
get to?"

He rummaged some more but didn't locate them, and I was
just as glad, it being a whole lot safer not to be in the neighborhood of an Allen revolver when it goes off, even standing behind it and ducking.

And now I seen two of the men from the riverbank coming
toward us on horseback and two more stringing along behind,
and in the lead was the one that swang at Pa. He had his hat
back on, a buckskin felt sombrero, flat-brimmed and looking
too clean and neat for being on the Trail, and a fringed buckskin jacket I'd never seen the like of and must of cost as much
as a saddle, and his horse wasn't no plow-jerker or cart-kicker
but some kind of rich man's horse, glossy and short-haired and
so full of muscles it couldn't hold still, and it was buckskin
too.

Pa drew hisself up and crossed his arms, holding that empty revolver like he didn't mean to use it unless somebody tried to take it away from him.

Ma stayed by the fire, and I was about twenty foot off between everybody and the hogs, and the man in the buckskin reined in and left the other three catch up. They weren't as fancied up, being dustier-looking and needing a shave (the buckskin man looked like he'd just come out of Bellini's Tonsorial Parlor in St. Joe), and they didn't say nothing but waited for the buckskin man to do the talking. They all seemed like only five or six years older than me.

"I believe we were having a conversation," he says to Pa. "It was rude of you to run off in the middle of it."

He had a funny kind of high drawl in his voice that must of come from back East someplace. I'd never heard the like before, but all kind of people from all over was on the Trail that year. And he was drunk, which I hadn't noticed right off, him being so straight-backed and high-chinned and his broad, sandy mustache so neat, but he was having a harder time balancing than he should of, even with his horse being shifty.

"I didn't notice no conversation," Pa says. "I heard some words spoke and I seen a fist coming my way, but that's about all."

"I see," the buckskin man says. "You should pay closer attention." He was wearing a black-handled sixgun and a rifle in a saddle scabbard, and he touched each of them like he was making sure he could reach that far. "And precisely whom do I have the honor of addressing?"

"My name's Saul Hunt and this here's my wife and boy," Pa says, polite and sounding like he could commence hoping nothing bad was going to happen.

"And hogs," the buckskin man says.

"And hogs," Pa says.

"They're the ones with four feet," the buckskin man says, and one of the others, a gawky, narrow-headed kid with his brown sombrero shoved back so's he'd have room to sweat give a high heehee up behind his nose.

"Except for the mules," I says. "They're the ones with the long tails."

I could see the buckskin man didn't like that none, though he tried not to show it. He hadn't give me no more than a glance, but now he checked back to see if I was anybody in particular and, whiles he was at it, give the hogs a good stare.

"Hush up, Zeke," Pa says.

"My name is Arthur Shadwell Parkhurst," the buckskin man says. "I don't ordinarily introduce myself to strangers of your station, but I'm doing so for a very good reason: I want you to recognize where your orders are coming from, so there will be no mistakes along the way."

First off, I'd thought his horse might of been moonblind on account of it being so bulgy-eyed, but now I seen it was het up and restless like it'd just shied from a snake and couldn't think about nothing but running itself inside out. It acted like it didn't want no part of what it was doing. But this Parkhurst didn't seem to mind none: he had it checked in tight and looked just as calm as it looked half-loco. I think if he'd of got off then, he wouldn't of seen his horse again for a week. It kept getting the bit about halfway betwixt its teeth, and if Parkhurst hadn't kept giving it jaw-jerkers, it might of been showing him the nearest way to mustang country.

"I don't intend to make no mistakes," Pa says. "Nor take no orders neither."

Which I had to admire him for, him standing there facing four armed men who was beginning to act mean. And him with that Allen revolver which he'd of done better to trade in for Ma's cooking fork.

"Well, you have just made two right there," Parkhurst says. "But it's more important to get to these hogs now." He looked around at the sky, which was glooming up and the red turning streaky and purplish. "I will go back to the beginning: you have camped upstream of us with a herd of filthy animals, and you are going to move them before dark—move them far, far away—or my friends and I will kill them all or drive them off, whichever proves to be more entertaining, and do the same to you and your family if you so wish."

Pa had changed color twice, and his voice went husky. "We couldn't camp downstream of you: you're at the mouth of the crick."

"Did I use any words you don't understand?" Parkhurst says. "I'd be glad to rephrase my orders."

"This land don't belong to nobody," Pa says. "I got as much right as you." Which was all right far as it went, and I might of said the same thing myself, but his voice sounded like it'd sprung a leak.

"Let's go, Saul," Ma says. "Won't take but a few minutes."

"Ma'am," Parkhurst says, touching his hatbrim, then turning back to Pa. "There's plenty of room on the other side of the river, and if you get started now, you may even be able to see what you're doing."

"Be glad to change places with you," Pa says. "You come on up here and make yourself at home, and we'll go down to the riverbank, and everybody'll be happy."

But wherever I looked, I didn't see nobody about to be happy except maybe the horseman furthest back—a tattery, blue-bearded, schoolteachery-looking kind of moonhead with his new rancher's hat too small for him—who was standing up in his stirrups so's he could see better. He was half-grinning, but nobody else was, and Pa had a look like the day we auctioned off our farm and all our barnyard caboodle and most of our house goods: he knew something bad was going on but couldn't tell how bad till he come to the end of it.

"Why, we couldn't stay here," Parkhurst says, glancing around and opening one dark eye further than the other. "You have desecrated this ground. You have allowed muck to fall upon it. I think it would be best for all concerned if you crossed the river right now. Yonder it is."

He didn't look at it, but I did, and the wagon that had lost its oxen was still stuck sideways, and the man and woman looked to be gone out of it, either swimming or drownding or sloshing after their beasts someplace, and one wagon had made it, but one of the others must of changed their mind and turned around: the clump of wagons was bigger on the shore, and except for the stuck wagon the water was empty, churning all kind of sunset colors and looking mean and oily. No hogs was going in there if I could help it, not till it come down about two foot at least.

Pa give me a look over his shoulder like he was about to ask my opinion (which he didn't customarily do), but Parkhurst didn't give him time.

"I'll remind you once again," he says. "My name is Stanhurst Parkman Postbody, and I am issuing you a direct order, and I am here to see it's carried out."

His name had got shuffled up, and he was either too drunk to keep it straight or he had some spares. The moonhead in back of him giggled.

"I'm a decent, law-keeping man," Pa says. "But I don't like being—"

"Others will determine the degree of your hypothetical decency," the buckskin man says. "It is unseemly for you to decide in your own behalf." He turned a little in his saddle. "Unseemliness is a punishable offense, is it not, Mr. Bunfried?"

The kid with the brown sombrero next to him grinned. "It surely is," he says. "Punishable by sticking."

"Sticking, do you think?" the buckskin man says, blinking. "Do you mean pig-sticking or are you referring to the cane?"

"Just good old sticking," the kid says.

"Nothing elaborate, you think?" the buckskin man says.

Pa raised his voice to get the huskiness out of it and says, "I have a wife to take care of, and I never forded nothing that deep or fast in a wagon or on foot, leave alone with a drove of hogs. Let's us work this out at sunup. I don't want to get stuck out there in the dark. It don't make no sense."

"You are going to be stuck in the dark in any event," the buckskin man says. "Mr. Bunfried has already determined that. As to sense, sir: sense is not made, it is born. Like poets.

You have nothing to do with sense. Give up the idea, and you will be a happier man."

"Hadn't we better get going?" the kid says.

"That's for *me* to decide," the buckskin man says, switching around to stare at the kid for a long spell of quiet. "You know, I want to give you my horse."

"Aw, Stull, for godsake, I don't want your horse," the kid says.

"Yes, you do," the buckskin man says. "And you're going to take him whether you like it or not."

"I *don't* like it, and I *don't* want him," the kid says.

"And I'm going to take yours," the buckskin man says, smiling a little crack of a smile. "I'm going to take yours and skin him and eat him. Then I'll know what you aim to do in this life. And I'll make myself a hunting outfit out of the skin and six pairs of boots. Then I'll have you inside and outside."

"I don't happen to be my horse," the kid says, glancing at Pa like he might be embarrassed. "Now don't get too stirred around, Stull. We've got a long ways to go."

"I want your horse for dinner," the buckskin man says.

Raising his voice some, the kid says, "You'll have to eat him out from under me then, because I'm not serving Archer up to nobody, not even you."

"You see?" the buckskin man says, looking around at the other two and nodding like he'd just cracked the wisdom out of a Bible text. "Disloyalty in the very heart of my staff. My rod and my staff discomfort me."

He clumb down off of his frothy, skittery-hoofed horse and trailed its reins just in time to keep it from seesawing halfway to the river. Even as it was, that swole-eyed gelding slid and humped six directions whiles bracing stiff-legged in the hard sand. And he stalked over to the kid and knocked his near-foot out of the stirrup with his elbow and grappled with the kid's leg for a couple seconds like he might be thinking of heaving him over out of the saddle, but then he stuck his whole right forearm under the girth, which shouldn't of been that loose,

braced hisself, and tried to take a bite out of the tight barrel of
the kid's horse, shoving his face up against the ribs and growl-
ing whiles he dug his teeth at it.

At camp meetings back home (I used to sneak out to them
some nights just for the scary fun of it) I seen people rolling in
the dirt and hollering glory-shouts and talking languages not
even a hog could understand, and it seemed like they really
enjoyed thrashing around and tearing at their shirt and sticking their tongue out and rolling their eyeballs white and
drenching theirself with sweat. I felt the buckskin man was
like that, even though he didn't exackly do none of them
things. I felt like he was showing off to hisself and just as surprised as anybody else over what he might say or do and twice
as pleased.

The kid didn't look pleased at all, and he says, "Stull, if you
eat my horse, what in the hell am I supposed to ride on?"

"Me," the buckskin man says, giving a cackle and backing
off and catching his horse before it could bolt. He swang up
into the saddle and took three deep, happy breaths, sobering
up.

I had to make a couple clucks and whickers at Granddaddy
Rockwell who was shoving a hogget named Armbruster too
close to the edge of the crick, just to remind him I was there
and could staff-whack him anytime he done something too
foolish.

The buckskin man looked my way and let a slit of a smile go
to work under his mustache. "Your son has got the right
idea," he says. "He's learning the language of hogs in an effort
to improve himself. Let me hear *you* grunt, sir."

Ma says, "Saul, may I speak?" She was standing stock still
by the fire which had went out.

"No," Pa says.

"I said I wish to hear you grunt, sir," the buckskin man says.
"I will remind you once more: my name is Asher Peerbilt
Whistover, and when I give you an order, it is going to be
necessary for you to obey."

"I'll harness up my mules and move on to oblige you," Pa
says, uncrossing his arms and aiming the Allen at the ground.
"And I won't quarrel with you."

"In good time," the buckskin man says. "But first I want
you to get down on your hands and knees and grunt for a
moment. I won't request any squealing. Perhaps later. For
now, a little grunting will do."

"And then sticking," the kid says.

"We shall see. All in good time," the buckskin man says.
Then to Pa: "Grunt, sir."

I begun walking toward Pa without knowing why, not in no
hurry but just pacing it off slow and not saying nothing.

"I'll just harness them mules," Pa says.

The buckskin man took off one of his gloves with a little
flaring gantlet on it and fringe down the little-finger side and
three embroidered stars, and he says, louder, "Down on your
knees and grunt, sir!" and swang the glove and knocked Pa's
straw hat off, stinging him across the forehead.

Pa only moved back half a step and had enough sense not to
raise that empty Allen which the buckskin man could probably see weren't loaded anyway. When I passed Ma by the dead
fire, she made a clutch at me and says, "Zeke," but missed,
and I come up next to Pa and waited.

"Your boy can show you how," the buckskin man says. "It
must not be too difficult. I judge it to be a language not much
different from your own. Say something in pig-talk, boy, and
lead your father into the paths of righteousness, for I must tell
you he is in the valley of the shadow of death."

"Yes, sir," I says. "I'd be glad to." And I took me a full breath
and done my best to out-call what Ed Hostetter could of done
on a cold, clear, windless day. I let out a Seeeeeeeeeeeeeeeeeee-
uuuuuuuuuuuuuuuuuuuBOY that started outside my head way
back behind my ears someplace and wound up hitting me
below the belt, but before I was a third of the way through,
the buckskin man's glossy horse had reared up and give a half-
turn like it was trying to climb out of a stall, knocking back

against the kid's horse and shuffling the other two, and Speck
and Long Tom gawped around at me (which they wouldn't
ordinarily), and Colonel Woppert come trotting stiff-legged my
way like a hound dog that's been whistled for, and the rest of
the hogs come stumping after, milling around and bumping Pa
and the wagonwheels and eating up the buffalo chips out of
the fire (which maybe tasted better half-cooked) and going
betwixt the legs of all these shifty horses and generally creating a disturbance.

A hog don't mind a horse, long as it stands still and eats its
own fodder and don't disturb the natural order of things
which consists mainly of a hog doing what it pleases, but when
a horse starts cutting up and flexing around all higgledy-peg
and kicking and taking up too much room where there might
be something worth snuffing over, a hog turns into a mighty
uncomfortable neighbor. So when one of them horses tried
stepping on Miz Atlas, she bit him in the pastern.

I picked up *Aesop's Fables* before it got stomped on or more
likely et and stuffed it in my pocket, and when I looked around
again, the buckskin man had drew his pistol and was trying to
settle his horse back down and was yelling something at the
moonhead whose bit horse had shied off about twenty yards,
and then he switched around and aimed his pistol at Pa and
says in a high, tight voice, "Sir, your snide, uncalled-for, ignorant, slurring remarks about fairies when you first forced your
company upon us were bad enough, but your stink is worse,
your stink and your stinking wife and your stinking boy and
your stinking hogs."

Pa says, "I only asked if there was—"

"Easy now, Stull," the kid in the brown sombrero says.

The buckskin man turned his pistol off Pa and aimed it
down at Lucy June who was doing a little rooting in the sand
for practice, since there wasn't nothing to root, and I swang
my staff and hit him a good crack across the wrist, and the gun
fell out of his hand and hit the ground. He let out a screechy
yip and yanked at the rifle butt sticking out of the scabbard

with his other hand, and soon as he had it all the way out, I whacked him on that wrist too, good and hard, and the rifle fell to the ground, and between Lucy June and Armbruster they'd of et it and the pistol too if Pa'd only give them five minutes instead of scooping up the both.

"Shoot him!" the buckskin man yells at the kid. "Shoot that bastard!"

Meaning me, which I didn't like to be called none but didn't blame him much for, since he was clutching both wrists to his chest and crouching over them and squinching up his face. I might not of busted both of them, but his right one hadn't had no gantlet to protect it. With all the swinging and commotion, his horse had shied around sideways and was still doing little steps and rolling its eyes, and I cocked my staff again, ready to hit anything or anybody I had to.

Pa was holding the rifle like he meant business, and the buckskin man says, "Shoot them! Shoot them all!"

The kid, glancing at Pa, says, "We can't just go gunning people down." He tried to get his horse in close to the buckskin. "Are you hurt bad?"

The buckskin man had his hands crossed over his saddlehorn now and wasn't crouching as much, but the sweat was pouring down his smooth, tawny skin, and he'd gone all shaky.

"I tried to be reasonable," Pa says, sounding scairt. "Now I'll just have to ask you to go on away and leave us alone and good luck to you." He wasn't aiming the rifle at nobody in particular, but to look at him you'd think he might know how to shoot it all right. I might of thought so myself if I hadn't seen him plowing up the dirt twenty foot short of the mark at the last turkey shoot back home.

The moonhead had brung his horse limping back in close, and he had his pistol out but was holding it like he didn't know if he should stick it back in his holster and clear off. The kid hadn't pulled his. And the third pardner had just set there with a five-day red beard, working on his sixth, and drinking in the show and not doing or saying nothing.

"Would you care to stay for supper?" Ma says.

The buckskin man blinked at her and took a good breath and seemed to pull hisself together some. Then he looked at his wrists and moved his fingers a little, not even making fists and wincing like he'd just had arnica poured on a cut, and then he looked straight at me, his eyes going narrow and steady. "I want your name, boy," he says.

"Well, you got everybody else's," I says. "Might's well have mine too. My name's Ezekiel Hunt, and I ain't giving you no orders whatsoever except leave our hogs alone."

"Sir, I believe you have broken my right wrist and maybe my left one too, and I—"

I says, "You should of used your wrists for something better than—"

"Don't you dare presume to interrupt me," he says, still sweating and pale and squinty and trembling a little. "You are alive at this moment only because my *friends* have been insubordinate jackasses."

The moonhead says, "Now, Stull, don't go—"

"Silence!" the buckskin man says. Then to me: "My name is Markham Millmont Penderby, and your name is mud. Your name is muck. You are going to die."

"Be glad to oblige you in about fifty years," I says.

"Zeke, why don't you take the hogs up the crick a ways and let me settle this," Pa says. "There's no use—"

"I wouldn't soil my hands or my reputation dueling with the likes of you," the buckskin man says. "So you will be summarily executed after proper sticking."

I didn't know what all that meant, though it didn't sound too enjoyable, but I held still to keep peace in the family.

Turning his deep-set eyes onto me and changing his voice till it was high and strange and syrupy, the buckskin man says, "How would you like to be a freebooter instead of a piggy boy?"

I didn't like talking to him, but you don't learn nothing if you just keep your jaw shut, so I says, "What's a freebooter?"

"Why, one who spreads the gospel of ill-will, a plunderer, a marauder, an orphan-maker," he says. "You'd have to steal yourself a horse somewhere, but for a young man as accomplished as you with the singlestick, that shouldn't take long."

"No thanks," I says. "I believe I'll find another line of work."

"You might find it very invigorating," he says. "It might rouse up your sleeping spirits."

"They ain't asleep," I says.

He looked me up and down. "Haven't you killed any salvages yet?" he says.

"No, sir," I says.

"Your education has been grievously neglected," he says. "By your age, I'd already killed a half-dozen, not counting squaws. You must do your part. You must share the burden of cleansing the land. No Muck, No Backtalk, and No Salvages is our motto. Wouldn't you like to ride under that banner?"

"No, sir," I says.

"In that case, I'm afraid we'll have to resort to sticking," he says.

Pa says, "It just don't make no sense to—"

"First, you will return my property to me," the buckskin man says to Pa. "You will put that pistol back in my holster and that rifle back in its scabbard."

Pa shuffled a little and made a move like he was half a mind to oblige, him being extra careful about property rights all his life, and if he'd commenced actually doing it, we'd of had our first wrassling match in five years. But he held back and says, "You aimed these at me and my family and my hogs, and I don't believe I'd care to arm you again right now when you've got your bile up."

"My what?" the buckskin man says. "What do you know about my bile or blood or choler, you stupid, comic lout?"

"Let's get out of here," the kid says.

"I don't recall giving you leave to speak," the buckskin man says, snapping around on him.

"Your friend's giving you good advice," Pa says, mild but worried-sounding. "We'll do our best to cross the river tomorrow, and I'll leave these here weepons on the other side, unloaded."

"You think you can steal my property and live to tell about it?" the buckskin man says.

"I never stole nothing in my life," Pa says.

The buckskin man's horse had just let fall a set of horse-apples (and they must of had a feed wagon along because they was a high quality), and Colonel Woppert moved in to inspect and take charge, making the horse shy off and almost unseat the buckskin man, who wasn't holding his reins. The kid grabbed hold of them and begun leading him off into the dusk towards the riverbank. The others followed along, and the buckskin man leaned around and yelled back, "You are going to see the wheel within the wheel, my stinking young Ezekiel. And it's going to be the last thing you'll ever see."

Chapter Four

BESIDES *Aesop's Fables* (which I had read four times) and *The Historie of Four-Footid Beastes* (which I had read too numerous times to mention), my third book was the Bible (which I had read once, once seeming like about enough), so I knew what the buckskin man was talking about, but it didn't seem to make no sense. That other Ezekiel had went on to live a long time after he seen his vision. He'd had a full life of yelling at people and carrying on about their sins and oraculating and fainting and seeing things. But I got the general message: he aimed to work some kind of vengeance on me and us and ours.

So when Pa commenced harnessing the mules in a hurry, I snuck some grain out of the back of the wagon and scattered it for the hogs before he could notice or stop me. It wasn't enough to feed a flock of chickens that size, leave alone hogs, but it made them feel good—or like they might be *going* to feel good—and it give them something to go on. Because it seemed certain sure they'd have to go somewheres else tonight or get hurt or kilt or scattered or stole or something.

A half-moon was trailing along after the sun which had already set, and there wasn't enough clouds so's I could hope for the kind of darkness you can hide twenty-seven hogs in where there's no brush to speak of nor ditches nor draws nor boulders. It was still light enough to see the riverbank and the water, though the other shore was misting up and glooming, and I seen the moonhead (who must of changed horses, since Miz Atlas had meant business) and the kid and the redbeard— all three—go trotting right into the water, swimming their horses a little when they had to but mostly walking and sometimes coming up to no more than knee-deep, zagging downstream towards a long skinny island where there was a grove of cottonwoods about fifteen foot tall, and at first I thought they'd called it quits and was laying in some firewood.

"That rifle don't have but the one bullet in it," Pa says. He'd come up behind me and sounded like he was apologizing for something. "And only four catridges in the gun."

"That ain't enough to fight *sane* people," I says.

"And I have to think of your ma," he says. "Let's get on out of here whiles there's still some daylight." He held up his hand before I could start talking. "Nobody's going to ford no rivers at night, so just forget about it. Let's head back downstream. We can get to the middle ford by tomorrow afternoon, and maybe it'll look a little better this time."

He was talking straight across to me instead of down, like we had an equal say in what was going to happen, and it give me an awesome feeling like I'd finally managed to climb a tree right up to the top and now didn't have no problems in the world except how to climb down. "All right," I says, hearing the far-off thud of an ax over on that skinny island.

"Ma's got some cold beans," he says. "Can you eat and walk and herd them hogs all at the same time?"

"I can try," I says. I felt light-headed and kind of dazy, like I'd already did everything I knew how to do and didn't need to think no more, and whiles Pa mounted up to the seat and wheeled the wagon around and headed northeast the way we'd come, I tried to shake that mood away, feeling like it might be the death of me. I was just in a lull, and I was going to have to do a whole lot more, whether I knew how to or not.

And after the five minutes it took me to get it into the hogs' heads they'd have to start moving again, and which direction, I seen the three pardners sloshing their horses back to the near bank, each dragging a couple of them young cottonwoods on each side of his saddle, and what made it worse was they'd already cut all the little branches off of them and left them behind—something no man would do that was scrounging firewood in this kind of country.

I felt cold, though it wasn't cold out, and wondered if Pa'd seen them too. He was having to go slow with Speck and Long Tom, even though the sandy ground was pretty smooth, sloping us down gradually towards the riverbank again but away from the clump of wagons where there was two or three cook fires going now. If we could only get in a steady half-hour of walking, it'd be night, I reckoned. Night, and us too far off to bother with, even with that blamed half-moon shining.

Ma showed up behind the tailbox and handed me down a sticky scoop of beans in a pie plate which hadn't had no pie in it for seven weeks, and she says, "You were brave."

"I was?" I says.

"Pa thinks so too," she ways. "He told me."

I felt embarrassed and glad of the dusk, it not being the kind of talk that was ordinarily passed around amongst us. "Well, you tell him *he* was brave," I says.

"All right," she says, and I could see her teeth shine.

"And tell him I hope he don't have to be braver yet in about ten minutes," I says.

She ducked back under the canvas, and I et my beans.

It took about fifteen minutes for them to catch up with us,

though it might of been less since I crammed the time inbetween full of so much useless thinking, I could of made a town clock slow down and back up. But I might as well of passed it whistling or whittling for all the good it done me. When them three horsemen (I couldn't see the fourth at first) come cantering up on us, looking black against the smudge of light left from the sunset, I didn't have no more in my head than to start out with.

Pa must of heard their hooves because he popped his head out of the back with the sixgun stuck in his belt and the rifle aimed over my head and says over his shoulder to Ma, "Now just keep going steady like we're minding our own business."

I got behind the last hog (that being Shaver, a smaller hoggaster than Colonel Woppert, acting disgusted with all this extra droving), and I give him a touch in the hock to speed him up a little with the rest. The three reined in about ten foot behind me and begun walking at our speed, which wasn't much, and when I glanced back I seen they'd brought them cottonwood poles with the branches lopped off and the pointy ends frontwards like lances, one for each of them, longer than my staff but sure not stronger which was about the only comfort I could think of.

The kid says, "We've come to collect that rifle and sixgun, mister. If you're heading back for Arkansas or Missouri or some such garden of earthly delights, you won't need firearms. Especially not when they belong to somebody else."

"I'm sorry about that," Pa says, sounding confused like he hadn't expected that particular subjeck to come up first. "It didn't seem like we could trust your friend's temper, so we decided to try the middle ford tomorrow or the next day."

"The fact remains you've stolen Mr.—uh, my friend's property," the kid says. "And he wants it back now."

"They say there's a kind of Post Office at the foot of Ash Hollow up on the North Platte," Pa says. "I'll leave them there for your friend if you're going that way."

"Which way we're going is *our* concern," the kid says. "Meanwhile, you're breaking the law."

"Don't seem to be a whole lot of law out here," Pa says, sounding miserable and giving his lip a chaw.

"You're dead right there," the moonhead says. "You've hit the nail right on the thumb, mister."

"What's them poles sposed to be for?" Pa says, and I'd been wondering when he was going to get around to that. The moonhead was holding his about two foot behind my back, and it was getting hard to tell who was doing the droving here.

"I'll tell you what I'll do," Pa says.

"That won't be necessary because I have already told YOU what to do," the kid says. "Hand over that rifle and sixgun and the whole regrettable incident will be forgotten."

"Zeke?" Pa says, like he was asking me a favor.

Walking sideways so's I could keep an eye on where them poles were aiming, I says, "Gents, you and your friend have been threatening us, and them are our only weepons. I reckon they'll just have to be the price you pay for your sins."

"Why, we haven't even got going on the sins yet, boy," the kid says. "How much does pork fetch by the pound?"

"Depends on who's buying and who's selling and what part of the Territory it's in," I says. "But these hogs ain't for sale." It was getting so dark, I couldn't see their faces plain. The half-moon hadn't brightened all the way up yet, and besides, I had to keep looking every which way—from them to the hogs to the poletips to Pa to the ground underfoot.

"Why don't we stop and talk a little business?" the kid says, sounding halfway reasonable.

But Pa wasn't fooled no more than I was. "We don't need no more business this evening," Pa says. "Much obliged to you. Just ask at the emigrants' Post Office at the foot of Ash Hollow, and you'll find these guns."

And then the fourth horseman come trotting along behind them. What with the wagonwheels squeaking and the hogs

gruffling and us getting nearer the river current, I hadn't heard
him as quick as I would of ordinarily. But the cut of his sombrero and the funny way he was setting, I didn't have no
trouble reckonizing the buckskin man, and I wished pigs could
fly and me with them.

"Damn it, Stull," the kid says, wheeling around and almost
knocking the moonhead off of his horse with the pole. "You
said you'd lie down and rest."

"When Duty whispers low, 'Thou must,' the Youth says,
'Pass the can,'" he says, sounding slurry now like he'd been
drinking some pain-killer.

"I've been conducting peaceful negotiations here," the kid
says. "And I believe I have come close to convincing these
two—uh, countrymen of ours it would be the gentlemanly
thing to to to turn over your property immediately, thus pre-
venting embarrassment all the way around."

"Shoot the bastards and slaughter the hogs," the buckskin
man says.

"Oh, for the love of Jesus," the kid says, disgusted.

Pa lifted the rifle and sighted along it, and I hoped he could
see the difference between me and them. "Back off from this
wagon," he says. "I never kilt nobody in my life, but I'm willing to start right now, and it'll be the fella with all the names,
right through the gut."

It sounded pretty good, but they kept right along following
us. I seen the buckskin man was wearing some kind of sling
on his right arm and something like sticks tied to his left wrist
to keep it stiff. "My guts are not the location of my soul nor
even the seat of my passions," he says. "How many punishable
offenses does that add up to now?"

He must of been talking to the kid because the kid says, "I
don't know," kind of offhand and still disgusted like he
wished the buckskin man had played this game some other
way.

"You got no right to torment and persecute folks," Pa says.
"If it'll do any good, I'll beg your pardon for whatever it was.

No offense intended, but there's been some *took* now. So clear off. I mean it. And I told you where you can find these weepons in three or four days, if the Lord permits."

"The Lord permits many curiosities, as you are about to bear witness to," the buckskin man says. "And it isn't your words that give offense, but your *selves* and your stench and that piggy boy."

Meaning me, I guess. "I'd just as leave be a piggy boy as any other kind," I says. "What kind of animals you reckon *you* are?"

The tip of redbeard's pole come swinging across near my neck, and I got a good look at the dull, lopped-off point he hadn't even bothered to char in a fire for a couple minutes to harden it like you would if you wanted to drive a stake. The buckskin man muttered something to him and then muttered something at the moonhead.

And when the moonhead swung away from the bunch and give his horse a touch with his heels and trotted along past the hogs and up towards the front of the wagon, Pa yells, "Keep off!" as fierce-sounding as he could and aimed the rifle at the moonhead and hesitated till he was too far past, and I knew he was thinking about that one bullet in there and wondering where it would do the most good, and by that time the moonhead had give Long Tom a jab in the rump with his pole and speeded him and Speck up some, and the wagon was jouncing Pa back and forth so's he couldn't aim even if he'd been any good at it.

Whiles the wagon commenced pulling away from me and the hogs (not too fast because it took more than a jab to get them mules working, specially at night), Pa says, "Jump in, Zeke. Come on, jump in."

But I had better things to do than go bouncing along in a wagon whiles the likes of these four done that sticking they'd spoke of. If I jumped in that wagon and crouched and ducked and clung to Ma or Pa and hoped for the best, I felt like there was going to be too much dead meat here on this godforsook

riverbank by daybreak, including mine maybe and some of the
hogs for sure, and I meant to come up in this world and improve myself and take some kind of equal place among my
fellowmen who happened to all be on horseback but me. So
the first thing I done by way of bettering myself was to dodge
back sideways past the tip of redbeard's pole and hang onto it
with one hand, same time sweeping my staff around hard as I
could, nor caring if the blow on the end of it turned out to be
murderous or not.

Even whiles I was doing it, the kid had stuck what looked
like Lucy June (and sounded like her too) in the butt, hard,
with his pointy pole, so hard it bent. And some part of my
brains took note of that limberness out of the dim corner of
my eye. My hickory staff didn't do no bending to speak of
when it whizzed over the top of redbeard's horse's ears,
glanced off of his shoulder with a whack and went *thonk* on
the side of his head, knocking him out from under his hat and
toppling him right over sideways and out of his saddle. Lucky
for me, he didn't hang up in his stirrup, so I was into his place
by means of shaking hands with grandma (which is what they
call it if you use your saddlehorn when you shouldn't), and
I almost lost holt of his pole in the scramble but kept it so's
he'd have to do the rest of his damned larking around barehanded which a hog has got enough teeth not to tolerate.

The buckskin man busted into a gallop back the way they'd
come, which seemed like mighty unhealthy exercise for his
horse in this squinty kind of moonlight and must of been unhealthy for him too since he was crouching forward and letting
out whiny yelps over what he was probably having to make
his wrists do. The kid quit sticking Lucy June and just set
there on his horse gawping at me, and the redbeard was taking
a rest flat on his back (I didn't have nothing against him and
even felt sorry for him, but I've come to find out in this life—
what there is of it—if you go pushing somebody too hard and
too far, you'd better be set for some pushing back), and the
moonhead was forty or fifty yards up ahead with the wagon,

probably still rousting the mules, though I couldn't see good enough to tell.

And the hogs was all strung out inbetween, some chasing the wagon like a dog might and some walking along, stopping and starting and beginning to wander a little, and some hanging back with me, snuffing and grunting and peering around to see where I'd went. I'd never done my droving on horseback, not having no horse (though I'd ridden off and on since I was five), so they didn't reckon on me having four feet or being up in the air.

Whiles me and the kid was staring at each other the best we could, the rifle went off up ahead and two shots from a sixgun (coughier-sounding and less of a whang) and in a few seconds two more shots, and if they'd all been Pa's doing, he was going to spend the rest of the night with two empties, three counting the Allen.

All of a sudden like he was coming out of a fog, the kid scratched for his own sixgun, and I tried to rein and kick this strange heavy-barreled mount in close so's I could swing my staff some more, but it was skittish and confused and I didn't even know its name, and before I could get enough balance to land a blow or even try, the kid was aiming at me and saying, "Hold still or you're a dead one."

But redbeard's horse couldn't understand no complicated instructions like that and probably didn't much care if I was a dead one or a live one, long as I was somewheres besides on him, so when redbeard down on the ground let out a big hog-sounding kind of groan almost underhoof, the horse bolted with me and went bucking. It wasn't no cool-headed night horse but a spooker ready to believe it was going to be et by six-legged hogs or bit by a snake the size of that sprawled-out redbeard.

Whiles the nearest hogs went scattering six ways from Saturday, the kid should of forgave and forgot, it not being *my* fault I wasn't holding still. Instead, he loosed off a shot at me and then another, not hitting nothing but moonlight and sand,

far as I could tell. I had only been shot at once before, and it
ain't a feeling I'd care to repeat any too often: it makes you
think some dreadful things about your flesh and bones and
don't exackly heighten your hopes for the near future.

I'm not a good rider, but I'm stubborn, and I stuck with that
horse for a spell. Lucky for me he was a straightaway bucker
and didn't do no pinwheeling, so he put a good distance between me and the kid in no time at all, even though he couldn't
see good enough to let out all the way. He went in the general
direction of the wagon but off at an angle towards the river
which scairt me some more because of that five foot bank
in most places and no way to tell if the water was deep or shallow in any particular place. I tried to rein him in hard as I
could, but I had that cottonwood pole in one hand and my
staff in the other, and all this ruption and trying to chin the
moon was making them two sticks flap around and whack him
now and then and sweep past his eyes, making him jerk his
head and veer off which I don't think he would ordinarily of
done.

After a couple minutes of that, we parted company and no
hard feelings. I didn't know if he bucked me off or I jumped
and still don't. But he was getting so near the bank and going
slewfooted with all this dodging, I reckoned I'd be better off
afoot after all, and whiles I was in the air, I seen him go over
the edge without me and don't know whether he busted a leg
and drowned or cooled off and come to his senses or just kept
going on across that river and up to the North Fork and beyond and headed for the hills. I was too busy laying myself
out cold on the ground.

It don't hurt to get knocked out, as most anybody can tell
you in case you been keeping your head to yourself all your
life. You just lose track of things for a spell and do a little
recollecting and don't seem to mind at all. At first. Afterwards
isn't so good. I don't know how long it lasted, but when I
come to, I seen the wheels, just like the buckskin man had said

I would, and the wheels inside of wheels too, and some stars and stripes and whirlicues that hadn't no business taking up that much room in the sky. Even the half-moon, when I tried to make it hang still by staring with one eye, went skating off southeast someplace, leaving what looked like patches of orange fire in back of it which I didn't remember that other Ezekiel mentioning.

I hadn't had a good bonk on the head like that (with a jolt up the spine thrown in to clinch the bargain) since I'd fell off of Pearly Hax's shed roof trying to scramble out of her pa's general neighborhood after he'd caught me trying to recite a poem (I used to know one, but I forget which) over her bedroom windowsill, back before I knew you could also climb over it if you was so inclined and didn't feel like talking no more. The bonk and jolt hadn't made me no wiser then, and the treatment had disimproved in the meanwhile. Least, I hadn't felt dumber the first time, but now I felt like I'd been left out for trash.

I didn't forget where I was or what I'd been doing or none of that. I just felt like I'd been out of touch with myself and had to get familiar with my hands and feet all over again. And what helped me over the hump was Colonel Woppert.

He give me a snuff and a good nudge in the side, and I set up (instead of trying to make sense out of that whirly sky) and smelt him too and hung onto his left ear and scratched it which he liked fine. "Colonel Woppert," I says. "Kindly report the military situation."

He give a wheeze and a grunt which summed it up pretty good.

After I'd practiced breathing and seeing some more, I stood up and tried to figure out what was going on. I couldn't see much in either direction, and when I looked in the river, I couldn't see no sign of redbeard's horse. The current was making so much noise, I couldn't hear nothing else, so I located my staff and the cottonwood pole and my straw hat laying nearby and walked away from the river fifty feet, wobbly at first but then better. Colonel Woppert come along like a pet dog, and I seen the shapes of four or five other hogs not too far off that looked to be rooting at weeds or brush or scouting for buffalo chips. And then I heard the gunfire.

It was from downstream of me, the way the wagon had went, and was spaced out slow, almost regular, not a rifle but a handgun, and I give three medium SeeeeeeuuuuuuBOY's to collect the nearest hogs, not going too loud with it for fear of busting my head all the way open instead of half and also scairt of bringing the kid after me, wherever he was. I rounded up six hogs all-told, including Armbruster and Aunt Fanny and Seldom, and commenced walking toward the gunfire which had now left off for a while. I couldn't of run for pay, pardon, or paradise.

Chapter Five

THE GUNFIRE NEVER did start up again, and me and the hogs
(with them stopping here and there to snuffle up some mess or
give their hope for supper a little more exercise) trotted along
stiff-legged just like we knew what we was doing. It wasn't
hard country to walk night or day, as I'd already learnt since
this was backtracking: mainly level packed sand with now and
then a rut or a small crick or a dished-in buffalo trail down to
the river where they done their fording single-file, not waiting
for no ferries nor bothering to look for the shallowest places.
You could walk pretty fast if you was a mind to and only fall
down once in a while.

I rounded up two more hogs in the first ten minutes (Shaver
and Silky Purse) but didn't see no trace of the wagon up

ahead, though the moonlight was as full as it was going to be and I could of made out a shape that big from a hundred yards or more. Then I heard the horse trotting along behind me.

First I thought it might be redbeard's horse come to apologize, but then I used my brains for something besides bag pudding. I crotched down as quick as I could to keep from sticking up like a moony landmark in that flat, mostly bare, dang near endless stretch of ready-made wagon trail that had already lured upwards of fifty thousand lunkheads along it that year alone, and I got on the far side of Colonel Woppert, who was big enough for two my size to duck beside, even though he'd trimmed down a good bit, and I kept my staff in one hand and hooked my other forefinger through Colonel Woppert's nose-ring so's he'd keep me company and not stray off. He didn't like it none since it usually meant he was going to have to do something he didn't feel like doing, but when I just stayed there not tugging or hauling, he grunted and whuffled a little and held still. He wasn't used to me being down on all fours next to him, but he seemed willing to tolerate it.

The horse come closer and closer now, and me being down on the ground like that, I could get a good look at the shape growing up against the paler sky, and the horse had a rider with a sombrero, carrying a cottonwood pole almost straight up in the air like a flagstick, though it didn't have no flag on it but something pointy and shiny like a butcher knife tied on, and then the buckskin man's slurry highpitched voice says, "Here, piggy-piggy-piggy-piggy-piggy. Here, piggy-piggy-piggy-piggy-piggy," kind of sweet like he might of had a bowl of mush for piglets.

He must of seen the hogs about then because he veered over our way instead of trotting on past, and the pole come wobbling down to aim. I held tight to Colonel Woppert's ring because he wasn't enjoying the sound of the horse or the voice none and wanted to switch around and stare and keep track. He tugged but I tugged harder, hooking two fingers through the ring now.

"Nice piggy-piggy-piggy," the buckskin man says, sounding like he was grinning too hard to talk straight, and I seen him make a jab at Aunt Fanny, and she went running and squealing off sideways, hurt or scairt or both, and I had all I could do to keep Colonel Woppert from taking me off into the dark with him. As it was, he drug me about ten foot before I got his nose turned and made him plant his trotters again.

He must of looked tempting to the buckskin man: the biggest hog of the bunch and the only one standing sideways. He got his horse reined around (maybe using his knees like some can do instead of his hurt wrists) and headed for the both of us, aiming his lashed-on butcher knife which I could see plain now. I couldn't tell how he was hanging onto that pole.

"Stay just like that, piggy-piggy-piggy-piggy," he says, high and happy and almost like a girl.

But when he was still a short ways off, coming towards us and leaning forward, I turned Colonel Woppert loose and give him a good swat on the ham at the same time and done just what I done to redbeard—or tried to. Once ain't enough practice at something like that, and it was darker now, and what threw me off my swing with the staff after I'd grabbed his cottonwood pole above the knife handle was him screaming. He done it high and loud, good enough for the middle part of a hog-call, and my staff hit him square on the shoulder instead of the side of the head, but I kept aholt of his damn pigsticker, and when his horse reared and went swiveling to get away from whatever I might be, the buckskin man come right out of his saddle like a beechnut out of a husk and landed smack on his rump, still screaming. Limber as it was, his pole busted on the way down, leaving me with the butcher-knife end and him with the butt tied to his right forearm with a thick leather belt.

He left off screaming as sudden as he'd started and laid back gulping for air whiles I made a pass at catching his horse but couldn't. It bolted off a good ways and then stood watching, just like Colonel Woppert and the others was doing, and I didn't dare get too far off from the buckskin man in case he'd scrounged up another gun and could use it. I searched him good as I could in the bad light and didn't find nothing.

"My God, my God, oh my God, my wrist!" he says, though what god was going to be listening to him, I couldn't guess. "Oh God, my shoulder!" And he let out a stream of cusswords, most of which I'd heard before but some new ones, though they come too fast to remember.

I remembered Aunt Fanny squealing off into the night, and I says, "How'd you like to be pig-stuck your own self?" And I showed him what his butcher knife looked like up close right under that mustache.

After letting out a few more strainy groans like a boy trying to get his tongue unstuck from an ice-cold ax blade on a winter morning (just ask me what it's like), he says, "No thank you."

I tried hard to keep reasonable about all this, but I started recollecting them gun-shots up ahead and not knowing if I should go or stay or choose up sides for Ducks and Drakes or maybe kill him. I had never thought of doing that to nobody before, and it made me shamed of myself. But where was Ma and Pa? "What's the matter with you?" I says, meaning in general, not just his shoulder and wrists and whatever. "Are you loco?"

"Nothing the matter with me, piggy boy," he says, gritting his teeth and talking through them like they'd stuck. "Except some grievous bodily damage, thanks to you."

"It's your own fault," I says. "You lead a dangerous life." I showed him his knife again. "You know what kind of dangerous life you're leading right this minute?"

He turned his nose out of the road an inch. "I believe so," he says.

"What you been doing to my hogs?" I says.

He took time to try feeling at his shoulder, but neither of his arms was working right, so he just groaned some more. "Nothing out of the ordinary," he says. "After all, what is the fate of pigs? This little piggy went to market."

I didn't know what the fate of pigs or anybody else happened to be. I think it's sposed to mean something like the Last Judgment, only without the general uprising, and if hogs get left behind when the trumpet blows, I reckon I'll stay behind and lead them off someplace else where we don't have to listen to the likes of this buckskin man who had mistook hisself for an Archangel.

"This little piggy had none," he says. "Many are called but few are chosen."

"Nobody's going to call my hogs but me," I says. "And nobody's going to stick them for fun."

"It wasn't fun," he says. "It hurt like hell."

"What do you use for brains?" I says.

He seemed to think that one over, then says, "I need a drink."

"So do my hogs," I says. "Wherever they might be, dead or alive or lost for good. I used to think my pa was dumb sometimes, but you beat all."

He commenced writhing and rubbing his wrists against each other, scraping the stub of busted pole back and forth in the sand. "Oh Jesus Christ it hurts!" he says.

"You're in the wrong part of the Bible," I says. "Let's get back to where it says a tooth for a tooth."

"You damn bumpkin," he says. "I'm lying on the cold ground, crippled. What more do you want?"

"How many dead hogs am I going to find on this here cold ground when the sun comes up?" I says.

"Too many unknowns in that equation," he says.

"What was that gunfire downstream?" I says. "Where's our wagon?"

"I wasn't downstream, I was upstream," he says.

I showed him his knife up close again. "The world was sorry enough already without you aiming to stick it and raise hell." I moved the point under his chin. "Why don't I just show you the way back home?"

"Wee wee wee!" he says halfway between a squeal and a screech. "Who gave you the right to humiliate me?"

I didn't know what that meant, but if it was what I was doing, I was going to go on doing it without no by-your-leave. "What happened to my ma and pa?" I says.

"Don't let the apron-strings stretch too far, piggy boy," he says. "Think for yourself. Cut your own meat. Wipe your chin. Sit up straight. Speak whether you're spoken to or not. *Carpe diem.* If music be the food of love, play on. If thine eye offend thee, pluck it out. If a job's worth doing, it's worth undoing. He hath pulled down the mighty from their seats. It's harder work getting to Hell than to Heaven. First come, first served. Everything is the cause of itself. Now, repeat after me."

He was talking quick and hard and not using the same high silky voice but still kind of slurry. I felt scairt of him, even if it was me holding the knife. "Why'd you want to go hurting people and poor dumb beasts?" I says.

"Suffer the little children to come unto me," he says, "and they'll get theirs. The race is not to the swift nor the battle to the strong. Nature delights in punishing stupid people. *De gustibus non est disputandum.* Travel makes a wise man better but a fool worse. Truth crushed to earth will rise again."

"All right, then, get up," I says. "You're coming with me to hunt that wagon."

But he just laid where he was, paying no mind to the knife and staring up at the sky which was maybe doing some wheel-within-wheeling for him now.

"I told you to get up," I says.

"Eat not thy heart," he says.

Well, I'd known all along the buckskin man wasn't what you'd call sensible, but now he'd lost me further than ever. I couldn't make no connections amongst what he was telling me except it all sounded like some kind of advice, and coming from him, it couldn't be nothing but bad, so I paid him as little mind as possible and stuck to the main bother. "I'm sorry I hurt you," I says.

"Kiss it and make it well," he says.

I stood up, trying to figure what to do. His horse was still a way off, acting shifty, and the hogs (I could only locate five nearby) had come drifting in closer, and then I heard the horse coming from downstream at a good canter.

It was too close too soon, and I didn't have a chance to hide or go hogback riding or get behind Colonel Woppert, so I just kept that knife close to the buckskin man and hoped for the best which turned out to be none too good.

I got my staff ready for business in my free hand, and by then I could make out the rider had one of them damn cottonwood poles held up tall. He reined in and circled a little, and I seen it was the moonhead (he'd lost his hat someplace, but that was the only improvement).

"Is that you, Stull?" he says.

"Yes, the piggy boy and I are having a little moonlight chat," the buckskin man says. "He's really *very* nice. But he happens to be holding a knife on me."

The moonhead come in closer, aiming what looked to be a nickel-plated sixgun at me, glinting along the barrel, and I says, "I'll cut his throat if you don't clear off." I didn't know whether I meant it or not, but I had to say something.

"He's really very, very nice," the buckskin man says. "But don't tell Roger."

"Roger got himself killed," the moonhead says. "That damn hog farmer shot his horse out from under him and he busted his neck." There was a long pause with only the sound of a couple hogs trying to root. Then in a whiny voice like a kid who knows he's in for a licking, the moonhead says, "I'm sorry."

Trying to sit up, the buckskin man says quiet and soft, "Roger's dead?"

I reckoned they meant the kid, since it didn't seem like redbeard'd be good for no more chiyukking that night.

"That's right," the moonhead says.

"You're *sure* he's dead?" the buckskin man says.

"Sure as I'm born," the moonhead says. "But it wasn't my—"

"You weren't born, you were whelped," the buckskin man says. "But Roger can't be dead. I need him. He loves me."

"Well, if you'd seen his neck, you'd know he couldn't—" The moonhead left off because the buckskin man had commenced screaming even louder than when he'd fell off his horse—higher and wavier and more like a real little girl. It scairt me and the hogs and his horse, and I pulled the knife back a little so's he wouldn't come lunging into it by accident and hurt hisself.

He come down out of the scream long enough to say, "Shoot him. Shoot this little pig. I've been telling everybody all night to shoot him. When's somebody going to shoot him?"

I brung the knife back close again and says to the moonhead, "I mean it. I'll cut his gizzard out if you don't clear off," but even whiles I was saying it, I seen him aiming at me, and I couldn't get myself to cut nobody's throat, and I couldn't do nothing else but duck a little, whiles he shot me in the head.

Chapter Six

SO THAT'S HOW I come to wake up what looked to be way past
dawn, laying on the trompled sand with nothing but Colonel
Woppert and two crows for company. The crows was standing
on Aunt Fanny about fifty foot off having breakfast (I could-
n't tell it was her right off, my eyes being blurry, but I went
and looked later) which was more than me and Colonel
Woppert was going to have, though I couldn't of stomached
nothing. I felt sick from head to boots. Even my hair felt sick.
And I was all swole up and crusty over my right ear, and if I'd
felt slow of mind and foot before then, I had now sunk so far
I could of give lessons to the biggest grout-head in the Territory. But since that was *me*, I didn't waste time learning.

Somehow or other I managed to get up on my knees and be

sick at my stomach, and then I tried to keep my feet out of each other's road long enough to go the short ways to the riverbank. I found a halfway shelvy place where I wouldn't drowned myself and took a long drink through my bandanna (to cut the yellow silt some) and soaked my face and got sick again, but had barely enough sense to leave the side of my head alone which didn't happen to be bleeding at the moment.

I seemed to strengthen up some after that, and I took my hat (it had a long bloody gash in it along the side just above the brim) and my staff, and took a last look at Aunt Fanny, getting a good crow-scolding whiles I was at it. She'd begun to go the way of all hogs. And men too. With a big disgusted grin along one side of her snout, which was about the way I felt myself.

I couldn't see no other corpuses, man or beast, in any direction and no live hogs neither and wouldn't of had the gall or gumption or lung power to call them anyways. I hadn't protected them proper, and maybe they'd be better off wild than letting me drove them into some more stupid perdition.

Then I begun doing what I'd been doing before I'd been shot: I went trudging and staggering downstream to hunt for our wagon with Colonel Woppert following, giving off gut-grumbles.

I don't know how far I walked, not even counting the zags, but I kept at it, squinting into the low sunshine that was creasing along the top of the river mist at me till I couldn't tell if I was seeing things for real or just for fun. Lots of times along that river I'd seen water where there wasn't none and upside down hills and wagons looking tall and skinny as some kind of trees, so when I saw some humps up ahead, I squinched my eyes against the sweat or tears or whatever it was lapping over my eyelashes and tried to make them go away. But they stayed put and slowly become two hogs, namely Lucy June eating the last part of a feed sack that looked like ours and Miz Atlas stretched out on her side with a broke-off cottonwood pole sticking out of her neck. A flock of crows went flapping away when I come close, and I seen buzzards circling and thinking things over, not only over the sand but out over the river too. And that's when I finally seen the wagon.

I hadn't been looking at the water, nor anything else much neither with my eyes feeling sore and my head making noises inside like a wheel hub needing axle grease, but all of a sudden, there it was, our wagon laying on its side in the shallows about thirty foot out from the bank. The water was only a couple foot deep there, and the yellowy white current was sloshing up against it. The ground I was standing on had got all chewed up with hoofprints and wheelruts, and the low bank had been broke down all the way like cattle had been drinking there, and Speck and Long Tom had went off someplace, including their harness far as I could tell, and the way the wagon was laying at a tilt, I could see there most likely wasn't nobody in it. But I waded out to make sure, getting washed over and almost swept off even in that shallow a run.

Nobody'd got caught inside and drownded, and the tailbox was empty and no trace of Ma or Pa or worldly goods nor nothing. Half the hoops had sprung out of their slots and through the canvas, and there was so many rips and holes in it I couldn't tell if they'd been bullets or pig-stickers or what. I give my face another good washing and stared upstream and downstream and across, and about fifty yards down from me two buzzards (and two more waiting in line) was at work on a hog carcass. I didn't wade down to find out who it was, feeling sad and strange and sick enough already without no extra help.

I went back to the shore and set down before I fell down, whiles Colonel Woppert helped Lucy June eat the rest of the sack and whatever grain dust might of been in the seams. I felt considerable perplexed, being orphaned without knowing for sure if it was permanent or exackly how it happened or who done what before, during, and after. I didn't feel like I was obliged to mourn a whole lot over the wagon itself: it had

never given me no rides to speak of, and I knew it best from
gawping at its tailbox and wishing I was laying on it and not
memorizing different kinds of dust for seven weeks.

But Ma and Pa made me feel lost. There wasn't nowhere
to look for them, no messages scraped on the sandbank, nothing wrote on the wet canvas, and too many tracks leading upstream and down to make sense out of—not even the corpus
of the kid (if there was such a thing). I had to make up my
own mind—what I had left of it between aches—if I should
set and wait (leaving them two hogs to starve along with me)
or head back home (which wasn't no home of ours but Abner
Small's who was trying to change over to chickens) or go on
towards this California I was already sick and tired of hearing
about.

I set a long while, puzzling it over, and finally decided to
keep on going if I could, reckoning Pa for stubborn enough,
dead or alive, to go on the way he'd been going. So all's I had
to do now was figure out how to stand up and how to make
two hogs (or more if I could ever get strong enough to hogcall)
learn how to fly or float and take me over this blamed river.

And I didn't know if I should pound some markers into the
sand (sposing I could locate anything to use) like I'd seen for
them that died off of the cholera, sometimes three or four in a
cluster near the best campsites, or just go on pretending Ma
and Pa had swam out alive and was going to find me someplace
along the Trail, waiting at that Emigrants' Post Office like the
buckskin man's weepons was sposed to (but was probably laying under a foot of silt already on the bottom).

What I done finally was just have a talk with them, like it
might be a letter or what I could of said at some supper but
never did, not like praying which I wasn't much good at, even
when wrote down first by somebody else. What I says was
something like this, not counting the places where I left off to
think up what come next:

Dear Ma and Pa:
   I can't stay here because me and the hogs are too hungry, meaning no offense. If you're dead, I'm sorry, and I wish you as well as

possible on the Other Shore if there is one, and please don't blame me for not jumping in the wagon like you said to help fight and fend off. I couldn't desert the hogs. I didn't even think of *trying* to. They needed me just as much as you and maybe more, even if I was no use to them like it turned out. Sometimes I have to do what I *can't*, just like the both of you. It must run in the family.

> Yours truly,
> Zeke

Then I remember I held still and thought I'd better end it a little more proper, so I says,

> Yours truly, your loving son,
> Ezekiel

And then all of a sudden it was like I was looking through hog's eyes, all squinched and bloodshot and mean, the way they turn when something gets to violating their life and limb too much and makes them think it's Now or Never, and everything I looked at turned beet-red, and I felt fit to kill, only there wasn't nothing to kill. My hands commenced clutching at the air in front of me all by theirself, and I stared at them, wishing there was something in them I could strangle. My teeth felt like *teeth*, I could hear singing inside my ears like my heart had pulled all its strings in tight as a banjo, and if something had got in my road right then, I'd of cleared it out for good.

But I didn't *have* no road except all this rutted-up mess underfoot, and there wasn't nobody to fight but Colonel Woppert and Lucy June, who'd already had enough. There's no use in biting dust or kicking stones or whacking water with a stick or flanging yourself around or yelling at the breeze. So I done the next best thing and set down and fainted.

Chapter Seven

WHEN I WOKE up or come to, whichever, an old man with a neck beard—grizzled and bushy like a fur collar under his chin and up around over his ears—was propping me up and holding a tin cup of water under my nose.

"Now try some more," he says, so I must of been gulping some without knowing it. "Think you can set up by yourself?"

"Yes, sir," I says.

He left go of me, and I fell back on the sand, and he says, "Well, just lay there then, and I'll make a bandage. What happened? That wasn't no mule-kick. Somebody shot you."

I heard him rustling around in back of me. "Where's my hogs?" I says.

He didn't say nothing but come back in a minute with two bandannas, one folded up like a pad and soaked with what smelt to be whiskey which I reckonized from fuming out of my Uncle Fred's mouth back home whenever he come to see Ma. He laid it on the side of my head where I'd been shot and tied it on with the other bandanna and says, "Least it can't do much harm."

He had me setting up again now, and I tried to peek around and see if Colonel Woppert and Lucy June was still there.

"So you're the hog drover," he says. "Let them get a little spread out, didn't you?"

He didn't say it unkindly or like scolding me, but sort of gentle like he already knew it weren't my fault. "Yes, sir," I says. "You seen any of them? Yesterday sundown there was twenty-seven of them, all told."

"Well, I can see four right this minute," he says. "But two of them's got visitors."

I could hear the crows without looking, but I heard Colonel Woppert's medium-size leave-me-alone grunt, so I felt some better.

"That your wagon?" the old man says.

"Yes, sir," I says. "You didn't happen to see my ma and pa and two mules heading downstream last night or this morning, did you? Red and blue calico and him with a straw hat, blue jeans, and a hickory shirt? No saddles?"

"Don't get all stirred around now, son," he says. "When you get hurt in the head like that, funny things can happen. No, I didn't see any folks like that, but I wasn't looking. I was too busy. Your pa a drinking man?"

"Well, he drinks water," I says. "And coffee when he can get it. And I seen him drink rhubarb juice one time, but he didn't like it."

He smiled at me with short stubby white teeth and give his beard a ruffling-through under his chin. "I meant whiskey," he says.

"No, sir," I says. "He don't drink none of that."

"Then likely I didn't meet him," the old man says. "I sell whiskey, and I'm generally too busy keeping my customers from turning into thieves to notice much else."

I could see part of his wagon behind me if I twisted my neck a ways. He had a two-mule team, and Colonel Woppert was standing in back of them, near as he could without getting under the off front wheel, waiting for mule-apple harvest time, and I thought I could see some of Lucy June out of the corner of my eye, but it hurt too much to twist.

"What're you aiming on doing now?" he says.

"Walking," I says. "Soon as I can walk."

"And what do you aim to eat?" he says.

"If the hogs can get along, so can I," I says.

He set still a while, then give me some more water and says, "I have to tell you, your hogs didn't get along any too well from what I could see. Why don't you ride along to the upper ford with me, then see how you feel?"

Since I didn't know which way anybody'd went, including the moonhead and the buckskin man, it didn't much matter where I tried first. "I'd be much obliged," I says. "But my hogs have to come along too."

"They're welcome," he says. "Long as I don't have to carry none." I let him help me to my feet, and long as I used my staff for an extra leg, I didn't keel over.

"Now I got a little surprise for you," he says and commenced leading me around to the back of his wagon which had XXX painted big along the side of the canvas. He took me to the tailgate and let it down, and there in amongst some lashed-together kegs and great big crocks and tubes and coppery-colored tubs I couldn't rightly make out was one of our gilts named Sugar Loaf, hogtied neat as you please. She begun squealing right away, like she'd had lots of practice lately, and Colonel Woppert give a grunt up front.

"Have to excuse me, I hope," the old man says. "I didn't know whose it was, trotting along free and easy."

"No offense," I says, feeling better. If I could find three, why couldn't I find more?

"I wasn't the only one," he says. "It's a shame to have to tell you, but I want to spare you some time. There's a couple more trussed up for butchering a half-mile back."

I almost asked him which ones, but then I realized he wouldn't know one from another.

He begun untying Sugar Loaf, and he says, "And a couple more spitted and pits dug, and if the folks can find anything to burn underneath of them, there'll be some whole roasters by nightfall." He waited for me to say something, but I didn't feel like it, so he says, "You don't look in good enough shape to go back and lay claim to the meat. You might have a whole lot livelier time than you'd reckon on. Lots of hungry people on the Trail."

"I wouldn't fancy eating none of it," I says. "Leave them be." He was about to turn Sugar Loaf loose up in his wagon instead of down on the ground, so I helped him lift her down to keep from getting his kegs stove in. Even a hundred pound gilt can cause a lot of turmoil if she don't have room to roam. Soon as she was loose, she scuttled around next to Lucy June to find out what was fitten for deportment hereabouts.

And I wished I had somebody to show *me*. The old man was looking me over careful now, and he says, "I won't ask you again who shot you, but maybe you wouldn't mind telling me if you're in any trouble I can't see with the naked eye."

No, sir," I says, which wasn't entirely true, but I didn't feel like mauling it over.

He seemed to perk up. "I don't mind a good slice of ham," he says. "But it takes near as long as whiskey to cure it right." He hauled out a half-full gunnysack. "Reckon those hogs could use some feed?"

"Yes, sir," I says, there being no doubt about that. I give them a little chucking call, and the three of them came trotting around back, full of hope, spite of all the solid evidence to the contrary. And that hope was rewarded for a change: the old man flung down a half a bucketful of corn and wheat mixed, and they had it crunched down in no time and was whuffling for more.

"They don't stretch it out much, do they," he says. "I don't believe I can spare much more right now."

"That'll hold them a while," I says. "Much obliged to you."

"Come on, I have to get moving," he says. "Will they follow if you're riding?"

"After that feed, they'd come along and start your fire for you and redd up the dishes too," I says.

"I'll settle for less," he says, slamming up the tailgate.

And he helped me around the side and up to the seat next to him which felt like climbing straight up the side of a two-story house with my head in a sack.

When we'd both settled and he'd left loose the brake and looked to be ready to persuade the mules to start walking, he hesitated and says, "A hog's a mighty valuable piece of property way out here. You sure you wouldn't want to go back and squeeze a little barter out of them poachers anyway? I can argue pretty good, long as guns wasn't to come into it."

I looked at our wagon already commencing to lose its canvas in the current and at the chawed-up ground that wasn't telling nothing I didn't know already and at the dead hog out on the sand bank in the river (that might of been Shaver if the buzzards had got out of the way long enough for me to see more of his spots) and at Miz Atlas who'd been pig-stuck (which maybe was no worse than spitted or trussed at that), and it didn't take no Lightning Calculator from a tent show to figure out the only difference between me and them was less than an inch where the moonhead's bullet had creased my head. It could just as easily have went through and put an end to all my rising and setting and dreaming and talking and hoping. It was the narrowest excape I'd had (including the time Mr. Foreman mistook me for a wild pig in the beech woods back home and loosed off a shotgun my way), and I meant to go right on excaping even if the places turned narrower still, because something had struck me hard and seemed like it had turned me over, not like a new leaf but a rock, maybe, and now I was seeing everything from the underside. Yet I felt out from under too. I felt like a newborn baby that's just been swatted and might not like it but was squalling for his own good. I valued my life better than ever and most everybody's and everything else's life too.

"I believe I'll let all dead hogs work out their own future," I says.

He give the reins a flick, and the mules started walking. "Now don't cry, son," he says, which was the first time I realized I was doing it. "There's more where they come from by the look of that boar down there."

"Colonel Woppert," I says, leaving my staff hang down over the side so's they could all three take a smell of it. I chucked at them, and they followed along.

"He's a whopper all right," the old man says. "Needs a little feeding up. Ever try hogs on marsh?"

"Marsh what?" I says.

"Marsh," he says. "Marsh. The leavings in a whiskey still. Wheat and corn marsh."

"No, sir," I says. "I never even seen any. They used to like beech mast best of all, but they don't grow no beeches out here."

"Now quit crying," he says. "You'll get the mules upset. I wouldn't ordinarily suggest it to one of your tender years, but would you like a sup of whiskey?"

"I don't know if I would or not," I says. "I never tried none."

"It's here for the asking," he says.

"I believe I'll pass," I says. "I can smell it just fine right now." The bandage was leaking a little down past my ear, and I wiped at it with my shirtsleeve. "Ma says whiskey kilt her brother Fred."

"With all due respeck to your ma, I'd say Uncle Fred kilt his*self*. Whiskey don't jump down nobody's throat where it ain't welcome. Sure you won't have a sup?"

"No, sir, I don't believe," I says.

He looked me over from my busted boots to my mashed hat and give me a nod and says, "Fine. I ain't heard a man or boy or woman neither say that since a year ago February, and she was an old Baptist lady too sick to spit."

We rumbled along for a spell with all that crockery and kegs and tubes and tubs making a muffled commotion behind and my mind drifting off into all kind of bad places, and then he says, "How'd you like to work for me when you feel better?"

"Doing what?" I says. I'd been imagining me and the three hogs surrounding the buckskin man and the moonhead and redbeard and the kid if he was still alive and slashing them up for catfish bait, and it weren't charitable of me.

"Selling whiskey and meanwhile not drinking it all yourself," he says.

"How do you sell whiskey?" I says.

"A gill at a time," he says. "And it mostly sells itself if it's any good. And I make *Kentucky* whiskey, not that watery-looking moonshiny nose-paint that passes for the real thing."

"I can do most things if I'm showed how," I says.

"I don't spose I have to show you how to eat cheese and jerky and cold beans, do I?" he says, reaching behind him for two tin dishes clamped face to face.

"No, sir," I says and proved it, though I felt half-sick.

I'd been feeling too blurry-headed to do much noticing, but whiles I et and the old man kept still for a spell, I seen he must of been washing pretty regular—his hands was callusy but clean, and he'd shaved close but for his collar of neck beard, and his soft black hat hadn't been used to wipe nothing with, and his dark-gray coat and pants made out of store cloth looked like they might of been a suit once. He didn't put on no airs (he talked kind of like me which ain't necessarily good but *plain* anyways), and he wasn't chawing or spitting. I was glad I'd been in the river to rench off a little so's I wouldn't shame myself.

After we'd went a mile or two (I seen a busted cottonwood

pole but no more hogs, standing up or laying down), he commenced talking. "I run off three others that worked for me," he says. "I hope you won't be the fourth."

I couldn't talk much with my mouth full, so I says, "Yes, sir."

"One watered my good liquor so much to cover up his guzzling, it begun to look like I was trying to sell the Platte River a keg at a time. Sounded like it too. You could hear my customers' teeth—them that had any—crunching and gritting every time they swallered. The other fell off the back of the wagon, which he was sposed to be guarding against bung-punchers, three-fourths drunk, and I didn't even know I'd lost him till he took a shot at me a quarter-mile off. And the third started calling me Charlie and asking me did I still eat raw eggs and what was the matter with my hair because it kept stirring around like there was something underneath of it besides me. Well, I don't mind a joke or two or a drink or two neither, but then he started jawing at some old lady who didn't happen to be there and kept giving him sassy backtalk, so I left him off at the middle ford to vex somebody else for a change. My name's Casper."

"Zeke," I says.

"I believe in human nature all right, but I don't like it much," he says.

"You know a man named Stull?" I says. "Or sometimes calls hisself three names at a time, only they keep changing?"

"No," he says. "Is that who rousted your hogs?"

"Him and three others," I says.

"And wrecked your wagon and shot you?" he says.

"Yes, sir," I says. "It was his idea."

"Why?"

I let the mules take five or six steps whiles I thought it over. "I believe he just plain enjoyed it," I says.

"Is he a drinking man?" Casper says.

"Yes, sir," I says. "He talked like Uncle Fred used to right before he'd start busting things just to hear them bust."

"Then don't worry about it," Casper says. "If you want to find him, you'll find him because he'll find *me*. You don't sell the best whiskey west of the Mississippi without the word getting around among drinking men. I just got one request: if any more shooting's going to start, you'd best get yourself a gun or practice up on manly apologies or just keep running. And whatever you do, don't get behind my kegs to do it. Don't even get in *front* of them."

He give me a smile to show he only half meant it, but he'd started me thinking, which is more than I can say for most people or even my own self.

Chapter Eight

AS WE RODE ALONG, I was half-dozing and dreaming about how I was going to rescue Ma and Pa from that Mortal Peril they must of got theirself into and how I was going to save all the hogs from a fate worse than market, and I was seeing pictures in my mind of me cleaning up on all pigstickers, clonking them on the head with my staff and generally being the Terror of the Plains, even if I didn't have no gun or horse.

And every time somebody'd take a lick at me, they'd miss or I'd duck, and nothing bad seemed like it could happen to me because I was too quick or smart or too good a dodger. There in my head I wasn't no dumb bystander but more along the line of Uncle Fred whenever anybody tried to take a bottle away from him that didn't happen to be stark empty yet. (He used to say people had been trying to take bottles off of him since he was a year old, only instead of bawling about it like he done at first, he'd got sense enough to learn how to bust jaws even when he was laying down.)

It didn't seem like I could be dozing and rampaging at the same time, but I done it, my eyes coming open now and then but shutting down again so's I could get in a few more whacks with my staff.

And one of the times they was open, I seen a wagon up ahead with a gray-haired man greasing its off-rear wheel, and as we come jolting closer, I woke all the way up. I don't know what it was I noticed—a smell maybe so faint I couldn't tell if I was smelling it—but all of a sudden I was down out of the whiskey wagon and reaching over this stranger's tailgate without a by-your-leave and tearing back the piece of canvas there before anybody could stop me, and there laid the split half-carcass of a hog with the ribs showing from inside and all still gleaming wet from slaughter. It'd been skinned, of course, and the head was gone, so I couldn't tell who it might be amongst the middle-sized ones (maybe whoever'd got the other half had flipped for the head and won), but it made me feel just as rotten as if I could call it by name.

The gray-haired man was clawing at me and trying to haul me off by the scruff, but I didn't pay him no mind to speak of except to land him one with my elbow which made him leave off yelling long enough to make sure his jaw hadn't skewed a hinge, and meanwhile I got my shoulder under the half-carcass just above the ham and heisted it back off the wagonbed and just started walking, having to keep my knees braced so's not to stagger.

"I don't want to have to shoot you, boy," the gray-haired man says.

He sounded like he meant it, but I didn't care one way or the other, being in what they call an Ecstasy.

"Are you a drinking man?" Casper says to him.

I took the half-carcass down the riverside a ways, not wanting to bother the hogs with it, and didn't get shot whiles I let it slump down on the sand and stretch out as comfortable as it could with so much missing, including most all the fat which I'd helped walk off it all these weeks.

Casper was talking and talking, using his whiskey-selling voice, and the gray-haired man didn't come after me or yell nothing else, and after a bit Casper went back to his wagon and plucked out a couple bottles and brung them back and only stopped talking long enough to pull a cork with his teeth.

I was seeing them both with my eyes and seeing the half-carcass too, but it wasn't your ordinary kind of seeing. It was like looking out a glass windowpane at night and seeing about as much inside as out and not being able to tell the difference, only the inside was me and not no parlor. And I remembered all the times I'd slaughtered hogs or helped to, and not just hogs neither but chickens and our cow Fanny when her milk dried up and a coon Pa made skin for hats (though I never once wore mine and nobody could figure out why, not even me) and rabbits and bobwhites and catfish. For a few minutes there it seemed like I'd been born with a knife in my hand instead of a spoon in my mouth, and I felt ashamed and disgusted, but then I remembered I didn't even *own* a knife, so it couldn't be completely true, and maybe I was heading in the right direction over the years in spite of my blood-soaker of an upbringing.

Then Casper was standing behind me. "You need any help doing whatever that is you're doing?" he says.

"Yes, sir," I says. "You can loan me a shovel."

He left and come back with a short-handled spade and says, "I swapped some whiskey for that meat, but it's yours to do with as you please."

"I thank you kindly," I says. I could hear the grayhaired man's wagon rumbling off, but I didn't look.

"Just plain self-interest," Casper says. "Whiskey stops a whole lot more turmoil than it starts, and it's less expensive."

I started digging a trench alongside the half-carcass, but struck gravel after about six inches, and it was slow going.

"That hog's going to have to scramble on Resurrection

Day," he says. "The rest of him's probably been et already, and if he can't locate his other trotters—"

He left off when he seen my face.

"All right," he says. "I'll keep still. But don't you go swinging any spades at me, son, or anything else either, because I don't fight fair, not even with my friends, and I wouldn't want to hurt you."

He didn't look like no kind of fighter to me, foul *or* fair, but I didn't say so, being too busy trying to sweat out my Ecstasy which might of seemed just like an ordinary tantrum if I hadn't been taking in two breaths for every one I let out, choking on them both ways.

"And if you don't mind a little advice, I'd do that gravedigging slower," he says. "The meat ain't in no hurry, and you look like my old Aunt Elma just before she had herself an apoplexy during Christmas dinner. I don't think your head's working quite right, and you don't want to get too jangled up."

I didn't know whether he meant well or not, but I set down before I fell down, with the trench only half dug, and tried to blink my head clear.

Standing beside me and taking small sips out of a tin cup, he says, "Sometimes a young man gets too damn much experience all in a heap and don't know what to make of it. It just sets there looking like a heap. But if you think about it one part at a time, it all clears up just fine." He paused a bit, then says, "Ah, hell, I don't know what I'm talking about. Don't listen to me."

And truth to tell, I wasn't listening any too good, what with all the blurs and dazzles and spots in front of my eyes to keep track of.

"You want me to preach over this half a corpus?" he says. "I can give you half a funeral service, maybe. It's about all I'd be good for, since I'm still about half a preacher, ordained fair and sober by the United Brethren Church which had ought to of known better and just goes to show you."

The meat was commencing to draw flies, but I didn't know

whether I was strong enough to dig, so I just shooed them off with my hat. My Ecstasy had started to go back where it had come from which felt like my gut.

"But I better warn you," he says. "None of my sermons ever did come out right at the end, so don't let me get past halfway. I'd always start out just fine—twenty years ago I could quote enough scripture to paper a setting room with and halfway up the hall—but somewhere along the way I'd always get off the track and start congratulating them pore innocent sinners setting there in front of me for having enough spunk to dredge up a little fun in such a godforsook place as Paducah. You know where Paducah's at?"

I shook my head and then had to hold it.

"Well, it's on the Ohio River whenever it don't happen to be under it," he says. "I *will* say it's good whiskey territory, but it started making me feel dumb and dead, so I got out of Kentucky and figured I'd find out what folks was using for brains someplace else, sort of like a missionary, and I ain't stopped moving since, and I be damned if there's much more brains anyplace else after all."

I shooed some more flies. "If your whiskey's so good, you could settle down and get rich," I says, my voice kind of thick and wobbly.

He give me a look like I'd took off my oatmeal poultice and showed him a carbuncle. "I don't want to be rich, boy," he says. "I want to be smart. Which means I want to find out why I was born. When you get to my age, you start thinking about fool things like that more'n usual."

Before I could think how stupid it sounded, I says, "Did you have a ma and pa too?"

He kept still a while, and I was afraid he was going to take me for a cone-hatted dunce like Miz Peasemont had made me be twice when I didn't put my "i" before "e" except after "c" like you're sposed to and then got mad when I made up a sentence for her that went "The weird financiers seized neither leisure."

But instead he smiled and says, "I thank you for that very

high compliment, Mr. Hunt, but you'd best reserve your admiration for somebody who's done something to earn it. I had
a ma and a pa all right, and I done them the injustice of imagining they didn't think highly enough of me, when all along it
was *me* hampering my eyes and my hands and feet and my
ears and that little puddle of over-cooked squash in my brain-
pan. I hope you haven't went and made any mistake like
that."

"If there's some kind of mistake I haven't made, I expect
I'll get to it later on if not sooner," I says.

He polished off his cupful and took the spade away from
me and helped me haul up to my feet, and he says, "You've
just wound your well-bucket up about two gear-notches, boy,
and you'd better rest a spell and enjoy your progress." He
tugged me back a few steps away from the half-carcass. "You
leave that meat be now. The birds know more about what to
do with it than you, and they'll give it a better blessing and say
a whole lot sweeter grace over it than you or me ever could.
Let it go to them."

So I done like he said and didn't look back. I concentrated
on the live ones instead.

Chapter Nine

WE COME TO the upper ford (where we'd camped or tried to only yesterday evening but seemed like a year ago) by mid-afternoon, and only when I seen the two wagons halfway across the river and the four more waiting on the near bank to jack up their courage or learn from other folks' mistakes—only then did I realize I was pulled as tight inside as new-strung fence wire. I'd been half-expecting to see the buckskin man and the rest of them waiting there for me and what was left of the hogs, but the closer we hauled in, the more likely it seemed I'd have to wait a while for that fine, strange day. For one thing, there wasn't any loose horses, not even none in harness. All the wagons on the bank had yokes of oxen, them being able to suffer longer and quieter than a horse and better to eat, I guess, if they should happen to cave out somewhere along the Trail.

It seemed like Casper knew what I was thinking because he reined in a ways off and looked from me to the wagons and back at me a few times.

"I don't reckonize anybody," I says. The two wagons out in the river didn't have no horses neither but looked like they could use a few: a horse takes better to water than an ox, and most mules would just as leave climb a tree as get wet. I'd been dreading this time when it was either going to be cross or don't cross for the hogs, but it turned out I wasn't going to have much say right off.

"This is what's going to happen," Casper says. "We're going to camp by that crick, and you're going to get some sleep, and then later on you're going to eat some more, and then you're going to sleep some more, and then we're going to cross that river in the morning. I know how to do it, don't worry. Hogs and all. And you'll need your strength. Meanwhile, I'm going to sell or trade some whiskey, and if them people know anything we'd ought to know, why, they'll just naturally tell us, won't they."

He didn't give me no chance to say yes, no, or maybe but stuck a pint bottle of whiskey in his coat pocket and a small tin cup in the other after he'd braked the wagon next to the crick. Then he helped me down amongst the hogs and started walking off on his thick, stubby legs. He turned and says, "Leave Jesse and Si harnessed till I make sure we're welcome. Some people don't like hogs."

Well, he didn't have to tell me that. I set down on the ground, still feeling dizzy, and watched him begin jawing with two men down by the river. After about a minute, he poured some of that whiskey in the cup and toasted it at them and drank it off, talking all the while, then poured a little more and give them each a sup of it and talked some more, and a woman in a gray bonnet come down out of one wagon and stood there with her fists on her hips for a spell, and Casper

begun jawing at her too and poured a little more and offered
it at her, and she finally straightened out one elbow and
opened one fist and took the cup and done her sipping nice
and dainty and handed it back.

Then two more men come out of a different wagon and
joined up with the bunch, and Casper went on talking and
pouring a dash here and there, and another woman come over
and three more men, but after about a minute more, Casper
corked that pint with a big wide flourish of both arms like a
preacher heading for the tail end of a sermon (when the angels
commence lining up on the rafters and the pump organ starts
hogging up its breath), and he give a little bow and touched his
hat brim nice and polite and headed back towards us.

They all watched him go, and even though none come running after, I got the idea some'd be coming to call before long.
It didn't look too hard to sell whiskey, except for the part
where you had to drink some yourself and talk.

Casper looked pleased with hisself, and he begun unhitching
the mules and hobbling them and dragging an armload of real
hay out of the back of the wagon. "They don't know nothing
about nothing down there, including how to ford a river," he
says. "Now you just set there and rest."

Which goes to show you how much Casper knew about hogs.
Soon as he heard that hay rustling, Colonel Woppert was first
in line, not letting no mere mules show him how to eat supper,
and I had to haul him off by the nose-ring and give Lucy June
and Sugar Loaf a couple of good prods to get them drove off.

When he seen what was happening, Casper hauled out another armload and brung it over and dropped it for them, and
it was like seeing a man fling his money away in the street (like
old Quincy Fortner back home done once for fun before his
wife could get him tied down and drug off for loco), hay being
so costly out here. "You're a kindly man," I says. "And I
thank you."

"I'm investing in you and them," he says, scowling at me.
"A starved hog's no use to anybody. Besides, I can always get

more. Whiskey opens many a locked door and many a shut
mouth and many a skinny coin purse—not to mention some
other things. And you better save your good opinion of me because it's going to get considerable exercise in a couple minutes."

I seen him looking back at the wagons, and the woman in
the gray bonnet was coming our way with a lanky, glum-
looking, stoop-shouldered man wearing blue galluses and a
cap with earflaps.

"She's got a carpet needle, which is the best kind," Casper
says. "Only she wouldn't part with it or leave me borrow it
neither."

"What you want with a carpet needle?" I says, trying to
keep the hay spread out enough so's all three would get some
and not bite each other.

"Well, she probably sews a better stitch than me anyway,"
Casper says. "And she says she's already done it once when
her boy cut his foot with an ax."

I opened my mouth to let some air in and out, not having
no words handy to use it on, and Mr. Earflaps says, "Howdy,"
peering all around and licking his thin lips.

"This is my assistant Zeke I told you about," Casper says.
"Child of misfortune. Take off your bandage, Zeke, and let
the lady sew up your head."

"Now wait a minute," Mr. Earflaps says. "My wife does
some of these chores and midwifing too, but—"

"No need for any of that unless that young sow's deceiving
us," Casper says. "She ain't about to farrow, is she, Zeke?"

"No, sir," I says. "But I don't think I—"

"My wife don't do this for the sheer pleasure of it," Mr. Earflaps says.

Nor nothing else neither to judge by her face under the
shade of the bonnet, which she had all pruned up and squinty
and disapproving. But even worse-looking was the size of the
hooknosed needle she was holding with a long stretch of black
button thread dangling out of it.

"I reckon it's worth a quart of that whiskey," Mr. Earflaps says too loud, like he knew he was driving too hard a bargain.

"We need hay," Miz Earflaps says, watching what the mules and hogs was up to.

"Keep still," Mr. Earflaps says, and why a man would want them things tied down over his ears in the month of June was a wonder to me, though the less seen of him, the better. "A quart of whiskey and a little hay on the side," he says.

Casper give a shy chuckle and tipped his head like he was listening to that one over again to hisself. "I don't believe I've ever heard nobody raise the price on a second offer before I'd even turned down the first. If you always act like that in the line of business, you must be a lonely man."

"I don't want my head sewed up," I says.

That must of worried Mr. Earflaps some because he says in a hurry, "All right, just a quart of whiskey then."

"You don't need whiskey, but them oxen need hay," Miz Earflaps says.

"I told you to keep still," he says. "Or I'll tell you what *you're* going to need is a crutch."

"Tell you what I'll do," Casper says, holding up his tin cup. "I'll give you one gill per stitch. It looks to be about four stitches if they're spaced out right, and that'll give you a pint of the finest whiskey ever dripped out of a copper worm and spent four long years growing old for you."

"I'm not going to have that needle in my scalp," I says.

"All right, done," Mr. Earflaps says to Casper, giving me a worried look like he might be about to go thirsty, which he was. They could think up something better to do with that needle such as sticking a chunk of meat on it and setting out a trot-line for sturgeon.

"I think I'll leave my head well enough alone," I says. I already had some idea what it felt like to be scalpted, and I didn't fancy it.

"Now don't be foolish," Casper says.

"I don't aim to be," I says.

"We struck a bargain, and I mean to carry through," Mr. Ear-flaps says, giving his wife an elbow. "Go on, sew up his head."

"He has to take the bandage off," she says.

"All right, take off the bandage and let's get started," Mr. Earflaps says, coming over towards me.

I held my staff where he could get a good look at it, and I says, "You're going to need some stitching your own self if you mess with me."

"Now let's just all calm down," Casper says.

A second man from down at the wagons had come strolling in, and I kept him in the edge of my eye in case they'd all made a pack to gang up on me.

"This a private quarrel or can a man get a drink of whiskey here?" the second man says. He had a nose like a bruised strawberry and a big thick mustache (which looked like he'd have to wet down first before he could get a drink through it) and was fanning hisself with a straw hat.

"Open for business," Casper says. "Two bits a half-gill or what you might care to trade." He went around to the tailgate and hauled a little keg out to the edge with a spigot sticking out of it.

"You can just go ahead and get my quart of whiskey whiles you're at it," Mr. Earflaps says.

"If my assistant don't want his head sewed up after all, I'm not going to force it on him," Casper says. "'Do good by stealth,' the saying goes, but I guess there just ain't enough stealth about a carpet needle. I made a little mistake."

"Just give me my quart of whiskey and you can go on making all the little mistakes you want to," Mr. Earflaps says.

"I got a couple fresh eggs to spare," the strawberry nose man says.

"A quart of whiskey ain't a little mistake, it's a big mistake," Casper says. Then to the strawberry nose man, "Fresh eggs?"

"Yesterday morning."

"They've found a happy home," Casper says. "A gill apiece."

Mr. Earflaps give me a thirsty, dusty, dang-the-luck scowl
and says, "I hope your whole head rots off."

"I thank you for them noble sentiments," I says. "I'll see
what I can do to oblige." He come a step closer, and I give my
staff a little heft.

"You going to make my wife, who come up here on an er-
rand of mercy, stand there like a damn ninny?" he says.

Colonel Woppert budged me out of the way where I was
stepping on some of the hay, and I says, "Your wife may stand
where she pleases and look like whatever you want her to," I
says. "But she ain't going to string me through with that
needle."

He turned on Casper who was unwrapping a blue bandanna
from around two speckled eggs about the size a banty pullet
might of squoze out her first try. "We come all the way up
here and went to all this trouble and now you're fixing to fault
out of our agreement," Mr. Earflaps says. "Well, you're not
going to do no such a thing. I want that whiskey, and I want it
right now."

He was trying to talk loud like a bully, but he didn't have no
natural turn for it. A hog wouldn't of paid no attention to a
voice like that, even up close, and Casper didn't neither.

"Did you happen to notice what laid these here eggs?"
Casper says.

"They're *good*," the strawberry nose man says. "We et some
of them this morning. You can ask my wife."

"My compliments to your wife," Casper says. "But prairie
chickens ain't in my line. I believe I'll ask two bits a half-gill."

"Are you deef?" Mr. Earflaps says, louder.

While the strawberry nose man wrapped up the eggs again
and grudged a coin out of his pants pocket, Casper turned and
give Mr. Earflaps a long straight look. Being more or less in line
with it, I seen what was on his face, and I'd been thinking it
was a soft, kind, scrubbed-up, cheery, it's-a-pleasure-to-meet-
you face with nothing scary about it. But it changed now,

went dead cold and seemed like it shrank back against the
teeth and cheekbones and the wide jawbone just above all
them whiskers, and even though Casper wasn't packing a gun,
it didn't seem to matter none. He says, "Friend, you may
stand there till you change color and your clothes fall off and
your wife turns gray-headed, but you're not getting my
whiskey for nothing. You've already had a whet of it free. If
you want more, it's for sale or trade."

Mr. Earflaps stood thinking it over, same as he would of if
he'd had two sixguns and three brothers carrying sledge-
hammers. I'd never heard no voice like that, and most likely he
hadn't neither. It would of cut through three foot of pond ice
or turned the milk if there'd been any around.

Now the strawberry nose man had settled for what he could
get and was leaning back on the tailgate, holding his mustache
up out of the way with one hand and taking little sips out of
the tin cup and smacking his lips and beaming around inbetween. "I have to tell you, sir," he says to Casper, "you drive a
bargain, but you make the best whiskey it's ever been my happy lot to pour down my throat."

"I thank you," Casper says, looking calm and jolly again and
pleased with hisself.

"What's the secret?"

Casper shook his head. "Now you're asking a very, very expensive question," he says. "And you wouldn't understand if I
told you."

"Well, what the hell are you doing way out here instead of
making a fortune back in Indiana or Kentucky or someplace?"
the strawberry nose man says.

I guess by that time Mr. Earflaps had forgot what he'd just
learnt, and he says, "I'll tell you what he's doing: he's robbing
poor people of their rights and breaking promises and lying
and making trouble."

"Let's go, William," Miz Earflaps says, tugging on his shirtsleeve.

And all considered, that was probably the best idea Mr. Ear-

flaps had heard in a month or more, but he didn't think so. He
didn't reckonize it. Instead, he went slouching over to the tailgate and give Casper a shove out of the way and commenced
rummaging amongst a box full of bottles.

Casper caught his arm kind of polite, like you might help
keep an old lady from falling down the church steps, and give
him a quarter turn, and punched him short, straight, and hard
up under the chin (which he must of had a good view of from
about nine inches lower down). Mr. Earflaps straightened up
out of his stoop, and a look come on his face like he'd just had
an A-Number-One idea, and then he went over backwards,
stiff, and hit the sand and laid there, trying to clutch onto it
with both hands. His cap didn't come off, but his earflaps
stuck out like he might be fixing to listen a little closer.

Whiles he was blinking and studying the sky, Miz Earflaps
didn't do nothing but stand by and wait for rain, and the
strawberry nose man got his cup out of the road by backing
off, and me and the hogs minded our own business except for
gawping.

Casper rustled up another tin cup and drew a little whiskey
into it out of the spigot and squatted and got his hand under
Mr. Earflaps' neck and heisted his head far enough so's he
could choke on it a sip at a time. When it was all either in his
mouth or down his chin, he sat up all the way and gulped and
coughed.

Very polite, Casper says, "You may have wanted whiskey
bad, but you done a bad job getting it. If you want any more,
all's you have to is mess in my property without my leave, and
I'll lay you out again, and then I'll give you another free swig
—if that's how you'd like to fill up all that vacancy you got inside you, including your head."

Mr. Earflaps didn't say nothing but set there, trying to find
his face with both hands.

Tipping his hat to Miz Earflaps, Casper says, "I'm sorry to
of abused your husband's jaw, ma'am. But he went and abused
it first. If I was you, I'd take that carpet needle and I'd sew his

mouth shut a few days before some undertaker has to charge you extra for it."

"Yes, sir," she says. "Come on, William." She hauled him to his knees, then to his feet, and they started wobbling off towards their wagon.

"I believe I'll see if that river's gone down any," the strawberry nose man says, setting his cup down. "If you don't mind." He stood there a few seconds like he might need Casper's permission to excuse hisself, then turned and hustled off.

Casper spit on his knuckles and rubbed them and shook his head. "I wish I hadn't had to do that till morning," he says. "Now I'm going to have to stay up all night to make sure that knothead doesn't Injun-up on us and bust something."

But he didn't do nothing of the kind or need to. After we'd et supper (I had to range pretty far to find any buffalo chips left), a few more men come up from the clump of wagons to sup a drink or two, paying cash mostly and one a small box of pepper (which Casper shook and chuckled over), but all as calm and polite as if they'd come to the new preacher's house for sarsaparilla. If Mr. Earflaps had any grievances, he nursed them to hisself that night, along with his jaw.

When it was good and dark and most of the little fires had gone out amongst the other wagons and ours had too and the hogs had decided to lay down with something to keep their bellies from caving in for a change and it was no use trying to watch the wagons getting stuck and unstuck and half-tipped out in the river, I wrapped up in the blanket Casper give me and laid down by Colonel Woppert (he let me use his belly for a pillow about a half hour at a stretch) to make sure him and the other two would keep body and soul together till morning.

Casper had fixed hisself to sleep in the back of the wagon (he said he always done so), up against his kegs like me with the hogs, and when it was all quiet except for a grunt now and then and a coyote having a hogcall at the half-moon (they're pretty good at it but don't know when to quit), I says, "That Stull I told you about, that buckskin man—you think it might of been whiskey done that to him? I mean make him like to hurt people and hogs and all?"

"Might of helped him along," Casper says. "I've seen it happen."

"Then why do you want to go making and selling whiskey for?" I says.

Sounding tired and exasperated both, he says, "Some people use religion to hurt who they may please. Or guns or knives or their brains or just the sound of their voice. Do you want to shut down all the churches because some's bad?"

"I'd just as soon," I says.

"Or guns or knives?" he says.

"I can do without," I says.

"Or their brains or their voice?" he says, starting to hone up his voice like I might be a hopeless case.

"No, I'd bar that," I says.

"Well, there you are," he says.

And I was too, though it hadn't got me much further forward. He didn't say nothing else, and pretty soon I heard him give off a regular muffled buzz like somebody snoring far off.

And whiles I laid there, the night breeze—coming downstream along the river and up slope along the shallow bank like it always done—started filling up with the smell of frying pork, a smell I was so familiar with, like my own, I didn't reckonize it right off. It was drifting up from the wagons by the crick's mouth, and the pork might of belonged to them, and then again it might not. And I felt bad and lonely about it.

If I went ahead tomorrow and done what Casper wanted, I'd be leaving a good many hogs on this shore, most likely forever, and some might still be alive. But how could I wear out and starve the few I'd found by going off hunting for the others when I didn't know where they'd strayed? Casper seemed to have lots of feed and know how to find more, and maybe it was best I kept these three healthy and didn't go chasing ghosts.

But in a minute, I got sick and tired of feeling cross and peaked and down-in-the-mouth and mad and gruntled and stuck and mournful, that not being my natural frame of disposition, and I decided to get my will power up where it belonged and get my scalp to do its own stitching, and then something funny happened. Whiles I was half-asleep, I made me up a Hog Song in my head, which I'd never done before, laying there and kind of singing it the way I'd heard many a hymn put through the wringer back home (I can't carry a tune, but I can follow along behind it), and it went like this:

> The hogs are full of beech mast
> And singing in the hills.
> Their snouts raise up to break their fast
> On golden slops and swills.
> If God can see from First to Last,
> He'll bless all scissor-bills.

I didn't aim to take His Name in Vain (though most times before I'd bothered to talk to Him it'd been in vain all right), specially after what I'd said about churches, but it made me feel like I'd brung all the dead or stole or lost hogs back to life and comfort, and then I done myself a favor and fell asleep, which that night was like falling off the back of a wagon like one of them other whiskey boys.

Chapter Ten

TWO OF THE other wagons had already started across the river by the time we got set to try in the morning. Casper tied down everything in his wagon even tighter than before, and then we hogtied Sugar Loaf and Lucy June (who didn't like it none) and got them stretched out in the back of the wagon, helping shore up the kegs, and lashed the tailgate extra strong in case there was any bouncing, thrashing, or sliding. But between us we decided not to try nothing like that with Colonel Woppert.

It wasn't *only* that he was too big for the two of us to heist (even sposing Colonel Woppert felt agreeable to it and didn't get his bristles up) or that there wasn't enough room left for him on the wagonbed or that he might of broke down the back axle or that he'd be almost certain sure to bog down the back wheels in all that muck out there waiting for us: the main fear was we couldn't tie him good enough to keep him from struggling loose and going hog wild in midstream and busting the wagon apart.

So what we done was tie a rope to an iron ring on the tailgate, and from there on me and Casper had a difference of opinion.

"Tie the other end through his nose-ring and climb on board," Casper says. "If he can't swim, we'll haul him."

"No, sir," I says. "I believe I'll go afoot. Can you spare an extra three or four foot of rope?"

"Now don't be a damn fool," Casper says. "Get up in back and set on one of them other hogs and enjoy the view. I know my mules and I know this wagon, and I could take it across the Missouri if I felt like it, leave alone a little shallow-bedded spit-and-trickle like this. If anything goes wrong with that boar, you'll be setting right there to help. You can jump in *then* if you feel like it."

My head still didn't feel a hundred percent, and I wasn't as strong as I'd of usually been, but my will power was operating full-boom now, so I says, "Colonel Woppert stuck by me, and I'm going to do likewise. If he sees me in the water with him, it won't come so unnatural to him."

We argued back and forth a spell, but he finally give up, which was sensible of him, and we went down to the riverbank, where I tied a hank of rope through Colonel Woppert's nosering like a leash and hitched the other end to my waist (though Casper told me not to) and hung onto the wagon rope with my right hand so's I could either stick with it or leave go. If Colonel Woppert was going anywhere, downstream or under or floating through the air, he was taking me with him, but meanwhile I'd be aiming him at the far shore best I could, using my staff like a ferryboatman.

Whiles I stowed my boots in the back of the wagon, keeping them clear of Lucy June and Sugar Loaf who might not have nothing better to do but eat them, some of the lunkheads in

the waiting wagons begun laughing and bullyragging at me,
which I paid no mind to. Some people think the mere sight of
a hog is funny, and they're welcome to that mis-conclusion.
Truth to tell, Colonel Woppert probably knew more about
both sides of that river than me and them put together. He had
enough sense to know there wasn't no more full troughs over
there than there'd been over here, and if he'd had his way, he
wouldn't be turning his bacon leaner than it already was by
fooling with no cornmush-looking water that didn't have
enough sense to settle down and pond itself up. But here was
all of us two-leggers (sposed to be the brains in the family)
straining to get across when most of us, if not all, didn't know
what we was fixing on doing once we got to wherever we
thought we had to get to. If Colonel Woppert'd been in charge
instead of Pa, all fifty-one hogs (and more by now) would of
been back home in the woods and me enjoying looking for
them.

Mr. Earflaps had took the plunge and was about thirty yards
ahead of us up to his hubs in the current, and I seen him
stretching around the side to look back now and then, and
Casper took his mules right on in, using the same route, and I
waded into that cold, roily, rolly mess, trying to keep track of
everything at once but specially Colonel Woppert who had
more temper than he knew how to handle sometimes, and I
didn't want him sloshing up behind me and giving me a bite
like a watchdog coldsnapping a trespasser.

I was getting a lot of free advice from back on shore such as
several humorous things to do with my staff, which I paid back
by holding it high in the air and then pointing the way they
was all worried about going. But the water was making so
much noise now, I couldn't hear nothing else. Casper leaned
around the edge and give me a wave, and I waved back, and
then Colonel Woppert begun getting his first swimming lessons.

They come in short spurts mostly, when the bottom would
dunk down a foot or two for a couple steps, then dip up shallow again, so little by little, he got customed to hating it which

is a whole lot better than big bad surprises full-scale. Of all the parts of his body a hog values his earflaps about the most (bar his unmentionables) because that's what keeps the sun and rain out of his eyes and earholes, so Colonel Woppert done his level best to keep them free and clear. He'd already took a crunchy mouthful or two of the river and decided it wasn't no good to eat nor worth much for smelling purposes neither, so he was keeping slack in the line tied to his nose-ring except when the current swept him sideways or he struck a hump and felt like standing still and I had to haul him on a little.

I'd dreaded doing this so long and had so many day-mares about hogs getting drownded and wagons broke down and me swept off or quicksanded, nothing ordinary could of flabbergasted me. If the whole river had dried up and steamed off or commenced running the opposite way or if a sea monster with thirteen heads and blue goathorns had come wraggling upstream to take his breakfast on us or a Mississippi paddleboat had come puffing by to take us for a joyride, I might of been short on words but not surprised. You can't hardly surprise a man that worries as much as me.

But whiles I was slumping and slogging and wearing myself out and unplugging my feet from that bottom sludge I couldn't never lay eyes on, not even when it shoaled up and didn't have no more than two inches of water rushing over it, and passing out all kind of advice to Colonel Woppert who was doing just fine without me telling him nothing, I begun to realize I'd get to the other side no matter what kind of calamity or contrariness come to call, and there wasn't no *use* worrying. It made me feel happy.

And once when we come to a shallower stretch than usual and Casper braked the wagon to give the mules a rest and clumb down to see how me and Colonel Woppert was doing, he found me standing there grinning like a skunk eating goose eggs.

"Well, I'm glad you're enjoying yourself," he says. "We're about halfway."

The other bank was maybe two or three hundred yards off and we'd been fording steady for more than a half-hour, but my head hadn't busted open and the sun was coming down sweet and cool through a high haze and Mr. Earflaps looked to be stuck up ahead and had got out to push or cuss or both, up to his knees, and take it all together, I felt fine.

"Would you like a drink?" Casper says.

I didn't know whether he meant whiskey or water, but I says, "I believe I'm soaking up enough just like this."

"That boar don't look too enthusiastic," he says.

"He's doing about as good as anybody else," I says. "Which is the way he usually does." Colonel Woppert had changed color some, being washed off and silted up, and he wasn't so much brown now as gold.

"How's your head?" Casper says. "Want some more whiskey poured on it?"

"No thank you kindly," I says. "I'm fine."

"Well, we better move on before them mules take a notion to think," he says and went back around front.

I didn't tell him I felt all springy-footed and dumb-lucky and cockeyed and good as gold and churned up for whistling and stomping. It wouldn't of made no sense and might of been worrisome and made him think I'd been taking turns and pulls out of the spigot unbeknownst like them other whiskey boys.

I couldn't claim enough *cause* for what I was feeling like, but I felt so good I couldn't even get myself to fret about it. It didn't seem to matter none that Ma and Pa was gone and most of the hogs and my head all wrapped up like a busted pump and us commencing to flounder and slewfoot and splash after the wagon again. I felt like singing which I can't, but I took a whack at "Holy, Holy, Holy! Lord God Almighty!" that Ma'd used to sing on Sunday mornings rain or shine, and I sung my Hog Song, using the same tune but it didn't fit right, and then I tried "O for a thousand tongues to sing my dear Redeemer's praise," but had too much trouble stumbling over the words and my own feet too, and it seemed to get Colonel Woppert

flustered and jumpy so I left off and tended to business, not
being any too sure about no Redeemer, though I felt re-
dempted all right, least for a while.

One of the thousand tongues that morning was sticking out
from betwixt Mr. Earflaps teeth whiles he shoved and humped
at his off-rear wheel and not doing no singing at all, and when
Casper kept his wagon right on without stopping (it not being too wise to even slow down where it was mushy or you'd
get stuck your own self, same as in snow), I left go of the rope
tied to the wagon and veered off to lend a shoulder, feeling
charitable for a change.

Mr. Earflaps give me a damn-you look and didn't say nothing
but commenced shoving twice as hard hisself before I could
get there, it being a little deep for Colonel Woppert to like
much. In fact, Colonel Woppert kept on going straight after
the wagon and started hauling sideways at my belly rope like
he knew better than me what was what, so I had a little
trouble getting where I was going.

In his rush to get that wagonwheel over the hump so's he
wouldn't have to be obliged to the likes of me, Mr. Earflaps
slid hisself half under water twice and commenced yelling
around the side at his wife in the driver's seat like she'd did
something wrong, and meanwhile I'd reached the rear wheel
on the near side, having to clang onto it to keep Colonel Woppert from hauling me off, and I hadn't had a chance to do no
good yet before Mr. Earflaps got his wagon budged again
(helped out by his water-logged ox team up ahead). I got off-
balanced and half-spun and dunked and had to swim a couple
strokes and use Colonel Woppert's leash to slow me down till I
could get my feet under me.

And oh you'd of thought it was the best joke and most
comical event to come along since Bailey Frizzell and his Ala-
bama Coon Show. Mr. Earflaps bent over double whooping
and hawing at me, and I didn't mind much, there being enough
good feelings that morning to stretch as far as him and maybe
farther. But whiles I was catching up with Colonel Woppert
and getting aholt of the wagon rope again, Mr. Earflaps come

to find out he'd been left behind twenty yards by his own wagon, and he had to splash and wallow on after it, going all the way under once till only his cap was showing. He didn't take it kindly, even though *I* didn't laugh at *him* but only smiled like a friend might of. He shook his fist my way and yelled something I didn't care to commit to memory (that's how Miz Peasemont used to say it when we had to get whole slabs out of *McGuffey's Reader* down by rote such as "Mr. Idle and Mr. Toil"), but by then I was too busy keeping track of my own self to fret about him.

I don't think Casper'd even noticed I'd been gone, him having to read the current and keep on moving, and I got me and Colonel Woppert switched around in the right order and kept aholt of the wagon rope and give him lots of chucking noises (about like you might use feeding hens) to leave him know everything was all right and couldn't last forever. The second half took less time than the first, and Casper drove just like he said he would, and pretty soon the bottom was shelving up with less and less in the way of deep eddies and half-marshy backwaters. I don't know if Colonel Woppert would of did it without that hay and grain in him for boiler fuel and ballast, but he come through just fine, jowls bobbling.

I led him into the last shallows whiles the wagon was already on dry land, both of us stiff-legged, him natural and me because I'd had a powerful lot of wading. Mr. Earflaps had made shore just a little ahead of us (maybe he thought we'd been racing, I don't know), and as soon as my bare feet come out onto the flat sand, I had a vision.

It didn't have nothing to do with wheels in wheels nor like what I'd seen and felt when I thumped off redbeard's horse. I didn't go into no spellbind nor transit nor fall down and lather at the mouth nor go jerking or talking tongues like I'd seen some at camp meetings back home nor hear no voices such as God's or President Millard Fillmore's nor get flooded by some Message I'd have to keep obeying and jawing about the rest of my life and vexing everybody with.

What happened was I seen the Light. Not just daylight or

sunshine, though there was enough of both, but some kind of Light in my very own head. It could of been the whiskey leaking through my scalp or something from the welt and bump the moonhead's bullet give me (and if so, I'm much obliged to either or both), but I don't think so. It filled me up, and nothing corked it, and it overflowed, and I knew then I'd passed through and come out the other side—and not just the river neither. I knew I'd never be the same again, but that there was more *of* me. That's the best I can say it, even if it's no good.

And the first thing I done to celebrate was leave go of the wagon rope (Casper'd stopped anyways, probably to see if he'd sprung anything loose in the wagonbed) and give the primest, fullest, longest, highest-to-deepest hogcall I'd give in all my born and unborn days. I took my time over it and it took *my* time, and I went Seeeeeeeeeeeeeeeeeeeeeeeeeeeeee-uuuuuuuuuuuuuuuuuuuuuuuuuuBOY!

Two things happened at once: Lucy June and Sugar Loaf in the back of the wagon commenced kicking and thrashing and banging up against the kegs and squealing, and Casper come running around to unlash the tailgate to haul Sugar Loaf out onto the ground all by hisself without getting bit or slashed by a trotter (which took some doing), and by then I'd come to my senses enough to help drag Lucy June out (who was lots heavier) before she busted anything. They calmed down when they seen and smelt me and Colonel Woppert nearby, but whiles I was getting them untied and half-listening to Casper cuss, I seen what was happening to Mr. Earflaps' wagon about thirty yards ahead of us and off to one side.

It was still moving but not half as much as its rear end seemed to be doing all by itself without no help from man nor ox. And then the tailgate busted down entirely and hung on one hinge, and one of the sideboards sprung off a ways, knocking two hoops loose so's the canvas started flapping, and there was a hog laying in there flopping and arching and rainbowing and squealing now, and it rolled right out the back, taking the tailgate all the way off to thump in the sand alongside it.

The ropes tying its trotters come loose, and before Mr. Earflaps could stop and get around back, that hog was up and running at me and the others (I seen it was Pattycake, a two-year-old sow not as big as Lucy June), and she slowed down and turned dignified whiles the others grunted and snuffled over her.

Mr. Earflaps come running partway after, then stopped when he seen Casper standing there with his fists on his hips and maybe even taking note of me and my staff. And then he just seemed to give up without no argument (Pattycake had our nicks in her left ear, and he'd of never talked them away) and slung his tailgate up into the wagonbed and clumb back up to his seat and drove off.

Casper didn't say nothing but looked at me and the hogs and shook his head like we was a mortal caution. He drawed hisself a gill of whiskey and downed it slow whiles I checked over my drove (which had now built itself back up to four) to make sure they didn't have no cuts or troubles I didn't know about. They all seemed good as new, except maybe a little wiser and warier, and I hoped I was likewise.

And it was a good thing Mr. Earflaps hadn't tied no leash on Pattycake or she'd of pulled his whole wagon inside out like a gunnysack (if I do say so, as shouldn't, being the hogcaller) and left him aimed back towards Jayhawk territory or wherever he'd yanked up his lanky roots and come to be so thirsty.

I felt something bulgy in my pocket, and when I pulled it out, it was what had used to be *Aesop's Fables*, but old Aesop was so sopped, he didn't look likely to ever make it back into anybody's eyesight but a Platte River shiner's, and the binding was all unbounded and the cover peeling, so I flang it away (having no books left at all now), and Pattycake went over and et it, which I spose was as good a lesson as any Aesop give.

Chapter Eleven

CASPER FED JESSE and Si some grain for a thank-you, and we rested an hour to get some of the grit out of our mouth and ears and because we'd be having to climb California Hill right up ahead and get across about twenty mile of plateau before we'd come to Ash Hollow and the fearful steep downhill stretch to the North Platte, and meanwhile we could watch other wagons doing what we'd already done and feel good and calm and safe and smart and full of fine ideas about zigging and zagging. I give every wagon that come by us a long looking-over now, but most of them looked too tired or mad or glad (depending on how wet they'd got crossing or how much gear they'd busted or lost) to be yelling hogcalls at. If the ones

I seen had any hogs on board, it was most likely in the shape of fresh pork which I couldn't do nothing about but mourn.

Casper sold some whiskey just by standing still and keeping the tapped keg in sight, and between whiles he says to me, "A riverbank's a pretty good place to set up a grog wagon. They're either getting their courage up on one side and willing to lighten the load, too, if it comes to swapping, or else they're looking to drowned their sorrow or give their joy a little firewater bath or loosen up the sheepshanks in their gut. Long as they don't put down enough to get drunk, specially on the near shore, you're all right. I don't aim to get any man drunk, though some'll sneak by all the stage stations on the way and fool you."

"What's them stations?" I says, figuring I'd ought to learn what there was to this new trade of mine which I didn't know if I was going to take to or even like, leave alone get paid for (a subjeck I hadn't brung up yet since I hadn't done nothing useful but eat and rench off plates).

"Your common, ordinary drinking man will start off sober and serious and thoughtful," Casper says. "He'll talk about crops and weather and horses and keep his ear open for what the other feller's saying or me or like it might be you and talk it over and maybe recollect what he done or said someplace else or what his granddaddy done or said or how the wind or the rain done something five years ago—all nice and sociable. But if he's drinking steady, he'll start talking a little comical and remembering only comical yarns and good old jokes (which I've heard so many of, I can't remember none, thank God), and if you're going to sell as much whiskey as you'd ought to, you'd best learn how to laugh nice and quiet and listen and nod your head through all of that, rendering sober or fool opinions of your own now and then, in case there's ever any quiet to get them into. But you got to watch out: the stage pulls out of that station kind of fast sometimes, and your drinking man may be on a downhill run to turning mean. If

you let him get too far along and don't shut up shop or ease
him off towards home or get his nose into a coffee cup, you're
liable to have a sour patch of arguing, which spoils your
business amongst them trying to drink proper, or a drag-out
fight in which you and your customers can lose bottles or
teeth or mirrors or whatever else is handy."

I says, "Old Uncle Fred, he used to—"

"Don't tell me about your Uncle Fred," Casper says, but
kindly. "I've known a thousand or more Uncle Freds, and I'm
talking about general principles here."

"Yes, sir," I says.

"And since you're no customer, I don't have to please you
out of the ordinary, do I?"

"No, sir," I says. "I'm already mighty pleased."

He stared me over and says, "By God, maybe you are at
that. Of course, I don't have no mirrors to bust out in the
open like this nor spittoons to sling around nor tables to up-
end nor chairs to make kindling out of, so it's more likely to
be knives or guns right off or at least fisticuffs like that hog-
rustler yesterday evening."

"How about Injuns?" I says.

He drew hisself up full height which wasn't but to my shoulder and took another pull on his tin cup which he'd been
exercising pretty good since we'd made it across. "I never sold
a drop to an Injun in my life and never will but at gunpoint,"
he says. "There's no third station at all for an Injun, the poor
damn suffering savages. Injuns don't believe in crying, so they
stay mean till they drop down cold as rocks, which is the
fourth station, by the way. Your ordinary mean drinking
man, if he keeps up pumping his elbow and don't get laid out
first or sobered up by the sight of his wife or scairt back into
his good nature, he'll get sad and sorry and tell you all about
it if he can still talk, and you don't have to worry about him
none except maybe for falling off of his horse or stepping into
a ditch or something. If you just put on your iron ears and
keep the bottle out of his claws—you can trickle a little his way

to quieten him and keep him from sobering back partway to mean again—why, he'll go to sleep still telling you how he's been did wrong by the worst woman in the world (who also probably happens to be the finest two sentences later), and if you can still understand him, he'll tell you nobody understands him."

"Sounds mighty complicated," I says.

"You'll get used to it," he says. "You may even get sick of it. And it even happens to the best drinking men—the kind that just stand there or set there and put that whiskey where it belongs and don't cause no trouble nor laugh too much nor hit nobody nor start bawling or commence retching up between snores. He just gets up and goes off home, if he's got one."

We shared out an extra ration of grain and hay to all four-footers so's the mules would keep going and the hogs keep following and not start thinking the world was made up entirely of hard work and pigsticking and river-fording and then climbing uphill to top it all off. The feed didn't last long, and after the wagon had started and I'd made sure the hogs would keep up, I clumb onto the front seat to rest a little, and I says. "There must be something awful good-tasting about whiskey, considering how some people soak it up. Maybe I'll have to try it someday."

Casper give a beautiful calm smile with his deep black eyes half-closed like a preacher watching the collection plates start coming down the aisle, and he says, "When the time comes, if you treat it right, it can teach you how to enjoy yourself even at the shank end of a bad day. It can sweeten your joys and dignify your woes." He snapped a look at me. "I'm talking about *good* whiskey, you understand."

"Yes, sir," I says.

"And not much of it," he says.

"No, sir."

He aimed us at that steep, tedious-looking, wagon-scarred, greasebush-and-sage-covered slope up ahead where I could count four wagons partway up it and where the thousands of

wheels passing through had dug a long bare stretch more like a
ditch than a road, and as soon as we come to the foot and
started up, I got down to give Jesse and Si a little less to think
about and the hogs a little more. I felt like I was acting natural
and quiet and not doing nothing unusual or different apurpose, but all the time—ever since I'd set foot out of the river
—nothing had been the same.

My eyes kept going over everything I could see, left, right,
behind, and ahead, and there wasn't nothing new I could
name. The colors had stayed put, there wasn't no heat-shimmer or upside-down rocks, no ghosty-looking dust devils nor
burning bushes nor strange beasts made out of silver and gold
nor talking birds nor voices out of the rocks or the sky. But I
wasn't looking at the same world no more, mainly because I
wasn't scairt of it or mad at it like you might think I should of
been. I couldn't explain it. It didn't make me talk no different,
and the hogs hadn't sprouted no wings and haloes, and Casper
was setting up there on the seat looking like a plain man that
had learnt his trade better than most and liked to talk and had
did me a kindness, and it was almost noon of a June day with
nothing extra about it, and by the time we'd clumb the hill a
ways, I could look back at the upper ford of the South Fork
of the Platte River and northeast along the slightly rolly but
most level road on the far side and count dozens and dozens of
carts and wagons strewn out behind us and some trying to
ford right now, and any fool could see there was nothing special about me carrying a hickory staff and walking behind four
hogs and sweating through my shirt.

But there was. And I knew it like a secret I didn't dare tell
for fear it would spoil. I'd always been different in *wrong*
ways. Back home in school, Miz Peasemont didn't fancy having nobody like me in her class who didn't know how to ask
the regular questions like you're sposed to. (There was plenty
that didn't know how to ask no questions at *all*, but they
didn't bother her none.) Her main complaint when I got put

back a year and told to mind my everlasting tongue—which
sounded like something so good out of the Bible, I almost
wished I really had it—was I didn't take to the direction she
kept steering us at but was forever lunging off sideways to call
up different subjecks that wasn't called for nor proper nor
seemly. I never did find out what that "seemly" meant,
though I hunted in the dictionary sometimes when she left it
unstrapped, but it doesn't sound to me like what nothing had
ought to be. I've got all kind of "seems" in my head, but why
would a schoolmarm try so hard to scrub them off of my slate
or soap them out of my mouth when they didn't "seem" to
nobody but me? They only took up a little air in that schoolhouse (which there was plenty more of coming through the
chinks), so I finally figured out all my "seems" had to square
up with her "seems" or they'd wind up "unseemly." And
that's when I quit going up them four and a half steps to
school and let Pa turn me out amongst the hogs where I might
learn something and never did find out where I'd went wrong.

But this here was a new kind of difference, and nobody was
going to strop it out of me or scold it till it hushed up. It
wasn't just mine, it was me.

I'd seen a few others going west with hogs the last weeks,
and some had wrote on the side of their wagon with a paint-
brush *Root, Hog, or Die*, which was a way of saying they
didn't have nothing to feed their droves except what they could
root theirself out of country so bare and hard, you couldn't
crack it with a mallet, leave alone a hog's nose. But lots had
wrote it on their wagon that didn't even have no hogs but
meant their own self and was like saying *I am going to make it
by hook or heck or crook or crock and don't ask me for nothing.* And now I felt like it was *Root, Hog, or Die* with me too,
and I was going to root up what I needed and not do no dying
along the way. It wasn't like I'd froze up and lost my charity,
but from now on I was standing on my dignity just like Colonel Woppert done whenever anybody messed with him or

tried to make him do something that wasn't fitten or hog-like enough: all four feet weighted down with everything he could muster from snout to tail whiskers.

When we topped that hill, I was too tired to get the good out of looking backwards at the view. Besides, I already knew what it looked like: I'd been down there. So I just clumb up in back (when Casper give me leave to) and wedged up against the kegs and kept one eye on the hogs and let the other one go to sleep, and we jolted along like that all day, and I was either blissful and happy or I'd all of a sudden turned too dumb to worry. It didn't bother me none which it might be.

It seemed like I might be half-drunk, though I didn't feel like them drinking men Casper'd spoke of, laughing or jawing or turning smoky or fighting or bawling their eyes out or even sleeping it off. I'd rode off to some different kind of stage station than them, probably doing it the "unseemly" way as usual.

Chapter Twelve

TOWARD SUNDOWN we come to the brim of Ash Hollow where dozens of wagons had already drycamped (which you didn't ordinarily do in a country with so many cricks, even the cornmush Platte being better than nothing), and I couldn't figure it out at first, nor Casper neither. And eight wagons had lined up where the trail dropped off downhill, waiting their turn to have a go at it and the men all jawing away and giving advice and getting it back double and generally hemming and scratching and hawing and hesitating.

Casper walked up ahead to look, leaving me to guard the whiskey, and I seen him mingle with the drivers and some of their womenfolk, not breaking out his pint nor trying to sell nothing yet but just soaking up the situation.

When he come back to the wagon fifteen minutes later, he
looked like he'd had hisself a Vision like mine: his mouth
wouldn't close up all the way and his hat was tipped back for
air and his neck whiskers had taken a ruffling up and his eyes
was so wide open I was scairt they'd tip out. "Well, now I've
seen it all," he says.

I knew Ash Hollow was sposed to be the hardest place on
the Trail, and I'd heard Pa talk about it, but that was back in
the days when I was sick of listening how to get to California,
so I hadn't exackly drank it all in. "Is it bad?" I says.

"Depends on who you are," he says. "If you're on burro-
back or if you should happen to be a full-fledged bird, it ain't
bad. Or I expeck a sidewinder wouldn't have too much trouble.
Go on, take a look. I've got to do some thinking." He got out
his tin cup and give the whiskey spigot a little exercise.

And I walked up to the edge, keeping out of people's road,
and seen what looked like one of them hand-painted pictures
they have inside the lobby of Causeby's Hotel in St. Joe where
Pa hauled me in one day when I was little so's I could be sick
from eating green cherries. You could see for miles, and I
couldn't even guess how many, but the North Platte was way
over yonder, looking a mile wide its own self, and bluffs and
purple hills on past it and big dark clumps of bushes or trees
or buffalo on the far shore. But it was what lay closer by that
made my mouth start hanging open too: a broad, sandy-bot-
tomed gully so steep, if it had bent down an inch or two
slantier, you'd of had to call it a clift, and it didn't just drop
off and give up. It went on for what looked to be a good two
mile before it bottomed out in a big green grove of trees. It
was half like what they call a canyon, with jagged limestone
sides (like back home, only more of it) with good-size cedar
trees growing out of cracks. I seen the glint of water here and
there down below like springs, and in all that country I'd been
through week after stumpy week past all them chop-hills without enough grass to whistle with, I hadn't seen this many
bushes and flowers and berry brambles and different kind of

weeds. It looked like somebody'd rounded them up and rustled them off from everyplace else and stuck them here for a joke. Off on both sides there was a labyritch of sandy gulches chockful of enough forage to keep a drove of hogs happy for weeks, the only trouble being the road going by (if you could call the zaggedy line of gouges and ruts and bashed-looking cross ditches a road) was so sheer, you'd have trouble pausing long enough to get a mouthful. It didn't look like you could even lay down and stay still but would just keep on rolling.

All this green didn't seem natural after the prairies. It made me want to get into it and clutch onto it and eat some and set down in it.

I watched whiles one family decided they'd take the plunge before sundown instead of thinking about it all night. A kid about fifteen set up on the spring seat with both feet jammed against the footboard so's he wouldn't pitch over between his oxen. He had the brake tied tight, and his pa had just chained both back wheels so's they wouldn't turn and was afoot, hanging on to one of them for good measure. His ma stood by on the slant, passing out advice and probably thinking of her pans and crockery and what-all, and as soon as the back wheels had scraped over the edge, the wagon come smack up against the butts of the oxen and shoved at them and made them go stiff-legged as hogs.

A fat man with a big chaw in his cheek come sidling over to me, shaking his head and fanning hisself with his hat and taking a spit over the edge. "That ain't no proper way to go down that damn slope," he says.

I just kept looking whiles the wagon skidded more and more sideways and the oxen got more confused. The kid was hollering and his pa was hollering and his ma was holding her bonnet on with one hand and trying to keep her feet from going too shifty.

The fat man says, "What they'd ought to done was—" He left off and helped me watch the wagon go completely sideways now, still skidding but slower, and if them oxen could of figured out how to walk cross-legged without tripping, it might not of been a bad idea, but the wagon was going a little faster than them, and pretty soon it commenced hauling back on them.

"They should of hitched them oxen on the rear end and—" the fat man says, leaving off again and watching whiles the kid did something or other he shouldn't of with the lines, probably jerking too hard to turn the oxen, which wasn't their fault they was looking back uphill now. You could see it dawn on them quiet, puzzled, long-suffering, thick, dusty-muzzled, splotched faces that they'd finally figured out what they was sposed to be doing: they ignored what the lines kept yanking at them to do and set their shoulders into the thick harness and commenced trying to haul that braked and chained wagon back up the forty foot where they'd started.

The fat man spit again and says, "What did I tell you?" like he was pure disgusted with all these fools making a mockery out of his wagon-driving lessons.

The oxen actually budged the wagon a yard or two up that impossible slope, which should of earned them pasture for life, but they stopped dead then and wouldn't do nothing.

"Leave go the brake!" the fat man hollers, and others up on the edge started giving more instructions, and the kid was hearing a good deal from his pa and ma and looking like he'd just as leave be off fishing someplace.

"All's they have to do is unhitch and turn them oxen around and—" the fat man says, dropping off short again.

I walked back to where Casper was setting. The hogs'd behaved theirself mostly because he had a two-thirds empty feedsack next to him and was dropping a handful down to them now and then. He hadn't opened up shop but had a cup of whiskey on his knee.

"It don't look too easy to get down," I says, hearing some shouting and hoorawing behind me, which meant I was missing part of the show but didn't much care, because it didn't look like there was no shortage of newcomers going to have to take their turn at clowning, including us.

"Don't worry about that," he says. "I just seen the finest place in the world to sell whiskey, and if that's real spring water down below and got any volume to it, I've found a happy home for my still. Zeke, can you ride a mule?"

"I can if he'll let me," I says, probably not sounding any too sure of myself because I knew he didn't have no saddle.

"No, that's not good enough," he says. "You'd have to carry two kegs of whiskey too, and you'd best look after your own hogs up here instead of me. I want to scout out that grove down below, and I'll bring back them two kegs full of water before dark. May taste a little like whiskey, but I don't think the hogs'll mind."

"No, sir," I says, glad I wasn't going to have to ride no mule bareback down that two-mile chute. "But what's going to happen to the whiskey in the kegs?"

"If I can't sell fourteen gallon in a place like that in two hours, I'd ought to quit," he says. He jumped down. "Won't be able to take nothing in trade that won't fit in a gunnysack, though."

He seemed excited, and I brung two kegs around which he roped together in a kind of sling like saddlebags, handling that rope slick as a riverboat sailor tying off a skiff. They weighed about seventy pound apiece, and I slung them over my back whiles he walked the mules forward almost to the edge but off to one side away from the place where most of the others was standing.

Then he unharnessed Jesse, and we got the kegs draped over just behind the withers, and meanwhile I could watch how the kid and the oxen was doing which wasn't any too promising. He must of took the fat man's advice because him and his pa was just finishing unhitching their team still aimed mostly uphill, and the chains on the back wheels looked to be either loose or busted or snarled different.

"Better not try selling no whiskey yourself yet," Casper says. "You reckon you'd know what's worth two-bits or more if you're looking at it?" He mounted up on Jesse with his legs sticking out wide behind the kegs.

"I don't know," I says, shamed to tell him I'd never had no two-bits to spend so's I could find out.

"Better just keep the wagon shut and not get blamed for making nobody drunk at the top of a clift," he says. "And keep that brake tight, and keep strangers off."

The kid and his pa was both trying to show them oxen what to do, but it didn't look like the same thing, so when the team took a shuffling step or two and felt they'd been unhitched from their load, they just made up their own mind and commenced plodding up slope, dragging the kid along, with him trying to haul back on the lines and set his heels in the sand and plowing a crooked furrow all the way past the fat man who was still standing there fanning hisself. The kid finally got them stopped on level ground and looked back down at his ma and pa and the stuck wagon, and none of them said nothing for a mintue.

"You, now, Jesse," Casper says, leaning forward to talk into his mule's ear which was sticking up fine for the purpose. "You know what to do. Show a little sense."

He paused like he expected the mule to say *Yes, sir*, and I wouldn't of been much surprised if it had, and if Jesse knew what to do, he was one of mighty few at the edge of Ash Hollow that late afternoon. Casper stuck a spare spigot and a bung-starter in his belt.

"Hold the fort," Casper says. "I'll be back by dark."

"Yes, sir," I says.

He give Jesse a prod, and they started off at a shallow slant just like there was a switchback trail there but wasn't, and when the fat man seen them coming by, he left off giving advice to the kid and says, "You can't haul that wagon up here with one mule, mister."

"I don't aim to try," Casper says, using his rope bridle to

switch Jesse around on the second lap of his zigzag. "I suggest them misfortunates unload that wagon and take it apart piece by piece and bring it up top and build theirself a shack and try homesteading."

The fat man give a spit and a nod like he wished he'd thought of it first and begun talking to the kid again. Meanwhile, Casper tipped his hat at the kid's ma and pa on the way by and turned and give me a wave, and Jesse kept taking little tippy-toe steps like a burro. Pretty soon they'd made a hundred yards down that scary-looking hollow, shortcutting now and then with Jesse hunkering his hindlegs and sliding a ways but never falling.

Another wagon was getting set to go over the edge, and I clumb up into Casper's seat to watch, keeping my staff handy and an eye on the hogs and feeling strange and lonely with all these worldly goods behind my back in my safekeeping.

The wagon was bigger and heavier than the other and had a four-ox team instead of just two, and three skinny little red-faced men that looked like brothers was handling it, one up front afoot, steering with the empty tongue and the other two on each side of the team that had been hitched behind but facing forward. It looked like a workable idea, though I didn't envy the one holding the tongue much.

About that time the kid's pa come up from down below (his ma stayed with the wagon, keeping one hand on it in case it might decide to fly off which didn't look too unlikely even with the wheels braked and chained) and not saying one word to kid nor oxen, give the kid a good hard swift kick in the rump for his wages. The fat man was still standing there, and he said something to the old man (maybe telling him he was kicking with the wrong foot or using too much toe and likely to bust it), and the old man give the fat man an even harder kick without changing nothing else about it, and then when the fat man went right on talking, give him another one and another, not having no trouble hitting a moving target that size. The kid flung down the lines and walked off back along the Trail like he was headed for Fort Kearny and points east with his pa hollering some name after him, but it didn't do no good.

The new heavier wagon was well down over the edge now, the four oxen hanging back like they was sposed to, not being used to having nothing tug at them, and from all the grinning at each other and nodding, the three brothers must of been feeling proud of theirself, already having made about thirty yards out of three thousand or more. One even give the kid's ma a little mock of a bow on the way by, but she snubbed him by aiming her chin off sideways.

A man with a pockmarked face and a gray felt ranch hat that looked like it'd cost plenty once was all of a sudden standing below me next to the wagon. I hadn't seen him coming, and I felt shamed of myself for a watchdog.

"You selling whiskey?" he says nice and mild and polite.

I opened my mouth to say no and then opened it again to say yes and then shut it and changed my mind twice more, then heard myself saying, "I believe I could spare a half-gill to a sober man for two bits." I was sorry I'd said it soon as it was out, but there was no use trying to back out now.

"Let's see the color of it, boy," the pockmarker says.

I clumb down, bringing my staff along, and went around back where Casper'd left the kegs under a tarpoleum. Lucy June got in the pockmarker's road—I guess coming along to see if there was anything in the line of feed going to be dished out—and he started to take a kick at her, then didn't which was the right idea on his part and sound judgment since I didn't aim to let nobody use my hogs for games again, even if they did have a sixgun like him.

I knocked some of the sand out of a spare cup and drew it half full like I'd seen Casper do it and give it a sniff whiles I was at it, and I don't know how whiskey gets that way, but it sure beats coal oil for character. It smelt like enough to raise blisters but kind of sweet too.

The pockmarker reached for it but I kept my elbow betwixt.

"Two-bits, please," I says. He wasn't quite as tall as me but thick through the chest.

He give me a little smile on one side, showing two teeth and a gap, and hesitated like he had half a mind to wrassle me for it, then dug in his jeans instead and come up with a coin. "It better not be no stinkabust," he says.

"Finest Kentucky bourbon whiskey west of the Mississippi and probably east of it too," I says, since Casper wasn't around to brag for hisself. I took the coin (which looked to be all right and not shaved nor bent), and the pockmarker took the cup and stuck his nose most into it without drinking.

He took a deep sniff, scowling all the while like he expected it to turn out rotten, then looked sort of surprised and took a sip and held onto it for a spell like he was fixing to spit it out.

We was close enough to the edge so's I could see them three brothers keeping their ox-team hanging back hard enough so's the wagon would stay on its wheels and straight. But one of the brothers must of goaded the lead ox too hard with a stick (they'd made good about fifty yards, and I couldn't see for sure), and the ox wasn't used to no command that was sposed to mean "hang back harder" and must of took it to mean "get going" and took a lunge into the rear end of the wagon, twisting the yoke on his pardner and generally throwing things out of whack, including the third brother hanging onto the tongue up ahead. Then all four oxen speeded up at once, and the two brothers clang onto them, pulling at their lines, some of which was dragging now, and the third brother was having to trot down that steep slant with the tongue under one arm.

Then all of a sudden the lead ox decided it was time to quit all this whatever-it-might-be and planted hisself stock still, and the other three done likewise after some ramming and rearing, and then the hitch broke, and when the third brother felt that tongue shove forward and the whole wagon commence going faster than he could run, he done the sensible thing and fell flat on his face and skidded straight enough so's the wheels passed on both sides of him. And the wagon begun that long, lonely ride downhill, not bouncing much and staying on its wheels far as I could see. I just hoped it wouldn't give Casper too much trouble getting out of the road towards the grove, if it was to get that far as kindling.

Whiles I'd been watching, the pockmarker hadn't drunk but a few more little sips and didn't seem interested in watching the wagons go through their jumps (which most folks, including me, take to be a way to learn something, even if it's only how to go wrong). Instead, I seen him take a little glass tube out of his shirt pocket and unstopper it and pull out a plug of cotton which he plucked a small chunk out of and dropped it into his cup on the whiskey. It sank right off.

I'd never heard of nobody drinking cotton with their whiskey and reckoned I'd have to ask Casper about it. But instead of drinking, the pockmarker dipped his empty glass tube in and scooped it half full and stoppered it up again and shook it and held it up to the dark-orange sunlight and stared through it and shook it again and done the same.

By that time Casper would of had the chatter going and had him talking about hisself and cracking jokes, but I didn't know how to go about it yet, this being my first customer and the pockmarker treating words like they was two-bits. So I give Colonel Woppert a good scratch behind the ears with the butt of my staff and watched the next folks go over the edge: a light farm cart without no canvas top and with a mule and a cow tied behind. An old lady with her skirts tied up to her knees tended the beasts, and an old man in a Jehu cut coat and corduroy pantaloons was up front between the shafts. They didn't seem worried about nothing and didn't speed up when the ground turned steep, just walked along a little easier, leaning backwards.

"Who made this whiskey?" the pockmarker says.

"Name of Casper," I says, realizing I didn't know the last name to go with it.

"Where is he?" the pockmarker says. He seen me hesitate,

so he give me the second half of that first smile. "I'd like to shake his hand."

I seen the fat man coming over towards the wagon, limping a bit and looking grieved, though what with the chaw and the other bulges in his face, you had to look twice to see how he was feeling.

"He'll be back," I says.

The pockmarker give another shake and squint at his tube, then stuck it back in his pocket. He fished the piece of cotton out of his whiskey with a dirty forefinger and flipped it aside (Colonel Woppert got his first taste of whiskey far as I know and seemed to like it about as good as anything else). He took a plain, ordinary drink then and let it trickle down and nodded, almost closing his eyes.

"Do them X's mean whiskey?" the fat man says.

I seen the pockmarker staring into the back of the wagon at Casper's still which was all took apart but might seem familiar to anybody who knew what he was looking at, and his face had gone all slack with wonder. If it hadn't been for his scars, he'd of looked like a little boy for a minute.

"How much does it fetch?" the fat man says.

"Two-bits a half-gill," I says, keeping my eye on the pockmarker who'd pulled hisself together and was trying to squint closer. I eased myself along the tailgate and got in his way some, but he didn't quit staring.

"Sold," the fat man says. "Long as it ain't all blue fishhooks or putrid."

I drew him a half a cup with a bashed-in bottom that was hard to judge by, so he probably got more than his share, and the pockmarker strolled off a few steps like he was thinking, still holding his cup and giving it a sip now and then.

"Did you see that damn dirt farmer kick me over there?" the fat man says. "Why, I had half a notion to leave his wagon stuck right where it is and not tell him how to get back up." The fat man passed over his two-bits, which looked like it'd been squoze to get the juice out of it first, and took his cup

and looked inside like he was used to being disappointed.
"This ain't corn whiskey," he says. "It ain't even mobby or
applejack."

My heart wasn't but half in it, but I says, "Finest Kentucky
bourbon whiskey west of the—" But I kept watching the
pockmarker who was looking the wagon all over now like he
was fixing to buy it or worse.

After taking a sniff, the fat man hooked his chaw out of his
cheek with one finger and left it fall to the ground where Lucy
June beat Colonel Woppert to it. (I don't know if she liked it
much, but she didn't spit it out nor do no plain spitting
neither.) Then he licked his lips and made sure his mouth was
all clear and give me a little toast with his cup and downed
enough to cut the dust, then downed a smack more. A smile
about a foot long stretched around back to both ears, and he
says, "'Lift up your heads, O ye gates, and be ye lift up, ye
everlasting doors, and the King of Glory shall come in.'"

Which he hadn't made up but got down by rote out of the
Bible, I do believe, though I didn't see no connection myself,
not being a drinking man.

"Since this is my last two-bits melted down to gold," the fat
man says, sloshing his cup around gentle and looking into it
and smiling and puckering up, "I'll give you a little business
advice. There's a cart over yonder doing elbow-to-elbow trade
and charging fifty cents for less than this here, and it's bad
applejack watered down till it ain't no more than ciderkin.
Raise your price, and if you give me a bottle of this to pray
over between here and Fort Laramie, I'll warrant you I'll have
a mob clustered around this wagon in fifteen minutes paying
gladly and drinking you dry and naming their babies after
you."

I didn't like the sound of that, me and the hogs both being
more inclined to keep to ourself and shy around company,
and I didn't know if Casper'd want to sell that much whiskey
in a rush and then not having nothing to do with his time.

But before I could say anything, the pockmarker, who was

only standing about ten foot off, let out one of the loudest
whistles I've ever heard come between human teeth. I don't
know just how he done it except he used the thumb and
forefinger of his free hand (Si Acker back home used to favor
two forefingers, but that's sort of awkward sometimes if
you've got muck on one hand). It made Casper's mule take a
step or two against the brake, and it turned all four hogs like
a real fence-lifter of a wind had just struck, and it made the
fat man spill some of his whiskey which he had to lick off
his wrist.

"Damn it, give a little warning if you're going to make a
racket like that," the fat man says.

The pockmarker ignored him, looking off towards a clump
of wagons camped a good ways back from the edge. In a few
seconds a man on horseback come trotting out of it and heading our direction.

"Whiskey like this had ought to be treated with a respeckful
silence," the fat man says, finding a few more drops to lick
halfway up his shirtsleeve.

"Then why don't you just keep quiet?" the pockmarker
says, mild and slow, favoring us both with that little smile that
had a hole in it.

I felt uneasy and give a glance down that long steep slope
(where the three brothers was leading their ox-team downhill
to start hunting the pieces and no doubt having an interesting
conversation like the one the kid's ma and pa was having by
the stalled oxless wagon), hoping I'd see Casper coming back
early, but didn't see nothing but the old man and woman
slumping along in the deep distance, doing just fine with their
cart and cow and mule.

"Well, I think I'm allowed to strike up a little conversation
over my bought-and-paid-for whiskey," the fat man says,
looking at me to counterdict him which I didn't.

The man coming on horseback reined up short and dismounted (a small, skinny-shouldered man with a shock of
iron-gray hair coming down from under a new-looking straw

stetson), and the pockmarker walked out a ways to talk to him, taking the cup along, and they kept on talking, the small man looking our way now and then like he wanted to see what he was hearing about.

"I believe I made you an offer, but I didn't hear no reply," the fat man says.

"You'll have to talk to the whiskey man when he comes back," I says.

Sounding a little anxious, the fat man says, "I can also do blacksmithing if I had a fire, trim hooves, shoe mules and horses, and do carpenter work."

"Talk to the whiskey man," I says, making up my mind all of a sudden. "I'm shutting this wagon down, and soon's you're finished up with that cup, I'll take it back."

"Don't rush me," the fat man says, holding his cup in against his belly. "This here aged slow, and it should be drank the same way."

The small man and the pockmarker had quit talking, and now they come towards the wagon, leaving the horse behind with its reins trailing.

"My friend here'd like a little bite of that whiskey, son," the pockmarker says.

I stepped far enough away from the tailgate so's I could swing my staff all right if the occasion called, and I says, "Sorry, gents, but I'm closing up for the day."

The small man had a sixgun too, which wasn't exackly a sight for sore eyes, and it was some kind of long-barreled special near as long as his forearm.

"All friends here," the pockmarker says. "One more won't hurt nobody."

"I'm fresh out of cups," I says.

"Then I'll take one of them bottles there in the basket," the small man says. "How much?"

"I don't know," I says. "You'll have to wait for the whiskey man." They'd stayed far enough off so's I couldn't reach either

of them with my staff, even if I worked up to be fool enough
to try.

"Then I reckon we'll do that," the pockmarker says, smiling.

"Me too," the fat man says, leaning back on one elbow till
the wagon creaked and taking a little sip.

Still sounding friendly, the pockmarker says, "You get on the
hell out of here and keep your mouth shut about this whiskey."

The fat man straightened up and pulled his belly in a couple
inches. "Why, you can't talk to me like that," he says.

"I already done it," the pockmarker says. "Git!"

Draining his cup in a hurry, the fat man set it down and
backed off, keeping his rear end protected, and bumped into
Pattycake who give him a fright by grunting, then headed off
towards the main bunch still clustered up at the edge of the
drop-off.

The pockmarker looked at me cold and steady. "Now you
just be a good boy and set down amongst them nice hogs and
think peaceful thoughts, and we'll all of us wait for this wonderful whiskey man to come home to roost," he says.

The small man had taken his big gun out and was too far off
to hit unless I slung my staff (which I didn't want to do because I couldn't do it but once), and I didn't want none of my
hogs shot, and Casper was coming back anyway without no
way for me to stop him, and leastways then it'd be two against
two instead of like this, so I done like I was told, even though
I didn't like taking orders from strangers.

"That's right," the pockmarker says, setting down too and
leaning back and smelling his whiskey. Then to the small man,
"Draw yourself a little of this, Tommy, if you don't mind the
cup."

When he seen me scramble around to my knees, the small
man stopped and aimed his gun my way. "Is your life worth
two-bits?" he says.

I reckoned it was, and I set back down again whiles he drew
a full cup (first wiping the rim all around and wrinkling his

nose). He give it a test and smiled down at the pockmarker, then shook his head like he didn't want to believe it and joined him on the ground almost shoulder to shoulder so's they could whisper, all the time keeping a wary eye on me, which I hope to tell you was a right smart idea because I was mad.

I hadn't sold but two half-cups of whiskey (and had one stole) in all my sinful days, and here I set, with my life, liberty, and pursuit of unhappiness looking ready to start down the chute with a hook in its snout and a chain heisting it up for slaughter. It didn't seem legal, leave alone right, and nowheres near the kind of joy I had all day long been expecting after having a genuine Vision and filling up on Light.

But then it come to me maybe I'd mistook what was going on. I must of misunderstood something like the time I'd thought Uncle Fred was mad at me because he hit me across the ribs with a bottle whiles he was half asleep and me listening to him so's I could learn how to swear good (Pa didn't know how), but turned out he thought I was Beelzebub (which is what they call the Devil in the back part of Jefferson County). I'd been wrong then and maybe I was wrong now. I'd leave Casper figure it out.

Chapter Thirteen

HE COME BACK when there was still light enough to see by if your ambitions for seeing didn't stretch no more than fifty foot, and he had the roped kegs slung over his mule. One of the kegs was sloshing and spilling out of a stove-in stave, but I scarcely had time to notice it before I was yelling, "Casper! Two men with guns!"

The small man made a move to hush me with a slash of his gun barrel but pulled back when he seen my staff all primed to land him one, and the pockmarker scrambled to his feet, gun out, peering around the edge of the wagon.

"Damn you," the pockmarker says.

But Casper didn't seem to pay no attention to the warning.

It was like he hadn't heard me: he kept Jesse plodding right up to the front of the wagon and slid off of it and hauled the kegs off to the ground, trying to keep the busted one from spilling too much. "Hay and water for all them with four feet," he says.

"Yes, sir," I says, and grabbed an armload out of the bale in the back whiles Casper took the bucket off of its hook on the near side of the wagon and commenced filling it without losing much.

The pockmarker acted a little uncertain what to do, but when he seen Casper didn't have no gun on him and I'd put my staff down to get at the chores, he relaxed some and holstered his gun, though the small man stood off a ways near his horse, looking ready for trouble. Colonel Woppert wandered over his way to see if his horse was going to do anything interesting, but before any kicking could start, I slang two piles of hay down and did some chucking in my throat, and Colonel Woppert come back to join an easier kind of fun.

"Been down in the Hollow?" the pockmarker says, keeping it low and friendly.

"Yes, sir," Casper says, not paying much attention. "Zeke, would you work this bucket around fair shares and don't let nobody nose it over. I didn't get as much as I wanted, but there's enough."

"Yes, sir," I says. "They've had a gun on me two hours."

"Now, now," the pockmarker says. "All friends here. Just keeping the rough boys away. Some get long on thirst and short on money this time of day. Just keeping a friendly eye on all these valuables with nothing but a younker and four hogs to look after them."

"Get me some of that jerky, Zeke," Casper says.

I got one foot up towards the wagon seat, but the pock-marker says, "You just keep out of there." He had his hand on his gun butt. "Just till we can clear up any misunderstanding here." Though he was trying to make it sound like apologizing, it didn't have enough fat on it.

I kept on going and rummaged for the jerky jar back of the seat, and I heard a hammer click back and a chamber turn.

"You heard me," the pockmarker says.

"I heard you too," Casper says behind my back. "And if you don't mind your manners—and that goes for your little sister over there too—you're going to sleep the Sleep of the Sixteen Lumps which I don't recommend for weeknights when you might have to get up the next day."

By that time, I had the jerky jar out and clumb down and hadn't been shot. Casper took it and helped hisself and passed it back, and I had me a chaw of it too.

The pockmarker put his gun away slow, shrugging, and treated Casper to one of them smiles, which looked a whole lot funnier by daylight than now. "I've been admiring your whiskey," he says.

Casper give me a glance, and I says, "He paid for hisn, but the other didn't."

"Then you're welcome to admire it," Casper says. "I hope you gave it a good home. Now if you'll just leave me and my assistant to our business here—"

"I aim to talk business," the pockmarker says.

"Why, I couldn't talk business with a thief listening," Casper says. "Wouldn't be sensible."

"What thief?" the pockmarker says, his voice going shallow and thick.

"Your little sister over there that owes me two-bits—"

"Fifty cents," I says. "A whole cupful."

"—fifty cents," Casper says, "and that don't know no better than play with a gun."

The small man was standing dead still with that long-barreled gun hanging down till it near touched his ankle, and I wished Casper'd scold me or the hogs for a change.

After hesitating and scratching his chin, the pockmarker

fished a couple coins out of his pocket and flipped them one at a time towards Casper, meaning for him to miss and have to stoop, but Casper caught them both without seeming to try, still chawing jerky.

"All right, now you can state your business, and I'll use both ears," Casper says. "Sorry I went and lost my good disposition. There was two gents down below tried to dislocate my kegs, and I had to do a little dislocating of my own. I'm a sunny man at heart, and I want to ask the pardon of the short gent with the long gun over there, now he's paid up. It's no sin to be short, and here I stand the living proof. Have a drink on me."

"I wouldn't say no," the pockmarker says. "What say, Tommy? The man's asked your pardon."

"He'll get my pardon right through his breastbone and out the back if he don't look to his tongue," the small man says.

Casper was letting his voice out soft and warm as a mackinaw blanket now. "I loosened that tongue with a little too much of my own whiskey whiles busting my crutch uphill on a mule," he says. "I'll ask your pardon again."

The small man didn't say nothing but come in closer when Casper and the pockmarker went around back where the spigot was hanging over the tailgate.

"You had a fight down in the Hollow?" the pockmarker says, taking his cup and handing the other to the small man who kept off a ways. "With who?"

"I wasn't innerduced proper," Casper says.

I didn't like what was going on but didn't know what to do about it besides keeping my eye on the hogs (who was still giving the hay a work-over) and staying close enough to help Casper if he needed it. I knew he had a rifle wrapped up in the wagon, but it wasn't doing him no good out here, and these two didn't seem interested in no fisticuffs, which was what Casper done best next to talking and whiskey-making.

"We work for Cole Selfridge," the pockmarker says. "Heard of him?"

"No, sir," Casper says, lifting up his own cup. "But I wish
him a calm night and many a happy day."

They all three drunk to it, and the more I seen of this toast-
ing and cup-raising that drinking men liked to do, the less I
understood it. If they're going to pour something like whiskey
down their throat, how's come they all want to turn into
preachers at benediction time or birthday boys blowing out
their cake or talking like they was going off on a long, long
journey? I knew it was something like grace before grub where
you thank God (if you should happen to remember to) for
having a dish of your own, but these here toasts never sounded
like that.

"Well, he gets his share of happy days, anyway," the pockmarker says. "We're up here selling whiskey for him." He kept
it slow and quiet. "With his permission."

"I wish you well at the trade," Casper says. "I'd like to
sample your stock."

"I wouldn't give you the insult," the pockmarker says. "Not
after tasting what you can do. And it's none of my doing anyway. It—" he turned on his smile a second or two "—comes
from here and there. It sort of collects in the Hollow, just like
rainwater."

He shifted his feet, and Casper shifted hisn to match, and the
small man come a step closer, holding his cup and his gun
both, and I had both hands on one end of my staff because it
seemed like—as it got a little darker—what the pockmarker
was saying turned darker too.

"Normally, in my territory—which this *is*—if a man tried to
sell whiskey, I'd just buy it all offen him and run him along,"
the pockmarker says. "You can understand that."

"I understand just fine," Casper says.

"But you're a different matter," the pockmarker says.

"I been noticing that since I was belly-high," Casper says.
"And them that have tried to get me to run along have noticed
it too."

The pockmarker made a little calm-down wave with his free

hand. "What I want is for you and your whiskey and Mr. Selfridge all to get together," he says. "I think you could do a deal
of business, and I think me and Tommy would profit too or I
wouldn't be talking so nice and drinking the sun down with
you."

"Why, I wouldn't mind obliging you gents with an idea like
that," Casper says. "Me and my assistant will be passing
through Ash Hollow tomorrow, and if this Mr. Selfridge wants
to talk or needs a drink, I'd be glad to stop and sell by the
smalls."

For a second, I seen the pockmarker was going to snap some
kind of answer back, but he caught hisself and let it out as a
plain breath instead. "I think that'll work out fine," he says.
"Don't you, Tommy?"

"Yes," the small man says, taking another pull at his cup.

"Long as there's none of this *permission*," Casper says, making it sould like something the hogs wouldn't touch. "I sell
my whiskey where and when I please."

"Shouldn't be no problem," the pockmarker says mildly.
"If I've ever tasted whiskey born to be sold, that's it."

"And *don't* sell it when I please," Casper says.

"I believe you'll find Mr. Selfridge a good listener and a good
talker," the pockmarker says. "Now, if you don't mind, we'll
camp right along with you here and see you get down that
damn slope safe and sound and not a drop spilt and no obli-
gation either way and no guns nor cross words nor nothing.
Let's keep this here a civilized world."

I could hear what was probably the last wagon of the evening commencing to jolt down over the edge of this civilized
world with some bottles or crocks busting and a great big snap
like an axle getting tired of it all, and the hogs whuffling in the
hay, and the mules snuffing hay-dust out of their nose, and far
off, the voice of the fat man going up to full pitch whiles he
told how somebody else had skipped his sound advice and
turned out sorry, and I begun to wonder if there wasn't some
other way to get to California.

"Fair enough," Casper says. "I'm a peaceful man, and the ground's willing to take all comers. Just don't bed down too near the hogs or they might root you up during the night to see what's going on underneath of you."

The pockmarker went over and whispered to the small man for a while, and he mounted up and rode off towards the clump of wagons, leaving the pockmarker who just set down and waited, finishing up his whiskey.

We decided not to make no fire, since we didn't have nothing to make it with, but just spread our blankets and had some more jerky and some dry pilot bread. After a minute, the small man come back with two bedrolls and a second horse, and the two of them spread out on the off-side of the wagon out of earshot. I bunched the hogs in close as I could, holding Colonel Woppert's nose-ring till he got tired of it and laid down and left me lay my head on him.

And when it was almost dark, Casper whispers, "Don't do nothing foolish. I'm going to sleep in the back of the wagon to keep my whiskey company. Just go along with these gents tomorrow and let them do as much of the work as they please. It's the direction we're going to have to go anyway, Zeke, and we might's well take one thing at a time and take it calm, same as you'd roll with a punch. All kind of people walking around this Territory carrying thumb-busters and thinking they're the Law. Just mind your manners and your hogs and leave the rest to me."

And he slipped up into the wagon without making a creak or a rustle and could of unwrapped that rifle and shot them two laying on the ground if he'd a mind to but didn't.

I laid there open-eyed a long while, my head raising and falling on Colonel Woppert's side bristles whiles he took the night air in and thought it over and passed it on and then took some more in, and I wasn't sure what had become of me. I felt like I'd improved some in the last few days, but maybe not enough to count, because I could hear a kind of fat man inside me, giving me all kind of advice I didn't need nor know how to

answer, and one of the things he says was for me to sneak out
in the night and round off my hogs and light off on my own
down that halfmoonlit slope and start picking out my own
kind of trouble instead of always using somebody else's.

But I didn't go, and it wasn't because I was scairt the pockmarker or the small man would catch me at it neither. I didn't
feel scairt of nothing but that fat man inside me. So I told him
to hush up because I was going to help Casper like he'd helped
me. My sore head was throbbing just about in tune with Colonel Woppert's lungs, and I was almost asleep, carrying my
load of worries down into the black watery mess I usually fall
into at night (full of squigglers and crawdads and bloodsuck-
ers), when I heard the pockmarker and the small man muttering together.

And I took it into my head I'd try to overhear what they
was saying and learn something useful and be more of a help in
keeping Casper's whiskey from going down the wrong throats
free of charge the next day.

So what I done was crawl under the wagon, keeping well
away from the mules so's I wouldn't get too much sense
kicked into me, but when I come to the inside of the near-
back wheel (which was as far as I could go without busting out
into the open and getting caught) I still wasn't near enough to
make out the words. Casper was snoring overhead kind of half-
hearted but loud enough to muffle my ears. But I did see the
pockmarker go crawling off by hisself toward the clump of
other wagons, leaving the small man behind and staying just as
quiet as he could.

It made me suspicion something was going on we'd ought to
know about, because why did he have to worry over whether
he roused us or not?—him being the kind of man who seemed
to do and go as and where he pleased. So as soon as I seen the
small man lay back against his saddle again and tip his hat forward, I backed up on all fours and crawled off the other way,
trying not to get the hogs interested in what I was doing and
follow me, hoping I knew about some midnight forage.

I circled a good ways before coming up to a crouch and

learnt more'n I cared to about what and who had been camp-
ing on this ridge since spring and probably earlier too: I run
into more kind of trash than I could name and was glad when
I could get my hands off of the ground and let my boots do
the dirty work by theirself. I cut across the open patch, steering by the last few campfires up ahead and having to guess
which way the pockmarker'd gone and walking upright now
because, if the small man looked this way, he'd think it was
somebody going between some other wagons or a call of
nature.

When I come to the tailboard of the nearest wagon, I commenced hearsing over what I might say if I run into a stranger
who might think I was up to no good and how I'd tell him I
was looking for this pockmarked friend of mine and did he
happen to see him passing through just now and where was the
fifty-cent whiskey being sold, but I didn't have no time to
worry about keeping out of trouble: I was in it with two more
steps, and if I'd of took three (going all the way past the tailboard where the firelight would of caught me plain) I might of
ended my days on the California Trail right then and there (or
maybe drug off a hundred yards someplace where the coyotes
and crows wouldn't have to be so shy) because the pockmarker was setting on the ground close to the fire and across
from him, blue-bearded and squinch-faced and his rancher's
hat tied on because it wouldn't fit over his bulgy temples, was
the moonhead. He had a sixgun and a rifle and was talking low
and fast to the pockmarker who was listening hard.

I ducked back and didn't linger around to overhear nothing
they might be saying for fear of getting caught. Whatever it
might be, it was bad news, and I didn't want no part of it. I'd
come without my staff (it seeming too clumsy to handle in the
dark), and I didn't fancy trying to wrench the story of Ma and
Pa out of him barehanded. I swang back around the way I'd
come and crept in amongst the hogs without flustering them
but for a few snorts, and I laid there for a spell, wondering
what to do. Already I was commencing to feel I'd been a
coward, but it's no joke being unarmed and trying to face

down a man who'd shot you once and would probably just as
soon come around for second helpings. I could wake up Casper
and maybe get him to help me, but I'd have to do a whole
mess of explaining and he'd said he didn't like guns and, besides, the small man was laying guard on us, and we'd have to
shoot our way past him first and shoot the pockmarker too,
probably, and get all the other wagons riled and ready to lynch
us for road agents.

Whiles I was mulling it all around, I heard the pockmarker
come sneaking back and muttering things over with the small
man, so for all I knew, the moonhead had walked off amongst
the dozens and dozens of other wagons someplace or rode off
backtrailing, and no matter what I thought up to do, it meant
me leaving the hogs behind and Casper dropping his guard on
his whiskey (which I didn't think I could get him to do for no
revenge of mine).

So I wound up doing nothing and cussing myself for it and
wondering what the moonhead had been cooking up with the
pockmarker, because even in the split of a second I seen them
together, they'd looked like they was talking about the near
future and not chatting about old times. I tried to get all the
voices and frets and wonderings to hush up so's I could rest
and strengthen up by daylight, and finally the dark come in so
close it seemed like I must of fell asleep, which would of been
fine with me if I hadn't seen the buckskin man standing in the
back of my head and staring at the inside backs of my eyes
just like he done to the fronts the day before. He looked
tattery now and falling apart like he'd been dead and buried
but had clumb out and come to call.

And then in this half-dream (because I thought I could still
hear Casper snoring) the buckskin man seemed to rip open the
front of his jacket and reach right into his bare chest and take
out a handful of his liver or lights or something and fling it at
me hollering "Eat! Eat!" I ducked deeper into sleep to get
away from him, then deeper, and he faded out, and everything hushed up like I'd been mulched over.

Chapter Fourteen

A HOG HAS MORE TROUBLE laying down than you'd think, him being so close to the ground already. If he lays on his side, he don't have nowhere to put his upper legs but stick them out in the air, and it's tiresome. If he lays flat on his belly with his legs sprawled, he can't tuck his chin back: he has to stretch it out flat, and after while he gets a crick in his neck. If he sets up on his hams, he can't do no more than doze, which ain't enough rest for another day of walking. And he can't lay flat on his back because it ain't flat and he tips over. If you sleep with hogs, you're going to try all them ways to get comfortable right along with them, and they won't work, and if you've got a troubled mind, you're going to wake up sleepy like I done.

It didn't seem to bother the hogs (they had more lard to go under them than me), and they commenced rooting around at dawn whiles I was still getting the hair out of my face and my hat on. The small man and the pockmarker rolled up their blankets and et something grimy-looking out of their saddle-bags and took another cup of whiskey when Casper offered it and didn't say much. Nobody else had started down the gully yet, but a few was getting set to try.

"I'd ruther be last than first, but anything's better than in-between," Casper says. "If we get enough of a head start, some of these knotheads'll have to fall down mighty fast to hit us."

Him and me was out of earshot of our two guards (though they'd been trying to act different: not drawing their guns and even dropping a friendly word now and then), and I says, "I seen something last night, and I don't know what to do."

"Well, don't let it bother you," he says. "If you hadn't seen nothing, you *still* probably wouldn't know what to do. Hand me over that bungstarter."

"I seen the pockmarker there talking to the man that shot me," I says.

That made him hold still a second. Then he stooped down to study the rear axle and says, "Where?"

"Over by them other wagons," I says. "He snuck out after you was asleep, so I followed him."

"You interested in getting shot again?" he says.

"No, sir."

"Then don't go crawling around amongst armed men at night," he says.

"What should I do now?" I says.

"Well, if you see him again, duck," he says.

"That's what I done last night," I says. "And I felt shamed of it. Maybe he knows where my ma and pa went."

He give me another long, still look. "Where do you reckon people go when they leave their hogs straggling along a trail and their son shot and their wagon laying in a river?" he says.

I tried to see it as simple as if it was somebody else instead of me. "I reckon they'd be hurt bad or maybe dead," I says.

"Now that's what I call a practical notion," he says.

Then with me and the two others doing the grunting and propping up one corner at a time, Casper unpinned and knocked off all four wheels of his wagon till it was setting on its axles and looked like it'd sank in a bog. Then he stowed the wheels inside, lashing them up against the parts of his still and not leaving nobody else do it but him. He left the mules harnessed and hitched up front but didn't set on the seat: it was so low down, he couldn't of seen nothing but leather straps, mule butts, and maybe a little sky, so he tied off the lines to keep them from getting tangled underhoof and clumb up on Jesse and says, "Now if you gents would oblige by roping onto my back corners and keeping this here land-sledge going straight and not sliding off cockeyed, we'll go right down this chute and enjoy the scenery too."

They done what he said, each playing out about ten foot of rope and giving it a couple turns around their saddlehorns, and the pockmarker says, "I've seen some others try this, and you'd ought to be glad we're back here hauling keel."

"I'm counting on all whiskey-lovers to do their duty," Casper says. "I don't aim to break my mules' legs nor anything else either, and you'll get your reward in Heaven."

The pockmarker made a face like he didn't figure on applying for that reward for a while yet.

"I don't have to tell you how to do nothing, do I?" Casper says to me.

"I won't be shy to ask," I says.

"You can't stampede four hogs, can you?" he says.

"Not so's you'd notice," I says.

"How do hogs like going downhill?" he says.

"Better than up," I says.

"Well, keep them off a ways in case something busts loose here, pray God it don't, or one of these deckhands leaves go of his rope to scratch," he says.

"Yes, sir," I says.

And Casper started over the side at a steeper angle than he done with the mule alone, not aiming at shallow switchbacks but deeper ones. At first Jesse and Si could barely move the wagonbed, but after it'd tipped onto the slant (I heard a few bottles clink and some rumbles out of the kegs but nothing else but creaking) it slid along easy and might of started going too fast (spite of the axles and wheel-span doing some gravel-plowing) if the small man and the pockmarker hadn't kept their ropes taut.

The fat man was up early so's he wouldn't miss nothing (I hadn't seen him treat a wagon like home, so for all I knew he planned on spending his whole life directing others down the chute whiles he educated hisself), and he opened his mouth to tell me all about hogs, but then he held still and watched the whiskey going away, maybe keeping track in case any kegs fell out and rolled off unbeknownst.

Colonel Woppert didn't like the looks of that steep slant no more than I did, but he come along at an angle like the wagon, and the others followed. I kept downhill of the hogs so's they couldn't see how far they could slide if they didn't mind their trotters, though they couldn't see much past Casper and the mules probably and had more blissful ignorance than me to go on. But they was probably smelling some of that greenery down there too and the bushes showing up on both sides of us, not far off, and that helped keep them moving. With the mules setting the example, Colonel Woppert got the idea of switchbacking right off, and I quit worrying long enough to see the wagon that'd been stuck there without its ox-team was gone now, and no way to tell if it'd been took apart, hauled up, down, or sideways. And this Trail had always been like that: you'd see somebody struggling with their troubles, and then they'd either fall behind you or something else'd happen and you'd fall behind them, and you'd scarcely ever find out what become of them. It didn't seem neighborly, but except for the wagon trains, you never got to know people well enough to put names to them.

The small man and the pockmarker wasn't enjoying theirself any too much, it being a very tricky kind of riding to keep a

rope tight like that on a slope and not let their horse get thinking so much about handling a wagon like it was a roped steer,
it'd forget it could fall down and bust an ankle without half
trying. I heard them cussing considerably (they wasn't no good
at it), but every time Casper looked back my way, he had a big
smile on his face like he was taking corn to market and didn't
have nothing on his mind but chicken stew and biscuits for
dinner.

There was so much that could of went wrong, I couldn't
even come close to thinking it up, though the remainders of
what that axle-cracking, beast-panicker of a gully had did to
others was strown all along beside us and underfoot sometimes
—splintered wagon parts and chunks of crockery and bottle
chips and ox bones and stray boots and the lid off of a trunk
and a mule skull picked clean and crumpled pie plates and
shredded canvas, and none of it worth picking up for fear
you'd fall over doing it.

The limestone sides with blind gullies running into them had
rose up higher, and by the time we'd made it halfway, I could
see grapevine and roses and currant bushes off left and right
and brambles that probably was going to have berries on them
in a month or two and all kind of scrubbery I hadn't seen since
back home. The hogs didn't want to keep going downhill but
could see and smell all that lovely forage passing them by and
wanted to rove off into it and quit eating dust for a change,
and if there'd been many more than four of them, I'd of had a
sweet time convincing them I knew where we was going. But
they'd got into the habit of following mules and a wagon, even
if it didn't have no wheels, so they put up with the butt of my
staff and their empty bellies a while longer.

I looked back a few times and seen other wagons coming,
but no runaways yet and no landslides full of wagonwheels
and happy families and pieces of their valuable contraptions.

We kept going another lathery, thigh-stretching, heel-digging,
hoof-slipping, trotter-scraping, mule-skinning half-hour, coming closer and closer to a thinned-out grove of big ash trees

that was such an unusual sight (including all the wildflowers
thickening up on both sides) that if we'd been out on the flat
on a hot day, I'd of thought it was one of them upside-down
Visions. But it was real, though the grove turned out to be
mostly stumps, and there was a spring of clear water in a
bushy cluster off to the right, forty foot across, and I seen the
glimmer of another beyond and a little further down, like
they might be part of the same underground crick that boiled
up here and there.

Gradually the sandy gravel leveled up under us, and Casper
reined in the mules as soon as the wagonbed quit sliding by itself, and the small man and the pockmarker let loose their
ropes and rode over to water their horses and theirself, too,
laying flat on the ground.

I tried to hold the hogs back so's there wouldn't be no
trouble (most people don't like to drink with hogs because
they get a little too enthusiastic about it, long as it ain't too
deep), but the best I could do was get them around on the
far side and make them use their snouts instead of trying to
soak it in all over.

Even so, the small man scowled up at me and says, "Get
them damn pigs out of here."

I couldn't of obliged him if I'd wanted to, and he probably
knew it, so I just let them go on drinking, joining in myself
next to Lucy June. Casper unhitched Jesse and Si and brung
them over for their share and whispered in their ear a while,
then left the wagon setting out there at the foot of the slope.

When everybody had wet their whistle all the way down to
the anklebones, Casper says, "All right, boys, let's get them
wheels back on."

I'd had time to look around, and I seen a nest of wagons
camped down towards the far end of the grove next to another
spring and off to the right among smaller clumps of bushes and
brambles and even some real grass, there was a big wide low
building, part plank and part doby, the first house (or whatever it was) I'd seen for many a day.

Without saying nothing, the small man just mounted up and rode off towards that house. The pockmarker and Casper give each other a long look, and if you'd added their smiles up together, they wouldn't of made a whole one.

"Well, I reckon the three of us can manage," Casper says, but he didn't sound like he expected a whole lot of help from the pockmarker, and he was right.

"Why don't we just rest up and wait for Mr. Selfridge?" the pockmarker says, setting by the spring and stretching his legs.

Casper nodded, but it wasn't the kind that means *Yes*. It was the kind meaning *I figured as much*, and he turned around, tipping his chin at me, and led the mules back towards the wagon in a hurry with their harness dragging, and I prodded at the hogs till they left the grass alone and followed after.

The pockmarker stayed put by the spring, and when we'd got out of earshot Casper says, "*Hurry*. But don't look like it."

Which is pretty hard to manage. "What am I sposed to be doing?" I says.

"Hitch the mules," he says. "And find us a branch low enough to get a rope over."

For a minute I was dumfounded, thinking we was going to get hung or try hanging somebody ourself, but then I used what little brains I had and straightened out the mules' lines after I'd backed them into place and Casper'd done the actual hitching, and I says, "I wish we had a windlass and pulley."

"Long as you're wishing, get us out of this Hollow and down to the river and up the road about twenty mile," he says, climbing up on Jesse. "There's too dang much to unload, and we probably don't have time anyway, so see if you can lend a shoulder here."

I got behind to push, and when Casper'd whooped and kicked a few times, the mules begun budging the wagonbed along, but it stalled after about fifteen foot, or else they just quit, and no matter how hard I shoved, nothing moved but my shoulder joints and my feet slipping.

"Can you get them hogs to shove?" he says.

"They might *haul* if we had any harness for them," I says. "Back home, Dr. Dewby had a hog cart he'd rigged up, and every Saturday, him and his sow named Alice—"

"Never mind, never mind," he says.

And I seen what he meant: out of the ash grove from the direction of that plank-and-doby house four horsemen was coming, one the small man and one an important-looking, square-shouldered, big-gutted, red-faced man in a pearl-gray stetson, wearing a fancy duck vest and a ruffled shirtfront and pointy-toed brown calf boots with a shine on them that must of cost a bucket of sweat. The pockmarker touched his hat-brim as they trotted by, then followed along afoot, leading his horse. The other two men didn't amount to much, except one had his left eye swole shut and his nose scraped raw and may-be busted.

"Ah, Jesus, here goes my whiskey," Casper says before they come close enough to hear. "Let me do the talking."

Which I was glad to do, since I didn't think I'd be able to get out enough words to keep that bunch listening for ten seconds: all five had guns and none of them looked sociable. They reined up, and the important-looking man stared everything over but Casper: the mules, me, the hogs, and a good long look into the back of the wagonbed, though he probably couldn't see the still too good or even the kegs with the four wheels lashed in there.

Still up on the mule, Casper says, "Something I can do for you gents?"

"I'm Cole Selfridge," the man says. "And I'd like a drink of your whiskey."

"It's a universal wish, whatever their name might be," Casper says. "But I haven't made up my mind whether I'm selling any today."

"Didn't seem to bother you yesterday, uphill *or* down," Selfridge says.

"I didn't know the local customs then," Casper says, dismounting and walking around back to get between Selfridge and the kegs.

I herded the hogs off a ways in case of more trouble or trompling and got my staff ready.

Selfridge tipped his hat back a half-inch, letting the sunshine play on four of the eight diamond rings he was wearing. I'd never seen a man with even one on before, and they made me feel shamed of him and shy and kind of embarrassed. He was no kin of mine, so I don't know why I felt like it was half my fault. "The local custom is *I* sell the whiskey here, what there is of it," Selfridge says.

"In that case, I wouldn't dream of selling you any," Casper says. He looked around at the other four dead-serious solemn faces. "I'm paying a dollar a wheel to get this wagon rolling again." He waited, but nobody said nothing. "Two dollars a wheel."

"These men aren't for hire," Selfridge says. "They work for me. And now I'll take a cup of your whiskey as a goodwill offering and an earnest of your good intentions."

Casper stood there, seeming to think it over, looking dry-faced and calm whiles Selfridge done the sweating for the both of them.

Finally Selfridge raised his voice a bit. "You injured two of my men yesterday," he says. "Andrews?"

The man with his eye swole shut says, "Yes, sir?"

"This the one?"

"Yes, sir."

"I don't deny it," Casper says. "Him and another stove in one of my kegs with us five hundred mile or more from the nearest barrelhouse and the nearest white oaktree. It's a damn crime against Nature."

Selfridge seemed to mull that over, then says, "Let's have a taste of that whiskey, and we'll see who's been committing what."

After another pause, Casper shrugged, rummaged in back for a cup, wiped it off with a clean bandanna from his hip pocket, and drew it half full. He handed it up to Selfridge like he didn't want to see it go and stared off someplace else with his mouth flat whiles the sniffing, sipping, mouthwashing, swallering, and breathing-out went on.

"Great day in the afternoon," Selfridge says, almost whispering. "I thank you, Albert."

"You're welcome, Mr. Selfridge," the pockmarker says.

"I thank you, Tommy."

"You're welcome, Mr. Selfridge," the small man says.

"Don't thank them," Casper says. "They didn't do nothing but haul rope."

Using a new kind of big bossy voice, Selfridge says, "Get the wheels back on this wagon and take it over to the shed and guard it. And be *gentle*." He looked down into his cup like a man might look at a piece of lode ore.

Still keeping quiet, Casper says, "Hold on now. This wagon ain't yours to move or guard or nothing unless I say so."

"Let's not have any trouble," Selfridge says, looking into his cup and not seeing what I seen on Casper's face.

"You can't go robbing me, Mr. Slipperage," Casper says. "I'd have to kill you, and it takes up too much time and interferes with my digestion and ruptures my business and generally turns a good life to hell. You'd a whole lot better go off someplace and kill yourself *for* me and save all the fuss."

That appeared to catch Selfridge's attention pretty good (and the other four too, who probably hadn't heard that kind of talk before, judging by the slack jaws), and he dismounted slow and careful and steady, not spilling a drop and come up about a yard from Casper and narrowed his eyes like he was lining up fenceposts. Then he checked around at the others to see if they'd heard the same thing, and then he done about the next-to-last thing I'd reckoned on, me being ready to swing my staff and get shot and lose my hogs. He giggled way up high and snorted at the end of it (most as good as Colonel Woppert could of) and says, "You sound like a moneymaker." He pitched one shoulder up higher than the other. "How'd you like to work for me?"

"I wouldn't," Casper says.

I could see that didn't peel too many apples with Selfridge, him not looking nor acting much like a man used to having his sass without cinnamon on it. "Well, that's just a sorry pity about you," he says. "You're hired."

"I quit," Casper says.

Selfridge took another sip of whiskey, and it appeared to calm him down. "Is that your still in there?" he says.

Casper didn't say nothing but after a long gap just give a nod.

"I've got the finest water in three hundred miles any way you'd care to point," Selfridge says. "I've got the only store of good grain in about the same distance and same directions —rye, corn and wheat. I've got malt. I've got yeast. What I don't have is a still and somebody to run it right. Why not start it cooking and let's all make some money?"

"I set up my still where and as I please," Casper says. "Which don't happen to include here."

"What more do you want?" Selfridge says, sounding easy and reasonable.

"Why, I want just exackly what you want," Casper says. "I want my own way."

"You're not going to get it," Selfridge says.

"And you're not going to get none of my whiskey," Casper says.

Selfridge lifted the cup at him like a toast and took another sip. "I've heard men of genius are balky and moody and stubborn, but I'll tell you what might just happen. I might take all the whiskey you've got and set up that still myself, and if I can't make it work right, I'll bust it. And I'll bust you and your wagon too so you couldn't tell it from the next sodbuster's rig that comes past here end over end."

"You wouldn't do that," Casper says, sounding dead sure.

"I'll lay you odds," Selfridge says.

"And I'll lay you down to sleep with an angel whistling through your earhole to see if anybody's home," Casper says.

Again, there was a hush which the hogs filled up with a little

restless whuffling. They could smell forage everywhere, and I
was holding them back and being a nuisance. But I was too
busy watching Selfridge turning even redder, specially between
the eyes. Finally he took another sip of whiskey and a big
deep breath and says, "I hate to do business with crazy people,
but I'll make you a deal. You set up that still and make me a
full run of whiskey out of those eight hundred bushels of
mine—"

"Where you fixing to age three thousand gallons of whiskey?" Casper says, looking around at the four lunkheads. "I
spose you could fill up boys like these and stand them around
for a year or two and tap a spigot in. But it wouldn't taste like
no whiskey of mine."

Acting a little eager now, Selfridge says, "I've got every kind
of wood in creation out back, everything any wagonmaker
ever used and more besides. Barrels too and casks and hogs-
heads. Some are busted, I'll admit, but they can be fixed. I'll
see to that. And I'll pay you a dollar a gallon when it's in the
barrel, and you can take the still apart and haul it off where
you please. Meanwhile, you can have your whiskey here—all
but one keg for board and room—and sell it for whatever it'll
fetch." He stood still now like a cat laying eyes on a grass-
hopper.

"Would you call that a hard bargain, Zeke?" Casper says.

I was so startled at being asked something, I didn't have
time to hear myself think, so I says, "Hard to middling." I
didn't want to see Casper (and maybe me and the hogs) left
out for the crows and buzzards over some whiskey and pots
and tubs and tubes and bottles. There was always going to be
more whiskey in the world, but (far as I could tell) no more
of us.

Casper give his neck whiskers a ruffling-up. "Well, I'll tell
you, Mr. Suffrage," he says.

"Don't make fun of my name, mister," Selfridge says.
"That's very costly humor in the long run."

"I figure I better get it whiles it's cheap," Casper says.
"Looks like a *short* run."

"Never pays to be cheap," Selfridge says.

"I get the feeling you don't pay at all," Casper says.

"That's wrong," Selfridge says. "I pay handsome, and I pay ugly. Take your choice."

"If I had my choice, I'd take my leave and my whiskey both," Casper says.

Selfridge finished his cup and smacked his lips. "If it's as good a batch as this, I'll pay two dollars a gallon."

"Even skullbuster fetches four," Casper says.

In a broad, heavy, rich voice, Selfridge says, "I pay wholesale or I pay nothing."

Looking mad but sounding mild, Casper says, "I want some of that room and board for my assistant and his hogs too, all of which are to stay alive and well and singing for their supper, or I'll do to your grain—without you knowing it's happening—just about what you said you do to me and my still. You do me wrong, and I'll make you whiskey that'd scorch this whole Hollow to cinders."

"Done," Selfridge says, letting a big smile break out of his red face for a change. "Be a pleasure to fatten up that pork." He switched a look around at the four lunkheads. "A man after my own heart."

"Just don't get me after it too hard," Casper says.

"And you quit threatening me, Whiskey Man," Selfridge says. "Or I'll have *your* heart for breakfast with scrambled eggs. Have to peel it first, but I don't mind." He got his big haunches up into his saddle, making it look easy except on the horse. "But first, why don't you make me those three thousand gallons and enjoy yourself for a while?" He flicked his chin at the lunkheads. "Get the wheels on."

Chapter Fifteen

SO THAT'S HOW ME and Casper went to work for Cole Selfridge, though we pretended like we was doing it for ourself to make it more interesting. The plank-and-doby house was bigger than it looked: they'd kept slapping more rooms on every time another wagon got crunched coming down the chute, which was frequent, and had plenty left over for kindling and stove wood and fireplace chunks and a big pile out back that'd been scavenged over good. Selfridge kept nine or ten men busy scouting up top and down in the Hollow both, selling whiskey (that's what they called it, but Casper called it something else it wouldn't be fitten to write down) and selling fodder and clothes and all kind of trade goods, and every bit of it had been lost or stole or bullied or claimed out of emigrants' belongings that'd been wrecked or not watched close enough or both.

Selfridge had set up part of the building as a general store and part as a tavern and rooms with all kind of different beds in them made out of busted planks and pieces of quilt and straw pallets and stinking bedrolls and what-all they'd scrounged up hither and yonder. In the tavern part they sold whatever they could find worth getting drunk on that wouldn't actually kill you outright, and the whole outfit was like one of them big machines they're commencing to build in sheds back East where you put cotton in one end and it gets mauled and mangled and shucked around inside and comes out calico the other end.

Only here it wasn't calico come out the other end but Cole Selfridge looking sleeker and richer and more satisfied with hisself every minute.

First off, Selfridge kept at least three lunkheads working for Casper to set up the still in a shed out back of the tavern part. They wasn't always the same three because it was hard work hauling the busted harness and wheel-spokes and iron wheel-rims out of there and leveling the ground for some planking and shoring up one wall that had commenced leaning so far in, it wasn't holding up its share of the roof, but they got it done with Casper barking at them. I wasn't much use at first because I was setting up a sty against one side of the shed, using some rusty fence-wire and split wagon-tongues that was most as good as real posts. By next day, I even had a kind of gate on it I could open or shut with a wire loop if I wanted to drive the hogs out to forage in the brush. I wasn't going to let them rove free, which they'd of been pleased to do in a Paradise like this until they run up against somebody with a butcher knife. Instead, I found me a sickle, bent but still good, in a heap of trash behind the general-store part and sharpened it on a rock and cut enough grass and brush to keep them from breaking out of the wire which wouldn't of been no problem if they'd a mind to.

Since we didn't know nobody we could trust, we had to be watchmen for each other—Casper keeping an eye on the hogs and me setting on his clump of full kegs—whenever Nature called or one of us wanted to stray off a ways to scout the lay of the land. Casper said it was slow-going from here down to the river: a couple miles through sloggy sand and no way to make a run for it, burdened down like we was and no way to make mules or hogs run besides.

There wasn't much noise out of the tavern the first night whiles we tried to get used to the idea of sleeping next to so much company (Casper in his wagon backed up into the door of the shed to block it and me out in the sty which the hogs hadn't had time to churn up yet), and come to find out they didn't have nothing to sell but a barrel of green beer some emigrant hadn't made right and was now getting his sour revenge on Selfridge's lunkheads for taking it off of him. We heard a fiddler going for a while and some stomping, but they left off long before midnight so's they'd have plenty of time to get sick without losing no sleep over it.

We hadn't had much trouble with skeeters before, it being mostly too dry and too open and too windy where we'd been on the Trail, but here in the calm brush and with fresh, barely moving water nearby, they come to call. If a skeeter was to lay an egg in the Platte, it'd be washed out clear to the Mississippi before it hatched, but here they had time to grow up and learn their trade and raise their own family and pass on what they'd learnt, which was mainly how to find one inch of skin left out in the open for five seconds. I cloaked up in my blanket best I could and left my hat on, but you can't slap too good when you're all bound up, so I done a deal of thrashing before I tuckered myself out and asleep. They didn't bother the hogs none: you can't teach a woods hog nothing about skeeters he didn't learn at his mama's teat.

But the second night was different. I'd spent the whole day (except for eating the washy antelope stew with wild onion

still growing in it that the old cook handed out to us from the
back of the tavern and a spell of brush-cutting) helping Casper
and the three latest lunkheads—one of them that Andrews
with the swole-shut eye—set up his one-hundred-sixty-five-
gallon still and the seventy-five-gallon doubler that went with
it, getting the big marsh tub set just right and polishing the
copper cap and coil—he called it his worm—and making sure
the brass cock worked right. The whole contraption must of
weighed five hundred pound and hadn't been damaged none,
as far as Casper could tell, by all the jolting uphill and down,
which had been enough to churn butter once a day. He told
me all that rocking had made the kegged and aged whiskey
even better than it was sposed to be. Between whiles, he'd had
a look at Selfridge's grain bin which was another shack with a
plank platform where they'd heaped up all different kind of
sacks on top of each other, some busted open and the field
mice going to work, but apparently enough good for plenty of
runs of marsh if you wasn't too particular. Some had commenced mouldering, and he smuggled out a sack or two past
the lunkhead who tended the latching-up, saying he wanted
to test it but stashing it away in his wagon for me to dole out
to the hogs who was ready to treat a little moulder like an
extra vegetable.

So that night we was both tired out, me as deep as my wish-
bone, and ready to lay down with the sun which set a little
earlier because of the bluffs. But then the tavern begun showing us why somebody'd braced up the outside with raking
shores made out of planks and sole plates dug in under them
on a slant.

It started off mild with the fiddler again and two or three
lunkheads half-yelling and half-singing offkey:

> Oh, they chew tobacco thin in Nebraska,
> They chew tobacco thin in Nebraska,
> They chew tobacco thin

And they drip it down their chin,
and they lick it up agin in Nebraska.

I didn't mind it much from out around in the sty, but I
heard Casper cussing them out and rattling his cup under the
spigot.

Now, if somebody's singing and carrying on almost right
next to you—even if it ain't no good—you feel left out. You
may not be much interested in doing what they're doing
exackly, but you'd like to know you was welcome if you felt
inclined. But me and Casper both felt like we'd been forced
to stop off here and set up our still and sty, maybe not at actual gunpoint but near enough, and we didn't feel like nobody's pardners. We'd seen some emigrants from down at the
camp by the next spring heading for the tavern around sundown, so it wasn't just Selfridge's men in there starting to
romp it up, and somehow it made me feel lonelier knowing
men had went in there of their own free will to enjoy theirself
(even if it was offkey), and I couldn't.

They bellered out another verse:

> Oh, the chickens they grow tall in Nebraska,
> The chickens they grow tall in Nebraska,
> The chickens they grow tall,
> And they eat them guts and all
> When they chop them in the fall in Nebraska.

Then the fiddler went whanging along whiles they stomped,
and Casper says, "Dog dag the dig ducky dogdots!" Them
wasn't the real words, but they sounded like that, sort of. "If I
couldn't sing better than that, I'd—"

I guess he couldn't think up nothing he'd do. I heard his cup
clink a few times after that, and pretty soon he set up his usual
steady snore.

I laid there whiles more laughing and yelling went on, and
when it had got as loud as it'd been the night before, I settled
back against Colonel Woppert, expecting it'd dwindle again so's

they could all get sick. Instead, it just kept on rising and swelling sideways and putting out shoots and runners and sending its roots deeper till my eyes wouldn't go shut for the commotion. Finally I got up and swatted a few skeeters and hung my blanket on the highest post so's the hogs couldn't eat it unless they felt like working for it, and I let myself out of the sty and went over to the back door where they throwed out the trash and dishwater or now and then come to retch up. There wasn't no proper windows, just some slots with scraped deerskin stretched over them (or left off, depending on the weather), but a couple was left open now and I could see most of the room.

It was lamplit at both ends and a couple of rough tables and benches against the two walls I could see where some of Selfridge's lunkheads was eating out of tin plates and drinking out of cups, and more of them, including emigrants and at least three women, was standing out on the loose-plank floor, waiting for the fiddler to tie up a busted string on his fiddle and yelling advice about how to do it. There was a cask about twice as big as Casper's kegs set up on one end of a table, and when the pockmarker let hisself a drink out of the spigot, I seen it run clear as water, so at least it wasn't none of Casper's whiskey, which was more honey-colored. They sounded like they was having enough fun for two taverns and enough left over for a husking bee and half a church social, but it didn't *look* like fun, even after the fiddler give up and started playing again with one string dangling (I couldn't tell no difference in the tune) and they all commenced stomping and skipping again and wheeling arm in arm and bumping against each other.

But I guess fun always looks peculiar from outside in, and even though I still had Casper's fifty cents in my pocket (he'd told me to keep it for practice), I didn't feel like drinking or dancing or setting up a conversation with the likes of the pockmarker, who was too steely-eyed for comfort. Two of the women was older, but one was a girl with her brown hair let

down to her shoulders in stringy curls and a blue bow on top.
She had on a blue-and-gray dress that was too big for her in
the front, spite of her being heavy-set, including her face, but
she looked so unhappy amongst all them others that was
laughing and jawing and calling each other comical names and
some throwing bread around, I couldn't take my eyes away
from her, even when somebody got in the road. A lunkhead
was making her dance with him, like it or not, tugging her
wrist this way and that showing her how to stomp, but she
wouldn't do it right, just like somebody else's dog might halfway take orders from you and not go so far as disobey, but
not doing nothing proper neither.

A bunch of the boys over by the cask had started singing
something the fiddler wasn't playing, hunching in close to each
other so's at least they could hear theirself yell, and most of
the people trying to dance give up except the lunkhead with
the girl, a middle-sized, round-shouldered, blurry-faced man
almost as old as Casper with a side-rolled sombrero tilted over
one eye. He kept giving dance lessons and tugging and hauling
and whispering in close whiles the girl hung back and tried
pulling away kind of half-hearted.

All of a sudden he swang in close to her again and violated
her privacy something dreadful, and if she hadn't hit him on
the side of the face, knocking his hat off sideways (which he
shouldn't of had on anyway, ladies being present), I'd of done
it myself by sticking my staff through the slot and using it like
a pool cue on the back of his skull.

I'd only seen Miz Selfridge once before when me and Casper
was getting our supper the first night and she come into the
kitchen doorway to cuss out the cook for a meat-burner
(which he was), but I didn't have no trouble reckonizing her
now through the slot: she come hoving into view built along
the same lines as her husband but stockier and corseted hard
to give her a little dent in the middle and a shove up-slope in
front, and she grabbed the girl's wrist before the lunkhead
could even locate his hat and yanked her off out of sight. In

about five seconds, the two of them come out the back door and stopped amongst the trash with Miz Selfridge still hanging on and the girl looking hangdog.

I kept flat against the outside wall, and I must of seemed like another piece of shoring in the gloom because they didn't even glance my way.

"Well, I never ever!" Miz Selfridge says. "What did I tell you to do?" She was wearing a shiny red dress (the color of her hair except next to the scalp), and there wasn't enough to go around.

The girl mumbled something.

"That's no excuse!" Miz Selfridge says loud and clear and probably making the hogs roll over out in the sty. "If you're not going to be friendly, what good are you?"

"No good," the girl says.

"Those boys have been working hard all week, and they earned a little heel-kicking," Miz Selfridge says. "What've you been doing besides eating and sleeping and mooning around like a virgin?"

I couldn't recollect nothing in the New Testament about her mooning around, nor Joseph neither, but then I only read it that once and might of missed it.

"Washing sheets and sewing and scrubbing floors," the girl says.

"Never mind that," Miz Selfridge says. "If you expect to earn your keep, you'd better look lively. You don't have much to offer, so you'd best give it a twitch or two while the twitching's good."

"I hate being mauled at," the girls says.

"I'll give you something to hate worse," Miz Selfridge says, shaking her by the arm and shoving her almost to the shed. "And you wouldn't get mauled at *all* if you learned how to say Yes a little better. Remember how I showed you to do it?"

"Yes, ma'am," the girl says.

"Then do it," Miz Selfridge says, shaking her by the shoulders now.

The girl wasn't resisting much, but I know stubbornness when I see it, even in bad light, being around hogs so much and mules and Ma and Pa and my own self and Casper too (who I could hear still snoring), and it seemed like Miz Selfridge had a good eye for it too.

"I'm warning you," she says. "You think just because there aren't any pretty young girls around, you can act like one yourself. Don't put on airs. The way things are going, we'll have a wagonload of dance girls here in a month—girls that know where their hands and butts and lips belong—and then do you know where you'll be?"

The girl either shook her head or was having it shook for her.

"You'll be out on your cold lonesome," Miz Selfridge says. "Or into the first stinking horny corn-dodger's wagon that comes by. Now get back in there and use your brains. What kind of underwear do you have on?"

I didn't hear what the girl answered, though I strained to catch it (I'm shamed to say I got an unnatural curiosity in that department, yet I felt shy and mad and flustered from what I was seeing and listening to), but whatever it was, Miz Selfridge didn't like it.

"The very idea!" she says. "After I gave you some of my very own with almost no holes!"

"They didn't fit," the girl says.

Which didn't surprise *me* none because, spite of her being heavy-set, Miz Selfridge made about two of her whether you looked frontways or sidewards.

But it set Miz Selfridge off like a sting from a yellow jacket. "How dare you call me fat?" she says, getting up to full boom and giving the boys inside the tavern a little pump-priming for their yelling. "I don't have an ounce of fat on me!" She held out both thick arms in the moonlight and shoved the sleeves of her dress back like she expected the girl to search her. "And what's there is more than *you'll* ever have."

I agreed with her there, but the girl just looked more hang-dog.

"I know where it is and what it is and what it's for and where it's going," Miz Selfridge says. "And you'd best find out about your own right quick. I'm going to send Halsey out here so you can apologize for slapping him, and you'd better do it right. If you're too shy for the bunkrooms, then take him out in the bushes and do it like I told you." Her voice quietened down some, but I could still hear. "It's no more than your own mother would have done. You have to get on *some*how."

Miz Selfridge stalked off through the back door, kicking a mashed lard can out of the way, and the girl stood there shaking her head like she wanted to clear the words out of it or maybe was telling herself No. But she didn't run off or duck under Casper's wagon like I half expected.

So when this lunkhead Halsey come out the back door a minute later, bumping into the jamb on the way through and tilting his sombrero even further, she was still there in plain view with the bulgy, lopsided moon shining on her.

"Where the hell did you get to?" he says, pausing to aim hisself in her direction.

"Nowhere," she says.

"How's my little Peggy?" he says.

"Fine," she says, not meaning it.

"Like it better out here?" he says. "It felt so good out tonight, I *left* it out. Did you ever hear the one about—?"

But he didn't get no further. I didn't like interrupting, but I didn't want him to insult her, and it's hard to tell exackly when an insult's coming till it's too late, so I edged along the wall and hit him a good one on the head with my staff and laid him out amongst the busted bottles and cans and scraps.

Chapter Sixteen

EVEN THOUGH I'd never swatted nobody with my staff but hogs and sometimes dogs chasing them (up till five days ago with the buckskin man and the redbeard), I was getting pretty good at it. I left Halsey taking a rest amongst the rest of the trash where I reckoned they'd spose he'd passed out from taking in too much fresh air, and I went over to the girl who shrunk back a step or two like I might be aiming at her next.

"Don't," she says. "Please don't."

"You better run on home before he comes to," I says. "Or Miz Selfridge comes out."

The fiddler and the singers struck up the same tune together this time, bellering out:

The monkey married the baboon's sister,
Kissed her so hard he raised a blister . . .

And on and on, loud and ragged and jagged, and her and me
moved off a ways around the side of the shed, same as you'd
try to put something between you and a bonfire without even
thinking about it, to keep from getting scorched. Then we
slowed down and stopped next to the hogs laying there restless and even bigger-looking than usual in the moonlight.

"I don't *have* a home to go to," she says. "Except in there,"
tossing her head a little and meaning the tavern or the kitchen
or someplace. "That Halsey, he'll kill you when he wakes up."

"I was just learning him some manners," I says. "Besides,
he don't know I hit him."

"He will if I tell him," she says.

I hadn't thought of that. "Why'd you want to tell him?"
I says, giving the moony side of her face a long look.

"I'd sooner have him kill you than me," she says.

"Me too," I says.

Then it was her turn to give me a looking-over, which I was
glad wasn't by daylight because I hadn't exackly washed myself off for Sunday.

"You *would*?" she says like she doubted me. "Why?"

"Well, you're a lady, and—" But I couldn't think of no way
to say it right. "You're too young to get kilt."

"You mean it'd be all right if I was twenty-one?" she says,
teasing a little.

I could see I was going to get tangled if I went any further
in that thicket, so I remembered my manners instead and says,
"I'm Ezekiel Hunt."

After a spell of looking me over sideways and still keeping
her distance, she says, "I'm Peggy."

She left a pause, and not thinking up nothing else to fill the
gap, I says, "Peggy what?"

Her voice changed then, turned cold and high and far-off

and hard to hear over that dang singing. "I won't say it," she says. "Never again will it cross my ruby lips."

Well, I'd never laid eyes on any rubies (and still haven't) but calculate from reading they're sposed to be shiny as ripe tomatoes. Hers was chapped or else just parched up and puckered and kind of lilac-colored, but nice even so. I didn't counterdict her. "I didn't mean to pry," I says.

"Pee-you," she says, pinching at the end of her nose and looking at the hogs, thank God, and not me.

"That's just my hogs," I says. "Ordinarily they don't smell at all, but if you pen them up, they can't help it. These are woods hogs and cleaner than most men and smarter too." I left off because most people don't want to know nothing about hogs except which part's the bacon. I told her some about Casper and me and the whiskey still.

And she says, "I heard all about that. Mr. Selfridge is going to make a fortune, which is what he's doing anyway, that fat lummox." She sounded hard all of a sudden and sour and not no sweet sixteen (which had been my guess). "If he comes poking and tweezing around me again, I'll lop off his butt and paint it purple and hang it out for the horseflies."

I'd never heard a girl talk like that—nor scarcely anybody else neither—but I sposed it was the company she'd been keeping.

She seemed to notice I didn't know what to answer, and her voice went high and far-off again. "I was left at the mercy of brutes," she says. "And they don't *have* any."

I tried to remember what *brutes* was, but couldn't (if only Miz Peasemont had left the dictionary unstrapped more often!), so I concentrated on the *mercy*. "How much mercy do you need?" I says. "I think I've got some to spare."

She smiled for the first time, and it made her look so much better, she turned almost pretty. "I want too many things," she says. "That's been my downfall."

"You haven't fallen down yet, far as I can see," I says, feel-

ing bold and glad it was half-dark so's I didn't have to keep
remembering who I was.

"Shall we take a walk?" she says, swatting a skeeter on her
forehead. "As long as I'm breaking rules anyway, I might as
well do it where it's quieter."

She commenced strolling away, and I followed along, not
wanting to leave her nor get too far off from the hogs neither
and at the same time going hollow-throated and cold-handed
that she might be taking me into the bushes like Miz Selfridge
had told her to do with that Halsey, because how would I
dare say No?

"Well, come on, slow coach," she says.

I hadn't been alone with a girl since back home and hadn't
been too handy at it even then, what with Rose Parmalee's
half-brother peeking at us through the berry bushes, and
Helene Rosker having the catarrh so bad most of the time she
had to carry Dr. Brautiberg's Tar Expectorant around in a bottle with her and the cork leaked, and Bessy Schneider being so
ticklish she'd start yelping before you even tickled her, and
Maud Blaines being so muscle-bound she could knock your
arm black and blue playing Flinch (which was all she wanted
to play and not no kissing games), and Edna Otterbein who all
she could do was talk about Jesus six days a week and bawl
all day Sunday, and none of them liking hogs much nor me
either. I'd even been alone with some of them at night, but
nothing much had happened in the way of Sinfulness, unless
hoping counts against you which it shouldn't, no matter what
the preachers say. Hoping's just a kind of hunger, only it ain't
your stomach that's empty.

She reached back and held out her hand to me, and I took
it, bold as you please. She squoze it then, and if she'd been
Maud Blaines, I'd of had to soak it in salts for three days. But
spite of being on the thick side and her fingers short and her
fingernails chawed down blunt, her hand felt gentle and dry,
which was more than I could say for mine.

"There's a path here," she says. "Goes up to the head of that little bluff. It's not far, and it's a whole lot cooler." She got us between some wild rosebushes without getting hooked, and we started climbing. "Do you always carry that stick?"

"Mostly," I says, letting her lead the way and making sure I could still see the shed and the sty.

"Halsey wears a gun," she says.

"He's welcome to," I says.

"He's one of Selfridge's crows, that little runt, may it rot off for him," she says. "They go picking over everybody that's in trouble and some that aren't, and to hear them tell it, being a road agent with wool in your teeth is the grandest form of human endeavor next to getting dead drunk. From now on, far as I'm concerned, they can all just put their pants on backwards and leave them that way."

I didn't know what she meant, but it didn't sound any too comfortable. We'd clumb up about fifty yards, and the bushes had thinned out, and the ground had turned crumblier and harder, and most of the skeeters left off singing in our ear. We'd come out in the open on a cut-off ridge, and though there wasn't far to fall, there was a long, long way to see: the whole North Platte Valley was laid out again, almost as good as I'd seen it up top of the ridge, but shallower now (me being almost in it myself) and moonlit so's the colors had dimmed down to nothing but glitter and shade. We set on the bare rock and admired it without having to tell each other what we was admiring, which is the best way.

She'd left go of my hand to get settled and her skirts tucked, but now she searched it out again where I'd left it available on my knee and held it like it was natural and easy and not something I'd dreamt about and worried over. You can't practice nothing like that yourself without no other hand to hold, so I was having to learn in a hurry.

After a bit, using that high, far-off voice again, she says, "I'm the daughter of a Queen."

She'd caught me by surprise, and instead of being polite

about it and letting her go on like she pleased, I says, "What kind of a Queen?" It come out sounding like I doubted it, which I half did but shouldn't of let on. I knew they had a Queen over in England and probably some more here and there, and if you stopped to think about it, some of them must of had their share of daughters now and then.

"A beautiful one," she says. "She's in exile, and so am I. She's been deposed."

I reckoned that to be something like *indisposed*, but kept my ignorance to myself for a change. "I'm sorry," I says, that seeming to be a pretty safe thing to say to judge by her voice.

"I had a wicked uncle," she says.

Well, I had her there. "So did I," I says.

"You did?" she says.

"Uncle Fred once drank a pint of Ma's vanilla extrack and hung out the parlor window by his knees and sang hymns." She didn't seem too impressed, so I says, "On Sunday."

"That's not wickedness," she says. "That's just tom-foolishness."

"Well, it was good enough for back home," I says.

She sighed, and her voice went far-off again. "Wickedness is like dire plots in antechambers, and Innocence chained in dank dungeons for years, and maidens locked in turrets with their long lovely hair turned gray overnight by horrors committed by fiends and such."

"Oh," I says. I couldn't match that with nothing of Uncle Fred's except maybe him cussing all through the hymns instead of the right words, but it didn't seem like a fitten subjeck.

"I could tell you about wickedness that would curl your toenails," she says.

I hoped she wouldn't, not because I didn't believe in wickedness (me having pig-sticking fresh in mind) but because she'd begun looking so strange out of the corner of my eye, which was the only way I could work up nerve to memorize her better and get her down by rote in case she wasn't ever going

to speak to me again: I couldn't count on Halsey and Miz
Selfridge to chase her out back *every* night. What was strange
about her, she had tears in her eyes and down her cheeks and
hadn't made no sound of crying, yet looked so calm and beautiful all of a sudden, it was like she'd turned older than me and
her put together.

Out of a clear sky (and it *was* clear, with the Big Dipper up
on its lip-end, pouring starlight into the river) she says, "Why do
you have that crazy-looking bandanna tied around your head?
It makes your hat all crooked."

"I got bunged up a few days ago," I says. "I'll take it off if
you want, but I think it's stuck."

She laughed, which I'd never heard nobody do whiles they
was crying. "Maybe you better show Halsey how to do it,"
she says. "He's going to have a lump like a darning egg."

That worried me some, and I looked back down at the shed
and what I could see of the tavern and the low house sprawling
past it where the ash trees wasn't in the way, but I couldn't
see no sign of extra commotion. Nothing was moving near the
sty, and the fiddling and yowling was still going on but faint.

"Do you get in fights a lot?" she says, sounding like she admired the idea.

"Not if I can help it," I says.

"Well, what got your vinegar so far up tonight?" she says.

We still had aholt of each other's hand, but hers had went
sort of offhanded about it, and it was mostly me doing the
holding. I recollected all the things I'd done wrong with them
other girls or had went wrong without my help, and I reckonized
this was one of those times I'd be mulling about for months
to come or longer if I didn't hurry up and use my half of the
wits passed out when I first hit daylight. "I wanted to touch a
Princess," I says, which was pretty good going for *me* who
customarily had a clovehitch in my tongue around girls.

But she didn't seem any too anxious to write that one down
in her album. "Is that all you wanted to do?" she says.

Well, I couldn't go down and wake up Casper and ask him

what to say next, but I wished I had some whiskey so's I could
loosen myself up to that first stage-station he'd told me about,
where drinking men start to joking and telling all about theirself and find it easy as rhubarb pie. So I done the best I could:
I turned her hand around and kissed the cool, smooth back of
it without knocking my hat off.

It didn't seem like too big a mistake, because she didn't jerk
back nor smack me nor tell me what Jesus would of said (that
Edna Otterbein knew more about what Jesus would of said
than Matthew, Mark, Luke, and John rolled into one) nor wipe
her hand on her dress. Instead, she stared way off north where
you could see bluffs and hills hanging in a kind of wash-water
light, and she says, "I used to wish I'd never been born, but
now I'm just plain mad."

"Why don't you move on then?" I says. "The Trail's open,
and somebody'd give you a ride. I don't know how long it's
going to take Casper to make all that whiskey, but *he'd* give
you a ride with us. I know he would. He done it for *me.*"

"Run off with *you*?" she says, smiling a little too broad for
comfort.

"I didn't say run off exackly," I says.

She glanced me all over, then sounded like half-teasing. "Miz
Selfridge wouldn't like it," she says.

"She's got plenty of room on her for lumps if she don't
like it," I says. "Why does anybody have to please her?"

"Why are you and that whiskey man trying to please *Mr.*
Selfridge?" she says.

"You mean she's threatening to hurt you?" I says, commencing to get riled and worried in about equal shares.

"About every five minutes, and I've got the welts to prove
it," she says. "Want to see?"

"No," I says. I did, but I didn't like the funny hard way
she'd spoke of it. "All the more reason to move on."

Peggy left go of my hand and stretched her arms forward
and up and yawned which made me yawn so deep, I almost
wrenched my jaw off of its hinge. "Oh, well, she pays me

good," she says. "Better than most. Even if I have to do chores." She'd quit her crying, but now her face turned solemn-looking again. Her eyes went wide and watery. "I hate old men and old women. Take my advice: never be an old man."

"Nothing much else *to* do, unless somebody was to croak me," I says, thinking it must be a joke. "Why, you'd make a wonderful old woman."

She rounded on me like Miz Peasemont hearing a recitation come out crooked. "Don't you ever say a thing like that to me," she says. "I'll be good and dead and in my white coffin with the lavender satin lining and lilies-of-the-valley in my hair and a wreath of red roses hanging down at the foot of it long before that day ever arrives, and be glad of it, and go to Hell happy where I belong, and take my eternal roasting with pleasure, thank you, and now I suppose you want to tickle my fancy up here like the rest of those yokels that don't know the difference between their manhood and a pinochle deck. Well, it's all right with me."

"No thanks," I says, and even to me it sounded like I meant it. "Much obliged."

But she acted like she hadn't heard me. "You'll have to hurry it up, though," she says. "If I get back before Halsey wakes up, I can tell him he got hit by a falling star." she chuckled a little up in her nose. "I can tell him we'd already been to the bushes and back and he just can't think straight." She held out both hands at me. "Come on."

I stood up and stretched, and offered her a hand up, and she took it, looking at me puzzled. "Don't you want to?" she says. "It's got to be quick, though, because Miz Selfridge is going to fall out of that corset before long, and I want to be there to watch."

"I'd like to kiss you on the mouth," I says, feeling the wonder of all these decisions I was making and words I was saying without no help. "I mean on the ruby lips."

She held out her face for me, and we kissed each other a

long, careful, quiet, soft-feeling kiss that felt like it had broke whatever I had under my breastbone for the sweet pain of it, and after we'd finished, I just stood there for a spell with my knees feeling unbuckled, and she keep still and helped me look off north at the night.

Back home they say a hog can see the wind, and if I didn't know it was true, I'd beg leave to doubt it. But I seen hogs too many times (when the air was still and you wouldn't think there was a breeze left in the county) all turn around at once and squint in the same direction and wait and look pleased with theirself—before there was a bent grassblade or a rustle in the beech leaves—and then it would commence finally over on the next hill or up at the top of the field, moving and rolling over and tumbling towards them and picking things up and laying them down and changing color and me watching too. They say if you've suckled at a sow, you can see the wind your own self, and I don't know what my ma and pa left me do when I was too little to know no better or no worse. But now and then, I'd see the wind too, though I never told nobody lest I'd take a hooting for it.

And that night on the bluff I seen it again, going upstream on the North Platte just like that stream of fool emigrants, including me, that didn't have a skeeter's notion in this world what they wanted except they was hungry for it.

I'd never seen the wind at night before, so I don't know whether it's always dark blue with purple streaks along it, but that's what it looked like this time. "There's the wind," I says without thinking, because it was muggy and dead calm where we was standing.

"Yes, isn't it beautiful," she says.

And then I knew she could see it too and must of suckled at a sow her own self.

"And you're a plain fool," she says.

Well, I knew that already and didn't need no extra telling. After a bit, we walked back downhill.

Chapter Seventeen

ALL THE NEXT DAY Casper worked back and forth between seting up the still and collecting all the sacks and jugs and buckets full of what he was going to need to make his marsh and showing his three daily lunkheads how to run a short pipeline (somebody had lost a load of wood gutters off of a wagon) from one of the uphill springs into the whiskey shed so's he could use it both for the marsh and later for cooling his coil, and one of the lunkheads turned out to be Halsey with a sore head and a suspicious eye on both me and Casper.

He hadn't been laying there anymore when I excorted Peggy home but had staggered off to soak his head someplace. I seen him looking from Casper's wagon to the doorway where he'd been clomped, then at me and rubbing his head and doing a good deal of blinking and thinking. But he kept his mouth shut about it, probably not wanting to let it be laughed over that he'd got laid out by a girl or another old man or the likes of me. I kept my staff as much out of sight as I could to keep the notion out of his head, though there wasn't too much room in there for notions anyway.

I hadn't told Casper nothing about it nor about Peggy neither, since I didn't want to be scolded or laughed over my own self. I didn't know how I felt: if I had put together all the worry and shame and wonder and doubt and glorification I had rattling and rumbling around inside me into a marsh tub and stilled it off and rectified it and barreled it and aged it good, then bunged in a spigot and ran myself a cup of it, I'd of probably choked. But I kept still about it and didn't clap an eye on her all day, though I gawped through the kitchen door every time I could. I didn't exackly feel moony or in love (like the week after I seen Isabel Shanklin in her green Easter hat going by in a phaeton, and she never looked at me nor spoke nor ever did), but I felt *some*thing.

One of the other daily lunkheads was the pockmarker who was mad at having to do chores like a farmer but done them anyway. Every time he could, he worked on Casper, starting off saying, "I'm going up to the top of the ridge tomorrow with Tommy. Long as you two are so busy, why don't you leave me take a couple of kegs of that whiskey and sell it for you and split the take?

Casper shook his head. "I believe I'll let it set there getting older and older," he says, knocking at the inside of an empty barrel with his bung-starter. "I don't know what they made some of these dang things out of, but the trees must of been growing in the shade."

And later in the morning: "Whiskey Man, what do you want to hog it for? Look what I got to try to sell to those fearful, trusting souls about to fall off a clift." He handed over a pint bottle out of his hip pocket.

Casper uncorked it and took a sniff and crinkled up his face like he'd just had bad news.

"Dollar a pint," the pockmarker says, half-smiling. "But they don't come back for more."

"Alcohol, ipecac, and tartar emetic," Casper says. "I'd sooner dry up and blow away."

"Then give me and Tommy something better to do," the pockmarker says. "No hard feelings, is there? I never laid a hand on you."

"Just get that little sluice-gate waterproof, and I'll take care of the whiskey, new *and* old," Casper says. "And it's a good thing you never laid a hand on me, mister, or you'd be wearing your ears inside out."

The pockmarker didn't like it, and he flushed a shade darker. "Get your whiskey made, old dog," he says. "Then I'll teach you a new trick."

"I got plenty of old ones you never seen yet," Casper says. "Now get to work or I'll tell Old King Cole on you."

Working around a still seemed lively enough (there was never no shortage of chores), but the trouble was it all *felt* like chores to me, and I didn't know if I was cut out for a whiskey boy or not. And the trouble in back of the trouble was I didn't know for sure what I'd be best at and most excited over.

I'd been wondering for years what I was going to be, but it didn't seem like I had enough to go on yet, as if I was still hunting through myself to find where I'd got to or where I was hiding, and I couldn't figure out *why* I was hiding neither, like I used to do to Pa when I was little and didn't want to take on some chore or wanted to keep my loose tooth to myself and didn't want it slammed out with a string tied to a doorknob. I felt like I'd lit out on my own all right and excaped but now needed locating, and there wasn't nobody to do it but me.

For instance, what was I doing out on this California Trail (even though I was stalled for the time being)? I was just letting myself be led by the hogs and trying to catch up with my future that seemed like it had got a head start on me and couldn't be bothered by no-account laggards.

I felt like I owed myself an explanation and an apology and a hand-wrote excuse from Ma or Pa like the kind Miz Pease-mont had to have before she'd stick you for being a truant and have to learn all kind of mottoes and sayings and Worldly Wisdom to make up for it, such as "Waste not, want not" and "Honor thy mother and thy father as thyself" and "A rolling stone gathers no moss" (though I never seen how moss would do a stone no good but cover it up and crack it to pieces and moulder it, and if you want to go rolling a stone, you'd just as soon it didn't clog itself over with moss or it couldn't budge).

And for twenty years I'd had the fearful example of my pa in front of me (or more usually behind me, with me aiming for elsewhere) as somebody who'd mistook his Call in Life entirely. My pa should never of been a hog-raiser. He didn't *like* hogs. He never did nothing but blame them for being their ornery self which he could of taught them lessons in. He wanted all them hogs to be *his* hogs and keep their opinions to theirself. You can't do that to hogs *or* men without a whip and four sides of brick wall and giving up on sleep. He'd of done better in the slaughterhouse, overseeing the chain-haul and the ramp and the stringing up and the quartering. Then he'd of had things just the way he wanted. Maybe.

But none of that was what *I* wanted.

I'd just finished helping Casper set up a big old black iron apple-butter kettle outside the shed to boil water in, and I says, "What do you spose I'm going to be when I grow up?"

"Why, I'd reckoned you for growed up already," he says. "Maybe it already happened and you didn't notice. Maybe you're *already* what you're going to be."

That set me back. "It don't look like much, does it," I says, feeling myself gloom over.

"Hush up that kind of talk and get a move on before somebody hangs harness on you for a fencepost," he says. "I'm going to make the first batch of marsh tonight. Don't say nothing. I don't want people watching me. But lay in a good heap of firewood because we're going to need about fifty gallon of boiling water, about sixteen gallon at a time, and I don't want to be standing around waiting for it and ruin a batch and lose a whole day amongst these bushwhackers."

"Yes, sir," I says.

"So find me something that'll hold about eight gallon so's one man can handle it. Or two at eight gallon apiece. Whatever it is, clean it out good."

"Yes, sir," I says.

"And what happened to you last night?" he says.

"Nothing," I says. "Nothing I didn't know better than to do." He had me scuffing and ducking like he was my ma or pa, and I didn't like the feel of it.

"These three girls here, you don't want to get messed up with them," he says.

"Are there *three*?" I says, wondering how I'd missed the others, then remembered what looked like old women to me might not to him.

"I seen you come back by here like you'd just been courting the governor's daughter," he says. "I hope your head's healing up proper. I hope it ain't leaking your brains out."

"Last time I tried thinking, they hadn't quit on me yet," I says, but it wasn't all true. I almost told him she wasn't no governor's daughter but a Queen's, just to see what his face would look like, but didn't.

"Then see if you can fetch me them tubs or whatever," he says.

"Yes, sir."

Long as I didn't know where to find what Casper wanted anyway (there was so much junk strowed around in the brambles, up slope and down, I could of picked any direction), I figured I might's well hunt where I might run into Peggy without seeming to try too hard. But she wasn't around front in the general store or the tavern neither, far as I could see, so I went picking and kicking amongst the half-overgrowed heaps of busted harness and homemade ditty boxes and wore-out shoes and dresser drawers with their knobs off and their joints sprung and all the rest that'd been left behind by people coming down the chute too fast or what had been hauled here and pecked over by Selfridge's crows.

Whiles I was at it, I looked back up the gully, able to see the last stretch and some beyond that and the white humps of wagons waiting up at the ridge and some partway down, and I couldn't remember why I'd been so bothered by it when I was up there nor why people was doing all this scraping and straining to get down. I remembered the fat man and wondered if he might not have the right idea: just pick yourself a comfortable place where there was sure to be plenty going on that didn't cost you nothing and then stand around and make yourself useless and you'll be a happy man.

It come to me like that because I felt *un*happy and couldn't tell why exackly. I'd thought that feeling of being full up to the stopper with Light had been going to last forever, but there I was, moping like I *had* sprung a leak.

One narrow-bedded wagon had most made it to the bottom and had even come to a rutted stretch where it shallowed out some, but either the twelve-year-old kid handling the reins let the brake go too soon or the mules took it into their head to trot the last fifty yards or the lanky, red-faced man afoot quit hauling back on the tailgate to do something else—or all three at once, because the wagon commenced going too fast and got thrown out of line by the ruts I'd stumbled through my own self, and it jounced around sideways and tipped over and broke its tongue and sent one wheel rolling down in my general direction and made the kid jump off and land hard and left the mules standing brace-legged in a tangle of harness, aiming back uphill.

The kid was rubbing both his elbows and trying not to bawl, and it didn't look like anybody'd got hurt, not even the mules much except maybe their butts scraped raw, but the wagon

looked ready for firewood. They must of come a long ways
and damaged it before because it had come half to pieces like
a wagon I made me out of a hen-crate once with four mis-
matched wheels and tried to give three piglets a ride in that
didn't want to stay put. Their goods, which looked to be
mostly carpenter tools, had come spilling down the slope.

I started walking their way to see if I could be neighborly
(though I didn't hold out any hope for their wagon, and they
was going to have to learn how to pack a mule if they didn't
know already), but just then the pockmarker and Halsey come
cantering along behind me and passed me by without saying
nothing, their eyes glued on that wrecked wagon. Halsey had
two poles trailing behind his horse like what they call a *travois*,
and the pockmarker had a load of rope and gunnysacks, and
Selfridge must of had some kind of lookout because they'd
dropped their sluice-making and mounted up quicker than
hired hands hearing a dinner bell.

They'd already dismounted and commenced talking or arguing by the time I clumb up within earshot, though the shoving
and shooting hadn't started yet. I don't know why I was
poking my nose in, even though I had a pretty fair idea what
was going to happen, but I guess people just naturally collect
around trouble, and I'm no different except I didn't have the
same reason as the pockmarker and Halsey, not being a crow
at heart.

The pockmarker seen me and hollered, "Clear off!"

But I didn't. I stayed off about thirty foot and kept my staff
handy, and the lanky man says, "*All* of you clear off. We don't
need any help."

"Why, sure you do," the pockmarker says bright and friendly.
"You not only need help, you need it *bad.*"

"And we specialize in bad help," Halsey says and looked
around at everybody, including me, like he expected a belly-
laugh but didn't get none.

"I'd say you might be in the market for a wagon," the pockmarker says, turning over one of the busted floorboards with

his foot and sending it a little further down slope. "We got lots of wagons to spare down below if you're in a trading mood. Or maybe you'd rather deal in cash."

"Ned," the lanky man says. "Start getting those tools boxed up again."

"Yes, sir," the kid says, looking sore and sulky and confused.

"Yeah, get them boxed up," Halsey says. "Save me doing it."

"Look at it the practical way," the pockmarker says, picking up a hatchet-adze and admiring it all over and touching the thin oil on its two blades. "You've got a serious transport problem, and I've got an easy solution."

"I'll pick my own help and my own solutions, thank you," the lanky man says. "I—I got some friends coming along right behind me. They'll lend a hand."

He wasn't no good at lying, and I seen the pockmarker smiling that one away as if he wouldn't bother them imaginary friends. The kid had picked up an armload of smaller tools like hammers and planes and augers and was trying to jam them higgeldy-skelter into long toolboxes, and Halsey found a three-foot-long wheelwright's reamer under a bush and held it up by both handles to admire its spear-point.

"Leave my tools alone," the lanky man says. "I made all those myself and loaded them and hauled them five hundred miles, and I don't aim to leave them rusting in this damned gully."

"Those tools are going to receive the finest of care," the pockmarker says.

"You bet your life they are," the lanky man says, trying to sound hard and strong and not making too good a job of it. "Because I'm going to give it to them myself. Now you just go about your business and leave me to mine."

"I'm going about my business right here and now," the pockmarker says. "Do you reckon it's one load or two, Halsey?"

Looking from the tools to the *travois*, Halsey says, "One, long as it's downhill." Then he picked up a frame saw and looked around the slope. "No, better make it two, so's we won't bust the poles."

The lanky man was wearing a gun, but he'd only halfway reached for it before the pockmarker had his out and aimed.

"Now, you don't want me to drive *that* hard a bargain, do you?" the pockmarker says. "Why don't you help us get your tools packed, and then we'll all go down and have a talk with Mr. Cole Selfridge and work you out a deal for a new wagon, and everybody'll feel rosy."

"And Rosie loves to be felt," Halsey says.

Turning splotchy-faced, the lanky man says, "Why should I bargain under a gun?"

"That's the best time of all," the pockmarker says. "It clears off the confusion and cuts down on the bickering and simplifies everything."

The lanky man didn't look like he was enjoying getting simplified, and he turned and looked down at me and says, "Do you know these men?"

"As well as I care to," I says.

"Are they robbing me?"

"I wouldn't be surprised," I says.

"I told you to clear off," the pockmarker says. "Now git! Or you'll beat those hogs to slaughter."

The next wagon was coming closer, ox team hitched behind and two men afoot and an old woman half laying down in a rope-tied chair at the front of the wagonbed, and the lanky man took a couple steps across to where they'd be passing before long if nothing broke loose.

"Easy now," the pockmarker says like he was gentling a horse.

Looking scairt and mad and uncertain and sort of hungry, the lanky man glanced back at me and says, "Why don't you run and tell somebody down there what's happening?"

"It's happening down there too," I says, since there wasn't nobody to tell but other crows and Casper (who was already working on his part of one of these hard bargains).

The other wagon had about drawed abreast now, creaking and dipping, and the two men glanced at the wreckage a couple times, then kept their eyes front like they might catch the same disease if they didn't ignore it, and the lanky man hollered, "These men are robbing me!"

Working at packing the tools into gunnysacks, Halsey grinned and says, "Louder."

The two men followed their wagon right on by, and one shook his head like he'd been asked did he want to buy any sweet potatoes.

The twelve-year-old had set down on a toolbox, watching and listening and taking in his lessons like me, and I felt sorry for him having to see his pa flop and flounder and probably have all his hard work stole from him, and I wanted to tell him not to judge his pa too harsh nor expect him to get kilt to prove how manly he used to be a minute ago, but there didn't seem to be no way to talk sense.

Halsey held up a thick-bladed two-handled chamfer knife that looked sharp enough to cut cross-grain on anything, including me, and that must of been what he had in mind because he give it a whirl and says, "Come on up, piggy boy, and I'll show you how it works."

I turned and started downhill and didn't even bother to say no when the pockmarker yelled at me to come on and make myself useful by helping pack up the tools. When I come to level ground, I glanced back long enough to see the lanky man had give up and was helping sack and tie his own goods, arguing and waving his hands and leaving his gun in its holster, and I couldn't figure out how I was sposed to be a Good Samaritan like the Bible says if I had to go starting a fight to do it. The lanky man had fallen among thieves all right, just like me and Casper had, but some thieves was awful gentle and persuasive and thoughtful about their trade and didn't leave no easy way to do good, even if you was a mind to.

I wasn't doing no good at finding some eight-gallon cans neither, and I come back towards the tavern, feeling more like

a waste of time than ever, and when I seen the top buggy with
a man and and a woman in it coming up from the campsite
below the next spring, I give it a thorough look-over just to
put my mind on something else. It was shiny clean like it had
just been renched off and buffed and looked too frail to of
come this far except maybe knocked down and crated, the
wheels being too skinny for sand. The hub bands and seat
handles and prop cuts and the dash rail was all nickel-plated,
but what made me stare the most was the lady setting next to
the driver. She had on a lace straw hat with a net and a bunch
of violets and coiled ribbon on it and a silky-looking black
double-cape choked up tight around her neck, spite of the
warm day, and she had her lips pursed up like she'd sucked a
lemon and was too puckered to spit.

The man had on some kind of derby with a curly brim,
which was a new one on me, and a suit like a banker with a
gray cravat and a stickpin and was wearing shammy gloves like
he was skinning six mules instead of one little bony bay gelding.

The buggy come right at me and pulled up alongside, and I
touched my brim like you're sposed to, and the derby man
says, "You there."

I couldn't figure out what he meant. It didn't sound like a
question, and he didn't have to call me because I was close
enough to rattle his spokes with my staff, so I just kept still
and nodded.

The derby man opened his mouth, but instead the lady says,
"I was told there was a halfway civilized tavern at which I
might stay." She had her voice pitched up behind her nose like
Miz Peasemont tried to show us when you're doing them dang
Exercises in Articulation such as "His *lips* *g*row *rest*less, and
his *sm*ile is cur*led* *h*alf into *scorn*" where they mark all the
hardest parts nobody can say right, specially me. I never even
got past "E*very* vice fig*hts* again*st* nature."

"Well, I wouldn't go as far as half*way*," I says. "But that's it
over there."

"Don't smart off at the Colonel's Lady," the derby man says. "And take off your hat, boy."

"I already touched the brim," I says. "I thought that was sposed to be good enough for outdoors."

"I said take off your hat," he says.

"Let's just get on with it, Mr. Arthur," the Colonel's Lady says.

"I don't mind, ma'am," I says, taking it off and glad it wasn't stuck to the bandanna. "Never too old to learn." Then I give the derby man a nice straight friendly look. "Now, how about you taking off yours?"

"Shall I thrash him, madam?" he says.

"No, I don't believe so," she says after hesitating a bit. "I'm hungry."

I was keeping my temper but not enjoying it none. Staying mild, I says, "What's your stomach got to do with him thrashing me?"

"Kindly do not address the Colonel's Lady at *all*," he says. "Especially not with vulgar terms. Or I'll get down and teach you a lesson."

"You're teaching me a lesson right now where you set," I says.

Raising his voice, he says, "Where's your master?"

"I don't know," I says. "He ain't been born yet." Casper'd told me that one, and I'd been saving it up, and it seemed to work just fine.

The derby man turned white, but before he could do nothing, the Colonel's Lady says, "Mr. Arthur. Lunch."

"Yes, madam," he says, sounding a bit relieved because I'd stuck my staff in the sand and hung my hat on it and was standing there waiting for him. I don't know if it was me getting more tetchy or if it just come natural to everybody on the Trail who was tired out and feeling ornery, but I was ready to do as good as Casper at holding up my end of an argument.

He turned the horse and wheeled off towards the front of the tavern where there was less junk laying around than usual, which meant somebody'd been taking it around back for a chore or hauling it off for trade. And they no sooner pulled up and the derby man flang down the parking weight on the end of its rope than Miz Selfridge was out the door in a pale-blue dress this time that seemed like at least the top part had been meant to fit, and Peggy was there, gawping from behind at the fine rig and the Colonel's Lady, so I drifted over that way (same as the fat man would of) so's I wouldn't get left out of this part of the tent show and stunt my education.

Peggy glanced my way, but there wasn't nothing much in her eye for me. I seen her look me up and side-to-side, and a little tilt come to her head like she was sizing up curtains without no tape-measure and calculating they wouldn't fit right but hang short. Then she turned back and fixed on the Colonel's Lady and Miz Selfridge who was already both talking.

And I felt my guard come up a little so's I wouldn't get heart-sore from her, and same time, I tried to look at her hard so's not to mix her up with too much moonlight. She *was* husky and a little blunt in the face, and she must of been doing a wash because there was a soapy splash down one side of her gray skirt, yet I still felt like I'd admire to take a stroll with her right now, anywhere she might please, and practice kissing her some more whiles I still remembered how I done it the first time.

"Well, I suppose that will have to do," the Colonel's Lady says. "Are you sure there are no vermin?"

Miz Selfridge stood up straighter and filled up her front. "Not so much as a flea," she says, lifting her chin and half-closing her eyes. "We had a very wet springtime, and it killed most all of them."

That seemed to satisfy the Colonel's Lady. "Mr. Arthur is goint to fetch the remainder of my belongings from that dreadful campground," she says. "Would you kindly place my portmanteau in my room?"

Miz Selfridge stood there a second, and if she was doing what I was doing, she was trying to figure out what a portmanteau was. But then the derby man reached around in the boot

and pulled out a leather case with a handle, and Miz Selfridge
come to life. "I'll *have* it done, ma'am," she says, her eyes
slitting more and going deeper. "Peggy, put Miz Landsour's
port—put her bag in her room."

"It's *Landseer*, Miz Siffridge," the derby man says good and
loud.

"*Selfridge*," Miz Selfridge says just as loud.

Peggy scowled, and I could tell she didn't like the idea of
fetching and carrying. She looked straight over at me and says,
"Ezekiel, would you put Miz Landseer's portmanteau in her
room, please?"

"Sure," I says, coming over and enjoying the way the derby
man was looking at me.

"Madam," he says. "I don't believe it would be wise to put
your valuables in the hands of this bumpkin."

"It's all right," I says, reaching. "I won't look inside."

"I should think *not*!" the Colonel's Lady says.

The derby man jerked it back out of my hands and says,
"Miz Selfridge, if this is one of your hired help, I'll tell you
he's been insolent and ought to be thrashed."

"That's just the hog boy," Miz Selfridge says. "You, what's-
your-name, what are you doing around front here? Go on back
where you belong."

I lifted my hat so's everybody could see it'd come all the
way off for them with daylight inbetween. "That's too many
hundred miles, ma'am," I says.

"And what's wrong with your head?" Miz Selfridge says.
"It's bleeding."

"Reckon I've been tipping my hat too much," I says.

"Well, get on around back," she says.

Peggy was trying not to giggle, and the Colonel's Lady,
sounding like she wanted to get on a higher subjeck, says,
"My husband is making a military survey of Sioux Territory
on the other side of the river, but he'll be along in a few days.
Perhaps you could slaughter a pig for him. He enjoys a good
porkchop."

"Why, I think we might arrange that," Miz Selfridge says.

"My husband used to be a butch—" She swallered it a bit too late. "He's had experience in dressing livestock."

"As long as they're not diseased," the Colonel's Lady says.

I didn't stay to listen to no more of that. I headed straight for the tavern door, meanwhile seeing Halsey zigzagging down-slope, trying to keep his overloaded *travois* from sideslipping or overhauling him, and the pockmarker with pairs of gunny-sacks tied like saddlebags both in front of and behind him, and the lanky man and his kid leading a mule apiece loaded up with whatever the crows had left them keep theirself (least till Selfridge had his high, fat, and handsome say in the matter), and I wished them well but knew better.

I barged right in and nosed my way through two or three rooms, bold as brass, having to duck under doorways and not running into nobody and giving the loose plank floors a little rumbly exercise, then off through a storeroom in the general-store part where a couple lunkheads jerked their head around to stare at me, but I just kept on going, making my way to-wards the back by guess and by gut, and located the kitchen but didn't go in because the cook was chopping vegetables and I didn't like the look of the knife, and then off left through the washroom where there was two copper-bottomed, copper-rimmed wash boilers with wood handles, both half-full of wet sheets that'd just been drained off and not put through the wringer yet, so I just dumped them and walked off out the low back door with the both. I didn't care who I was going to make trouble for, even if it was me.

I stomped over to the shed where Casper was polishing the copper tube and running a cloth through on a long wire, and I let the boilers clang on the floor whiles he sized them up and nodded, then caught the look on my face before I could take it off.

"What's the matter with you?" he says.

"Nothing a little walking won't fix," I says and went around to the sty where Colonel Woppert stuck his nose-ring out through the wire for me to twiddle for him (I think it give him a scratch inside his nose where he liked it but couldn't get at no other way), but the kind of walking I was thinking about wasn't no stroll to cool my brow.

I went around to give Jesse and Si their share of hay where Casper'd tied them on the shady side of the shed, then come back to fork some more over the top of the wire amongst the hogs. Lucy June and Pattycake and Sugar Loaf come over to join Colonel Woppert trying it out, and I says, "Looks like we might be traveling soon, folks, so eat up."

Chapter Eighteen

THE FAT MAN SHOWED up in the door of the shed about sun-down and couldn't get through because the butt end of the wagon was in the road. I was inside helping Casper get the cornmeal and ryemeal and wheatmeal and all the rest lined up and set to run whiles the boilers and the big black kettle come up to boil. Nobody had come hunting for the boilers (which we'd renched the soap out of), so they must of had spares somewhere amongst all the storerooms.

Casper wheeled around on the fat man, who looked like he'd been left out in the rain for a month and then brushed off some with a broom or else had done a considerable part of the chute by rolling down.

So's Casper wouldn't think he was about to get raided, I says, "It's all right. I met him up top."

Casper relaxed, but not much. "Private business in here, mister. And you're making the ground tilt."

"Feel like an old friend by grace of that whiskey of yours, and I'd like to shake your hand," the fat man says.

"It's already shaking," Casper says.

"Portman, Everett Portman," the fat man says, still stuck outside too far to reach. "I won't make no bones about it nor no pretense nor empty promises: I don't have two-bits to my name, but I'd like to work my way up next to some of that whiskey for any kind of chores. I can lift and haul and do carpenter, shod horses and mules, and I'm down on my luck."

"And it makes a man thirsty, don't it," Casper says, like he might possibly of heard something like this before once upon a time.

"It surely does," the fat man says. "Specially this time of day. I don't know what it is about whiskey, but it gets to looking better and better as the day wears out."

"Is that water up to boil?" Casper says.

"Won't be long," I says.

"I see a lot of miserable-looking kegs and barrels out here," the fat man says. "I've did barrelmaking from well buckets to casks."

That seemed to perk Casper up some. "You see a hundred-gallon cask out there with a sprung stave?" he says.

"Yes, sir," the fat man says.

"What kind of wood's it made out of?"

The fat man backed off for a bit, then wedged hisself in again. "White oak, and I could fix it if I had a day to leave it soak and a mallet to persuade it."

"Well, go soak it, and you're good for a gill," Casper says.

"Yes, sir, thank you," the fat man says. "Call me Ev. Could I have a little sup on account?"

"No," Casper says. "Now get out of here."

"Won't take but a few minutes to get it soaking, and after that, I'll just be standing around," Ev says. "I know what you're doing. How about leaving me help? Is it just the two of you?"

"Tend the fire, Zeke," Casper says.

When Ev cleared out of my way, I poked up the fire under the grid I'd made out of half a brass bedstead and added some more chunks of planks and wagonbeds, not letting it get too roary so's I couldn't come close without scorching myself. Both boilers and the kettle was coming up to bubbles.

"Put in a good word for me," Ev says. "I stood by you up on top of the ridge, didn't I?"

"You stood by just fine," I says. "And you walked off just like you was told." His face sagged, and I says, "I don't blame you." I hadn't expected him to take on the pockmarker and the small man for me and get hisself kilt for a stranger, but now he acted like I'd showed the forgiveness of a walking and talking Jesus.

He took off his hat at me, which I couldn't recollect anybody ever doing before. "I hate to drink around a grudge," he says. "Spoils the taste. I don't mess in other people's quarrels, and I don't make none of my own. Now, I've made corn whiskey in my time, but never nothing like this. What do we do first?

"Clear off," Casper says from the doorway. "Or else go fix that cask."

"Yes, sir," Ev says.

"Bring one of them boilers now," Casper says.

And I done like I was told, going slow so's not to scald myself, and when I was halfway in, Casper took the other handle and we poured the whole sixteen gallon into the empty marsh tub, and he tossed in two good handfuls of hops and three sacks of cornmeal and commenced stirring it with what looked like an old canoe paddle and says, "Bring the other boiler. You'll have to haul it your own self this time. I can't quit rocking the baby."

When I went out, Ev was still there, pretending he hadn't
been looking in, and whiles he fiddled with the cask, he says,
"Is he using rye or wheat?" keeping it down to a whisper.

I didn't do nothing but grunt and hauled in sixteen more gallon of simmering water. Casper helped me pour with one hand,
stirring with the other, and he showed me how to add in another three sacks of cornmeal, him stirring all the time, then
sent me out to fill up another boilerful (which I had to ladle
out of the kettle with a bucket), and Ev was still watching
everything he could.

"It ain't oatmeal, is it?" he says.

But all I done was go back and help Casper do the same
thing a third time. I didn't want to tell on Ev and get him laid
out if Casper decided to take time off to punch him, so I kept
my peace. So far, this marsh was looking like something
dredged up for breakfast at a camp meeting, and Casper kept
stirring it slow and talking to it now and then, but I couldn't
make out the words. Then after a bit he quit stirring and took
the paddle out and held it up and watched it drip and smelt it
and waited a long while, then put one hand down flat about
four inches off the steamy surface like he was blessing it.

He smiled and says, "It ought to just sting a little" and
nodded and says, "and a gallon of malt" and poured that in
gentle without stirring and then poured in three sacks of
wheatmeal and commenced stirring slow but only about halfway down. Then he took the paddle out again and looked it
over and nodded and says, "And now we're going to stand
here about ten minutes and not do nothing. Don't talk. Let
that marsh start *thinking.*"

And we done so. After that, he stirred it all the way to the
bottom, going round and round and across and figure-eight,
and then waiting ten more minutes and stirring again and waiting ten more minutes, not talking (which was the most work
of all for me but Casper didn't seem to mind) and not paying
no attention to anything but the marsh and the paddle. He let
it set a while longer without stirring, then going slow, stuck his

bare hand down in it past the wrist and seemed to think it over
and says, "All right, it's cool enough. Let's fill her up."

We used the gutter sluice and poured cold water into the
marsh tub till it was most full up. Then Casper chunked in a
half-gallon of yeast or more and stood over that great big tub,
watching the bubbles commence and sniffing it all around.
Finally he backed off and says, "There she stands. When that
blubbering stops, we'll stir it up and still it, and if we don't get
fifty gallon of passable whiskey out of it, I'll retire and start
learning how to spit higher'n my shoes when they're propped
on a porchrail."

He seemed pleased with hisself, and he patted the side of the
tub like he often done to the mules. "If it was cold, we'd have
to cover it," he says. "But this is fine. It'll work all night."

"Only fifty gallon?" I says. I'd never been much good at
arithmetic, but I didn't have no trouble chalking that one up
or coming close. "You mean we got to do this fifty times?"

"More or less," Casper says. "Depends on how much of that
grain's gone mildew and whether them lunkheads bust the
meal grinder."

I was trying hard to calculate. "But if it takes two or three
days to make fifty gallon, it'll take three or four months to get
through that heap of grain."

"Something like that," he says, holding the coal oil lamp
close enough to the tub so's he could see the bubbles.

The sun had went down a while back, and our shadows was
leaping all around amongst the copper coils and the shed walls
and the wagon. I'd seen Ev's fat outline looming up now and
then outside but didn't care. I couldn't figure out what was
going on in here right under my nose, so I reckoned he hadn't
learnt much from out there.

"But me and the hogs could be in California before that,"
I says.

"I spose you could," he says.

"It'll be coming on for fall and maybe snow, and I can't
drive hogs in the winter nor feed them, not even just four," I
says, hearing my voice going hollow with worry.

"You're free to roam," he says. "This wasn't my idea. If you want me to, I'll trade Selfridge some more *old* whiskey to turn you and the hogs loose. Think you could make it on your own? Lots of Injuns from here on."

"They'd sooner take your whiskey than my hogs," I says, but I could tell from Casper keeping quiet that I wasn't answering straight. Trouble was, I couldn't make up my mind. "I not only don't know what I *can* do, I don't even know what I *want* to do."

"Well, just make sure the second fits inside the first, and you'll be all right," he says. "Now go round me up something to eat."

"Yes, sir," I says.

"I'm going to watch over this big bubbly baby here so's some stray cat don't try to steal its breath," he says.

"Yes, sir. And I'm much obliged for you offering to trade me and the hogs. I've been a burden. Come springtime, maybe I can pay you off in pigs."

"Well, I've heard worse ideas," he says.

But by the time I'd slopped and foddered the hogs and mules and brung the stew for the both of us, Casper didn't seem interested in his. He'd been taking more pulls at the old whiskey and had another cupful handy, so whiles I et mine and his set there on the tailgate and cooled off, he says, "The beauty of selling whiskey is it's all right if you don't try too hard. Folks even like it better if you don't try, and they'll honor you and respeck you and watch over you as if you was the very spigot out of which the whiskey come."

"I don't notice you collecting any too much honor around here," I says.

"I didn't get kilt, did I?" he says, looking a little vexed with me.

"Not yet," I says.

He scowled and took a pull at his cup and went over and snuffed the marsh. "You're right, there's others that want to treat you like the spigot and nothing else," he says. "Now and

then you run into a Selfridge. But I'll show him and all the
other rough-housers and deadbeats and four-card-flushers and
overcooked mangelwurzels and pigeon-droppers and whip-
crackers that want to make me do what I don't feel like doing.
I'm a *gentleman*." He give me a look like he expected to be
counterdicted, but I et some stew instead. "And a gentleman
can always spot them people that's got a handful of Gimme
and a mouthful of Much Obliged."

"And what does he do after he spots them?" I says.

"He shuts off their whiskey," he says. "And if they don't
like it, he puts out their light for them, and if they don't like
that, he turns down the damper on their damned windpipe."
He got his nose into the cup of whiskey again.

"Meaning no disrespeck, you don't sound a whole lot like
you was ever a preacher," I says.

"I didn't say I was any good at it, did i?" he says.

"No, sir," I says, swatting a skeeter and losing a spoonful of
stew.

"Now look at that," he says. "You just put out that skeeter's
light and shut off its windpipe both. Don't go hauling up any
moral authority on *me*. That skeeter wanted to live, didn't
he? And didn't your blood taste just as good as whiskey to
him?"

"I spose so," I says, looking at the little fleck of remainders
in my hand. "But it sure got him in a lot of trouble."

"Your blood was the Elixir of Life, and your palm was the
Angel of Death," he says. "And a drinking man has to keep
one eye over his shoulder, or the same thing can happen to
him." He took another sup and glanced over his shoulder and
I guess didn't see nothing to worry about yet, because he
reached over and drew another gill.

"What if everybody was to just quit making whiskey?" I
says. "Then you wouldn't have to waste so much time looking
behind you and worrying."

"I seen you looking behind you and worrying many a time in
our short acquaintance," he says, and he had me there all right.

"And the problem is *thirst*, boy, not whiskey. Blood come before skeeters, didn't it?"

"Well, *mine* didn't," I says.

He looked at me like I'd just squeaked my chalk on my slate. "Go on out and give the rest of the skeeters some business," he says.

I was setting out in the moonlight an hour later, propped up against one of my sty poles and trying to keep the skeeters from getting drunk on me and thinking about my Future and wondering if Peggy liked hogs (but knowing she didn't and wouldn't) and generally muddling over what I'd been doing since I'd lost Ma and Pa, when fat Ev come lurching up to the sty gate kind of top-heavy and stood with his legs spraddled, looking down at me. "Stingy old bastard," he says. "Keeps all that whiskey to hisself. Wants to dole it out by the damn drop. Wants folks to beg."

"Go tell it to him," I says. "I don't have none."

"Me neither," he says, sounding thick-tongued and sorry.

"I wouldn't be surprised if you'd had some a bit ago," I says, keeping my staff handy and hearing what sounded like a couple of banjos start jangling inside the tavern.

"That wasn't no proper way to make whiskey," Ev says. "That was all foolery. Why, I could make better whiskey'n that if I had me a still." One leg bent a little too much, and he went sideslipping and knocked one of my sty posts half over.

I stood up and give him a prod in the side with my staff to get him out of range if he was to keel all the way over. I didn't want him falling on my hogs and hurting them.

"What the hell are you doing?" he says.

"Keeping you out of trouble," I says and give him another prod to back him up.

He tried to swat at my staff, but all he done was scuff his knuckles. "You leave me be or I'll crack you open like a musk melon," he says.

"All friends here," I says, but knew it wasn't true. I didn't want to go busting somebody else over the head and making another enemy, which I'd been doing too much of lately. Seemed like all's I could do was get people quarrelsome at me, even though I didn't feel like I had bad intentions.

He stood and cussed me a bit from out of reach, and I left him do it if it made him feel any better, which it didn't appear to. Then he staggered off around to the front of the tavern.

I set there a long while, wrapped up in my blanket and feeling like I was getting older and dumber by the minute, not aging into something better like whiskey nor bubbling up and changing for the best like the marsh inside the shed (where I could see the coal-oil lamp flickering through the chinks with Casper probably dozing over it and whispering and maybe praying—or whatever it was he had to do), and then I heard Colonel Woppert give a big deep happy grunt behind me and a long sigh after, which meant he'd relocated hisself in his sleep and was nice and full in the stomach and wasn't troubling his mind about tomorrow because he knew exackly who he was and what he wanted.

And all of a sudden, all my good gumption come back to me like somebody'd doused me with a bucket of water, and I got up and scuffled over to the nearest spring and took off my hat and my blanket and my shirt and crouched down and dunked my head all the way under, giving them bandannas a good soaking and getting water in my ears and up my nose and not caring. That sharp cold chill seemed to set my brain to working, and by the time I'd peeled off the outside bandanna and the inside one folded like a pad and give my crusty scalp another cold soak, I thought I had my aims all figured out, and I went whistling back to the sty and wrapped up again and slept all the noisy night just like I knew what I was doing as good as Colonel Woppert and maybe even better than Lucy June and sure enough better than Pattycake and Sugar Loaf, which just goes to show you how easy it is to get above yourself.

Chapter Nineteen

WHAT I DONE was I got up before dawn and told Casper what I was going to do (I couldn't tell if he'd took any sleep—he was red-eyed and gaping and scratching and fussing at the marsh), and when he didn't try to talk me out of it, I used the extra energy I'd been saving to argue with on sneaking the hogs through the brush away from the sprawling heap of joined shacks and down past the second spring, keeping on the bumpy, scrubby side away from where the wagons was camped and hardly got barked at before I was headed downhill on the rough road to the North Fork of the Platte where I hoped to find that Emigrants' Post Office I'd heard Pa tell about and maybe track down some news that would tell me what I'd ought to do on this earth instead of just bogging down amongst thieves.

It was the worst excuse for a road I'd seen yet, the only good part being it wasn't as steep as Ash Hollow. I was glad I didn't have to get a wagon along it through the mixup of rocks and sand and mudholes and every kind of ankle-buster known to man except roots: nothing had stayed alive where the wagons had been going, though a fair share of stumps was sticking up on both sides, where most of the trees and brush had got logged off long since. My main problem was keeping up with the hogs well enough to steer them away from the gullies that led up to each side, though I did have to leave them browse from time to time to fill their belly halfway, and I done likewise on a half a loaf of rye bread I'd swiped from the cook the night before, and I hope to tell you half a loaf is better than none.

The sun lightened things up slow and smoky, keeping behind a sheet of what looked to be high fog, but before long, I could see good enough so's I didn't have to shuffle and wonder and scuff rocks with my boots to keep from dislocating myself. And me and the hogs commenced enjoying what felt almost like freedom for a change, with the road (if you could call it that) empty ahead and behind, and nothing plaguing us yet, and nobody herding me, and nobody herding them except me which they didn't seem to mind, long as I stayed reasonable enough to let them crop off berry leaves and some kind of seed grass they'd took a fancy to.

I hadn't been alone like this on the Trail except for a short spell the night and morning of the pigsticking, and it felt good and made me feel old and stiff-chinned and frowny-eyed, and I even done a little strutting whenever the ground leveled enough for it which wasn't often. It begun to give me the idea that if I found any good word at that Post Office, I might just keep on going then and there, and might do it even if there wasn't no word but just go stomping along and taking care of

my own self without fear nor favor and see what this here
California was all about, if anything.

Casper didn't really need me, far as I could tell. I couldn't
get him out of the trouble he was in and maybe could only
get him in deeper if it come to me defending my hogs with life
and limb and maybe crowning Selfridge with my staff and
Casper fighting for me (like I suspicioned he might do) and the
both of us getting shot. It might be better with me off on my
own, letting him decide how much blood he wanted to shed
for whiskey. Least it wouldn't be hog's blood nor mine. And
Peggy seemed like she might be growing a little too high on the
vine for me to reach just yet or maybe had ripened too soon
and drawn the birds before picking time. She was a puzzler
and a strange discomfort, and the further off I got on the road,
the easier it seemed like for me to think about something else
besides her hand and her lips and her throat and so on down
the line.

Pretty soon I was feeling plain independent and springy-
footed over it, and even though my drove had been cut down
to a mere four, at least I'd be more likely to find feed for that
many instead of half-starving twenty-seven.

By the time the road begun to shallow out and the ground
turned sandier and I could see the river glinting up ahead
through the blurry gray light, I'd almost decided to turn myself loose on the Trail, spite of having no food nor shelter like
a blanket or a piece of canvas nor no gun. I reckoned I might
do chores at the campsites up ahead between here and Fort
Laramie and maybe pick up a new trade along the line of
whiskey boy without the whiskey. And then I seen three
things just about the same time.

Off to the left where the scrubby brush ended and the bare,
hard-packed sand of the river valley commenced was a clump
of tombstones made out of old planks but most of them
rounded on the top like you're sposed to do it so's it looks like
Moses's tablets and some with crosses instead and four or five

of them looking too new to be comfortable. And the second
thing I seen was the Emigrants' Post Office which I had mistook for a wrecked wagon from a ways off. It wasn't but a
lean-to about fifty yards past the graves, an empty, lonely-
looking shack and not what I'd had in mind. Post Offices back
home was likely to have folks setting in front of them all day
whittling and spitting and picking their teeth and lying and
swapping stories about the Mayor and the Government and
arguing about which way the weather was headed and waiting
for somebody to get a letter or a package so's they could
guess what was in it. But this one didn't look like it had nothing at all worth waiting for, not even a flag up top.

And the third thing I seen off to the right maybe a half-mile
down near the riverbank was an Injun camp with five tepees
giving off smoke or mist or both. I could see a few Injuns
moving around there and one fetching water, and I begun to
lose some of my independence.

Because I'd stopped and not been minding them, the hogs
strayed off a ways into the brush without knocking down no
tombstones, though Colonel Woppert started scratching hisself on one before I staffed him away from it. Well, it was no
surprise to me that people had been dying on the Trail. I'd
seen many a grave before and wagons with the red flag hanging
out which meant somebody was smallpoxed and might be
headed underground. With the cholera, there wasn't no time
even to put out a flag before it was time to be put to bed with
a shovel. But something felt different about this cluster of
dead ones, and somehow I was scairt I was going to get my
news from Ma and Pa in what'd been chiseled or scratched on
one of them plank slabs.

So when I got down on my knees, I reckonized I was doing
so for a lot of reasons: to see better, out of respeck, to be half-
praying against what I was afeard I might find and half-praying
for whoever was under there (whether it was my own flesh and
blood or not), and partly to keep out of sight of them Injuns
because this was Sioux country down here, unless a Pawnee or

Arapaho hunting party had got ambitious, and I'd heard many
a tale about the Sioux being short on hospitality.

I tried to read the old tombstones first, them being the safest,
but didn't have much luck except to make out a few names
and ages (mostly under twenty-five which was discouraging),
the chisel marks already weathering and splintering off and
generally turning forgetful. But when I come to the new ones I
become wary as a raccoon sniffing bait under a box. When I
finally let my eyes focus, they turned out to be two baby girls
and one of them's mother, a young man my age, and a fifty-one-
year-old farmer where somebody had scratched "The Seeds He
Planted Come to Life Again, May He Do Likewise," which was
a pretty high order of hoping in sandy soil like this and a
winter on its way that was likely to put three foot of snow
across where I was kneeling.

I walked on to the Post Office, taking my hat off and half-
hunching and keeping an eye on the Injun camp where the
sight of me hadn't raised no fuss yet (if I could see them,
Injuns could probably see me twice as good), and I went into
the lean-to where there wasn't no postmaster but a field mouse
that scattled out of my way, probably taking a mouthful of
somebody's letter with him to use for bedding. There was
notes and notices and letters and messages stuck here and
there in chinks or on pegs or some nailed, half of them wea-
thered till you could hardly tell what was wrote and some
ripped in half and wrote on the back of by somebody else.
I begun the long stretch of leafing through.

After I'd spelled out a whole batch of them slow enough
to make Miz Peasemont shamed of me (but I couldn't help it,
penmanship not being part of the upbringing of most on the
Trail), I begun to get the idea nobody'd ever located nobody
else in Nebraska Territory and everybody was vexed or disappointed or worse like the one that went:

Dear Thelma Lou:
    I wated 2 days past what I said and you never come along like
you was spose to. I cant wate no longer being without proper vitals

to feed my ma and have to get on tords Scots Bluff or resk starving
her she has took a fever and vometing regular. I love you but dont
drink nothing but way up cricks. Will wate 2 more days at the first
honest sutler, then God knows.

Truely yours,
Amos W. Bradley

It didn't look like Amos was having much more fun than
most of the others, and judging by the rain-streaks on the
piece of butcher paper it was wrote on, Thelma Lou hadn't
come by yet and read the good news about her mother-in-
law-to-be (or whoever), and there was twenty more on the
order of "Why wasn't you at where you said you was going to
be?" and I reckoned the cholera and the Injuns and maybe
friendly folks like Selfridge and the buckskin man might of
had some say in the matter.

And there was some that was short and tart like the one
on the back of a handbill for Dr. Rademacher's Arrowroot
Stoolbinder that says, "God Damn you, William Dexter," and
underneath of it somebody had wrote with what looked to of
been a burnt stick "The Blasphemer Names His Own Perpetual
Torment!" which seemed like a mean trick to get back at an
angry man with (who might be more sensible five minutes
after letting loose), but I wouldn't of put it past the kind of
God who couldn't think up nothing permanent for His creatures on earth but didn't have no trouble creating permanent
torture afterwards.

But there wasn't no trace of anything from Ma or Pa, both
of them being pretty fair writers for country folks, though I
hadn't got down to the oldest-looking papers next to the wall
yet which seemed the unlikeliest. Then I heard the shooting
and whooping.

First I thought the Injuns had seen me and was heading my
way for a barbecue with Colonel Woppert and his three nieces
on spits and me tied to a stake, but when I ducked out in the
open and peeled my eyes towards the camp, I could tell they
was keeping their fights at home that morning and using their

weepons on theirself: a small party, maybe a half a dozen, was trotting around amongst the tepees on horseback and firing handguns and rifles both and I even seen a few swinging swords (though I'd never heard of no Injun using a sword), and after a bit, two of the tepees commenced burning and a third toppled all the way over, and I seen one Injun running along the riverbank get stabbed from behind by one of the raiding party on horseback, and then two riderless pintos come busting out from behind a tepee and galloping my way (though I stood there wishing they'd picked any other direction) and an Injun on a fine big black horse turned and galloped after them.

Even whiles I was gaping and feeling desperate worried, I still noticed all the raiding party's horses looked like whitemen's mounts and not the usual piebald ponies or half-cayuse skin-and-boners you'd usually see Injuns with. Then a whole string of rifle shots come from near the tepees, and the Injun coming towards me slumped forward till his face was down against his horse's mane, but he stayed on somehow, and the two pintos begun galloping even faster. Just before I got behind the Post Office and called the hogs, I seen the rest of the raiding party riding away east along the river with more rifle fire coming from the two tepees still standing.

The hogs didn't enjoy the commotion no more than me, even at that distance, but I got them in close before something worse happened, and in a few seconds the pintos come pounding past, keeping between me and the river just outside the brush-line where the valley sand commenced, and they didn't stop for no mail nor messages, and I crouched low when the wounded Injun come by, going full tilt after them. But he didn't look like he was thinking about much except that bullet he was carrying along inside of him someplace and stayed bent over, his bare back gleaming with blood or warpaint or both and his buckskin leggings slapping too free for safety against the sides of an expensive-looking saddle. He'd only got fifty or sixty yards past me when he slid off the near side without trying to. His horse kept right on going after the others, then slacked off and walked for a bit, and then finally stopped and turned and looked back like maybe he'd misunderstood what he was sposed to be doing and needed some reminding.

But the Injun didn't get up. From where I was standing, I couldn't see him, but the bushes was so low there, he'd of had to be laying flat to keep out of sight. His horse begun coming back, browsing the bushes along the edge on the way and stopping now and then.

I looked off towards the tepees again where the two on fire had turned into nothing but tall sticks which was still pouring smoke downstream, but I couldn't hear no more gunfire and didn't see nobody else on horseback. It was a small camp and it'd been a small raiding party, and maybe they'd shot each other up so bad, they all wanted to lay down and bandage up and think about something different or maybe die in peace. I'd been running into a good deal of unneighborliness back uphill in Ash Hollow and points southeast, but nothing on this order where you just up and start shooting at everything in sight or set fire to it, and if this was the way Injuns treated each other, I was surprised they hadn't run theirself short-handed by now, since they'd been out here a considerable number of years before we come.

I didn't feel much at home, and since I had to do some of the thinking for the hogs too, I tried to imagine what Colonel Woppert would of advised me to do, and I could hear him saying, When are we getting back to that nice sty with all the hay and brush and grain?

Whiles I was making up our mind whether to take the plunge alone and head upstream along the North Platte and take our chances with the Sioux and starvation and cholera or go back and wait till Casper'd earned our way out and then stick with his whiskey wagon, I walked a ways to get a better look at the Injun, not having much hope of helping him since I didn't know nothing about doctoring. In the back of my mind I was commencing to nag myself about being such a Poor Samari-

tan and not having no more charity than a chigger, because
all I could think about was me and mine, and at the same
time I was half-thinking if it so happened the Injun was dead,
I'd sure admire to have that horse of his because then I'd have
a better chance of defending myself and the hogs and keeping
clear of all this trouble I kept running into and which it didn't
seem likely there'd be no shortage of in the future.

The Injun was laying on the sand curled up and not moving,
and I crouched for a spell to watch him and make sure, glancing back at the camp now and then so's not to get surprised,
though it would of took a band of angels playing jew's
harps to surprise me by then. I was about thirty yards off
from the Injun and could see everything pretty clear, and
when he still hadn't moved after another minute, I crept up
on him closer. His horse seen me about then and stopped cold
to think me over and the hogs too, since they'd come straggling along and might look like dogs to a plains horse. I did
everything nice and slow so's not to spook him, meanwhile
noticing the blood streaked down the Injun's back, some of it
caked with sand or mixed over yellow and black streaks of
paint. The rest of his skin that showed was a funny chestnut
color, not much like other Injuns I'd seen up close, but I
reckoned they must have their different-complected ones like
us.

I didn't see no kind of gun, so he'd either dropped it along
the way someplace or been too busy stealing horses to keep
track of it, and besides, I wasn't sure I wanted to carry a gun
anyway. I give a medium whistle at his horse, but he didn't
seem interested. Maybe Injuns called them some other way I
couldn't even guess at. Then I stood up straight and held out
my free hand to show I didn't have no rope in it and walked a
little ways, letting my staff trail, but by the time I'd come
close to the Injun, his horse heaved up its head and shied off
and looked ready for more if I was to try him again, so I give
up.

Kneeling by the Injun, I felt sorry and shaky and ready to

scuttle on back to the stable and sty, having learnt a lesson and the wiser for it, and then I felt dumb all over gain and numb too, because when I shifted his shoulder a little to get a look at his face, the black pigtailed wig skewed half off his red hair, and under the smeary streaks of face-paint I seen my old friend redbeard (he'd been too proud of it to shave) who hadn't had no luck pigsticking and had now done even worse playing Injun.

Chapter Twenty

ALL MY LIFE I'd heard it complained of that I didn't move fast enough nor think fast enough nor do chores fast enough nor eat fast enough nor even sleep fast enough, but whiles I was still kneeling there for what couldn't of been no more'n five or ten seconds (I wasn't breathing fast enough neither nor at all) I managed to get the following through my skull: 1) if redbeard was raiding Injuns dressed up like one, the buckskin man wasn't far off and 2) if they'd been killing real Injuns (and I knew it was so because I'd seen it), then the real Injuns would be painting for war right now, even if they was down to only one left and 3) if a real Injun had kilt the redbeard, he'd be heading this way as soon as he could make it to get the pintos, to claim redbeard's horse, and to take home a chunk of hair

(the red kind, not the wig) and 4) if the real Injun was wounded
and laid up back in one of them tepees, then it wouldn't be no
time till the buckskin man come riding this way to find his
pardner and 5) I had best make me and the hogs as scarce as
possible.

I commenced running in a crouch, chucking at the hogs to
follow, and as well as I could make out between times when I
was checking to keep from wedging myself head-first into a
bush and getting stuck and turning out like that Ram in the
Thicket that got hisself burnt just for being nearby at the
wrong time, the hogs was willing to trot along. I knew neither
of us could keep it up, specially when the ground would be
rising soon and laying them rough two miles uphill betwixt us
and Casper. But I done the best I could and got past the
tombstones, keeping on the bushy side so's I'd be near cover,
even if it meant considerable zigzagging. A woods hog is built
for running through brush, no matter how thick, being narrow
head-on and bristly and hard-snouted, but a two-legged man's
got too many forks and crutches on him, including my staff
which sometimes didn't want to go on the same side of a
clump as me.

I heard more rifle fire then and crouched even lower in case
the Injun back at the tepees was aiming at me and the hogs
who'd been counting coup on the redbeard before he could get
there hisself. When I heard still more, I laid low and held still,
chucking the hogs in close as I could, though they seemed inclined to stray since I'd got their blood up trotting. I didn't
hear no nearby whines nor ricochets, and when I stuck my
head up to scout around, I seen why: three Injun-looking men
on whitemen's horses was galloping along the edge of the
brush past the burnt camp, heading for redbeard's corpus, and
whoever was still left firing from the tepees (it might of been
more'n one because the shots come pretty frequent) was giving them good cause to hurry on by.

Nobody seemed to get hit, and I was far enough off—pretty
near a hundred yards—to feel halfway safe, long as they stuck

to the sand and didn't head up the road my way and the hogs
didn't decide to go wild. A little further up the road, the gully
sides commenced rising, and there was no brush worth trying
to hide in left or right. So I stuck where I was for a while,
about ten yards off the road in the scattered, hip-high bushes
where I could peek down through and past the Post Office
and see the three horsemen reining up where the redbeard was
laying. The rifle fire had stopped since they was out of range
now, but if it'd been me, I wouldn't of taken no comfort from
that nor been as careless as them: one trotted up ahead and
got hold of redbeard's horse without no trouble, and the other
two had dismounted and wasn't even looking back at the Injun
camp. From where I was setting on higher ground, I could see
an Injun come crawling out of camp, keeping flat on the sand
and using the little swells and rises in the valley floor for cover
whiles he went along upstream between them and the river. He
was snaking along pretty quick, not heading straight for them
but aiming to wind up about two hundred yards off or maybe
closer.

I kept straining my eyes at the three horsemen whenever I
could snatch a clear look at them, and no matter what else
they was doing, they didn't look to be sculpting the redbeard,
so I took them to be whitemen too, and the one wearing a
blood-red blanket and three feathers stuck straight up from
the back of his head carried hisself like the buckskin man,
which I mean he held hisself like a flag or like he was posing
for a stone statue or like he was aiming to take up a collection
after everybody'd got a good look. My heart was racing like I
was still running, and I chucked the hogs again, doing it as
loud as I dared, and they at least kept in sight, which was right
nice of them because so much was going on they wasn't used
to, I couldn't expect them to behave perfeck.

One reason my heart was racing was I felt scairt I'd do something foolhardy and get myself butchered and not be no
smarter at the end of it than now and not even find out if Ma
and Pa was up ahead someplace, waiting at an honest sutler's

(if there was such a place) for me to show up like Amos W.
Bradley waiting for Thelma Lou. And the other reason was I
couldn't make up my mind what was the smart-hardy thing to
do next.

The three make-believe Injuns was getting the redbeard tied
across his own saddle, and the real Injun had made it about
halfway to where he seemed to be going, and the hogs was
snouting around in the brush nice and quiet (I'd managed to
keep them away from the road so far, having to use my staff
on Pattycake twice before she got the idea), but laying down
like this left me short on choices if anybody come my way,
which is what them three now proceeded to do.

They mounted up and walked their horses east, then turned
up the road past the Post Office, leading redbeard's horse like
a kind of funeral party, only looking back at the Injun camp
once apiece to make sure it was minding its manners. After
they'd come a short ways and wasn't looking back no more,
the real Injun got up on his feet and commenced running low.

There wasn't even any rocks good-sized enough for me to
hide behind, but I located one that must of tumbled down
from the gully-sides lately and stuck up against the root of a
bush, and the two together made just about enough cover to
keep me mostly out of sight if nobody looked right at me, so
I scrunched down behind it and laid my staff flat and tried
my durndest to look like sandy ground and kept my face
pushed up so close to the rock, I could barely make out the
cracks and loose chips in it where it had left go of the rest of
the gully-makers up above and come down here to start turning into sand. It looked like it was aiming to take its time and
should of been a lesson and a parable to me, but I was too
jitter-headed to learn it then.

I could hear the horse's hooves coming closer, and I laid
still, trying to melt or crumble or steam off to nothing, and a
deep voice I didn't reckonize says, "If only he hadn't gone
chasing off like that."

And the buckskin man says, "A sure instinct for blood sport, sir. If something runs, you chase it. I shall honor his memory, and I shall name a city after him."

"What the hell *was* his name?" a third voice says, which I also didn't reckonize and which meant the moonhead wasn't along on this game or maybe had got kilt over amongst the tepees.

"By george, isn't that a hog?" the deep voice says. "Or a wild boar?"

"Where?" the third voice says.

"Over past that elderberry bush or what the hell ever it is," the deep voice says. "If that isn't a hog, I'll eat it. In fact, I'll eat it if it *is*."

"Gentlemen, this is a burial detail," the buckskin man says. "And may I remind you we are in full view of what's left of those salvages back there? Move on."

"Yes, sir," the deep voice says. "But it's still a hog."

"I don't doubt that there are hogs in this world," the buckskin man says. "I have already collected considerable proof of that fact, and I require no further evidence. Move on."

"Yes, sir," the deep voice and the third voice says together.

They was well past me now and hadn't scouted me out, and I laid still, feeling helpless and half a coward for not getting in amongst them with my staff and at least killing the buckskin man before they shot me. But it didn't seem like the right time nor place nor worth dying over just yet.

And I found myself peeking downhill again, even though I knew it was dangerous to show my face to the real Injun amongst the twigs and stems and parched leaves, because I guess I was born to nose into what didn't *have* to be none of my beeswax. And I seen him still up on his feet, running in a crouch as low as a coyote and taking shelter behind the Post Office, scuttling quick and crooked and not looking like no man at all but something you could only catch in the corner of your eye and never see straight on.

Then, when the barrel of his rifle showed up sticking around the edge of the left-hand corner post and aiming up the road at the three of them hand-painted left-overs from a murder party, at least one a part-time pigsticking marauder and as near a devil as I'd ever seen outside my own head, plus one corpus on his way to a thrilling new heap of fun underground, I didn't do nothing but wait and lay still and hope he didn't shoot a horse by mistake. I didn't raise no warning nor even think of it.

The rifle went off, and I heard the bullet zinging way up the gully, and the three make-believers fired back and rode off uphill as fast as they could whiles the real Injun was reloading, and then the rifle went off again, and some handguns answered from far off, and I kept still and laid low through it all, not wanting to interrupt nothing or get mistook for belonging to either side, though I'd of picked being with the Injun if I'd had to choose.

I waited a long while before chancing a look, and when I finally did, I seen the Injun walking off west along the riverbank towards where the pintos had headed. The fact he hadn't come up the road meant there wasn't nothing there to scalpt, so I reckoned he'd missed. The road up the gully was bare, and he hadn't felt like chasing them afoot, though it looked like that was what I was going to be obliged to do, like it or not, being stuck with a mighty poor choice of directions. About all I could do if I wanted to keep my hair on was go on up the road to Ash Hollow and hope they didn't turn around after they done their burying and meet me and the hogs face to face and snout.

After I'd rounded up the four and got the notion in their head it was time to do some climbing, I done it as slow as they pleased, letting them browse along the edges. I wanted to keep quiet and not overhaul the raiding party and not get bushwhacked. There was nothing up ahead for them to be aiming at except the little campground below Selfridge's or Selfridge's own place or that dang chute they was commenc-

ing to call Windlass Hill up to the ridge, and I didn't know
which to hope for. I wanted to talk to the buckskin man—and
maybe do considerable more too—but I didn't want to be
took at a disadvantage, which was where I always seemed to
be. I wanted to make trouble for him if I could figure out
how, and I needed to talk to Casper because he seemed to of
had about every kind of trouble there was.

I kept wary for a slow hour uphill, inspecting every hint of
a side gully before I passed it by. For all I knew, the buckskin man had some kind of robbers' den or secret camp up
one of them brush-filled draws, though it didn't look likely.
Then, whiles all five of us was taking our bittersweet time
along one of the leveler places before it turned steep again,
Lucy June found the grave about ten foot off to the right in
a place where there was some loose, gravelly ground.

And I don't know what they'd used for a shovel, but it
hadn't worked too good because I could see part of redbeard's
leggings sticking out through the mess of stones and dirt and
brambles they'd heaped over and tried to tamp down on him,
and up front they'd drove in a stick with a piece of paper
stuck on it and had wrote in lead pencil as follows:

Hic Jacet Alexander Bottomley

(which was even more peculiar for a name than them three-
handled ones the buckskin man had kept making up).

And below that:

Died June 1852 in combat while loyally
serving in the 1st Regiment of the
Territorial Pacifiers. R.I.P.
"The slayer follows the slain."

The redbeard had took some of his own medicine, and I
hoped he was enjoying the taste of it. He'd got pacified right
back and sent off on a different Trail where he was going to
have some tall explaining to do if the Bible was right, which I
doubted then and still do.

I kept the hogs off, though they probably wouldn't of done nothing impolite, being pretty full up on forage, but in lean times, I wouldn't of put it past them to show the redbeard how to get through some Pearly Gates consisting of forty-four teeth and making him hard to reckonize when he turned up at St. Peter's even pearlier ones.

When I come to the campsite below Selfridge's, I stayed as far off as I could whiles skirting around it. I was half-scairt I'd see the three of them there at the spring, washing off their paint and joshing and splashing and ready to shoot hogs for a change. There was seven wagons all-told and folks walking this way and that, getting their supper-and-sundown fires going and horses and mules tethered in three clumps and some oxen, but nothing or nobody I reckonized, so maybe the buckskin man had led them right on up the chute to the ridge so's he could get a good view and start naming them cities after all the dead friends he was accumulating. Nothing else he'd done made much sense, so I didn't expect him to start this evening.

No horses was tied in front of the tavern and none in back neither (the crows all off striking bargains before dusk, most likely), and soon as I got the hogs styed and foddered, I sidled up to Casper who was setting on his tailgate, yawning, and staring at his marsh tub and holding his empty cup, just like I hadn't been no place and nothing had happened.

Before I could open my mouth, he says, "It's almost quit bubbling, boy, and everything looks sweet as a nut."

His voice was a little slurry, and I felt embarrassed for him, but I says, "I need some advice, Casper. Bad."

"Well, you come to the right shop," he says.

"I seen another one of them pigstickers," I says. "The main one. The boss. He's around here someplace with at least two others, and if he sees me, I think he's going to kill me."

"What for?" he says.

"I pretty near busted his wrist," I says. "Maybe both wrists. And I think he's crazy. He was down along the North Fork

dressed up like an Injun, shooting and burning a camp of
Sioux."

"Then he didn't have no broken wrists," Casper says, drawing a drink out of his keg. "Maybe it was somebody else."

"No, I heard him talking," I says.

Casper give me a long, squinty look. "Sounds like you had
a full day," he says. "How's your head? Is it making any noise
inside there? You been seeing things?

I shook my head, and truth to tell, it *was* hurting and buz-
zing some. "You don't know what he's like. He's crazy-mean,
and I don't want him hurting you or me or the hogs. Maybe I
should get on the road and—" But even as I was saying it, I
knew I couldn't go back down there myself afoot.

"Where is he?" Casper says.

"I don't know," I says. And I realized how lame it sounded.

"Well, if you see him again, ask him over for a drink, and I'll
have a word with him," Casper says. "Nothing like pouring a
little whiskey on a wound."

"But he maybe kilt my ma and pa and *did* kill some of my
hogs," I says.

"You're a long ways from the Law, you're young, you don't
pack a gun, and you don't even know where he is," Casper
says. "If I was you, I'd have a drink and think it over."

Whiles he followed his own advice, I stood there, smelling
that strange marsh and my head pounding and wondering if I'd
dreamt it all up.

He looked at me slit-eyed and crooked, like he was making
sure he was seeing me clear enough to tell what I was thinking.
"You don't believe in whiskey, do you," he says.

But I was thinking of Peggy and some of them spare wagons
Selfridge had stowed in an extra stable and wondering if I
could be so bold as to steal mules from him. "I'm not too well
acquainted with it," I says to be polite. "It seems—respectable."

"Don't go thinking it's just a painkiller," he says.

"I don't think about it much at all," I says, wondering if a wagon with Peggy and a rifle would be safe enough to get us through them Sioux if we tagged behind somebody else or whether it might not be best to haul it back up the chute and head for Missouri.

Casper looked mad. "Then wait till you've earned yourself some pain and can't find nothing to kill it," he says.

"Yes, sir," I says. "That's how I feel right now."

"Then take a drink," he says. "I don't mind being the one to lead you into that particular temptation. Somebody'll do it next year if I don't this year."

"No, I thank you kindly," I says. I was having enough trouble thinking without adding tanglefoot to it, but didn't say so.

"Then go on out and find what's bothering you and spit in its goddamn face," he says. "I'm busy."

I went out and scrounged some food off of the cook and swiped some extra when he wasn't looking and set down outside the sty, thinking and doing guard duty both, and where the idea'd come from, I don't know. I'd never thought much about getting married and having kids. I'd been too busy getting over being a kid my own self to notice I might have to wind up starting some kind of mess like Ma and Pa done. I'd probably had it in the back of my mind, same as you might carry the notion you was going to get old and croak someday, but I'd never felt inclined to trouble hunting up some girl who might say Yes instead of choking herself laughing like Alfrieda Molesworth nearly done to Uncle Fred one summer night in our hayloft which I just happened to hear because I was down below listening through the planks. (I'd always sort of studied Uncle Fred because everybody said he was the worst example around, and I figured I might learn more from him than somebody inbetween like Pa.)

But now, after that bleak, lonely, scary feeling I'd had amongst the tombstones and in the Post Office and seeing how easy it was to get yourself kilt and never have nothing else good happen, it seemed possible I might actually try this here marriage, if Peggy'd have me, which I doubted—and Casper being handy if he was still a preacher like he'd said.

I set there watching the night clump down into Ash Hollow and listening to the hogs gradually leave off their munching and settle down in the sandy dust, and I decided not to let nothing haunt me I wasn't looking straight at, including the buckskin man, no matter what he dressed hisself up as. I was going to keep my share of life and not spill it from shaking.

Chapter Twenty-One

I GOT UP BEFORE dawn again and went around the far side to
what I hoped was Peggy's room (I'd seen her twice late in the
day coming out of a low doorway next to it to dump a basin),
and spite of there being no window, I started calling her name
through a chink.

Finally an old lady's voice says, "What? Who?"

"Peggy," I says for about the twelfth time.

"Get the hell out of here," the voice says. "She's in back."

So I moved along the plank wall a ways and found another
chink and started in again, and after a bit, Peggy's voice says,
"Go away."

"It's me," I says. "Ezekiel."

"I know, I know, I know," she says, sounding half-asleep. "Who else could it be?"

Which meant she reckonized my voice, so that was a pretty good start (a whole lot better than the night Maud Blaines called me Herman after I done a recitation for her from half-way up a peachtree outside her window). "Will you walk out with me today?" I says.

"Will I what?" she says.

"I'm taking the hogs out rooting," I says. "And I thought you might like another stroll."

She kept still awhile, then says, "I've got chores to do."

"I'll do them for you later," I says.

She come up close to the other side of the chink, and I seen one eye peeking out at me, and I begun losing my confidence. She was younger than me, but maybe *I* was too young for *her*.

"Been selling any whiskey, Mr. Hog?" she says.

"I've been doing worse," I says, not minding the name since it was so close to true. "I've been helping make it, and that's the difference between me and just an ordinary sinner."

She switched over and looked at me with the other eye. "You're not as dumb as you act," she says.

"I never quarrel with a lady," I says.

"Well, *that's* dumb," she says. "All right, I'll meet you out front. But don't make any noise."

"I won't," I says, already running back to Casper's wagon to stuff some ship's biscuit and jerky in one of his spare bandannas and tie it up (he was rolled up asleep in his blanket next to the marsh tub that had quit bubbling) and then around to the sty to herd up my drove of four and then out around front past the store and tavern to the far end, feeling tiptoe and looking at the grand day which had clouded over some but who cared? I could see a few people stirring down at the campsite, and from this far off they looked happy and natural and friendly and neighborly and decent and honest and full of lovingkindness that the Bible keeps on and on about, so I reckoned it'd be a good idea to keep away from them so's they'd stay that way, maybe including the buckskin man.

A couple of the ash trees that hadn't been chopped down was shimmering their leaves, and one of the stumps nearby had put out a mess of shoots about the size of switches and hadn't give up entirely, and the fat man was nowhere to be seen nor even a stray lunkhead out early to start the wreckage business whiles the dew was still on the dead oxen, and there didn't look to be a pig-sticker for miles around.

In about five minutes she come out of the low doorway wearing gray bloomers and a blazer jacket to match that I hadn't laid eyes on before but in pictures, and I must of left my mouth open because she chucked me under the chin to close it.

"Am I that dreadful a sight?" she says, dabbing at her hair which she'd tied back with a ribbon.

And either I was imagining things (which I wouldn't put past me) or she had some face paint on and a little crust of red all the way round her lips, like she'd et some red raspberries and forgot to use her sleeve after. "No, indeed," I says. "I was just admiring the view."

"Let's get away from here before somebody sees us," she says. "Miz Selfridge would get in a purple snit if she saw me. But I did her a good turn last night, so at least she won't whip me. Let's go."

I was glad to see she wasn't heading uphill or down but across to a brush-filled gully where there didn't seem to be nobody camped and the hogs could enjoy theirself in peace and us likewise. "What good turn?" I says.

"Oh, what she likes best," Peggy says, giving me a quick slanty glance. "Money. And I also gave that Colonel's Lady a come-uppance, which Miz Selfridge couldn't have done in a month with an instruction manual to go by. She's no more a Colonel's Lady than I'm a—"

She either couldn't think of nothing she wasn't or else didn't want to. "What kind of money?" I says.

"Cash money, Mr. Hog," she says. "Come on. I want to show you something."

She led the way up a kind of goat path amongst the roses and brambles, something like the one we'd took that first night but on the other side, and after we'd clumb to the top, we was at the start of another gully leading down this time. It took quite a while because the hogs fancied berry leaves and green berries too, and I had to let them browse their way up to keep on their good side.

Peggy pointed. "We go down to the mouth of this one," she says. "It isn't very far."

Her bloomers was a sight to linger over, but I couldn't leave myself do it for long, not even when she was leading the way and couldn't catch me at it, because it put painful ideas in my head, and I didn't want to disappoint myself, same as you wouldn't dwell on supper if you knew all's you had waiting for you was an empty dish.

"Come on, don't dawdle," she says.

"It ain't me, it's the hogs," I says, and we hung back awhile and watched them enjoy theirself which they're mighty good at if they've got room and something worth chomping. It wasn't worth trying to root in craggly country like this, but it was a wonder for browsing.

"That Colonel's Lady," she says. "She keeps talking about pork chops and pork roast and spareribs, and Miz Selfridge too. I told them they were *your* hogs, and they both cussed me out. Miz Landseer—or whatever her real name is—she can cuss better than Miz Selfridge, and that Mr. Arthur swiped a bottle of brandy. I saw him do it. He's no more a gentleman than—" she took a look at me, but picked Colonel Woppert instead "—than that hog."

"Colonel Woppert's better off being what he is," I says. "He may not be a gentleman, but he's gentle. And he's manly. Which is more than most get to be."

"I think Miz Landseer and Mr. Arthur are imposters," she says, glancing around to make sure the hogs wasn't listening.

And there I was, up against Miz Peasemont's strapped-shut dictionary and nothing to do but grunt. If Mr. Webster had meant for his book, which I don't doubt he'd worked hard to think up, to be strapped-shut all the time, he'd of had it sewed up all four sides instead of just one and called it a door-stopper.

"I think they're out to steal things," she says.

"What things?" I says.

"Have you seen Miz Selfridge's jewels?" she says. "Sometimes she wears enough to sink a keelboat. Have you seen Mr. Selfridge's iron safe?"

"No," I says.

"He's making money hand over hand," she says. "I've never seen such a place. Don't they have any marshals out here?"

"Not so's you'd notice," I says.

"Isn't this the United States?"

"I think that left off back at the Missouri River," I says. "Somewhere along there. My pa used to say it was every man for hisself and the Devil take the hindmost."

"Well, Mr. Selfridge thinks everybody's the hindmost but him and his crows," she says. "He's going to get his comeuppance too. Maybe we *all* are."

Which left the door wide open for me to tell her about my idea, but I had a knot in my tongue and another one between my ears, and when she started down the stony slope, I couldn't do nothing but follow like she was the drover and me and the hogs just another drove on its way to market.

"I have to show you this," she says.

She was lightfooted for her size, and her pointy brown shoes didn't touch down no more than a goat in a hurry, but I had to use my staff like a crutch here and there on the crumbly limestone to keep from doing myself an injury or ripping off a boot-sole. The hogs straggled along after. Finally I says, "You already showed me something."

"What's that?" she says, not turning.

"How to start the day off right," I says.

She stopped and squinted up at me against the pale sunshine

that hadn't worked its way through the morning mist yet. "That's a pretty compliment," she says. "Been keeping that one on the tree till it was ripe?"

"I just now thought it up," I says.

"Well, think up some more, and someday you might make a halfway respectable beau," she says. "Hogs or no hogs."

"I don't want to be a beau, from what I seen of them back home," I says. "Nor respectable. And I'll likely always have hogs if they'll have *me*."

She heaved a sigh and started on down again. "You're a stubborn case," she says. "I'm glad you don't have any money."

It took me about fifty foot to figure out what she meant, and then it made feel sad and skin-tailed and careful again, just when I'd commenced getting over it.

But now she'd stopped in a little clearing where the ground had flattened out next to a caved-in overhang in the side of the gully. She was pointing at a jumble of what looked to be big gray bones, some laying flat, some sticking up out of the limestone like they'd been buried and half washed out, and some sticking out of the chalky layers of the overhang. I'd never seen the like, and when I picked up some kind of a loose legbone that could of belonged to an ox if it'd been half the size, it was as heavy as stone. In fact, it *was* stone, and it didn't make no sense at all.

She was watching me to see what I'd do or say, so I kept still so's I wouldn't make no mistakes right off, gradually forgetting what she'd said about me and maybe meant about herself. I turned over a few more strange-looking bones or stones or whatever and poked a couple more with my staff and give my jaw a scratch and waited.

Finally she couldn't stand it no more and says, "Well? What do you think?"

I picked up another that looked like a chunk of a spine. "Well, it ain't buffalo nor ox nor horse nor mule nor deer nor bear nor nothing else either," I says. "And they're all stone."

"Yes," she says, looking happy and scairt.

I thought it over some more whiles the hogs went browsing amongst the bushes nearby, and then over next to the back of the caved-in part I seen another kind of shape half-stuck in the wall, and I dug it out the rest of the way with my staff and brushed it off some and hefted it and looked it all over, and I says, "I don't know what them others might be, but I know what *this* is. It's a hog's jawbone."

"Great sweet sainted day in the morning!" she says in a whisper like a prayer and left her mouth open.

"Only it's too big, and it's made out of stone," I says. "Now why would somebody want to go and carve a hog's jawbone out of stone?" I turned it over again. "It must of took months. And then just to leave them all laying out here."

"I don't believe anybody made it," she says, using that high, far-off voice I'd heard the first night.

"Well, you don't think there's such a thing as stone hogs, do you?" I says.

"I think there used to be," she says.

I didn't want to insult her, so I just made a chucking out of the side of my mouth, and Colonel Woppert come over to see what was going on. I held the jawbone out at him, and he smelt it and took a nudge at it, but then left it be as not fit to gnaw and turned off into a bush again. I don't know what he'd of done with a real ancestor bone, but he treated this like it was no-account. "A hog this big could of hauled a wagon," I says. "Only if he was stone, he'd just stand there taking up room, like one of them statues I seen in St. Joe."

"I don't think they were stone to begin with," she says, soft and high. "I think something turned them to stone. I think this is an Enchanted Valley."

Ordinarily I'd of smiled and gone along easy with an idea like that, it being my policy not to give girls no extra offense beyond what I was always doing naturally. Once I even let Edna Otterbein tell me she had a piece of Jesus's fingerbone in a locket without cracking a smile, and whenever Helene

Rosker wasn't hawking and spitting or taking a slug of Tar Expectorant, she used to tell me about how the stars was the personal peepholes of angels and how snow was their lace nightgowns falling to earth (I never did find out how's come they wanted to rip them up and shred them around so often come wintertime).

But here I was, holding the stone jawbone of a giant hog, and the idea of an Enchanted Valley didn't seem any too strange, though Enchanted Gully might of been more like it.

"Now just sposing," I says. "Why would anybody want to turn a giant hog into stone?"

"A Sorceress might want to do anything," she says. "They might've been men before she turned them into hogs and whatever these other creatures were. It might've been a judgment."

"Then she must of et them first because there's nothing but the bones," I says, going along halfway with it because Peggy looked like she was enjoying herself and, truth to tell, it *did* seem like a dead-certain wonder, and as long as you were hav-yourself a wonder, there didn't seem nothing to bar Sorceresses. "And she must of been a mighty big eater."

Peggy's eyes widened some more and peered all around. "I think you've hit on it," she says.

"But if she was going to throw them bones away, what's the use of bothering to turn them to stone?" I says.

She'd moved off about twenty foot on the far side of some brush and was hauling at the end of what looked like a stone stump about four inches across, and when I tagged along and helped her with it, having to use my staff for a lever and coming near to breaking one or the other which ain't easy with hickory, it all of a sudden come popping loose of the clay kind of limestone it was half-stuck in, and it was a chunk of round bone about four or five foot long that tapered and done a loop like a fish-hook and come to a point.

We stood looking at it and then each other, and I think we both knew what it was right off. Ever since I'd been on the

Trail I'd heard talk about the Elephant people was going to see. Sometimes they meant California, but mostly they meant like when you was outside a circus or a tent show and the man tries to get you to pay extra to see an elephant or a wild man or something, and maybe you do and maybe you don't, but it come to mean somebody was trying to fool you. And some emigrants that'd give up and turned back would pass you by, going the other way, and tell you they'd seen the Elephant, meaning they'd had enough of this craziness and they'd come to their senses again, though most looked sadder and dumber both instead of wiser.

I'd seen them in picture books, and I think I heard one once back home when a show come to town. I couldn't go, but I heard something yelling high-pitched and long and clear from miles off like the finest hogcaller could ever of done or better. Pa said it was a lion, but I knew better. Nothing that didn't have a long nose could of made a high wail with a pure bleat all through it like that, but I wasn't counterdictory in them days, so I left him have his lion and more power to him.

I hefted this piece of a tusk (it was broke off jaggedy), and Peggy give it a lift too, and I says, "She et an elephant."

"Yes," she says, nodding and pinching her lips like that Sorceress had the right idea all right. "Yes, she did."

"And then turned the remainders to stone," I says.

"Yes."

"Why?" I says.

"I don't know," she says. "I just work here."

"Maybe she didn't like crows and didn't want to leave them nothing worth pecking at," I says.

"I wish she'd come back and start on Ash Hollow," Peggy says.

Another fifty foot down the slope, Peggy showed where there was a small spring, and we set there in the shade of the rosebushes and had some jerky and biscuits and good cold water which we was pleased to share with the hogs (I left them come and go as they wished now) and with a stream of little birds that flittered in and out of the scrubbery, some yellow and gray, some rusty and white, some black and blue, and all having a lively time.

"I like you better with your bandanna off so I can see whether you're wrinkling your forehad at me or not," Peggy says. "But is your head going to be all right? It looks like a fearful wound. And I believe you might lose some hair if it scars over." She touched it with her fingertips like it might be hot.

It'd crusted over pretty good and wasn't bleeding none or hurting much and didn't seem swole too lopsided, so I'd left it out in the air. "Well, a man's wife wanted to sew it up for me with a carpet needle, but I'd just as soon have a crease," I says. "Pa used to say I was so homely, if I'd been a girl, I'd of had to take my callers by lamplight. A *small* lamp. So I guess there's no harm done."

"Your pa doesn't know anything about women," she says.

"It runs in the family," I says. "Maybe it runs in *all* families."

"You have craggy good-looks," she says, sounding angry about something. "And don't let anybody tell you any different."

My mouth dried up, and it wasn't from the jerky and biscuit but hearing something like that which I'd never heard before, not from none of them girls back home who never done more than take a peek at me now and then and duck and giggle. "Ordinarily people don't say nothing about my looks," I says. And then it dawned on me I was getting pretty far behind in the compliments. "I think you're very beautiful and interesting to look at and not like nobody else. You've got—" I fished for the right word and caught it just in time "—dignity."

She scanned over my whole face, tracking down everything that showed, and I watched her doing it, spite of it being a scary feeling and nothing like standing up to somebody in an argument but harder.

"What are you aiming at?" she says, not smiling or troubling to look pleased or flattered. "Why did you come calling for me this morning?"

I had to get a drink of water to rench my mouth out, and four or five of them little birds cleared off and hid in the twigs, peeking at me till I was finished. "I wanted to show you how easy it would be," I says.

"It's never easy," she says, looking dead serious and a little downcast.

"I mean how easy it'd be for you and me and the hogs to light out some morning—or even earlier if there was a moon— and I could buy one of them spare wagons from Selfridge, if Casper was to pay me enough for being his whiskey boy—or maybe give me whiskey to trade—and I could get a team of mules too, and we could just light off back uphill and back to Missouri." It was coming out in a jumble, and I knew it didn't sound good.

"I've already been there," she says, like that made it no good forevermore.

"Well, then we'll find someplace better," I says. "But there's Injuns up ahead, and—"

"What makes you think it wouldn't be someplace worse?" she says. "That's what's happened every time I've moved on before."

"I'd *make* it better," I says, but it didn't sound likely, even to me, leave alone a girl in gray bloomers with a crumb of biscuit stuck in the corner of her ruby lips that was still more lilac than anything else.

"Do you know who I am?" she says.

I reckoned she meant that Daughter of a Queen story, so I says, "You already told me."

"Do you know *what* I am?" she says.

"I got a pretty good idea," I says. "You think you're one of them Soiled Doves or Crushed Roses they talk about in the newspapers, but you're not. You're just misfortunate."

She stared at me a long while and bit her lip and lost that crumb, and she made me feel terrible uneasy like out of all the fool things I could of said, I'd picked the foolishest. Finally she says, "*I* can turn men into pigs. Into stone too."

I don't know where the courage come from, but I kissed her then, mostly on the mouth but missing some because she flinched a little, not like she was trying to get away, but like she was too busy thinking.

Then she seemed to make up her mind, and I'm not going to tell what happened next, because once you tell, it changes too much and don't sound the way it was, and I don't ever want that part of the day to change wherever I might carry it in my head and my heart (I was sure I had one long before noon). Neither of us turned into hogs so's you'd notice, nor stones either, but I knew I'd changed all right, maybe me more than her, but when you're dumbstruck and confounded and goggle-eyed (even with your eyes closed), you can't keep track of everything perfeck.

We was laying down in the grass and looking at the sky full of the kind of clouds that make you want to hang names on them like "The Time the Snow Drifted Over the Fenceposts" or "Two White Sows Trying to Stand on Their Head" and doing a new kind of thinking. Least it was new for me. I felt like I'd been walking or running all my life and just this minute finally figured out you could lay down if you wanted to and let everything find *you* for a change, let it all come pouring and purring into your eyes and ears and mouth by itself instead of you chasing it and having no more luck than trying to catch up with prairie heat-shimmer and drink it. It was a scary kind of contentment I'd never felt the like of and made, me wonder if I was going to lose the little ambition I had. (No, that's not true: I had a world of ambition but just hadn't used it much yet, not having nowhere sensible to aim it.)

Yet with Peggy laying beside me in the grass on a day like that, I felt what they call spellbind, as if she'd passed some kind of a spell on me, so's I couldn't move unless she let me. I knew more or less what I was and where I was (grass in that kind of country ain't what you might be customed to in

bottom-land meadows but has more sharp corners and spikes
and burrs and cracklers in it and don't flatten out for man nor
beast without getting back at you some), but I didn't care
what I'd been or where, and there was no such a thing as being
uncomfortable, even getting gouged with rocks and scraped
with stems, and I didn't much care what I was going to be
neither or where I was headed. I had the feeling I could sprout
roots if I felt like it. Or horns or wings or grow hair all over if
I was a mind to or float in the air like thistle-puff.

It must of lasted ten minutes or more, with the whole sweet
world passing in and out of my head like it wanted to memorize me, and then Peggy spoke up and says, "Well, what are
you going to give me?"

But I was still in a spellbind and didn't feel like nothing
could budge me out of it. "Anything I got," I says.

She kept quiet for a stretch, and I thought maybe she'd
gone back to floating or sprouting too, but then she says,
"What's that?"

For a second I thought she'd heard something, and I rousted
up a bit and looked around, but there was nothing but the
hogs foraging below us a ways and some more small birds taking their turn at the spring. "I don't hear nothing," I says.

She come up to one elbow, fussing a little with the green
ribbon that was still tying her hair mostly back but had sprung
loose. "No, I mean what have you got to give me? You want
to get in practice being a gentleman, don't you?"

The spellbind was commencing to show a few cracks here
and there, but I clang onto it, not wanting to let that contentment get stirred in with anything else. "I'll practice whatever
you preach," I says and laid down again, hoping she'd do
likewise. "If you want to turn me into a gentleman, I'll give it
a try, though you might have more luck turning me into that
pig you mentioned. Or stone. I'm halfway to both, so take
your pick."

"Gentlemen give ladies presents for their favors," she says.

"Well, I got fifty cents, and you're welcome to it," I says. "It ain't burning no hole in my pocket way out here anyway." Soon as I'd said it, I knew I shouldn't of mentioned no small amount of money like that but steered her off towards a likelier subjeck instead.

She sat up straight, steaming. "How dare you flip any old coins at me, you raggedy-assed pig-pusher you!" she says. "I expected better than that."

"But it's all I got," I says, feeling the last pieces of spellbind fall off and leave me my plain old self laying on the grass and taking up too much room.

"I mean I expected better *talk*," she says. "Can't you talk?"

"Yes, ma'am," I says, hoping it was true.

Her voice went light and sad and younger, and she says, "Then tell me what it's *going* to be like. Tell me what you'd give me if you could. Flatter me. Get the lid off the butter tub and tell me something beautiful and reckless and noble."

She had me so off-balance, I didn't try setting all the way up for fear of caving over, and she'd give me such a tall order I didn't know if I could muster. I shuffled around in my head, hoping maybe something Miz Peasemont had learnt me might still be stuck there, and I stumbled across chunks of Psalms and lines of poetry and a few clumps out of the Constitution and some jingles and a stretch out of *Pilgrim's Progress*, but none of it fit right. It wasn't pretty enough and didn't suit, and she was waiting for me, and the silence was getting too long for comfort, so I just took enough breath to get going on and hoped for the best.

"I imagine us walking in the woods someplace," I says. "Green woods in June, beech and hickory and dogwood and hazel, and it's soft underfoot and the sun coming through on us like gold coins."

"Why not make them real coins while you're at it?" she says.

But I stuck to it, closing my eyes so's the sky and clouds wouldn't confuse me. "And you're beautiful and calm and

easy and hanging onto my arm and—" I choked off because I
didn't know how to bring up the subjeck of her maybe loving
me.

"What am I wearing?" she says, sounding halfway interested.

She had me stuck there because I couldn't think up nothing
for her to wear that was better than what she had on now. Or
half-on. So I took a chance and says, "A silver gown."

"Oh," she says like she'd try it for a minute and see.

And lucky for me, she didn't ask what kind of a silver gown
because I couldn't think of none but nightgowns. "And we're
both happy and feeling full of blessings and there's nothing to
be scairt of anywhere," I says.

"What're we doing walking in the woods?" she "Why aren't
we riding in a carriage or on gorgeous big racehorses?"

But I ploughed on, even though I knew I wasn't doing no
good at it. "Because we like the woods," I says.

"I suppose it's full of pigs," she says.

And truth to tell, I *had* been thinking of a drove of half-wild
hogs snouting around on the forest floor and enjoying theirself
too, but I didn't dare say so now. "And all of a sudden we
come to a clearing, and there off in the distance—"

"Is that all that happens?" she says. "Aren't you going to
fight any damn beasts or robbers or wizards? Aren't you going
to dig up any treasure for me?"

I still had my eyes closed, so I couldn't tell how much she
was joshing at me exackly, but it was more than somewhat
which at least meant she was staying mostly good humored.
"What kind of treasure have you got in mind?" I says, ready
to tell it her way to keep the peace.

"Cole Selfridge's cash and Miz Selfridge's jewels," she says
flat and cold and clear.

I come rearing bolt upright, blinking at the glare around me,
and tried to get her face straightened out, but she'd turned
half away like she was thinking about the birds still twitting
around the spring. "I don't believe I'd be very good at finding
that kind of treasure," I says.

She leaned in close to me and tried to get her eyes fixed straight into mine all of a sudden and says, "I know exactly where everything's kept and exactly how to do it. All I need is somebody with more spine to him than that Halsey."

"I'm no kind of robber," I says. "I never got practice. Nor wanted any." She had me all flushed up and half-stammering.

"I thought I saw traces of a little spine and sand in you," she says. "Maybe I was mistaken. Maybe you want to be a namby-pamby dirt-poor back-of-the-stables pig boy all your life. Wouldn't you like to own a forty-dollar worsted wool suit and a hat made out of something besides straw and get an Italian haircut and wear some fancy silk embroidered half hose and get something to hold your pants up besides galluses and put on a pair of pointy-toed dongola nullifiers instead of those clodhoppers with a busted heel and wear a linen collar?"

"I don't know," I says. "But I'd sure look a sight, wouldn't I. I'd scare off the hogs."

"You aren't going to be on this Trail forever," she says.

"I hope not," I says.

"Then why not take your big chance now and be rich when you get where you're going?" She softened her voice like she was pouring just a little vanilla in the cookie dough. "I'd be very nice to you. I'd show you all kinds of things to do and places to go, and we'd be just as happy as if we were walking in those woods you were talking about. Happier."

"I couldn't rob nobody," I says. "I'd be too embarrassed."

"You'd have a gun, don't worry about that," she says. "I know where Selfridge has a whole barrel of them."

"I believe I'll just do without," I says.

She snapped her chin away from me and scowled and give her head a shake and says, "All I ever meet are liquored-up grunts and damn lily-pads."

By that time, I was so far from being in a spellbind, I couldn't hardly bear to look at the sky I'd been drinking in earlier, and the gully was looking bleak and dingy and scrabbly and nothing enchanted about it whatsoever.

"There's nothing wrong about stealing from thieves," she says. "Why should you care?"

"I don't care enough about money and jewels to get myself and you shot for them," I says.

"You're scairt," she says.

"Scairt of you, but not much else," I says.

"Really?" She left off scowling and looked pleased and pulled her knees up and clung her arms around them. "What scares you about me?"

"I'm not sure," I says.

"Does *this* scare you?" she says. And she done something to me I can't tell about.

"Some," I says.

"Does *this* scare you?" she says. And she done something else I can't tell about neither.

"Yes," I says.

"How about *this*?" she says.

But when she tried to do something still different, I turned the tables on her and commenced doing something to her which I can't even begin to describe and won't try except to say she wasn't scairt a bit, and in a little while that spellbind was back stronger than ever and deeper and fuller of feelings I couldn't of named even if Mr. Webster hisself had come along and unstrapped his book and hunted up the right pages for me.

It was near dusk when we come back to Ash Hollow, and because no excuse of mine was going to saw any ice in Miz Selfridge's pond, Peggy made me leave her go ahead and sneak in by herself and told me she'd take care of it.

Me and the hogs watched her go on ahead, admiring, and then stood for a while amongst the junk and the stumps, admiring everything else too—ourself and the tavern and the campsite down the shallow slope. The hogs looked to be as near content as me and as tired and happy and ready to spend every day of their life over in that Enchanted Gully, stone bones or none, and if that was Seeing the Elephant, they wanted more of it and me too.

So whiles I was at it—and for joy and practice and not meaning to spoil nobody's supper nor ruin Casper's marsh—I left out a middle-size SeeeeeeeeeeuuuuuuuuuuBOY!, taking off my hat first so's I wouldn't snap it off at the end.

And I noticed the commotion down at the campsite right off because somebody commenced yelling about it. I had a full view of the three hogs trotting towards me right from the start. They was about seventy-five yards off and coming steady, spite of what they'd had to haul along with them. Ordinarily you couldn't leash a woods hog without him slipping the leash (he's got more neck than a sty hog but still not enough to count) or without him eating the rope off, but these looked to be half-starved and lean and they'd been chained, so when they Answered the Call, they each brung their chain along with them, including what it was linked around which I judged to be the back axle of a light wagon with the two wheels still on, and they come running at me and the other hogs, the wheels jouncing and bucking behind them and rolling along at hog speed, which is about as fast as a man uphill.

Before I could read their spots and figure out who they might be, I seen the moonhead come running out from between two wagons and light out after them, making some kind of barking noise, which I could of told him wasn't going to slow down no hog. He was gaining on them, holding his little hat so's it wouldn't bounce off, but then the buckskin man come jogging after and hollering and looking just like some of my nightmares of him.

Chapter Twenty-Two

I FELT KIND OF SHY facing them again without expecting to. Underneath, I'd *known* I would because I'd been going to *try* —soon as I could figure out a way to try without risking my neck and the hogs' bacon and maybe Casper's whiskey— though I hadn't known what I meant to say to them, and couldn't think up no kind of talk now.

But I held my ground, and when the hogs was still about thirty yards off and the moonhead about fifty and the buckskin man about ten behind him, the two of them seen me. The buckskin man stopped cold, and the moonhead slowed down and then stopped too when the buckskin man yelled something at him. They just stood staring whiles the three lost hogs (a half-runt hogget I'd named Uncle Fred after Uncle Fred and a sow named Honey Snout and a gilt named Bucket that had nearly died of the thumps when she was a month old) come to join the drove, chains jangling and the axle creaking.

Whiles I got their chains loose, busting a couple of finger-nails on the wires they'd used to link the collars, I kept my eyes on them two men standing down-slope of me. The buck-skin man was wearing his old tawny clothes again, and now he'd added on an ankle-deep duster unbuttoned down the front. I couldn't tell how he was getting along with his wrists, but he had the same flat hard level look aimed square at me. They both had guns in holsters but hadn't took them out yet nor made any kind of move. They was probably doing about what I was doing: trying to figure out how to be smart instead of stupid, which takes up a lot of most people's time. I wanted to talk to both of them gents—and even do a good deal worse than talk, if I could—but I had the hogs to worry about and my own skin too (which meant a lot more to me after that morning and afternoon, because what use would it be to me and Peggy if I went and got it shot full of holes?), and I knew they was both loco, least part-time.

So as soon as I'd freed the hogs and they'd had a good whuf-fling grunt-around with the other four, I started backing off, giving a touch here and there with my staff so's they'd know what to do. The buckskin man and the moonhead started talk-ing quiet now and still watching me but didn't move when I did. I aimed for around back and chucked at the hogs, and they followed along, and I kept watch on them two men I hated more than anybody else on the whole grunting earth. It was near enough for me to shout at them, but I didn't, and they didn't neither, but as soon as I passed the saggy edge of the doby store-part, I commenced running for the shed and got the hogs into the sty and the gate shut and around through the doorway where Casper was down on his hands and knees tending the little fire under his still and banking it with coals and char.

"Casper, I need help," I says.

"Me too," he says. "That marsh stopped bubbling hours ago, so I've started the first batch running." He was humming and happy, and I could tell he'd been putting down his share of the old whiskey whiles waiting for the new, though he wasn't drunk or near it.

"Can I borry your rifle?" I says.

"You'd do better to learn to spit birdshot," he says. "Go on, open up that sluice-gate about another half-inch. I want that cold water running good down here and doing its duty, and you'll be glad to hear them three helpers done your chores for you without actually busting nothing important."

"I'm in trouble," I says.

He went checking over the copper hood and the coil and rectifier and brass stop-cock and giving it all little touches to make sure the temperature was right everyplace, and I was getting my fill of the sweet, strange smell of cooking marsh but didn't have time to enjoy it or disenjoy it. "Sluice-gate," he says.

So I run up the slope and fixed it like he said and took a good scouting-around whiles I was at it, not seeing nobody but a couple lunkheads, and I run back to the edge of the store-part and looked, expecting most anything, but nobody was in sight except some strangers going into the tavern. The wheels and axle had been hauled off, and when I went out far enough to be able to see down to the campsite, I couldn't see nothing unusual. The dusk was piling up in the Hollow, and it seemed like the buckskin man and the moonhead had decided to hold off, least till they got their wagon fixed, and all of a sudden it come to me: maybe they was scairt of *me*.

If they'd kilt my ma and pa, they might be scairt I'd want to kill them. Maybe they'd sobered up and wasn't in no pig-sticking and rousty frame of mind and didn't care to be accused of hog-stealing or run afoul of Cole Selfridge who, for all they might know, I was working for.

I tried desperate hard to work it out so's I didn't have to worry too much, because it was spoiling all the joy I'd rounded up in the last hours, including the homecoming of three more of the drove that hadn't been kilt after all but was up to their hocks in hay right now, but mostly the full brand-new comfort I was feeling all through my veins and bones over Peggy.

I went back to the shed, puzzling it out, and Casper showed me a fair-sized barrel waiting under the stop-cock with its bunghole unplugged, and he give it a thump and says, "Take a whiff."

It smelt burnt, far as I could tell, but my mind was doing a good deal of wandering.

"Filled it full of straw today and burnt away all the blisters," he says, looking proud. "Not going to have *my* whiskey turning putrid."

"That man's back," I says.

He run his fingers along the nearest stretch of copper and give it a knock. "Know what it's like in there? All that copper's been planished, over and over, and the rivets burred, and the seams so tight, nothing comes or goes or gets left from last time, and ain't she a beauty far from home? Made by Benjamin Harbeson, God bless him, of Pittsburgh, Pennsylvania, and come all this godforsook way at the age of twenty-nine years, and nothing sprung open yet and not one patch on her, knock on wood." He hit the nearest plank with his knuckles. "What man?"

"The one that shot me and his boss or whatever he is," I says.

"Well, have the both of them over for a drink and let bygones be bygones," he says. "I'm busy."

I tipped my hat to one side to give my crusty patch of scalp some air because it felt throbby. "This time they both seen me," I says. "They know I'm here, and I think they're going to come get me."

"Don't get in a turmoil," he says, drawing off an inch of clear liquor in a little glass and holding it up to the reddish sky out the shed door. "If they show up, I'll have a word with the gents."

I didn't know how to get him as worried as I was, him not

having nothing extra like Peggy added on except maybe for his marsh and still. "I'll ask again to borry that rifle," I says. "Even if I can't hit nothing with it, I can put up a show."

"You'd do a whole lot better to climb up in back of the wagon and pull a blanket over your head and think about that hog farm you've got in mind—or whatever it is—and maybe those men'll just forget and forgive, and tomorrow'll be Tuesday or Friday or something, and the next thing you know, you'll still be alive," he says.

"Then I think I should get on the road with the hogs tonight," I says. "Even if I have to head back uphill. I don't care if I—" I spun and ducked and got my staff out for action because I heard somebody coming.

Casper give a jerk and spilt his sample when he wheeled around too, but Selfridge come squeezing in past the wagon, trying to keep his shirt ruffles from getting snagged on slivers. He had on a dark-gray felt stetson newly brushed and so rich-looking you could of et it with a spoon. Past him, I seen the pockmarker lingering in the yard.

"Somebody going to run off with my hogs?" Selfridge says, which was the first I'd heard out loud about him thinking he'd rustled me. "Better be a mighty good runner and have a cast-iron butt to boot." He tipped his hat back and smiled like he didn't mean no offense. "Not that I mind taking on more boarders, but where'd the three new ones come from? Keep that up, boy, and I'll have to open up a regular butcher shop."

He kept on smiling and didn't seem to expeck no answers from me, so I didn't give him none but reckoned I'd *show* him before long, instead of bothering to tell him.

"I understand you're running your first batch, Whiskey Man," Selfridge says. "Without telling me."

Casper had drawn another glass out of the stop-cock and was looking through it again. "I didn't agree to tell you nothing, not even the day of the week or the year of Our Lord," he says.

Selfridge stayed agreeable-looking. "Well, let's have a taste of it," he says.

"It's about one hour old and just starting to come through the doubler," Casper says. "Give it a chance to grow up."

"Let's have a taste anyway," Selfridge says.

"No, sir," Casper says. "It ain't fit to drink yet, and it's got to be left alone and barreled."

"Let's have a taste," Selfridge says.

"Just take a deep breath and smell what's cooking," Casper says. "If you know anything about whiskey, that'll tell you all you need to know."

Selfridge looked over his shoulder at the pockmarker, maybe just to make sure he was there, then says, "You put a cup of that in front of me right now, Whiskey Man, or I'll shoot holes in your still, and if you get in the road, I'll shoot them in you too."

It cost him a big effort, and I don't think he'd of done it for nothing but his still, but Casper handed over his glass. He looked to be steaming as much as the marsh but kept it tucked in like his neck whiskers.

"Albert?" Selfridge says after taking a careful whiff.

The pockmarker come in far enough to hand him a little paper packet, and Selfridge tore a corner off and poured a couple of pinches of black powder into the glass and set it down on the tailgate. Casper didn't look surprised nor raise a fuss when Selfridge struck a sulfur match and held it over the glass and set it afire. It burnt steady and blue, and we all stood watching it a minute till it went off with a whoof and a little cloud of gunpowdery smoke.

"Satisfied?" Casper says.

"Partly," Selfridge says, smiling again. "Always only partly." He nodded at the coil and stop-cock. "It looks good. Keep it coming."

"I'll do just exackly what I said I'd do," Casper says, turning away.

And just when I was trying to figure out how I could possibly sneak out to tend the hogs and keep an eye out for trouble with the pockmarker blocking the way, Selfridge turned his slab of a face my way and says, "You. What's your name?"

"Ezekiel," I says, keeping half for myself.

"You're wanted inside," he says.

"Who wants me?" I says, going chill and wondering if the buckskin man had come to call.

"*I* want you inside," Selfridge says. "Albert?"

"Yes, sir," the pockmarker says.

"Take him in to see Minnie."

"I need my assistant here," Casper says.

"He's just going to get a little talking to," Selfridge says. "Don't you worry. I'll get him back to you. Wouldn't want to disturb a pure batch like that."

Casper give him a long look, then glanced at me and says, "What you been up to?"

"Oh, just playing a game of shag with one of my girls is all," Selfridge says. "Nothing a little talk won't straighten out. Minnie's good at that kind of talk, isn't she, Albert?"

The pockmarker flushed dark and says, "Yes, sir."

After a few seconds Casper nodded like he meant it was all right, so I had to make up my own mind whether I felt like being scolded for what was nobody's business but mine. I'd been free of scolding for days and days now and was getting used to taking care of the blaming and danging my own self. But this was complicated. If Miz Selfridge was raising hell, I wanted to make sure Peggy didn't get punished on my account, and there wasn't no quicker way to find out than to go along and not start swinging my staff and getting people hurt, including me.

So I went. Selfridge lagged behind to talk to Casper some more, and I give the hogs a quick look-over on the way and didn't see nothing wrong with them nor any trace of trouble in the yard or bushes yet.

"Better leave that stick here," the pockmarker says. "Miz

Selfridge don't ordinarily bite, but if she sees you with that, she might think you're aiming to drive her out to that sty of yours, which is about where she belongs."

"I'll keep it, thanks," I says.

"Suit yourself," he says.

And I meant to, if I could manage.

Chapter Twenty-Three

IN THE MAIN ROOM of the tavern Miz Selfridge was setting in a platform rocker that didn't look wide enough to suit but had got into it somehow without ripping her dress nor scraping off none of the shiny fish-scales sewed all over it, and Peggy had hunched herself down on a short three-legged stool next to the wall. Miz Landseer and Mr. Arthur both switched around to stare at me when I come rumbling across the loose planks, and Mr. Arthur had his elbows up on the table where they'd been drinking something out of cups (which you ain't sposed to do with your elbows, and if Miz Peasemont had been there, she might of backed me up for a change), and the fat man, which surprised me, was wearing an apron and renching out cups in a tub over next to a pair of kegs in the corner, and *he* switched around to stare too. And the pockmarker hung in the doorway behind me to listen.

Miz Selfridge made a persimmon mouth and says, "What's all this about?"

I didn't like to peel my soul in public, and besides, I didn't know what Peggy was going to say or do, so I took off my hat (before that Mr. Arthur could butt in and tell me to) and says, "I'd like to have a word with you in private, Miz Selfridge."

"You'll have what I tell you to have," she says. "Now speak up. What've you and this biddy been up to, as if I didn't know perfectly well? And why'd you bring your damn pole in here instead of parking it outdoors?"

"Are you all right?" I says to Peggy. She had a red welt next to her eye, and she looked like she'd been bawling.

She nodded once without looking at me and snuck a glance at Miz Selfridge instead, seeming scairt.

"Never mind whether she's all right or not," Miz Selfridge says. "She'd be a whole lot more all right without the lousy likes of you sniffing her up."

"I don't have no lice," I says.

"I seen him sleeping with his hogs," the fat man says.

"Speak when you're spoke to," Miz Selfridge says.

"Yes, ma'am," he says, no doubt remembering how comfortable it was being next to them kegs, since it appeared he'd took up a new line of work.

In her high, half-singing voice, Miz Landseer says, "My husband the Colonel says you should praise your men in public but only reprimand them in private."

"If you don't want to listen, why don't you go take yourself a stroll?" Miz Selfridge says.

"I'm drinking my tea," Miz Landseer says. "And foul as it is, it is nevertheless *tea.* Am I correct, Mr. Arthur?"

"As ever," he says, watching me and letting one corner of his flat little mouth turn up.

Miz Selfridge glared at me like all the backtalk was coming from my direction. "I don't consider you hired help," she says. "And you don't earn any of its rights and privileges, including messing with my girls, night *or* day, rain *or* shine, with their half-witted help or not. As long as you're in this Hollow, you're not going to be taking any free rides in *this* wagon. Is that straight?"

"I'd still like to talk to you in private, ma'am," I says, feeling shy around all this company.

"Tell her the truth, Mr. Hunt," Peggy says. "She won't believe me."

It was a tall order, but before I could make a pass at filling it and shaming the Devil and me both, Miz Selfridge says, "Stand up, girl."

Peggy done so, scowling and her lips stuck forward.

Beckoning with her finger, Miz Selfridge says, "Come here close and bend over."

Peggy took a half-step towards the chair and bent a couple of inches, looking wary.

"Didn't I tell you to hush up?" Miz Selfridge says.

"Yes, ma'am, but —"

Miz Selfridge took a swing at her but missed when Peggy tilted her cheek back out of range, and Miz Selfridge cracked half of her ring-fingers on the chair-back. "You stand still when I'm slapping you!" Miz Selfridge says.

"You'd better not strike me any more," Peggy says nice and quiet.

"Why not?" Miz Selfridge says, looking like she never heard such a fool notion.

"I don't take kindly to it," Peggy says.

"I don't care how you take to it," Miz Selfridge says. "Just hold still. Why should I care what trash like you thinks?"

"This gentleman is going to defend my honor from now on," Peggy says, nodding at me like it was my turn to recite.

"That's right," I says, not fancying no fisticuffs with Miz Selfridge, but ready to try.

"Honor!" Miz Selfridge says, grinning. "Honor?"

Mr. Selfridge come in the door, bumping the pockmarker

out of the road, and give the planks a workout even louder
than me. "How's it going?" he says. "She eaten you down to
the cob yet?"

"No, sir," I says.

"You must not be very hungry today, Minnie," he says.
"Draw me a cup of that mobby, what's-your-name."

"Yes, sir," the fat man says.

"You mind your own affairs and leave the girls to me," Miz
Selfridge says.

The fat man spilt some of the liquor on the way over, partly
from hurry and partly from shaking. Mr. Selfridge scowled at
him whiles he let the cup drip. "Don't waste my damn
brandy," he says. "Only time it grows on trees is when it's still
peaches, and no telling when some more'll come rolling by.
You've got too big a rump to miss if you start serving my boys
like that."

"Yes, sir," the fat man says. "I mean no, sir, I won't."

In a rump contest it would of took a horse-auctioneer's
eye to pick amongst the Selfridges and Ev, but I didn't say so.

"Minnie, turn him loose and let him go back to helping at
the still," Selfridge says. "We've got us a batch of whiskey on
the way that'll bring you more trade in here than you and the
rest of them can shake a leg at, so boys will be boys and girls
will be girls and you ought to be glad, and just charge him a
dressed hog and be done with it. Matter of fact, I'll dress it
myself."

Looking mad, Miz Selfridge says, "I was getting around to
that, and now you went and spoiled it."

"Wouldn't get between you and your fun for the world,"
Selfridge says, putting down some brandy and smacking his
lips and acting all fired up and gingery. "If this keeps up,
we'll own the whole damn Territory in six months. And you
there, Peggy. Figure you're worth a hog?"

Peggy stared at the floor and didn't say nothing, and I was
going to say it for her, but Selfridge went right on, using a
great big joshing voice now.

"If you keep up the tricks, we'll have to call you Piggy from now on," he says.

The pockmarker give a snort and a haw from the doorway, and Selfridge glanced that way like he appreciated the encouragement.

"The din is becoming obnoxious in here," Miz Landseer says. "Am I correct, Mr. Arthur?"

"As ever," Mr. Arthur says, picking up his teacup and sipping at it and almost poking his eye out with his stiff little finger.

"Well, now, isn't that just too extraordinarily bad for mere words," Selfridge says, smiling kind of fishy. "Isn't that just too beastly to contemplate with our cerebrum and cerebellum. You think you're the only one that knows any words?"

"Don't speak to Miz Landseer so loudly," Mr. Arthur says. "*If* you please."

"Yes, I'm not hard of hearing, sir," Miz Landseer says. "Not *yet*. Though I expect our eardrums are being put to the test. I don't believe I have ever heard such appalling stomping and yelling and wailing and shouting and bellowing and howling and, for all I know, hog-calling—" (and she had me dead to rights there) "—as I've heard night, morning, noon, and evening since I came to this establishment. Not even drunken salvages make such a commotion."

Mr. and Miz Selfridge looked at each other a long while like they couldn't decide whose turn it was going to be first, but Mr. Arthur beat them to it.

"Exactly," he says. "Precisely."

There wasn't much light coming through the window slits and only two coal-oil lamps going in the whole wide room with its low canvas ceiling (which was probably up there to keep the leaks organized), so I couldn't follow the looks on people's faces too close, but what I seen on Miz Landseer's and Mr. Arthur's puzzled me. They acted like they wanted to pick a quarrel and seemed glad to have it fetched up fresh and didn't seem to mind putting theirself in danger of being thrown out in the evening air without no lodgings.

Miz Selfridge says, "Well, hoity-toity."

But Mr. Selfridge wasn't going to leave it go with anything sweet and teasy like that. "Just what kind of silence do you happen to be used to, Miz Landseer, darling?" he says, turning on his biggest grin. "Maybe you'd like to go outdoors and listen to the crickets all night. Or wouldn't that suit a Colonel's Lady from back East?"

"Whose gloves don't match," Miz Selfridge says as dignified as she could manage.

Mr. Arthur stood up slow, brushing at crumbs down his front where there wasn't any. "Sir," he says.

"And why don't you pay your bill while you're at it," Mr. Selfridge says. "Have they paid?"

"No," Miz Selfridge says.

"I can only conclude that you are inebriated," Miz Landseer says. "Kindly finish your drunken ravings elsewhere and leave your customers in what little peace they're able to find in your vicinity."

"Well, I'll be damned," Mr. Selfridge says.

"Undoubtedly," Miz Landseer says. "And for excellent reasons, no doubt."

Miz Selfridge tried to get out of her rocker too fast but didn't have herself leveraged enough, and when she tried a second time, something commenced ripping. She was aiming to cuss at Miz Landseer but was wasting too much of it on the chair and not doing a good job on neither.

So Mr. Selfridge took over and says, "Clear off out of here, both of you deadbeat bilkers. You're spoiling my dinner which I haven't even started enjoying yet."

"I will not allow you to speak to Miz Landseer that way," Mr. Arthur says. He leant over the table and tried to take a swat at Mr. Selfridge with his gloves but couldn't reach far enough. "I demand satisfaction."

"I've heard it highly spoken of," Mr. Selfridge says. "Just you both run along now and find it where you can. You'll get no more food and drink under my roof."

A couple of lunkheads, including the small man who I hadn't

seen for more than a day, come through the doorway either to see the show or looking for their share of brandy at sundown or both, and Selfridge nodded at them like he was glad to think about something else for a change.

Settling back in her chair like she didn't want to do her dress no more injury, Miz Selfridge says, "Cole, you've been challenged to a *duel.*" She looked real pleased and interested and flattered.

"Don't be silly," he says. "I don't fight duels."

"You are no gentleman, sir," Mr. Arthur says.

"You're damned right I'm not," Mr. Selfridge says. "And neither are you. And if you go pulling that little parlor gun on me, I'll stick it someplace you'd have a hard time reaching."

"Choose your weapon, sir," Mr. Arthur says.

Looking like he was tired of it all, Mr. Selfridge jerked his head at the pockmarker and says, "Albert?"

But the pockmarker stayed where he was by the door like he'd turned deaf, and Miz Selfridge says, "We've got that whole box of swords in the storeroom."

"Never mind the swords," Mr. Selfridge says. Then he raised his voice. "Albert!"

The pockmarker still didn't move, and Miz Landseer says, "I've mentioned this bellowing before. It's unwholesome and probably damages your throat tissues nearly as much as that poisonous alcohol you keep swilling in the presence of a lady. The presence of *one* lady," she added, pointing her nose a little bit away from Miz Selfridge and Peggy (who was drinking all this in like me without taking no part).

Selfridge seemed to forget about the pockmarker for a minute and turned back to Miz Landseer, squinting at her like she was getting hard to see. "Madam," he says. "How would you like that abusive tongue of yours removed and divided into two portions and stuck in your earholes for you? That'd give you a little peace and quiet and us too."

"If you won't name your weapons, I'll name them for you," Mr. Arthur says.

"Or we've got that whole heap of flintlock pistols," Miz Selfridge says.

"Hush up," Mr. Selfridge says, putting his hands on his thick hips and staring straight at Mr. Arthur "All right. Let's use fists."

It would of took two Mr. Arthurs, maybe two and a half, to stack up to Selfridge's size and wouldn't of been no contest but a one-puncher.

"Fists are not a gentleman's weapon," Mr. Arthur says. "Swords will be perfectly satisfactory. Are they rapiers or cutlasses?"

"Only sharp on one side," Miz Selfridge says, sounding like she hoped that didn't spoil them none.

"I used to be a butcher," Selfridge says. "And I—"

"Cole!" Miz Selfridge says, acting shocked and shamed.

Louder, he says, "I used to be a butcher and proud of it, and if you want to put me to a sweet temptation like that, I'll have you upside down in a smokehouse by tomorrow morning, getting a little flavor in the both of you. Now git!" Without looking over his shoulder, he says, "Albert, you'd better come when you're called and show these people how to git, or I'll have to start teaching you how to git yourself."

But the pockmarker kept on standing where he was, half in shadow. He'd took his back off the wall but hadn't moved no more than that, and then three more men come through the doorway, and one of them was a Selfridge wagon-wrecker whose name I didn't know, and the other two was the moonhead and the buckskin man.

Over at the table Miz Landseer lit up and smiled and give a wave of her glove. "Oh, here's the Colonel at last, back safe and sound. Stull dear, please come and reason with this dreadful man. He's being loathsome, and I'm afraid you'll have to chastise him."

Chapter Twenty-Four

AND IT BEGUN to look like I wasn't going to get a chance to ask Peggy if she'd marry me and make an honest woman out of her, which was what I'd been planning on doing if I could of stuck a word in with a bradawl someplace amongst all this talk. Instead, it seemed more like I'd ought to bust right out through the wall of the tavern, spite of it being shored up outside, and get my hogs on the road.

But when the buckskin man come up closer, he didn't give me much more than a glance and a twitch of his sandy-colored mustache. He still had on his long duster, wearing it like a cloak, and now he took off his flat-brimmed sombrero and shook his long straight hair (it most touched his shoulders) like he was getting the dust out of it and held his hand up to his chest and give a little bow around generally, saving Mr. Selfridge for last. He had some kind of leather straps around both wrists but no sticks or splints or bandages, and all his fingers looked to be moving when he took a primp at his mustache and shifted his duster to one shoulder so's he could flick the fringe of his buckskin jacket.

I'd hated him so hard, it seemed like I'd come out the other side of it and was looking back now to see what I'd been tearing chunks out of to get through, and I had to admit it was *different* being around him. He smelt of burnt gunpowder (or was my nose just trying to turn him into a devil?), but it wasn't only that: something terrible seemed like it was always about to happen around him, and *did*, but you got the feeling it could of been worse and *would* be if you'd just wait a minute. If I'd hit him on the head the other evening instead of the wrists and he'd acted like he done, I'd of thought he was forever having something like my kind of Ecstasy. So I felt half-kin to him, and it shamed me and dumfoundered me and kept me from doing my damnedest around him.

I felt cold being near him. And he was near enough for me to have another go with my staff, even if I got shot for it by the moonhead who'd stayed with the lunkheads in a cluster over by the door, but I didn't do it.

Mr. Selfridge looked sort of embarrassed, what with the buckskin man being armed and taller than him and sposed to be a Colonel and all, but he took an extra breath or two and says, "I run an orderly house here. Let's keep it that way."

"You run a *dis*orderly house," Miz Landseer says.

Using that drawly back-East voice I remembered and hated, the buckskin man says, "My name is Egmont Fitzhenry Stapleton, Lieutenant-Colonel, United States Cavalry, sir. Is there some difficulty here?"

"You'd ought to tell your wife to get her name straight," Miz Selfridge says, settling back in her chair like she meant to enjoy some more arguing. "She says she's Miz Landseer."

"My wife and I frequently travel incognito," the buckskin

man says, calm and dignified. "It helps confuse the salvages
and their scouts and other lawless riffraff who have excellent
reason to worry over our whereabouts. You needn't trouble
your mind, dear."

"Don't call my wife *dear*," Mr. Selfridge says.

The buckskin man didn't pay him no mind but looked over
at Miz Landseer and Mr. Arthur and says, "Is everything in
order?"

They both nodded, and Mr. Arthur says, "Yes, sir."

"If you're a Colonel, where's your damn uniform?" Mr.
Selfridge says, turning his voice hard and clear and getting his
belly behind it.

The buckskin man swung around slow and give him an in-
spection, looking vexed. "Are you trying to deafen me, sir?"
he says.

"Oh, Jesus, another one," Selfridge says. "Albert? Williams?
I think we're going to have to have a little removal party here.
I'm tired of these three people. Run them down the road a
ways and take their guns and boots off them and let them go
spoil somebody else's dinner."

But none of the lunkheads moved except the small man
who took out his long gun and cradled it in the crook of his
elbow, acting casual.

"I have some bad news for you, Mr. Selfridge," the buckskin
man says.

"Save it for the coyotes," Mr. Selfridge says, resting his big
hand on his sixgun. "Albert, damn you, do as you're told."

"The United States Cavalry is taking over all this land by
right of waterhole and these structures for housing and pro-
visioning," the buckskin man says. "As Commanding Officer
of the Territorial Pacifiers, I hereby declare this government
property in the name of President Fillmore, may he soon rest
in peace."

"The United States Calvary had better show me a piece of
paper saying so first," Selfridge says. "And I tell you what I'll
do: I'll take that piece of paper and stuff it down the nearest
lieutenant-colonel's throat."

Aiming it towards the doorway, the buckskin man says, "Is everything in order?"

"Yes, sir," the moonhead says.

"Very well, you may proceed," the buckskin man says.

But instead of the moonhead doing something, the pock-marker slipped out the door, and the rest of them stood where they was.

"What in the hell is going on?" Selfridge says, looking worried for the first time and leaving his hand on his gun.

I seen the fat man get around behind the brandy kegs and crouch a little, but he was bigger than both of them and stuck out on both sides of their rack.

In a sweet proper voice, Miz Landseer says, "The jewels are in a strong-box under Miz Selfridge's bed in the northwest corner of this building, and the cash is in a floor safe in the office directly behind the general store, and the keys are both on their respective persons: the one in what I shall dignify with the name of *bosom* and the other in the fob pocket."

"Thank you, dear," the buckskin man says. "You are a pearl among swine. And thank you too, Mr. Snyder."

"Not at all, sir," Mr. Arthur says.

Selfridge was standing dead still now, his eyes flicking this way and that and his brains trying to work, and it seemed like as good a time as any (since it appeared like there was going to be gunfire before long), so I says, "Where's my ma and pa?"

Spite of him keeping a close watch on Selfridge, the buckskin man spared me a glance and another half-twitch of his mustache which must of been all he could muster for a smile. "Why, they've gone on the Glory Road," he says. "Do you know what that is, my child?"

I had a fair idea, but before I could say anything back, Selfridge says, "You get your wife and friends out of here right now, and there won't be any trouble. I'll even wipe their slate clean for board and room. But if there's any more foolish talk about jewels and cash, everybody here's going to get a good look at the bottom of your boots while you're dying in them."

He made a pretty fair job of sounding sure of hisself, but I seen the sweat commencing to run into his eyebrows and knew better. What I didn't know was how to get me and Peggy out of the line of fire because I couldn't tell for sure how many lines there was apt to be, except they'd all probably be coming Mr. Selfridge's way.

"There are going to be revolutionary changes here," the buckskin man says. "And you're going to do most of the revolving, Mr. Selfridge. You may even turn over in your grave if you see fit."

"Thomas, go get that box of swords," Miz Selfridge says, but none of the lunkheads moved.

"Swords?" the buckskin man says. "What swords?"

"I challenged the proprietor to a duel, and his missus wanted us to try some old swords," Mr. Arthur says—or Mr. Snyder or whoever he was. "But he refused to accept."

"Excellent idea," the buckskin man says. "You must get over your timidity, Mr. Selfridge. A man of your bulk. You'd scarcely feel a sword unless by some lucky chance it encountered one of those tiny organs you must have squeezed in there somewhere. Fetch the swords." One of the lunkheads jumped out the door like a dog turned loose. "You'll have to pardon a certain solemnity in my manner, Mr. Selfridge, but they say a teacher should be sparing of his smile. And I'm going to be your teacher. I'm going to show you how to run this place properly. For instance, you haven't been charging the emigrants for their water." The buckskin man shook his head. "A shameful omission."

"You'll pay for every minute of this," Mr. Selfridge says, glancing around for help and not finding none but Miz Selfridge setting wedged in the rocker with her mouth open like Elias Stokes's old granny back home that they'd used to put on the back porch on good days to air her out.

"Why, I'm not going to pay you anything," the buckskin man says. "Except maybe my compliments for the fair extent of your greed. But times are changing, and a man of vision is called for, and I'm the man."

He didn't seem drunk like he had on the night of the pig-sticking, but there was something strange and stiff about him like he was hanging on hard in a high wind and apt to fly loose.

"I'll see you in Hell," Mr. Selfridge says, quiet and clear, but not looking like no Merry Old Soul at the moment.

"Not if I see you first," the buckskin man says. "And besides, you needn't wait that long. Take a good look now."

Miz Landseer giggled and had to put her teacup down for fear of spilling it, and two muffled shots come from out front of the tavern, then three more, louder. Mr. Selfridge jerked his head that way, listening, and tightened his hand on his gun but didn't draw. The sweat was getting in his eyes now.

"You were born before your time but not long enough before," the buckskin man says. "And now you will kindly oblige us by dying before it, which is a pretty pattern, especially for a former butcher."

Mr. Selfridge yanked at his gun then but didn't have it all the way out before the small man shot him from the other side of the room, knocking him over backwards, and then shot him again before he had time to hit the floor. Miz Selfridge had reared forward screaming and half-crouched with the rocker stuck to her and her dress ripped, and she was clawing at a little purse and trying to get what looked to be a little nickel-plated Derringer out of it but had snagged it somehow. Mr. Arthur, holding it out at arm's length to aim, shot her with a small pistol, and she tipped over sideways with a thump, chair and all, and Mr. Arthur excused hisself to Miz Landseer and come around the table and leant over Miz Selfridge and shot her once more in the side of the head for good luck.

In the middle of it all, Peggy had dove down flat against the edge of the wall, head turned away and not looking, and I hadn't even had a chance to flop on top of her, and the fat man was on his hands and knees now behind the keg rack with his hands over his ears, and the Selfridges was both letting out a good deal of blood and not budging nor showing any other sign they might miss it.

The buckskin man, who'd stood quiet and calm through it all, turned and took a step towards me whiles the smoke was still spreading and yanked the staff out of my hand before I could whack him with the end of it. I made a snatch to get it back, but Mr. Arthur was looking right at me with his pistol in good working order and the small man on the other side of the room where I couldn't see him good, so I held off, not wanting to join the folks on the floor except maybe if it was to be laying next to Peggy, sleeping this bad dream away.

The moonhead come over, grinning at me and rubbing his stubbly jawbone, and he located a couple places on the floor where he could kneel without getting blood on his pants and begun digging in Mr. Selfridge's front pockets. He fished out a key and handed it to the buckskin man, then went to work on the front of Miz Selfridge's dress. In about two seconds he come up with a key on a string and a tight roll of greenbacks, which he give to the buckskin man.

"Congratulations, dear," Miz Landseer says.

The buckskin man tossed the key on the string at her, and she caught it like a hound dog catching a piece of fat. Then he peeled the roll of greenbacks open, riffled them, handed them back to the moonhead, then tipped his chin at the lunkheads still clumped up at the doorway (a couple more had joined in, including the pockmarker), and says, "Equal shares."

They all had a good crow over that, and whiles the moonhead was doling it out, Mr. Arthur knelt down beside Miz Selfridge like he was going to give her smelling salts but commenced peeling off her rings instead, having to wrench most of them three or four times before they come loose. Then he plucked all the rings off of Mr. Selfridge, and when he'd got the whole crop, he brung them over to Miz Landseer in his cupped hands and laid them next to her plate like a heap of dewy grapes. But instead of eating them, she swept them off the edge of the table into her draw-neck purse.

The buckskin man says, "Clayton, Lassiter, Nye, and Boggs for burial detail, and what's in the kegs?"

"Peach brandy, sir," the fat man says in a high voice from down behind it.

"And brandy for all," the buckskin man says.

They give another hooraw over that.

"How many dead outside?" the buckskin man says.

"Three, sir," the pockmarker says.

"Is that all?"

"The rest all wanted in with us, sir," the pockmarker says.

Four of the lunkheads begun carrying the Selfridges off, having to take the platform rocker after they tried to wedge Miz Selfridge out of it and couldn't, and the buckskin man says, "Albert, a couple buckets of water here to wash down the planks. We'll keep a tidy messroom, please."

"Yes, sir," the pockmarker says and went out.

The buckskin man took his duster off all the way and handed it to Mr. Arthur and did a couple stiff-legged struts, using my staff like some kind of walking-stick (which I hated to see but couldn't do nothing about), and says, "And now that we've settled that score, let us consider a slightly older score, lest we be accused of carrying fire in one hand and water in another." He spun and looked straight at me and didn't pay no attention to the lunkheads passing him by on the way to the brandy kegs where the fat man was up on his feet and commencing to do business. "My child, no man is a hypocrite in his pleasures, so you see before you a plain truthspeaker: I'm enjoying this, and I'm *going* to enjoy this. What would you suggest we do to you first, piggy boy?"

Chapter Twenty-Five

I WATCHED THE SELFRIDGES heading out the door, ladies first, with a lunkhead at each end, and wished them well at their new line of work which would be mostly turning theirself into bones, and I wondered if maybe that Sorceress had commenced operating on Ash Hollow, the way Peggy'd hoped, and if we was all going into the bone business directly. I couldn't catch Peggy's eye because she had them both shut, though she hadn't fainted: I could see her fists clenching and unclenching. There wasn't no advice available, so what I done was try to imagine myself looking back on this minute years later (sposing there was going to be any years to speak of) and calculating what I'd most of wanted me to do, and I had the

250

answer right off: speak up, speak your mind, be yourself, talk back, don't give up. It sounded too hard to do, so I checked with myself again, years off from now, and it still turned out the same, like it or not.

So I says, "My name's Ezekiel Amalgamated Hunt—" the middle part wasn't real, but I had to stretch it out to show the buckskin man he wasn't the only bucket with three handles "—and you, sir, ain't fit to be left walking around. You helped kill my hogs and run off the rest and maybe kill my ma and pa —if you'd ever tell the truth—and wreck our wagon, and I mean to have your hide for it. Hung on a stick to dry." I added on the last part in case he'd think I just meant to give him a licking.

Everybody had hushed up to listen, though the brandy spigot kept on going without hardly being turned off, and Miz Landseer poured herself another cup of tea.

The buckskin man looked half-amused, though he had a hard face to read, his mouth being mostly haired over. "That is a pitifully inadequate list of my sins, my child," he says. "You ought to be able to do better than that. Or should I demonstrate?"

"If you want to confess, go to it," I says. "All I know is what you done to me and mine or tried to."

In a soft, quiet drawl he says, "It was bad enough injuring my person—that in itself is a capital offense—but you killed my best friend, my only friend."

"Oh, mercy sakes," Miz Landseer says. "Is *he* the one?"

"Be quiet," the buckskin man says.

And I remembered the kid too. "I never touched him nor did nothing to him," I says. "*He* shot at *me*."

With a choke in his voice now, the buckskin man says, "He was buried with full military honors. With a broken neck. Do you know what happens to a man with a broken neck?"

"Same thing that happens to a hog with a pole stuck through it, I expeck," I says.

"Do you know the meaning of full military honors?"

"No, sir," I says. "I seen soldiers from time to time, but they was mostly drunk like you."

The whole room had hushed completely now, and the buckskin man kept still for a bit like he was still listening to what I'd said. "Do you know what it means to be buried?" he says.

"No, sir, but I reckon I'll find out," I says.

Miz Landseer piped up and says, "If I might make a suggestion—"

"Silence!" the buckskin man says, and I seen she wasn't any too pleased. He kept his glinty, deep-set eyes on me. "Do you know what I feel towards you?" he says.

I nodded and says, "I got a fair idea." And I did too, but it didn't daunt me none. I was already about as daunted as I could be, and it was a good deal less than I'd of sposed. Peggy had sat up and was gawping at the two of us, mostly at me, and it must of helped spruce me.

"I consider you loathsome trash," he says.

"Then you'd best leave me alone," I says. "Or put on your gloves and your old clothes."

"No, I intend to make an example out of you," he says. "For the benefit of all future piggy boys. I intend to make a horrible example of you."

"I already beat you to it," I says. Out of the corner of my eye I seen the pockmarker come into the room with two buckets of water and stop still, trying to figure out what was going on. The buckskin man motioned to him to slop it on the blood, and I shifted out of the road whiles he done so, but didn't wind up no nearer the door and didn't feel like running anyways. "Mr. Arthur or Mr. Snyder," I says. "Would you mind loaning me them gloves of yours?"

"I most certainly would mind," he says.

"Then does it count just as good if I slap him barehanded?" I says.

"Do you believe in a God of Wrath?" the buckskin man says.

"It's enough trouble believing in a God of Peace," I says. "But I'm willing to learn."

"All you need to do is believe in *me*," he says, leaning in close and showing me how he could lift his mustache up off of his upper teeth which was set fair and square in his jaw like lavatory tiles in a St. Joe hotel.

"I believe in you all right," I says. "I see you."

"But if the organs of perception were cleansed, we should all see the world as it is: an abomination. Help me to reveal it." He was talking in a soft, joshy way now, like he wanted me to do an easy little chore for him. "Die for me," he says.

"I think I'll herd swine instead," I says.

"Do you realize how close you are to meeting your Maker?" the buckskin man says. "Don't waste your final minutes with tiresome frivolities and obscenities. Slap me? Do you really suppose I'd allow you to slap me?"

"I challenge you to a duel to the death as a mortal stink in the nose of God, so name your weepons and let's get going," I says. I glanced at Mr. Arthur. "Did I do it right?"

He didn't say nothing but kept watching the buckskin man like he expected something might bust, and Miz Landseer chuckled and tinkled her spoon against her cup.

After keeping still a few seconds, the buckskin man says, "Am I never going to hear the last of your lip?" But before I could tell him he was likely to hear a good deal more, he turned to the fat man and says, "Is that brandy any good?"

"Well, it's *strong*, sir," the fat man says.

"Any whiskey?"

"Yes, sir, Mr. Selfridge had a special keg here nobody was allowed to touch, and it's the finest Kentucky bourbon whiskey I ever tasted in all my life," the fat man says.

"Find a clean cup and pour me some."

Whiles the fat man scrambled around to the tub to rench out a cup, I says, "You're a coward if you won't fight me."

"You don't have any honor to defend, piggy boy," the buckskin man says. He thumped my staff on the floorboards. "What we ought to do is strip you and grease you and see how long you take to catch."

A couple of the lunkheads got a hawhaw out of that, and the fat man handed him a cup of Casper's whiskey which he took a whiff of and raised his sandy eyebrows, then sipped at and shut his eyes and opened them wide and poured the whole cup down in a string of gulps. He held his mouth open and let out a breath and snapped his teeth shut like he was biting something and says, "In the Name of the Father and the Son and the Holy Spirit and all their livestock, *where* did this come from?"

"From the whiskey man out back right now," the fat man says. "Selfridge made him set up a still."

"Has he got any more of this?" the buckskin man says, handing over his cup for another.

"Yes, sir, lots more, and he's running another batch too," the fat man says.

Turning to the pockmarker who was getting hisself some brandy, the buckskin man says, "Bring him in here and his whiskey along with him. All of it."

The pockmarker hesitated. "That's apt to take some doing," he says. "He doesn't like doing what he's told."

"Apparently you don't either, mister," the buckskin man says. "I've explained the nature of my orders several times before in your hearing. Do I have to do it again?"

Acting quiet and patient and careful, the pockmarker says, "Do I have leave to shoot him or knock him out? He isn't likely to come any other way, and he takes his whiskey serious. He knocked out Andrews and Cliff here with one punch each a few days ago. I just wanted to make the problem good and clear before I started working on it."

"I suppose it was too much to expect diplomacy from the ranks," the buckskin man says. "Send him the compliments of Lieutenant-Colonel Alexander Vanvoorhis Singletree, and would he do me the honor of joining me in a light supper."

The pockmarker shrugged and started out the doorway, taking his brandy with him, and the small man followed along when he give him a sign.

I didn't like the idea of Casper getting in a fight without me there to help, but it seemed like there was too much going on for me to keep track of.

Hollering after them, the buckskin man says, "And don't injure him. The man's a genius." He tossed down a second cupful the fat man had handed him, a little slower this time, and shook his head over it and exercised his face and jaw some more.

"Now, dear, be careful," Miz Landseer says. "You know how it disturbs you. You mustn't poison your tissues."

The buckskin man ignored her and handed his cup to the fat man again, and then (making me turn cold) he fixed his eyes on Peggy like he was seeing her for the first time. He give her a little touch on the shoe with my staff and says, "And what kind of a piece might you be?"

She pulled her foot back but stayed setting on the floor. "A gentleman should not address a lady—even one much younger than he—without being properly introduced," she says.

He seemed to enjoy that. "Why, I've introduced myself to one and all here," he says. "I've introduced myself into every fiber of this establishment and made it my very own, including you and your undoubtedly inadequate services, and the other doxies too—where are they, by the way?"

"In their room with the door nailed shut," the moonhead says. "Didn't want them getting in the road."

"I'm the daughter of a Queen," Peggy says, but she didn't sound like she meant it a whole lot.

The buckskin man only took down half his cup this time and swished some around in this mouth before swallering. "Well, let's have a look at your royal birthmark then."

"Leave her alone," I says.

"Be quiet, piggy boy," he says. "When I sentence you to

death in a little while, then you may have leave to speak your
last words. But not now. I would suggest silent prayer. All
things, whatsoever ye ask in prayer, believing, ye shall receive. Except your life. Don't get your hopes up about that."
He turned back to Peggy. "Stand up."

Whiles she was getting on her feet, I got between him and
her and says, "You're going to leave her alone, coward. Liar.
Murderer." I kept my voice low and calm so's it'd be more
convincing. "Or I'll kill you barehanded."

He almost smiled, crinkling up his eyes and pulling his chin
in. "Oh, is that what you've been doing?" he says. "Getting
this little sow in farrow? I'd hardly have thought a shoat like
you would be up to it yet."

I took the insults for both of us without moving, since I
didn't want to give my life over some words. "You heard
me," I says. "I mean it."

"Zeke, damn you for a fool, get out of the way and keep
still or you'll get us both killed," Peggy says. "I don't need
the likes of you defending my purity and chastity which I
don't happen to have. Go sit down and keep your mouth
shut." She shoved me out of the way and says to the buckskin man, "Now which birthmark did you want to see, soldier
boy? The red one or the blue one?"

"How about the pink one?" he says.

"Stull, you behave yourself," Miz Landseer says mildly.

If one of the lunkheads hadn't come in carrying a three-foot
wooden box with a busted lid and spilt half the swords out of
it when his boot caught between two wobbly planks, I might
of made a Fool for Love out of myself and got shot, but the
buckskin man took time off from messing with Peggy's collar
to look through the swords.

He swept one back and forth till it whistled (never letting
go of my staff because I watched close in case I could grab
it) and says, "My wrist may still be a shade weak, but—"
he made a couple more jerks and jabs "—but has my right
hand lost its cunning?"

"No, sir," Mr. Arthur says.

Having the sword seemed to work him all up like a preacher when it's getting late at camp meeting, and he climbed up on a chair and then up on the table where Miz Landseer and Mr. Arthur was still setting, and he pulled the chair up after him and set it on the table and jammed the point of the sword into the wood hard enough so's it stuck upright, swaying back and forth, and set hisself down with a thump, kicking a spare teacup out of the way and says, "Barkeep, once more into the breach."

The fat man brung him another cupful whiles he kept thudding the tabletop with the butt of my staff and saying, "Oyez! Oyez! Oyez! Oyez! Oyez!"

At first I thought he was calling hogs and not doing no good at it, but as soon as the boys had quieted down, he says, "The court will come to order, Territorial Pacifiers' Tribunal, Year of Our Lord 1852, trial of Ezekiel Amalgamated Hunt, crimes of assault with a deadly weapon, to wit, one hickory staff ordinarily used to prod hogs, defamation of character, talking back, refusing to obey a direct order from a superior officer, being out of uniform, horse theft, accessory to murder of the most—" he left off and took a pull on his whiskey cup "—let's just say *murder*, disturbing the peace, befouling the highways and waterways with pig dung to the immediate danger of the public health, causing the wreckage of the rear axle of a new wagon worth sixty dollars, cohabiting with a minor to the disgrace of public morality, uttering threats to life and limb of a Territorial officer, and interfering with the orderly extermination of the stinking salvages of the Sioux Nation in the valley of the North Platte, and being unre*pentant*!" He took a deep breath and a sip of whiskey, and there was some mumbling and chuckling amongst the lunkheads, who didn't look any too sure what was going on, which put them just about even with me.

"How does the prisoner plead?" the buckskin man says.

"Any way but on my knees," I says. At least he wasn't doing nothing to Peggy yet, so I didn't mind too much.

"My child," he says, touching the sword hilt so's it went

bobbing back and forth harder. "Didn't you come from God-fearing people?"

"Yes, and they had good cause to be feared of Him," I says. "And I reckon you do too."

"I have passed beyond such ordinary judgments," he says. "But *you* must consider them. The road left to you is short, very short. And it leads to Doom. Do you know what Doom is? Doom without hope of promotion?"

"I'll take my Doom from higher up the ladder, if it's all the same to you," I says. Miz Landseer didn't look worried, but Mr. Arthur had commenced sweating, and some of the lunkheads looked like they was uneasy at all this talk. Usually by this time they had the fiddler going and the ladies out and begun the singing and stomping.

"I don't mean to beat a cripple with his own crutches," he says, giving me a jab with the end of my staff but getting it back before I could grab it. "Therefore, I'll simply pronounce you guilty as charged and declare your property, including all pigs, confiscated by the Territorial Pacifiers and sentence you to death by sticking, which is the way it should have been in the first place, is now and ever shall be. But first I'm going to grant your dying wish and marry you to this little sow here so she can get in some early practice being a widow." He turned to Peggy. "What's your name child?"

"Amelia McReedy Langford," she says politely, not even hesitating a second.

"It's Peggy something," Miz Landseer says. "And she's a twit and a snippet."

"Well, then, we'll have to twit her and snip her later on," the buckskin man says. "But right now she's going to get married, like it or not."

"I don't believe I've heard anybody propose yet," Peggy says, staying calm, which seemed like a good idea. "Isn't that customary?"

The buckskin man took another pull on his whiskey and squinted at me. "Go on, propose, piggy boy. Man proposes and God disposes."

I give her a look and she didn't seem half as embarrassed as me. I hated for us to be mocked at, but it was still better than lots of other things that could of been happening, so I braced myself and says, "I don't mind asking a question like that. I might of asked it anyway. Will you marry me?"

"I might someday," she says offhanded.

But the buckskin man didn't like that. "Say yes, little sow," he says. "Or I'll turn all my men loose on a game of Up Smocks All."

She shrugged, not acting scairt. "All right," she says. "Yes."

Which was a dreadful way to hear it but maybe better than nothing or never.

The buckskin man raised my staff, and it went right through the canvas ceiling and through whatever was past that and probably up into the night air where I wished I was with me and mine instead of here listening to the buckskin man saying, "Dearly beloved, we are gathered together here in the hindsight and foresight and rotten eyesight of God, and in the dirty face of this company, to join together this piggy boy and this little sow in Holy Patrimony, irreverently, indiscreetly, inadvisedly, drunkenly, and if any man can show why they may not unlawfully be joined together pig-fashion, let him now speak and I'll lay him out cold."

Nobody said nothing, though I thought of plenty, and the buckskin man raised his voice like he was trying to auction off a heifer before anybody got a good look at it, staring blurry but straight at me, and says, "Wilt thou have this sow to thy wedded sty and hate her and dishonor her and leave her sick and forsake all hope as long as ye both shall live?"

"I won't do no such a thing," I says.

"Likewise, I'm sure," Peggy says.

"To have and be stuck with from this day forward, for worse, for poorer, in sickness, to hate till death do you part which won't be long now," he says. "Who's got a ring? *Two* rings. I want a ring for each of their noses. Better yet, two links of a chain so they can see eye to eye." He leant sideways at Miz Landseer. "Give me some of your rings, dear."

"I will not," she says.

Whiles the buckskin man polished off his cup of whiskey, I whispered to Peggy, "Don't worry."

She smiled a little shaky. "I'm the daughter of a Queen," she says.

Going up to full pitch, the buckskin man says, "Therefore, by the powers invented by me, I mispronounce you piggy boy and sowlet. You may do anything to the bride you please. That's your dying wish." He sank back and give the sword a twang and seemed to be waiting, and when I didn't do nothing but stand there and hold Peggy's hand and wonder if the wall would cave out if I took a dive at it with her, he says, "Well, get to work, let's see some action, it's your wedding night."

"Much obliged to you," I says, taking a step backwards. "We'll just be going on our way then." I nodded all around, trying to imagine how it'd be to give a party. "Drink up and enjoy yourself."

"Hold it right there," the buckskin man says. "Prisoners come and go only at my pleasure, and right now my pleasure is to see you both disrobe and consummate your marriage. I want you to try making a silk purse out of this sow's ear, for the benefit of all these hard-working soldiers of fortune."

The pockmarker come through the doorway, rolling a whiskey keg ahead of him with his foot and carrying the small man over his shoulder like a sack of oats. His hat was gone, and his nose looked like it'd come up against the butt end of something in too much of a hurry, and he dumped the small man down on the floor planks and took a deep breath, looking disgusted and having to snort and spit blood.

"Report," the buckskin man says, trying to shift into his colonel's voice. "Scouts' Special Detail, report."

"I think Tom's jaw's busted," the pockmarker says. "And I know damn well his gun's busted and maybe my nose too. The whiskey man says he's too busy and didn't feel like coming, but he sent a keg of whiskey to keep the peace."

Sounding halfway sober, the buckskin man says, "I said I wanted *all* the whiskey."

"Well, I'll tell you where it's located at if you want it," the pockmarker says, blowing his nose and giving it a touch like it might be going to fall off.

"How much is there?" the buckskin man says. He clumb down out of his chair, using my staff for a prop and yanking the sword out after he'd made it to the floor without falling down.

The pockmarker shrugged. "Five more kegs, I think, and some kind of a cask," he says.

Swishing the sword around and making Mr. Arthur duck back, the buckskin man says, "Then go ahead and tap that one for the men."

There was a big rouse over that, and I seen two or three lunkheads spill their brandy out and get set.

"I see we're going to have to press this whiskey man into the Territorial Pacifiers," the buckskin man says. "We'll make him a supply sergeant and official sutler in charge of stills."

The fat man rolled the keg over into the drinking corner and went to work wrenching the spigot out of the upended brandy keg. It didn't seem like Casper to give up any of his whiskey without being shown Death's Door swang wide open, but there it was, the fat man tapping it with a mallet and bunging the spigot into its new home and the lunkheads lining up to get theirs, including Mr. Arthur with two teacups and the moon-head with his rancher's hat about to fall off sideways and a tin can ready for business. Miz Landseer kept setting at the table like this didn't have nothing to do with her and she was actually off someplace else listening to a band concert in a park.

"Averill," the buckskin man says.

Looking like he didn't want to lose his place in line, the moonhead says, "Yes, sir?"

"Guard duty," the buckskin man says. "Tie this piggy boy's hands behind him. I don't want him laying them on me. Where's this still?"

"Right out back," the moonhead says, sounding miserable.

"And where are the hogs?"

"Same place."

The moonhead rounded up a chunk of rope from someplace and lashed my wrists in back of me.

"Bring one of the lanterns," the buckskin man says. "The men don't need to see to get drunk."

The moonhead picked up the lantern closest by, and Peggy says, "I'd like to be excused."

"Wouldn't we all?" the buckskin man says. "But be patient, my sowlet. Your reward will come. However, the prize is not without dust." He staggered a bit, and it wasn't just the loose floorboards, then shook his head and bucked hisself up, getting his back and neck stiff. "As you salute, so you will be saluted."

He give me a prod towards the door, and I went because the sooner I could get us where there was only a few to fight, the better, and tied hands or not, it was dark now, and Casper knew more about handling trouble than I did.

"Whiskey-making is a *gentleman's* business," the buckskin man says kind of slurry, whiles I led them out through a store-room and the wash room to the back door. "If you treat a whiskey-maker like a gentleman, he will respond like one."

"Yes, sir," the moonhead says.

"And if you treat a man like a pig, he'll *be* a pig," the buckskin man says. "And if you treat a girl like a sowlet, she'll be a sowlet, won't she."

"And if I treat a man like a customer, he pays up like a customer," Peggy says. "So keep your hands to yourself unless that's what you want."

"I'm your commanding officer," the buckskin man says.

I spun around and crouched a little and wished I had something to fight with besides my teeth. The moonhead poked the lantern at me so's I couldn't see much but it and the butt end of my staff aimed at my gut. "You leave her be or we'll see who gets sentenced to death," I says.

The moonhead shoved at me, and I stumbled cross-legged outdoors, and the buckskin man says, "I wouldn't expect a bumpkin to have heard of *droit du seigneur*, so I'll simply choose to pardon a nervous newlywed on his honeymoon. Where are the hogs?"

"This way, sir," the moonhead says. He had his gun in one hand and the lantern in the other.

And I couldn't see Casper when we went past the shed door, the wagon blocking most of the view, but the air was full of the smell of cooking marsh.

The buckskin man took in deep breaths of it like he was having another drink, and I says good and loud, "Two men armed, a girl, and me with my hands tied."

The moonhead rapped me in the ribs with the barrel of his pistol, but the buckskin man says, "Never mind, let's see the hogs first."

When the moonhead shoved his lantern through the wires, Colonel Woppert was already up and facing us square with the others bunched behind him like piglets ducking behind their mama, his nose-ring gleaming where he'd worn it smooth. They'd had time to root up the sty pretty good, though there hadn't been any rain to make it muddy.

"Admirable," the buckskin man says. "I ought to give that one a commission."

"I already done it," I says. "His name's Colonel Woppert, and if you go giving him a uniform, he'll show you what to do with it: he'll eat it."

"You called a pig a colonel?" the buckskin man says, his face seeming to go even darker in the heavy shadows from the lantern.

"Yes, sir," I says. "But I wouldn't of if I'd met you first."

He give me a thump on the back that was so hard, I couldn't tell if it was sposed to perk me up or knock me down. "This is where you'll spend your wedding night. This will be your Bower of Bliss. But of course when I say night, I mean more like a half-hour. Then we'll have you executed so we can all get a good night's sleep. How's that?" He was talking like a storekeep that had just threw in a free pickle along with the week's groceries and expected to be thanked.

"Why don't you just leave us alone?" Peggy says. "Why don't you just go back and get drunk and enjoy yourself?"

"Why, I *am* drunk, sowlet," he says. "And I *am* enjoying myself. Revenge is a dish that should be eaten cold, and I'm eating it right now." He leant on one of the sty posts and made a move with his hand like he was giving it away. "It's all yours, my children. The Kingdoms of This World. All you have to do is bump some of the pigs out of the way, which is what I've been doing all my life. Go on, enter the Garden. Every hog to his trough."

Of course going into a hog sty didn't mean nothing to me, but I could tell Peggy didn't fancy the idea none, so I brung up an old sore subjeck. "Where's that Glory Road my ma and pa went on?" I says.

"Everywhere," he says. "It's at every corner, at every threshold you cross, it's lying there under your feet right this very second, it's right under your tongue."

"You mean you kilt them," I says.

"I kill nothing," he says. "I only dispatch messages and messengers. I'm looking for a golden life in an iron age, and that calls for transmutation and the refiner's fire. Are you going to live tomorrow?"

"Yes, sir," I says.

"It's already too late," he says. "The wise, like me, lived yesterday."

"So did I," I says. "But I didn't kill no Injuns whiles I was at it."

He shrugged. "If you buy land, you buy war," he says. "The salvages must be driven out or put to death. Destroy the nests, and the birds will fly away."

"I'm ready to fly right now," Peggy says. "Why don't you let us take a wagon and go and you'll never see us again?"

"No, no," he says. "As soon as your honeymoon's over and

we've given the piggy boy his message to deliver, you can get right back to work. For me. And nothing is secret that shall not be made manifest."

"I want some of Miz Selfridge's rings," Peggy says. "And I want to pick them myself."

I couldn't tell whether she meant it, but I guess the buckskin man thought so because he says, "We'll see, sowlet," and grinned and jiggled my arm to see how I liked it. "Piggy boy, you'd love me too if you knew me better. To be great is to be misunderstood."

"I don't misunderstand you," I says.

"And I want that green silk dress with the pearl collar," Peggy says.

"First look for your pearls among the swine," he says. "You're likely to have more luck." He turned, bumping the moonhead out of the way, and headed for the shed door. "I want to meet this Whiskey Man. What's his name?"

"Casper," the moonhead says.

"Casper!" I says, making it loud enough to wake him up if he'd missed hearing me before.

It seemed like our honeymoon was over before it begun, which was fine with me, so we come along when the moonhead shoved at us. The lantern was still burning inside the shed, and when we got to the edge of the wagon, I could see the copper gleaming and the steam rising and smell the fire and the marsh but no trace of Casper who, I hoped, had remembered where he'd put his rifle.

"You first," the buckskin man says to the moonhead.

And the moonhead give a look like that was just about what he'd expected to hear but went anyway, holding his lantern high and his sixgun ready. We waited whiles he peered all around and looked in the back of the wagon. "Nothing here but whiskey and some food and clothes," he says, sounding like that was a big improvement on somebody who could bust jaws and noses. "Still's cooking, so he can't be far."

"Well, bring that kegged whiskey indoors," the buckskin man says. "I want it under lock and key. It's worth its weight in gold bullion."

"But there's five kegs and a cask," the moonhead says. "I can't carry—"

"One keg at a time, dunderhead."

"Yes, sir." The moonhead set his lantern down and rolled a keg towards him off of the tailgate and come out grunting and leaning back with it cradled, and when we backed out of his road, a rifle whanged from behind us, sounding like it come from uphill a ways, and the moonhead pitched straight over backwards in the shed doorway with the blood pouring out of his throat, and the keg come rolling toward us.

The buckskin man ducked sideways into the dark patch between the shed and the tavern, hauling me with him by my tied wrists and half fell to the ground, pitching me off-balance to my knees, and I hollered, "Run, Peggy, run. Get out of here. Go hide where the bones are." I seen the glimmer of her dress going along the shored-up wall of the tavern, but the moon wasn't out, and I lost sight of her. So I hollered, "You kilt one, the girl's safe, the other's still here armed." But by the time I'd finished, I could feel the gun barrel gouging me under the right ear.

And the buckskin man says, "No more talk, piggy boy. You just put aside any more ideas about squealing now or I'll shoot you *and* your hogs and go find that sowlet and give *her* something to squeal about."

I hushed up then, figuring to bide my time, if I had any to bide. Maybe Casper had worked something else out I didn't know about or maybe the buckskin man would make some fool mistake without me making it instead.

We waited a couple of long minutes, and everything turned real silent and the skeeters got interested in us, and I couldn't figure out why somebody hadn't come running from the tavern, unless a little gunfire didn't seem as important as whiskey. But there wasn't any yipping or singing going on neither that might of drownded out the noise of the rifle.

And the buckskin man must of been thinking the same way because all of a sudden he commenced yelling, "Andrews! Michelson! Where the hell are you? Tommy!"

But nobody was answering, and nobody come running.

"Snyder!" the buckskin man yells.

He kept his gun barrel up under my ear where it didn't feel good nor give me a whole lot of confidence in the future, and he waited another spell for something to happen, and I spent it hoping nothing would.

Then after cussing a bit under his whiskey breath, the buckskin man says loud, "Whiskey Man, are you in the mood to talk sensibly?"

There was a gap, and I begun to think Casper'd snuck off someplace or had went circling to creep up on us, but then his voice come from up towards the spring, sounding like he might be fifty foot off or so. There was enough trash strewed up that slope, some of good-sized, he could of been crouching in ten or twelve places or laying flat with a bead on us. "Tell me the tale, Colonel," he says. "I'm fresh off the farm and hunting for a friend."

I felt the buckskin man give a little start, but he kept his gun shoved up against my adenoids. "You know me?" he says.

"I've been listening to all your comical talk, Colonel," Casper says. "You've got a good parade-ground voice on you."

"I've also got a young man here who's about to experience the thrill of a hand-poured lead bullet through his occiput if you do any more rifle drill around my headquarters," the buckskin man says.

"Why, I don't mind who you may wish to shoot, long as it's not me," Casper says. And I had to hope he was just trying to throw the buckskin man off his plan to use me for some kind of shield or horse-trade.

"You've just killed a major in the Territorial Pacifiers and are therefore due for an appearance before our specially trained Execution Squad," the buckskin man says.

"I'm likely to appear most anyplace you can think of," Casper says. "But not there."

I could smell the buckskin man giving off a kind of rancid-buttery smell now like he was dripping tallow, and he says, "You'll be interested in their weapons, Whiskey Man. They use small knives."

"The smaller, the better," Casper says. "I'll stick to this good old-fashioned rifle, and I'm going to let some air into that little chicken-coop you've got for a head. I can see in the dark like a barn owl, Colonel."

"I'll kill this young man if you fire," the buckskin man says.

"You'd best be putting that soul of yours in working order," Casper says. "You're going to need it."

"And you'd better hit the road, Whiskey Man, because you're going to have my army after you in a minute."

"I have dismal news for you," Casper says. "You don't have no army to speak of, least not for a while."

With his mustache up against my ear, the buckskin man says to me, whispering, "You're going to crawl right alongside me over to the back door of that tavern." He still had my staff because he stuck it along my back between my wrists and commenced using it like a handle on me. We spent another minute or two getting to the door, and the rifle didn't go off again, and whatever it was Casper'd figured out, it hadn't happened yet.

As soon as we was indoors, the buckskin man jerked me to my feet, coming up wobbly hisself, and shoved me ahead of him to the door of the main part of the tavern. But we'd only took a couple of steps inside (me expecting to get slaughtered any minute and him probably thinking up what he was going to tell the lunkheads for not coming out like bonafied reenforcements) before we seen what the trouble was—though it wasn't no trouble for me but just for him: everybody in the room was laid out cold, except for a couple of lunkheads whose legs was still moving like they'd went out for a stroll but forgot to take theirself along.

After we'd had a good gawp at everybody (though the single lantern didn't help a whole lot with details), the buckskin man pushed me ahead of him towards the main table so's he could get a clear look at Miz Landseer laying back in her chair with her mouth hanging open and her hat dangling off sideways on a couple of pins. She was snoring through her nose and mouth both and didn't look too extra much like Sleeping Beauty. The rest in the room looked like they'd been caught in the middle of enjoying theirself with no place to set down: the fat man was laying slumped up against the keg rack like he'd wanted to stay close to home, and the pockmarker had pitched straight over frontwards on his face with his bloody nose down between two planks, and Mr. Arthur was under the table like he'd been hunting for something he'd dropped and got tired of looking. There was a good deal of snoring going on, and the smell of spilt whiskey was enough to set me dizzy.

"Knockout drops," the buckskin man says in a low sluggy voice like he was thinking about going to sleep hisself. "If it isn't one damn thing, it's after another."

But he wasn't through getting surprised yet, because he didn't see what I seen. Now that there was only me and him left, I was looking harder than ever for someplace to duck and run, even if it meant getting shot at, and whiles I was sweeping my eyes around to locate something to help me—a knife to cut my rope with or a loose gun or anything—I seen the barrel of a rifle come sticking through the dark window slit, aiming in our direction but (I hoped) mostly in his.

And then Casper in his hardest voice says, "I want that gun on the floor right now, mister, or I'll put you there with it."

The buckskin man spun to look and flang me around in front of him and yanked my staff out from betwixt my wrists and tried to aim a shot over my shoulder at the window slit, but I kicked backwards at him and disobliged him further by setting straight down on the floor to get out of the way. His

pistol and the rifle went off at the same time, and the buckskin man yelped like he'd been hit someplace, and whiles I
was scrambling to get my feet under me so's I could run for it,
I seen him sweep my staff around and knock the lantern off of
the wall hook, dousing it, and he must of gone right on swinging the staff because when I come up into a crouch, he caught
me what felt like a good one on the side of my head (not
where the scab was, but the other) and laid me out as cold as
well water.

Chapter Twenty-Six

I DON'T KNOW how much time slipped out from under me before I come to, but it was still dark, and at first I thought I'd fell asleep in the back of the wagon, and Ma and Pa'd let me lay down on the tailgate for a change instead of walking all day like the rest of the hogs. But then I figured out they wouldn't be traveling at night like this and remembered they was lost or dead or something, and it must be Casper making up a little lost ground and wanting to rest me up for selling whiskey somewhere up ahead, maybe Chimney Rock or Courthouse Rock or even Fort Laramie if they'd let us.

But then I went on figuring, and it didn't seem like he'd tie me up like this to keep me safe, even if I was amongst the whiskey kegs, because he knew I wasn't a drinking man, and this wasn't his wagon I was in anyway but something broader abeam and smelling like camphor instead of whiskey, and when I took a blurry look out the back and seen the full-moonlit shape of Colonel Woppert trailing behind with a rope tied through his nose-ring and no other hogs behind him, I come awake as complete as I ever will and recollected the buckskin man and the shooting and realized this wasn't no happy, lazy ride I was taking but some more Doom.

My head was swole up enough to make my ear squeak, and I'd been hogtied with some extra rope, shaking hands with my ankles and not enjoying it because it kept me hunched up. I was laying on my side, and I'd lost my hat someplace, and the wagon was on a rough road, and all in all I'd just as soon been out behind with Colonel Woppert who was having to go faster than pleased him. I didn't reckonize none of the country I could stretch far enough to get a glimpse at, but there was no gorge now, no trees, only what looked to be a high bluff far off behind.

I thought about hollering, but couldn't think of nothing worth hollering, and if it was the buckskin man up in the driver's seat which I couldn't see, I didn't want to listen to him no more than I had to. From time to time I could hear a man singing a snatch of a song, a note here and there, but not enough to make out, more like somebody enjoying some music going on in his own head and only letting out the loud parts or the notes he could reach without stretching.

It seemed like an hour before we stopped, and I commenced sweating worse than I had been, even though it was chill out, because I didn't feel like getting any more bad news. Yet that's all there was: the buckskin man come around to the tailgate and let it down and poked at me, smelling like a tubful of marsh and weaving a little to keep the ground from tipping too far.

"Time for the feast, piggy boy," he says, sounding soberer than he acted.

He tried to haul me out by the shirt but cussed at his wrists and finally just rolled me out to thump on the ground which I was glad turned out sandy. I didn't say nothing so's not to rile him in case he meant to untie me.

But he just left me lay there, and Colonel Woppert come up to snuff me and be a comfort, whiles the buckskin man worked at getting the whiskey kegs arranged some way on their sides. "Just in time for the revolution," he says. "Every revolution was first a thought in one man's mind, and I'm the man. Exterimation. Exter—" He backed up and got his tongue untangled. "Extermination with pork and whiskey: what could be sweeter?"

I didn't know if I should answer him back or not. I couldn't think up no way to soothe him down, and he didn't need any more riling. I blinked around at the moonlight, looking for some kind of help, but there was only Colonel Woppert.

"I don't like to kill my enemies," he says. "Not really. I miss them too much whenever I do something particularly brilliant they would have envied. And out here in the unformed wilderness, I'm wasting my sweetness on those too dull to comprehend it." He struck a sulfur match and lit a dark lantern, mostly shaded but a streak aimed at me. "Would you like to see a map of a New World?"

The words come out of my mouth by theirself. "I can't see," I says.

He opened the slit on the lantern a little more. "A New World which will eventually encompass these tired old Disunited States," he says, unfolding a crackly piece of parchment and holding it down near my face. "How does the name *Stullvania* strike you?"

"I can't see nothing," I says.

"Then imagine it," he says. "Roll it on your tongue. Use your mind's eye if you have one. Can't you see me as a king?"

I felt like I knew what he wanted me to say, but I wasn't going to say it. He wanted me to tell him I thought he was a damned, doomed fool so's he could kill me for it. I laid there, breathing his double-distilled bourbon whiskey thick as hickory smoke, and says, "I've went blind. I can't see nothing."

"You *what*?" he says.

I heard a bottle click against his teeth, and I says, "It must of been that whack on the head."

"Are you *really* blind?" he says like it might be too good to be true.

"Yes, sir," I says, blinking and squinting and trying to keep going long enough for him to pass out maybe, and the same time trying to remember how Lucy Clary used to act up for Miz Peasemont when we was doing Scenes from Great Dramas when you have to really and sincerely believe you're something you know you ain't. I rolled my eyeballs and squinched till I had some tears coming out of the corners. "I'm blind. Oh, God, what am I going to do for a living?"

"Why, you have a staff," he says, smiling. "You're free to wander and grow wise and prophesy."

"Thank you, sir," I says, choking it a little. "Just aim me and my hog in the right direction, and I'll get started."

He laughed and says, "Why don't you practice prophesying right now? If you're blind, you can let that mind's eye rove over the waters like a dove. Let it rove."

"Yes, sir," I says.

"Is it roving?" he says.

"Yes, sir," I says. "Sort of."

"Then tell me what you see and prophesy," he says. "That shouldn't be too difficult for a budding little Ezekiel." His voice turned hard as an oak root. "Speak well, sir, and I might even take you with me into the Higher Civilization and fatten you up and let you live in a cage."

I kept still, and my mind's eye wasn't doing nothing but falling down on the job and turning out Bible-story pictures of rocks and wasteland and me praying.

"Well?" he says as harsh as an ax-chop.

I give myself a nudge to get going and says, "I see a rock."

"What kind of a rock?" he says. And all of a sudden he clutched my head and heisted both eyebrows with his thumbs and come in close and says, "You couldn't *really* be blind."

"I see a rock coming out of the water," I says.

"You're an amusing liar," he says, leaving my head thump back on the ground. "I'll grant you that." And he took another good slug out of the bottle, leaning back like he was blowing a bugle. "Be *more* amusing."

"And you're laying on the rock," I says.

"What?" he says, turning dead serious.

And I knew I was on the right track if only I could keep from committing some mortal offense. "Laying chained to the rock," I says.

He held quiet for a few seconds like he might be coaxing his own mind's eye to catch up with mine. "What am I wearing?" he says.

He caught me short, so I had to fish a little. "Well, it looks like some kind of skin," I says.

"*Skin*?" he says, making a snarly face which I had to pretend like I didn't see.

"Maybe goatskin," I says.

He nodded, narrowing his eyes. "Yes," he says. "Yes, I see. So I'm to be the scapegoat for all of it. A typical whim of History."

I could tell I was holding my own as a prophet so far, so I got four notches above myself and says, "Amen."

He jerked back like I'd scalded him. "I'll be no one's goat!" he yells. "I can put blood on the moon. I can foretell the annihilation of the Ark of the Covenant. I can see into the blood-filled heart of man's impurity, and I shall not weep but rejoice. I have held the Lamb in my arms, and He has forgiven me all things, past, present, and future. I have weighed man in the balance and found him wanting. The whole world shall be my sepulcher."

"If you was in the sepulcher next to me, I'd get up and move over," I says, forgetting to act right.

"You're not blind," he says, turning the lantern up full.

"But you will be."

Off to the left someplace a half a dozen dogs commenced barking. When I looked that way, I seen a group of pointy-topped tepees and a couple of small fires, and the same time (whenever the dogs hushed up a few seconds to catch their breath) I realized I could hear the river running and been hearing it all along. The sound was on the right, so if it was the North Platte, that meant we'd come upstream a ways after getting down out of the bluffs.

Cupping his hands around his mouth, the buckskin man hollered *"Hi-wan!"* Then he smiled down at me and give Colonel Woppert a kick in the ribs to move him off to the end of his rope (which was about where I felt too) and says, "Try to behave for the company now."

We didn't have long to wait for it: the dogs come first, a couple of them big and mean-looking and maybe part mastiff, and they acted like there was nothing they'd rather chase than Colonel Woppert, only he wouldn't run so they had to make sure he wasn't some kind of over-growed wolverine that would tear their throat open if they got too ambitious. But two come crouching in close on him from in back to see if he was fit for hamstringing, and I tried to flop myself over so's I could at least make some kind of commotion or take a thrash at them. Using my staff, the buckskin man jabbed them away, staggering but doing most as good a job as I'd of managed.

"Not yet, boys, not yet," he says.

All at once the dogs hushed up, and everywhere I looked—out at the edge of the lamplight where it turned as pale and silvery yellow as the moon—there was Injuns standing and staring at us, wearing raggedy skin shirts with beads and bones on them and their hair in pigtails and a few feathers stuck up top of their heads on some and none on others and their dark skin shiny across their wide faces like they'd just been greased. And there wasn't a one of them that had what you could call an expression on that face nor anything but a straight mouth.

"O-hi-ka," the buckskin man says, tapping hisself in the

chest. "I bring much whiskey and *ku-ku-se.*" He touched Colonel Woppert with my staff.

One of the biggest and closest, with a clump of feathers laying down flat on top of his head, all pointing forward, says, "*E-ze!*" and there was a general mumbling and jabbering then, and when the buckskin man drew hisself a cup out of one of the kegs and held it up and took a swig and offered it, the one with the most feathers come in even closer and tapped his own breastbone which he could reach because his shirt was ripped and says, "*Chehu-pa. Oiyo-pe-ye mani-cha.*"

The buckskin man took a step at him, holding out the cup and wobbling a little, and says, "*Chehu-pa*, you don't need any money. *Hi-ya* two bits."

The Injun took the cup and downed the whiskey straight and let the fire settle in and took a deep happy breath and grinned as broad as ever the fat man could of and nodded.

"He says his name's Jaw," the buckskin man says. "And I'll give that jaw and all the rest a workout before this night's over."

Jaw handed the cup back, and him and all the rest seemed to be waiting to see what would happen next, it probably not being their usual experience to get something for nothing—or even to get something at all. But when the buckskin man commenced filling the cup again, they made happy murmurs, and when he went right on to filling a second, I heard grunting and laughing like the world had just turned into the dandiest place anybody could think of.

I didn't know which kind of whiskey the buckskin man was handing out, but if it was the knock-down kind, I didn't see how he was going to get them all laid out quick enough to keep the ones on the tail-end of the line from using the rifles and knives and bone clubs I could see here and there amongst the bunch, and I started working on my ropes again (I'd been doing it off and on since I'd woke up, but the knots had got soaked somehow and wouldn't budge) so's I could try to get away before slaughtering time.

The buckskin man must of brung a whole basket of cups because he went right on passing them out till everybody had one, even a couple of squaws crouching on the outskirts, and they all set down crosslegged with me and Colonel Woppert in the middle like we was roasting over a campfire—which wasn't the kind of idea that give me any comfort.

As soon as he got the first round out, the buckskin man showed Jaw and another Injun how to work the spigot for theirself, and then he come over to me and knelt down, grinning, and all of a sudden stuck an apple in my mouth.

I was so surprised, I got my teeth jammed in it. It was small and hard and half dried-out, and before I could spit it loose, he rammed it in past my teeth with the heel of his hand and it stuck there.

He had a cup of whiskey for hisself, and he drunk some now, kneeling and looking me over like I was just about right. "I want you to know I appreciate everything you've done for me," he says. "I can't talk this damned language of theirs very well, but when the time comes, I'll do my best to get them to kill you without straining their ingenuity." His mouth was working slower than before, and he was picking his way through the words like a man trying not to trip over nothing in the dark. "How do you like the stink?"

And truth to tell, the Injuns was raising a pretty good whiff, but I didn't have time to think about it, being too worried about coughing out that apple and getting loose.

Pointing at Jaw and then at me, the buckskin man says, "*Ni-ta ku-ku-se*." He pointed at Colonel Woppert. "*Ni-ta ku-ku-se*."

Jaw give a grunt and says, "*Han-ma-ni-pi-se un-ya-kon-pi*," and he looked in his half-full cup like he was puzzled over it.

"You'll understand later," the buckskin man says. "*Every*body's in the dark. Blessed is he that gets the gift, not he for whom it is meant. Great gifts are from great men." He paused and swayed a little, bracing hisself against the tailgate. "Don't these salvages make you sick, piggy boy? I've killed twenty-eight of them so far, and I think I'll double it tonight, not

counting you because you don't count." He rubbed the side
of his ribs, and his hand come away bloody. "That damn
whiskey man creased me."

If I could of said so, I'd of told him where I wished he'd
been creased, but the apple was in the road, and I didn't like
thinking about Casper because that meant I'd have to figure
out how the buckskin man got away with all this whiskey
without killing him first.

"*Mah!*" the buckskin man says in a loud voice, and most of
the Injuns stopped laughing and talking to listen. "*Chan-te
owechu-nicha.*" He put his hand on his chest like he hurt
there. "*Aki-chita-kte.*" And he pointed at me and Colonel
Woppert.

"*Echa-non shni to?*" Jaw says, taking down the last of his
cupful and getting up for more.

"Because I want *you* to do it and get the blame, you damn
ignorant salvage," the buckskin man says. "*Hi-ya ma-ka-he-ya.*"

Whiles the Injuns commenced talking among theirself again,
the buckskin man turned back to me and says, "If you live
with a lame man, you'll learn to limp, piggy boy. I've stuck
with you through thick and thick, and now we're going to thin
it out." He smiled and nodded so slow and even and steady,
he looked like a piece of crockery I seen at Miz Peasemont's
once when she had four of us in to quit being so hopeless. It
was a little old man all painted to look real, setting in a chair
with a blue shawl on him and wire specs, and if you tipped his
head with your finger, he'd just keep nodding Yes Yes Yes Yes
as long as you might like, even if you come up close and told
him No No No No like Miz Peasemont caught me doing.

I'd chawed some of the apple loose with my side grinders
and caved it in a bit with the roof of my mouth, and now I
give a big hawk and spit it out on the ground. "What's the
matter with you?" I says, though I knew it wouldn't do no
good to ask. "What do you want? What do you think you're
doing? Why can't you leave folks alone?" I wasn't just thinking of me and the hogs and the Selfridges (though they'd been

near as bad as him) but the Injuns too. This was their ground I
was laying on, and it looked like there was going to be more
blood spilt on it over nothing. They'd started ganging around
the kegs now, and one spigot wasn't enough, and when one
husky barebacked Injun with fringed leggings on tried to hoist
out another keg, the buckskin man yanked at his arm.

"*Hi-ya na-pi-skan-yan*," the buckskin man says, but the
Injun give him an elbow in the gut and hauled the keg off a
ways and commenced hitting the bung with a stone. "Damn
it, it's too soon. *Chan-te oki-chun-maya-ya!*" But the Injun
kept right on pounding, and it didn't seem like the buckskin
man felt like shooting one for fear of the rest, so what he done
was unload all the whiskey kegs (at least he hadn't took the
cask) in a hurry with a couple of Injuns, half-drunk already,
helping him. Then he turned to me and says, "Well, I've got
to be going now, piggy boy. They don't have a word for *mercy*
or I'd teach it to you. You want to know who I am? Why,
I'm the judge and the jury. The preacher and the congregation.
The sinner and the sinned-against. The wreckage and the
wholeness. The tumult and the silence. So you might as well
get used to it."

"I am," I says. Then I took a deep breath and let him have
it out of my spare hog lung (which you save to coax faraway
snouts out of the sweet potatoes): "*I am!*"

He staggered back a step and blinked, and some of the Injuns
left off drinking a few seconds. But the Injun that had been
pounding the keg give it one more rap and bunged it in, and
him and a couple others started splashing it around into cups
and chattering and chortling over it.

The buckskin man looked worried, but he paused to give me
one more look-over. "You remind me of someone," he says.
"Someone who used to make me sick when I was a boy."

"Well, you don't remind me of nobody, thank God," I says.
"If there was any more like you, I'd as leave be an Injun."

"You *are* going to be one," he says. "At least, you're going
to belong to them. You'll be one of the tiny morsels flung

their way in the midst of this whiteman's banquet I have been chosen to preside over. You have been privileged to take a small part in the founding of a new empire. You have listened to historical utterances. You have been witness to events which will puzzle and delight whole generations of scholars and proselytes and acolytes as yet unborn. Your insignificant life has been lent a specious importance by my presence. Do you realize I have actually paid *attention* to you? Your life is about to be put back where it belongs, to fertilize the great Vine of Necessity. And now, may the Lord damn you and not keep you, may the Lord bow down His countenance upon you, may the Lord make His face to shadow you and be vicious unto you and give you no peace. Amen." He turned to go.

"Likewise, I'm sure," I says.

And I seen a newcomer standing just beyond the wagon. He was wearing some kind of canvas around his shoulders and up over his head like an old lady's shawl but looked more like a big horned owl, hunched but watching everything, even what nobody else could see. He wasn't drinking or waiting in line to start, and he had black paint smeared over most of his chest and up across his face.

He was staring at the buckskin man, and he pointed and says, "*To-ka! Shu-shka-ka!*"

Getting up on his feet and trying to balance, Jaw says, "*Kto?*"

The buckskin man tried to get past them to the driver's seat, but Black Face shoved him back and yanked the shawl half off, showing a bunch of feathers hanging higgledy-scraggly out of his long braided hair and rattled off a whole string of talk, pointing towards the river or across it and then at the buckskin man. Everybody was listening, though they went on drinking too.

I'd never been so close up to Injuns before, and the main thing I kept thinking every time my eyes could see them good enough by the lamplight (which somebody was always shad-

ing out by crowding around the spigot) was they looked like
they'd been made out of all kind of birds and beasts and
stones and grass and clay from right nearby, as if the land had
just rose up and squoze itself into men with what was handiest
and strangest. It hadn't ever dawned on me I could stick
feathers in *my* hair or wear colored rocks around my neck, but
there sat some of the fiercest and manliest-looking men I'd
ever come up against—spite of them pouring down whiskey
and probably heading for a whooping drunk—and some had
paint on their face and what looked to be claws and fur hanging down from their neck and ears on thongs and some with
no pants on to speak of and some with deerskin skirts, and all
seeming like they wouldn't blink if it commenced raining or
snowing or whirlwinding but would treat it like a neighbor
come to visit.

"*Hi-ya to-ka*," the buckskin man says. "*Oho-ka.*" He patted
hisself on the chest like he was his own horse. "*A-ki-cita.*"

Jaw glared at him, getting his eyes in focus. "*He-canon he*?"
he says.

The buckskin man shook his head so hard it would of rattled
if he'd had some dried peas in it. "*To-hini-echa-man shni,*" he
says. "It must've been somebody else, somebody that looked
like me. *Wa-na-hna-yan.*"

Black Face spit and says, "*Ke-cha,*" and he grabbed the
buckskin man by the collar of his jacket and says, "*Nish-na-na.
Umaya-kah-niqa.*"

"I killed no one," the buckskin man says in a high voice.
"*Ta-ku-dan toka-mon shni!* Whiskey! A whole hog! *Ku-ku-se!*
And a prisoner to torture. *Ana-chi-gop-tan.*"

Black Face ran off another long string of talk at Jaw who was
looking soberer and madder every second, and Casper must of
really loaded the one keg with knockout drops—or else they
worked faster on Injuns, specially if they'd been drinking
already—because the first one keeled over then, almost knocking the keg down, and whiles the Injun that'd done the busting

shook him and talked to him, another keeled backwards and laid flat in the sand.

One of them hollered, "*Wo-ha-ka!*"

"It's *not* poison," the buckskin man says, trying to wrench his collar loose. "They're just drunk. *Yah-di-ya-ku!*"

Then the bungstarter Injun slumped to his knees and seemed to think it over before pitching forward and laying in the sand. He rolled over once and then held still after waving his hands for a bit. That made three down, but they was the only ones that'd got to the new keg, and now nobody else would go near it.

"*To-hini-echa-mon shni,*" the buckskin man says.

Whiles Black Face wrenched him around backwards and took his gun away from him, Jaw went over and took a good look at the three laying on the ground. He picked up one of their cups and sloshed it half full from the stove-in keg and come back to the buckskin man and held it out. "*Nis,*" he says.

Not looking any too thirsty, the buckskin man says, "*Tan-hdu-sa-ya shni,*" shaking his head. "I have many—oh, what the hell's the word for *blankets*? *Ni-na* whiskey. *Ni-na* two bits. For everybody."

Jaw jammed the cup at his mouth and splashed it down his chin and up into his mustache, and the buckskin man spit it out best he could and hollers, "Men are punished *by* their sins, not *for* them."

Reaching out, Jaw tore the buckskin man's shirt open all the way to the waist, and what must of been that map of Stullvania fell on the ground. Black Face snatched it up and opened it out and nodded and took a good spit on it and crumpled it in a ball. "*Wo-wa-pi,*" he says, making the sourest face of all.

"No, no, that's no treaty," the buckskin man says. "It's an image of a Glorious Future."

But he didn't say no more because Black Face stuffed it in the buckskin man's mouth harder than the apple had went into mine, and he took out a tomahawk that had a top-shaped rock lashed with rawhide to one end of a stick and says, "*Wanzhi ket-pi ktelo*," and he swang and hit the buckskin man on the back side of his head so hard, he cracked the skull first try. It made a sound like a watermelon dropping on a rock, and the buckskin man sank down in a crumply heap that looked too uncomfortable to hold for long, but he never budged out of it.

Then Black Face knelt and took a thick shiny knife out from under his canvas shawl and cut hisself a piece of scalp about as big around as a jar lid, yanked at it till it popped loose, and held it up in the air by a long sandy-colored hair handle.

He got a big roar out of the drinking Injuns, and as soon as they'd quieted down, he says, "*Ado-wan manka.*" And he commenced singing in a high waily voice that seemed to come from someplace so far back in his head, he must of had a crack there like the buckskin man. I wouldn't of been able to make out what the words was if he hadn't kept going over and over them, and what he sang was "*Ta-te-yo nawa-zhin-ye.*" An old-timer who could speak some Sioux told me later it meant something about being in the middle of the wind, and that Black Face looked like he was in the middle of *some*thing, all right, and he sounded like some winds I'd heard on bad nights out on the prairie before Ma and Pa had went on the Glory Road, coming down from the north out of the place on Pa's paper map that was mostly empty and run off the edge up towards the North Pole. It didn't look like no place a sane man would want to go apurpose, and when the wind come from there, it seemed mad and sad about where it'd been at, and that's the way Black Face made it seem now.

I felt cold, and whiles the singing went on, a squaw come crawling in and untied Colonel Woppert's rope and commenced leading him off towards the tepees. The drinking had started up again out of the good keg, and nobody seemed to mind where the hog was going except me, and I couldn't do nothing about it but thrash.

Jaw come over to me, giving the buckskin man a kick on the way by, and he looked down at me with that blank face they have most of the time that makes them look a thousand years old and brave and smarter than you. He touched the scab on the side of my head and says, "*Nun-ga.*"

He sounded gruff but at least not riled at me, and I says, "Please, that's my hog. He wouldn't be fit to eat. He'd be stringy as a riverboat hawser."

"*Wan-na ob-lu-la,*" Jaw says, sounding calm but not doing me no good.

Black Face had left off singing and was carrying the piece of scalp around through the crowd so's they could touch it, and the squaw was off beyond the lantern light someplace with Colonel Woppert, and I couldn't think of nothing on earth to do but hogcall, so I let out the loudest and best one of my life, spite of being sore-mouthed and bump-headed and half laying down so's I couldn't use my gut muscles easy, yelling, "Seeeeeeeeeeeeeeeeeeeeeeeeeeee uuuuuuuuuuuuuuuuuuuuuuuuuuu-BOY!"

Jaw straightened up and backed off with his mouth open whiles I done it, and Black Face come running towards me like it was him being called, but I figured if I was going to lose my scalp, I'd sooner do it in the company of the only hog I appeared to have left. Drunk as most of them was by now, there was a dead silence when I quit, and then I heard Colonel Woppert coming at a hog trot.

He don't like having his nose-ring pulled, but he goes along with it because it hurts if he don't, and lucky for him and me the squaw must not of been hanging on too hard—or else she stopped to listen to me calling and got caught by surprise. Anyway, she was trotting along after when Colonel Woppert come straight through the clump of Injuns (some having to flop and scramble out of his road) and up to me and stuck his snout in my armpit for a second like a dog would of to make sure it was me in all this mess of new smells.

Some of the Injuns was laughing at the squaw, but Black Face hushed them up by yelling, *"Hi-wan!"* Then he pointed at the squaw and over at the dark tepees and says, *"Ya-di-ya-ku!"*

She backed off out of the rim of light, and Black Face took out his knife and bent over me, grinning, and I stared back at him as good as I could because Miz Peasemont used to tell us Anything Worth Doing Is Worth Doing Well, and this might be the last time I'd get to do anything halfway respectable.

"Tan-hdu-sa-ya shni," Black Face says, and Jaw give a grunt that sounded like Colonel Woppert seeing something he liked. Black Face cut my ropes with two or three slashes, and if he was trying to hit me too, he was missing. *"Na-zhin,"* he says, motioning me to stand up, and after two or three tries, I done so, limbering some of my blood back into where it belonged and getting my knees straightened out.

"Yah-di-ya-ku," he says, pointing the opposite of the tepees, and since it was the same thing he'd said to the squaw, I reckoned I was being told to go back where I belonged (wherever that was), so I picked up Colonel Woppert's rope and my staff and starting walking, still not sure if I was going to get clubbed for doing it. Five steps seemed longer than a whole day's walk.

But the drinking Injuns got out of my way and didn't try sticking Colonel Woppert, and we went off in the near-dark that turned silvery as soon as we was off from the lantern a ways and kept going. I only looked back once and seen Black Face still standing there with some of the buckskin man's scalp in one hand and the knife glinting in the other and the buckskin man still heaped crooked and not pacifying no territory but what he was laying on and not even that for long.

Hollering, Black Face says, *"O-hi-ka!"*

Which was the last thing I heard and learnt later it meant somebody with a special kind of power, and if he meant me, I wish I'd known how to thank him for turning me and

Colonel Woppert loose. Hogcalling *is* a power, I guess. At least, it's powerful loud, but what surprised me most about that whole part of the night was I hadn't been very scairt, not even when I thought I might be down to my last breath or two, which meant I'd turned even dumber or crazier.

Chapter Twenty-Seven

THINKING ABOUT IT kept me from being tired through the hours of walking till the first part of dawn. I'd located the river whiles the moon was still up and was following it downstream, hoping I wouldn't miss the Emigrants' Post Office and turn-off up to Ash Hollow. I wanted to find the rest of my hogs and Peggy and Casper before something bad happened to them, and there wasn't no use trying to sleep. My eyes felt like they didn't have no shutters on them.

I hadn't seen nobody camped out along this barren stretch where even the little scrubby cottonwoods had been chopped off of the small islands, and when I finally seen the Post Office up ahead and let my eye go scanning along the riverbank off to the left, the Injun camp that had got half-burnt had pulled up stakes too, and no wagons was coming along yet this early, and I didn't have no company but my thoughts which was on the bleak side.

Whiles Colonel Woppert took some breakfast amongst the bushes, I set down by the cluster of tombstones and thought about the Glory Road. The buckskin man had said it was right underfoot all the time or under my tongue, and I didn't doubt but what he was right. But wherever it might be, there wasn't no news coming back from it yet, nor nothing pointing the way. If Ma and Pa was on it someplace, I wished them joy in the morning and hope at noon and peace at suppertime, and that seemed like all I might ever be able to do.

I set a long spell till the morning light had turned as pink as a shoat's nose back East, and then I seen the wagons coming. As they jolted down out of the gully, I didn't have no trouble reckonizing Casper's whiskey wagon and him up on the seat by hisself and the shapes and colors of hogs milling along behind. But the second wagon (a rickety-looking market wagon with no cover and the near-front wheel about to come off and a fine big riding horse hauling it) kept me guessing for another minute till I finally made out Peggy all bundled up in a gray fur coat and Miz Landseer's hat with the violets.

Casper let out half a whoop when they was still a ways off, but I was too tired to act happy and too wrang out to do any yelling myself. I just hunkered down and waited.

And the first thing Casper says was "Come on, get on board, we've got to keep moving."

He stopped his wagon, and Peggy stopped hers after the horse shied and backed up and done a little shuffle and took a bite at his harness, and it seemed like she was sort of embarrassed to see me and kept shifting her eyes off, even though I stood up and took off my hat.

"Can you fix this wheel?" she says, snapping it at me like I was a hired hand.

"I might if I had some tools and a spare wheel," I says. "Looks like the hub's cracked. Why don't you ask Casper?"

"He refuses," she says, pinching her lips together and narrowing up her eyes. "And what happened to you? Did you fight that duel?"

"Sort of," I says. "The Colonel got hisself demoted to a corpus about five mile up the road. You can pay your respecks on the way by."

"Did you kill him?" she says, her mouth dropping open.

"I done what any gentleman would of," I says, not meaning to brag or give myself a puffing-up but willing to stretch it some.

Looking uphill behind us, Casper says, "Son, I'm going to wait one more minute for you to get aboard."

"Don't ride with him," Peggy says. "Ride with me. He's been horrid. And after I helped save his life too."

Casper had a bloody-looking pad tied under the side of his chin amongst his whiskers, and between the two of them counterdicting and interrupting each other, I finally made out Casper'd been wounded in the neck and run out of bullets and had to doctor hisself to stanch the blood and hadn't been spry or foolhardy enough to keep the buckskin man from carting off most of his old whiskey and me with it, but Peggy'd showed up and helped him some. He'd rescued the lightest and most important parts of his still, taking it apart whiles the first run was only half over, and some kegs of new whiskey.

"I tried to tell her we had to get running—them knockout drops don't last forever—but nothing would do but she had to have a wagon of her own," he says. "I seen which way that Colonel took you, and I reckoned we'd catch up somewhere along the line, dead or alive. And before you get in her wagon, you'd best take a look at what she's got in the back of it."

"It's none of your business!" Peggy says.

She had drawed up beside Casper's wagon with me between, and they scowled at each other something fierce.

"That's a load of death she's got there, son," he says. "Bad enough me hitting that bunch up in the Hollow with a kegful of sleeping whiskey. They'd likely chase us a ways for that alone. But when it comes to money and jewels, they'll dog us a thousand miles or more."

I seen a jumble of women's clothes in the bed of Peggy's wagon and Miz Landseer's portmanteau and what looked to be a strongbox and some kind of a wooden chest.

She was flush-faced and still not meeting my eye. "If one of you nincompoops would fix that wheel, we could make better time," she says.

"I hope it falls off right now and stays off," Casper says. "I'm leaving, son. Make up your mind."

"What do you have in the wagon?" I says to Peggy.

"I have as much right to the jewels and cash as anybody on earth," she says. "Why should those stinking crows get it all? They stole it. And I've already offered half of it if he'll help me, and I'll do the same for you. Or if you'll both help, we'll go equal shares, long as I can pick ten rings out of the bunch first." She shoved Miz Landseer's hat up off her eyebrows. "I call that fair."

"And I call that plain old death," Casper says. He got his mules going, and I walked alongside, and Peggy tried to keep her horse even with us.

Using her wheedliest voice, Peggy says, "Zeke, you didn't even have to do it. I did it all. And all you have to do is get him to help. Do you want to just be a mud-butt all your life and never amount to anything?"

What I amounted to about then was worse than any mud-butt: I'm better at thinking sometimes than others, and this was one of the others. I'd been lopped on the head again and drug hither and elsewhere and given too much education in what seemed like a mortal hurry, and here I was: clomping along the hard sand with seven hogs, too much advice, and the full-scale morning commencing to burn off the haze and stretch itself up, and the river running the other way, and Casper shaking his head over me and giving me a flick of his near eye.

"You'd best pick your poison very, very careful, boy," he says.

I didn't want to pick no poison at all, but before I could say so, Peggy says, "You've got plenty of room in the back of your wagon for these few goods of mine, and if this wheel breaks all the way down, that's exactly where they're going."

And truth to tell, the wheel didn't look like it was any too interested in staying on the axle much longer, but Casper says, "There's plenty of room for *you*, young lady, but I'm not taking on them valuables. If I could of moved these mules a little faster, I'd of put a mile between us already. And that stump-sucker of a horse you got there's stolen too or I'm a bow-legged Turk."

"This horse has been stolen so many times already, one more won't count," she says.

"Tell that to the boys when they come pounding down the gully after you in about fifteen minutes," he says. "Nobody hates to be stole from worse than thieves."

She was glaring right at me, angry, like she'd already seen how I felt and knew what I was going to say, but I started saying it anyway. "Why not give it up like he says? You can forget about it if you try. Let's us just go on and try and be happy without no extra help."

"I guess boys just never grow up anymore," she says. "I haven't met a man in a year and a half."

"I'll buy you some rings and dresses later," I says. "I can be a hard worker."

She reined in her horse to keep it from busting into a slant-wise canter. It was acting like it'd never been harness-broke, and the front wheel was letting out regular squawks now. "I'll bet you are," she says. "Just like the rest of those salty-necked dirt farmers, all those red bandanna blowers parading through that wouldn't know a bottle of champagne if they got hit over the head with one. Have you ever even slept between sheets?"

"Well, not exackly what you'd call sheets," I says.

"I'm not going to wait till you or anybody else saves up a teapot full of pennies and buys me a genuine linen dish-towel from Vermont," she says. "I want my life right now!"

"Right now you're about to lose it if you don't use your brains," Casper says, looking backwards. "And I'm not going to heave mine in to haul yours out. Here they come."

I looked back over the stretch of up-slope bushes and seen three riders trotting out of the gully and starting to speed up where the ruts and rocks ended. They only had about a half-mile to catch up on us, and there was hardly no more time to argue. "You said you could turn men into pigs," I says. "Don't do it to your own self."

Casper had his rifle across his knees now and wasn't bothering to switch at his mules since they couldn't of beat Colonel Woppert if their hay depended on it, and I hefted my staff, trying to unwrinkle the rights and wrongs of all this, and Peggy reached back into her heap of worldly goods and pulled out a sixgun and tossed it at me. I caught it without thinking, and before I'd even got it turned right way around, she had another one pulled out.

"Are you going to defend me or aren't you?" she says, staring down and looking desperate at me and half-beautiful.

"I'd be glad to defend you," I says. "But I'm not going to defend that trash you're hauling."

"That *trash* is more than six thousand dollars and at least as much more in jewelry," she says. "You help me keep it, and we'll go shares."

"Sorry, but I don't believe I'll use this here," I says and tossed the gun back amongst the tangle of dresses. I felt shamed and downcast and peculiar.

She pointed the gun at Casper and says, "You start aiming that rifle, mister, and if you don't start picking off those three riders when they're in range, I'll shoot you dead, and don't think I don't mean it."

"If you get us in a gunfight before I can talk sense to those
damn bandits, you'll likely get us all killed, young lady," he
says. "What you'd ought to do is throw that gun away and
climb down out of that busted wagon and get in the back of
mine and keep your sweet mouth shut till next week."

She looked vexed as deep as she was ever likely to be, and
she unhooked the collar of her fur coat (I couldn't tell what
kind of animals it'd come off, but it looked to of been about
forty of them, sleek and skinny), and she says, "If I could
shoot straight, I'd show you what gumption is, you old fool.
I'd show you both how to make a fortune instead of being
damn butter-heads all your lives." And she commenced bawling and let the gun drop beside her, which was a good idea and
kept me from having to knock it away with my staff like I'd
been about to.

The three riders had about caught up with us, and I didn't
have no trouble reckonizing the pockmarker and Halsey and
somebody whose name I didn't know but had seen scrum-
maging around the feed shed. They hauled up about thirty
yards short of us and had a little talk. Halsey and the third
man both had rifles, and the pockmarker had two sixguns,
but Casper had turned his wagon and stopped so's he could
take a good look at them and had his rifle not quite aimed
their way, and they must of been calculating what to do first.
I stopped the hogs and waited too, since this didn't seem like
a whole lot of my business no more.

Peggy give her horse a crack on his big jittery rump, and he
heaved forward like he was going to jump a fence and jerked
the wagon about three or four lengths before the wheel
cracked and the axle slumped and dug into the sand, and the
whole wagonbed slouched frontways and sidewards and come
near to pitching Peggy out on her hat. The horse kicked some
and snarled hisself in the harness (the lines had gone flying
out of her hands whiles she clang on to the seat and kept bawling) but then had enough sense to stand still as if he'd been
roped.

Holding both his guns crossed on his saddlehorn like he was

willing not to use them, the pockmarker says, "I believe you've got something belongs to us."

"I figured you might be of that opinion," Casper says. "You'll have to ask the young lady there. It's all in her keeping and none of mine to give or take."

The white, sick look on the pockmarker's face brightened up a little, and Halsey opened both eyes instead of just the one he'd been using, and they all three walked their horses towards us, though the rifle barrels didn't shift off of our line much. I got the hogs off a little ways to keep them out of trouble.

The pockmarker was doing all his breathing through his mouth (his nose was darkening towards purple along the bridge), and it give him a kind of dumbstruck look which he might of had anyway, considering what Casper was doing. "Where's Stull?" he says. "We can't find him."

Casper shook his head. "I don't know nobody called that," he says.

Peggy had flung her hat off on the ground and was setting there crooked on the seat, running her fingers through her hair and crouching forwards, and I wanted to get this over with, so I says, "The Colonel got kilt by the Sioux in a camp up the road a ways. Gave them doped whiskey and didn't leave town in time." From the way Casper winched at me, I reckoned I hadn't been sposed to say nothing, but I didn't care.

"The Colonel's *dead*?" the pockmarker says, his face turning about as happy as it could, considering the interference it had took on lately and one eye watering regular. "Really dead? You *saw* him dead?"

"They seemed like they admired his scalp too," I says.

The pockmarker and Halsey exchanged a long, squinty look and then both started nodding and smiling at the same time. Peggy had quit bawling and rubbing her face and raking at her hair and had turned to watch and listen.

"Glad to see you boys woke up all right," Casper says. "I'm sorry about that sleeping whiskey, but there didn't seem no other way. Sorry about your nose too."

But the pockmarker was acting absent-minded and jittery,

like he didn't want to think about them unimportant matters. "I *told* the Colonel you didn't take to shoving," he says.

"I just don't want nobody gunning for me," Casper says. "Long as a word of mine can sweeten the air. Bad for business otherwise."

"Take your business and head west," the pockmarker says. "But I want a load of cash and jewelry."

Peggy says, "Halsey, now's your chance. If you go taking this treasure back to that flock of crows, you'll have to split it so many ways, all you'll get out of it is a couple of wiggles and a good drunk. You've got a horse, I've got a horse. All you have to do is use your brains and that rifle, and we can be on the road in five minutes, rich."

Looking embarrassed, Halsey says, "Hush up." He glanced from the pockmarker to the third man like he was afraid they might turn on him or might take up the idea theirself.

"Well, isn't she a sweet one," the pockmarker says. Then to the third man: "Unharness that gelding and see if he'll take a pack. If he won't, use your own and ride the other. Forget the dresses but lash that strongbox on tight."

The third man commenced doing like he was told, making Peggy climb down onto the sand with her fur coat dragging in it, and she says to the pockmarker, "Are you going to be in charge now, Albert?"

"I do believe," he says, snuffling.

"Is that right, Halsey?" she says. "Is he the one?"

Not looking too sure he dared to say so, Halsey says, "I guess that's right, Peggy-Leg."

"Then you might as well take me back to work," she says. "I don't like it out here on the Trail where the mooncalves think they're running the world. I want to go back to Ash Hollow. You're going to need somebody to run your girls now that Miz Selfridge is pushing up sweetpeas, and the others are too dumb." She was talking hard, but there was a weepy catch in her voice sometimes, and her eyes looked dead worried.

"Well, if Halsey's willing to give you saddle-room, it's all right with me," the pockmarker says. "I'd hate to leave you way out here without that coat to keep you warm nights, and it'd probably be more polite to find out what you've got hid under it in private, instead of outdoors."

She give him a fiery look, but it died down like a sulfur match, and she nodded and pulled her neck into her fur collar and stared at the ground whiles the third man started unloading the broke wagon and getting the saddle off of his horse, not seeming to like the idea of riding the gelding which I didn't blame him for.

"Well, that sounds like it's all hung up to air out," Casper says. "I believe my assistant and me will be getting along unless there's some more hard bargains I don't happen to know about."

"I don't even feel like *remembering* whiskey, leave alone fighting for it," the pockmarker says, looking sick.

"There's some just been born up at the stable," Casper says. "See if you can figure out how to help it reach a ripe old age, which is what I aim to do." He give the mules three twitches before they'd go.

I staffed the hogs into following along, but hung back myself to try and catch Peggy's eye, but she wasn't giving me none of it. "I wish you every happiness," I says.

She stared off at the river, looking frozen-faced. "Oh, for God's sake," she says. "How many kinds do you think there are?"

"I aim to find out," I says.

She didn't say nothing else nor give me that last look, and I followed along behind Casper and the hogs, wondering how I was going to feel as soon as I could feel something, and the reason I knew she hadn't given me no last look was because I kept giving her my half of it and not getting the other. Even before I was out of eyesight, she'd begun looking like a patch of gray fur amongst the lunkheads and horses, and it was a downright pity to see her fading off and looking as skimpy

as I might of looked to her if she'd troubled to try me, when
she'd been so earthly important for days and days and now
was going to take her leave like some new Miz Peasemont
latching up the schoolhouse door to keep me and the hogs
from using it all summer.

We camped a few miles up the road, since neither of us had
et or rested lately, and whiles Casper was getting the hogs
half-drunk on a boiler full of marsh he'd brung along in case
he had trouble keeping them close to the wagon coming down
through the gully before dawn (they'd took to it like they was
the sperits of Uncle Fred), I says, "I don't seem to be getting
much further along out here amongst all these civilized people.
Maybe I should turn in at that Injun camp up ahead and
learn how to be somebody different."

"They'd be glad to eat your hogs for you," Casper says.

"So would most others," I says.

"And you can't talk their style of talk," he says.

"I haven't been doing much good with all this they stuck in
my mouth back home."

"Don't you go turning hard and bitter and sour-whistled
while you still got fuzz on your face, damn it," he says. "Get
some sleep and let your marsh quit bubbling. We got a long
ways to go yet, so let it all settle before you start stilling it."

So I done what he said with my back up against Colonel
Woppert, and whiles I was sagging there, half-dozing, half-
watching over the hogs and listening to Casper warm up to
snoring in the wagonbed, it come to me I might not raise no'
more hogs than this after all but keep them for company,
maybe, same as some do with dogs or cats or birds, or just find
a good big rich woods someplace (like that one I'd dreamt up
to walk in) and turn them loose to root and farrow and go
wild as they pleased and maybe turn myself loose with them
and find a girl that wasn't no Daughter of a Queen but might
be half-hog like me and put together we could be a whole one,
because all people wanted to do was kill hogs and each other

and raise more and then kill the next ones, and I wanted to try it some different way: there'd been too much blood spilt for breakfast (and worse reasons such as none at all) along the riversides and corduroy roads and plains trails and mud and dirt and bedrock and desert clear across from back East, and nothing to show for it but bones in ditches or alongside the wheel-ruts or up in the gullies or along the cricks, both hog and human, and not even good for turning to stone. I figured I'd keep my hogs whole, since I had ambitions along that line myself.